"A BLIZZARD OF TREACHERY AND VIOLENCE...AN ADRENALINE-PUMPING THRILLER."
—**The Associated Press**

"[A] FEVERISH PLOT."
—*Rocky Mountain News*

"MOVIE-STYLE TWISTS AND HAIRBREADTH ESCAPES."
—*The Wall Street Journal*

"UNDENIABLY SUSPENSEFUL."
—*Entertainment Weekly*

"RIPPED...FROM TOMORROW'S HEADLINES."
—*The Raleigh News & Observer*

"SCARY... PROVIDES A RUSH OF FEAR."
—*New York Post*

KEN FOLLETT
"A hell of a storyteller."—*Entertainment Weekly*

Like no other suspense author in his genre, Follett reinvents the thriller with each new novel. But nothing matches the intricate, knife-edge drama of Whiteout. . . .

A lab technician bleeding from the eyes. Twelve missing samples of a deadly virus. Toni Gallo, the security director of a Scottish medical research firm, knows she has problems, but she has no idea of the nightmare to come.

As a Christmas Eve blizzard whips out of the north, several people, Toni among them, converge on a remote family house. All have something to gain or lose from the drug developed to fight the virus. As the storm worsens, the emotional sparks—jealousies, distrust, sexual attraction, rivalries—crackle; desperate secrets are revealed; hidden traitors and unexpected heroes emerge. Filled with startling twists at every turn, *Whiteout* rockets Follett into a class by himself.

"Filled with treachery, intrigue, and action-packed scenes. . . . Follett holds readers captive until the novel's final pages." —The Associated Press

"[Follett] takes the standard device of an isolated house on a stormy night and injects a modern and thoroughly frightening twist to it. What he ends up with is another book that forces you to put your life on hold. . . . Black out your schedule for a day or two and pick up *Whiteout*. It's as close to a sure thing as there is." —*Rocky Mountain News*

"Almost nonstop action with a plausible and sufficiently frightening plot . . . a page-turner, pure and simple." —*The Tennessean*

continued . . .

KEN FOLLETT

WHITEOUT

A SIGNET BOOK

SIGNET
Published by New American Library, a division of
Penguin Group (USA) Inc., 375 Hudson Street,
New York, New York 10014, USA
Penguin Group (Canada), 90 Eglinton Avenue East, Suite 700, Toronto,
Ontario M4P 2Y3, Canada (a division of Pearson Penguin Canada Inc.)
Penguin Books Ltd., 80 Strand, London WC2R 0RL, England
Penguin Ireland, 25 St. Stephen's Green, Dublin 2,
Ireland (a division of Penguin Books Ltd.)
Penguin Group (Australia), 250 Camberwell Road, Camberwell, Victoria 3124,
Australia (a division of Pearson Australia Group Pty. Ltd.)
Penguin Books India Pvt. Ltd., 11 Community Centre, Panchsheel Park,
New Delhi - 110 017, India
Penguin Group (NZ), cnr Airborne and Rosedale Roads, Albany,
Auckland 1310, New Zealand (a division of Pearson New Zealand Ltd.)
Penguin Books (South Africa) (Pty.) Ltd., 24 Sturdee Avenue,
Rosebank, Johannesburg 2196, South Africa

Penguin Books Ltd., Registered Offices:
80 Strand, London WC2R 0RL, England

Published by Signet, an imprint of New American Library, a division of Penguin
Group (USA) Inc. Previously published in a Dutton edition.

First Signet Printing, November 2005
10 9 8 7 6 5 4 3 2 1

Copyright © Ken Follett, 2004
Excerpt from *Night over Water* copyright © Ken Follett, 1991
All rights reserved

Ⓤ REGISTERED TRADEMARK-MARCA REGISTRADA

Printed in the United States of America

PUBLISHER'S NOTE
This is a work of fiction. Names, characters, places, and incidents either are the
product of the author's imagination or are used fictitiously, and any resemblance to actual persons, living or dead, business establishments, events, or
locales is entirely coincidental.

The publisher does not have any control over and does not assume any
responsibility for author or third-party Web sites or their content.

CHRISTMAS EVE

1 A.M.

TWO tired men looked at Antonia Gallo with resentment and hostility in their eyes. They wanted to go home, but she would not let them. And they knew she was right, which made it worse.

All three were in the personnel department of Oxenford Medical. Antonia, always called Toni, was facilities director, and her main responsibility was security. Oxenford was a small pharmaceuticals outfit—a boutique company, in stock market jargon—that did research on viruses that could kill. Security was deadly serious.

Toni had organized a spot check of supplies, and had found that two doses of an experimental drug were missing. That was bad enough: the drug, an antiviral agent, was top secret, its formula priceless. It might have been stolen for sale to a rival company. But another, more frightening possibility had brought the look of grim anxiety to Toni's freckled face and drawn dark cir-

3

cles under her green eyes. A thief might have stolen the drug for personal use. And there was only one reason for that: someone had become infected by one of the lethal viruses used in Oxenford's laboratories.

The labs were located in a vast nineteenth-century house built as a Scottish holiday home for a Victorian millionaire. It was nicknamed the Kremlin, because of the double row of fencing, the razor wire, the uniformed guards, and the state-of-the-art electronic security. But it looked more like a church, with pointed arches and a tower and rows of gargoyles along the roof.

The personnel office had been one of the grander bedrooms. It still had Gothic windows and linenfold paneling, but now there were filing cabinets instead of wardrobes, and desks with computers and phones where once there had been dressing tables crowded with crystal bottles and silver-backed brushes.

Toni and the two men were working the phones, calling everyone who had a pass to the top-security laboratory. There were four biosafety levels. At the highest, BSL4, the scientists worked in space suits, handling viruses for which there was no vaccine or antidote. Because it was the most secure location in the building, samples of the experimental drug were stored there.

Not everyone was allowed into BSL4. Biohazard training was compulsory, even for the maintenance men who went in to service air filters and repair autoclaves. Toni herself had undergone the training, so that she could enter the lab to check on security.

Only twenty-seven of the company's staff of eighty had access. However, many had already departed for the Christmas vacation, and Monday had turned into Tuesday while the three people responsible doggedly tracked them down.

Toni got through to a resort in Barbados called Le Club Beach and, after much insistence, persuaded the assistant manager to go looking for a young laboratory technician called Jenny Crawford.

As Toni waited, she glanced at her reflection in the window. She was holding up well, considering the late hour. Her chocolate brown chalk-stripe suit still looked businesslike, her thick hair was tidy, her face did not betray fatigue. Her father had been Spanish, but she had her Scottish mother's pale skin and red-blond hair. She was tall and looked fit. Not bad, she thought, for thirty-eight years old.

"It must be the middle of the night back there!" Jenny said when at last she came to the phone.

"We've discovered a discrepancy in the BSL4 log," Toni explained.

Jenny was a little drunk. "That's happened before," she said carelessly. "But no one's ever made, like, a great big drama over it."

"That's because I wasn't working here," Toni said crisply. "When was the last time you entered BSL4?"

"Tuesday, I think. Won't the computer tell you that?"

It would, but Toni wanted to know whether Jenny's story would match the computer record. "And when was the last time you accessed the vault?" The vault was a locked refrigerator within BSL4.

Jenny's tone was becoming surly. "I really don't remember, but it will be on video." The touch-pad combination lock on the vault activated a security camera that rolled the entire time the door was open.

"Do you recall the last time you used Madoba-2?" This was the virus the scientists were working on right now.

Jenny was shocked. "Bloody hell, is that what's gone missing?"

"No, it's not. All the same—"

"I don't think I've ever handled an actual virus. I mostly work in the tissue-culture lab."

That agreed with the information Toni had. "Have you noticed any of your colleagues behaving in a way that was strange, or out of character, in the last few weeks?"

"This is like the sodding Gestapo," Jenny said.

"Be that as it may, have you—"

"No, I have not."

"Just one more question. Is your temperature normal?"

"Fuck me, are you saying I might have Madoba-2?"

"Have you got a cold or fever?"

"No!"

"Then you're all right. You left the country eleven days ago—by now you would have flulike symptoms if anything were wrong. Thank you, Jenny. It's probably just an error in the log, but we have to make sure."

"Well, you've spoiled my night." Jenny hung up.

"Shame," Toni said to the dead phone. She cradled the receiver and said, "Jenny Crawford checks out. A cow, but straight."

The laboratory director was Howard McAlpine. His bushy gray beard grew high on his cheekbones, so that the skin around his eyes looked like a pink mask. He was meticulous without being prissy, and Toni normally enjoyed working with him, but now he was bad-tempered. He leaned back in his chair and clasped his hands behind his head. "The overwhelming likelihood is that the material unaccounted for was used perfectly legitimately by someone who simply forgot to make entries in the log." His tone of voice was testy: he had said this twice before.

"I hope you're right," Toni said noncommittally. She got up and went to the window. The personnel office overlooked the extension that housed the BSL4 laboratory. The new building seemed similar to the rest of the Kremlin, with barley-sugar chimneys and a clock tower; it would be difficult for an outsider to guess, from a distance, where in the complex the high-security lab was located. But its arched windows were opaque, the carved oak doors could not be opened, and closed-circuit television cameras gazed one-eyed from the monstrous heads of the gargoyles. It was a concrete blockhouse in Victorian disguise. The new building was on three levels. The labs were on the ground floor. As well as research space and storage, there was an intensive-care medical isolation facility for anyone who became infected with a dangerous virus. It had never been used. On the floor above was the air-handling equipment. Below, elaborate machinery sterilized all waste coming from the building. Nothing left the place alive, except human beings.

"We've learned a lot from this exercise," Toni said in a placatory tone. She was in a delicate position, she thought anxiously. The two men were senior to her in rank and age—both were in their fifties. Although she had no right to give them orders, she had insisted they treat the discrepancy as a crisis. They both liked her, but she was stretching their goodwill to the limit. Still, she felt she had to push it. At stake were public safety, the company's reputation, and her career. "In future we must always have live phone numbers for everyone who has access to BSL4, wherever in the world they might be, so that we can reach them quickly in an emergency. And we need to audit the log more than once a year."

McAlpine grunted. As lab director he was responsible for the log, and the real reason for his mood was that he should have discovered the discrepancy himself. Toni's efficiency made him look bad.

She turned to the other man, who was the director of human resources. "How far down your list are we, James?"

James Elliot looked up from his computer screen. He dressed like a stockbroker, in a pin-striped suit and spotted tie, as if to distinguish himself from the tweedy scientists. He seemed to regard the safety rules as tiresome bureaucracy, perhaps because he never worked hands-on with viruses. Toni found him pompous and silly. "We've spoken to all but one of the twenty-seven staff that have access to BSL4," he said. He spoke with exaggerated precision, like a tired teacher explaining something to the dullest pupil in the class. "All of them told the truth about when they last entered the lab and opened the vault. None has noticed a colleague behaving strangely. And no one has a fever."

"Who's the missing one?"

"Michael Ross, a lab technician."

"I know Michael," Toni said. He was a shy, clever man about ten years younger than Toni. "In fact I've been to his home. He lives in a cottage about fifteen miles from here."

"He's worked for the company for eight years without a blemish on his record."

McAlpine ran his finger down a printout and said, "He last entered the lab three Sundays ago, for a routine check on the animals."

"What's he been doing since?"

"Holiday."

"For how long—three weeks?"

Elliot put in, "He was due back today." He looked at

his watch. "Yesterday, I should say. Monday morning. But he didn't show up."

"Did he call in sick?"

"No."

Toni raised her eyebrows. "And we can't reach him?"

"No answer from his home phone or his mobile."

"Doesn't that strike you as odd?"

"That a single young man should extend his vacation without forewarning his employer? About as odd as rain in Glen Coe."

Toni turned back to McAlpine. "But you say Michael has a good record."

The lab director looked worried. "He's very conscientious. It's surprising that he should take unauthorized leave."

Toni asked, "Who was with Michael when he last entered the lab?" She knew he must have been accompanied, for there was a two-person rule in BSL4: because of the danger, no one could work there alone.

McAlpine consulted his list. "Dr. Ansari, a biochemist."

"I don't think I know him."

"Her. It's a woman. Monica."

Toni picked up the phone. "What's her number?"

Monica Ansari spoke with an Edinburgh accent and sounded as if she had been fast asleep. "Howard McAlpine called me earlier, you know."

"I'm sorry to trouble you again."

"Has something happened?"

"It's about Michael Ross. We can't track him down. I believe you were in BSL4 with him two weeks ago last Sunday."

"Yes. Just a minute. Let me put the light on." There was a pause. "God, is that the time?"

Toni pressed on. "Michael went on holiday the next day."

"He told me he was going to see his mother in Devon."

That rang a bell. Toni recalled the reason she had gone to Michael Ross's house. About six months ago she had mentioned, in a casual conversation in the canteen, how much she liked Rembrandt's pictures of old women, with every crease and wrinkle lovingly detailed. You could tell, she had said, how much Rembrandt must have loved his mother. Michael had lit up with enthusiasm and revealed that he had copies of several Rembrandt etchings, cut out of magazines and auction house catalogues. She went home with him after work to see the pictures, all of old women, tastefully framed and covering one wall of his small living room. She worried that he was going to ask her for a date—she liked him, but not *that* way—but, to her relief, he genuinely wanted only to show off his collection. He was, she had concluded, a mother's boy.

"That's helpful," Toni said to Monica. "Just hold on." She turned to James Elliot. "Do we have his mother's contact details on file?"

Elliot moved his mouse and clicked. "She's listed as next of kin." He picked up the phone.

Toni spoke to Monica again. "Did Michael seem his normal self that afternoon?"

"Totally."

"Did you enter BSL4 together?"

"Yes. Then we went to separate changing rooms, of course."

"When you entered the lab itself, was he already there?"

"Yes, he changed quicker than I did."

"Did you work alongside him?"

"No. I was in a side lab, dealing with tissue cultures. He was checking on the animals."

"Did you leave together?"

"He went a few minutes before I did."

"It sounds to me as if he could have accessed the vault without your knowing about it."

"Easily."

"What's your impression of Michael?"

"He's all right . . . inoffensive, I suppose."

"Yeah, that's a good word for him. Do you know if he has a girlfriend?"

"I don't think so."

"Do you find him attractive?"

"Nice-looking, but not sexy."

Toni smiled. "Exactly. Anything odd about him, in your experience?"

"No."

Toni sensed a hesitation, and remained silent, giving the other woman time. Beside her, Elliot was speaking to someone, asking for Michael Ross or his mother.

After a moment, Monica said, "I mean, the fact that someone lives alone doesn't make them a nutcase, does it?"

Beside Toni, Elliot was saying into the phone, "How very strange. I'm sorry to have troubled you so late at night."

Toni's curiosity was piqued by what she could hear of Elliot's conversation. She ended her call, saying, "Thanks again, Monica. I hope you get back to sleep all right."

"My husband's a family doctor," she said. "We're used to phone calls in the middle of the night."

Toni hung up. "Michael Ross had plenty of time to

open the vault," she said. "And he lives alone." She looked at Elliot. "Did you reach his mother's house?"

"It's an old folks' home," Elliot said. He looked frightened. "And Mrs. Ross died last winter."

"Oh, shit," said Toni.

3 A.M.

POWERFUL security lights lit up the towers and gables of the Kremlin. The temperature was five below zero, but the sky was clear and there was no snow. The building faced a Victorian garden, with mature trees and shrubs. A three-quarter moon shed a gray light on naked nymphs sporting in dry fountains while stone dragons stood guard.

The silence was shattered by the roar of engines as two vans drove out of the garage. Both were marked with the international biohazard symbol, four broken black circles on a vivid yellow background. The guard at the gatehouse had the barrier up already. They drove out and turned south, going dangerously fast.

Toni Gallo was at the wheel of the lead vehicle, driving as if it were her Porsche, using the full width of the road, racing the engine, powering through bends. She feared she was too late. In the van with Toni were three men trained in decontamination. The second vehicle was a mobile isolation unit with a paramedic at the wheel and a doctor, Ruth Solomons, in the passenger seat.

Toni was afraid she might be wrong, but terrified she might be right.

She had activated a red alert on the basis of nothing but suspicion. The drug might have been used legitimately by a scientist who just forgot to make the appropriate entry in the log, as Howard McAlpine believed. Michael Ross might simply have extended his holiday without permission, and the story about his mother might have been no more than a misunderstanding. In that case, someone was sure to say that Toni had overreacted—like a typical hysterical woman, James Elliot would add. She might find Michael Ross safely asleep in bed with his phone turned off, and she winced to think what she would then say to her boss, Stanley Oxenford, in the morning.

But it would be much worse if she turned out to be right.

An employee was absent without leave; he had lied about where he was going; and samples of the new drug were missing from the vault. Had Michael Ross done something that put him at risk of catching a lethal infection? The drug was still in the trial stage, and was not effective against all viruses, but he would have figured it was better than nothing. Whatever he was up to, he had wanted to make sure no one called at his house for a couple of weeks; and so he had pretended he was going to Devon, to visit a mother who was no longer alive.

Monica Ansari had said, *The fact that someone lives alone doesn't make them a nutcase, does it?* It was one of those statements that meant the opposite of what it said. The biochemist had sensed something odd about Michael even though, as a rational scientist, she hesitated to rely on mere intuition.

Toni believed that intuition should never be ignored.

She could hardly bear to think of the consequences if the Madoba-2 virus had somehow escaped. It was highly infectious, spreading fast through coughs and sneezes. And it was fatal. A shudder of dread went through her, and she pushed down on the accelerator pedal.

The road was deserted and it took only twenty minutes to reach Michael Ross's isolated home. The entrance was not clearly marked, but Toni remembered it. She turned into a short drive that led to a low stone cottage behind a garden wall. The place was dark. Toni stopped the van next to a Volkswagen Golf, presumably Michael's. She sounded her horn long and loud.

Nothing happened. No lights came on; no one opened a door or window. Toni turned off the engine. Silence.

If Michael had gone away, why was his car here?

"Bunny suits, please, gentlemen," she said.

They all climbed into orange space suits, including the medical team from the second van. It was an awkward business. The suit was made of a heavy plastic that did not easily yield or fold. It closed with an airtight zip. They helped one another attach the gloves to the wrists with duct tape. Finally they worked the plastic feet of the suits into rubber overboots.

The suits were completely sealed. The wearer breathed through a HEPA filter—a high-efficiency particulate air filter—with an electric fan powered by a battery pack worn on the suit belt. The filter would keep out any breathable particles that might carry germs or viruses. It also took out all but the strongest smells. The fan made a constant shushing noise that some people found oppressive. A headset in the helmet enabled them to speak to one another and to the switchboard at the Kremlin over a scrambled radio channel.

When they were ready, Toni looked again at the house. Should someone glance out of a window now, and see seven people in orange space suits, he would think UFO aliens were real.

If there was someone in there, he was not looking out of any windows.

"I'll go first," Toni said.

She went up to the front door, walking stiffly in the clumsy plastic suit. She rang the bell and banged the knocker. After a few moments, she went around the building to the back. There was a neat garden with a wooden shed. She found the back door unlocked, and stepped inside. She remembered standing in the kitchen while Michael made tea. She walked quickly through the house, turning on lights. The Rembrandts were still on the living room wall. The place was clean, tidy, and empty.

She spoke to the others over the headset. "No one home." She could hear the dejected tone of her own voice.

Why had he left his house unlocked? Perhaps he was never coming back.

This was a blow. If Michael had been here, the mystery could have been solved quickly. Now there would have to be a search. He might be anywhere in the world. There was no knowing how long it would take to find him. She thought with dread of the nerve-racking days, or even weeks, of anxiety.

She went back out into the garden. To be thorough, she tried the door of the garden shed. It, too, was unlocked. When she opened it, she caught the trace of a smell, unpleasant but vaguely familiar. It must be very strong, she realized, to penetrate the suit's filter. Blood, she thought. The shed smelled like a slaughterhouse. She murmured, "Oh, my God."

Ruth Solomons, the doctor, heard her and said, "What is it?"

"Just a minute." The inside of the little wooden building was black: there were no windows. She fumbled in the dark and found a switch. When the light came on, she cried out in shock.

The others all spoke at once, asking what was wrong.

"Come quickly!" she said. "To the garden shed. Ruth first."

Michael Ross lay on the floor, faceup. He was bleeding from every orifice: eyes, nose, mouth, ears. Blood pooled around him on the plank floor. Toni did not need the doctor to tell her that Michael was suffering from a massive multiple hemorrhage—a classic symptom of Madoba-2 and similar infections. He was very dangerous, his body an unexploded bomb full of the deadly virus. But he was alive. His chest went up and down, and a weak bubbling sound came from his mouth. She bent down, kneeling in the sticky puddle of fresh blood, and looked closely at him. "Michael!" she said, shouting to be heard through the plastic of her helmet. "It's Toni Gallo from the lab!"

There was a flicker of intelligence in his bloody eyes. He opened his mouth and mumbled something.

"What?" she shouted. She leaned closer.

"No cure," he said. Then he vomited. A jet of black fluid exploded from his mouth, splashing Toni's faceplate. She jerked back and cried out in alarm, even though she knew she was protected by the suit.

She was pushed aside, and Ruth Solomons bent over Michael.

"The pulse is very weak," the doctor said over the headset. She opened Michael's mouth and used her gloved fingers to clear some of the blood and vomit from his throat. "I need a laryngoscope—fast!" Seconds later, a paramedic rushed in with the implement. Ruth pushed it into Michael's mouth, clearing his throat so that he could breathe more easily. "Bring the isolation stretcher, quick as you can." She opened her medical case and took out a syringe already loaded—with morphine and a blood coagulant, Toni assumed. Ruth pushed the needle into Michael's neck and depressed the plunger. When she pulled the syringe out, Michael bled copiously from the small hole.

Toni was swamped by a wave of grief. She thought of Michael walking around the Kremlin, sitting in his house drinking tea, talking animatedly about etchings; and the sight of this desperately damaged body became all the more painful and tragic.

"Okay," Ruth said. "Let's get him out of here."

Two paramedics picked Michael up and carried him out to a gurney enclosed in a transparent plastic tent. They slid the patient through a porthole in one end of the tent, then sealed it. They wheeled the gurney across Michael's garden.

Before getting into the ambulance, they now had to decontaminate themselves and the stretcher. One of Toni's team had already gotten out a shallow plastic tub like a children's paddling pool. Now Dr. Solomons and the paramedics took turns standing in the tub and being sprayed with a powerful disinfectant that destroyed any virus by oxidizing its protein.

Toni watched, aware that every second's delay made it less likely that Michael would survive, knowing that the decontamination procedure had to be followed rigorously to prevent other deaths. She felt distraught that a deadly virus had escaped from her laboratory. It had never occurred before in the history of Oxenford Medical. The fact that she had been right to make such a fuss about the missing drugs, and her colleagues had been wrong to play it down, was small consolation. Her job was to prevent this happening, and she had failed. Would poor Michael die in consequence? Would others die?

The paramedics loaded the stretcher into the ambulance. Dr. Solomons jumped into the back with the patient. They slammed the doors and roared off into the night.

Toni said, "Let me know what happens, Ruth. You can phone me on this headset."

Ruth's voice was already weakening with distance. "He's gone into a coma," she said. She added something else, but she was out of range, and her words became indistinguishable, then faded away altogether.

Toni shook herself to get rid of her gloomy torpor. There was work to be done. "Let's clean up," she said.

One of the men took a roll of yellow tape that read "Biohazard—Do Not Cross Line" and began to run it around the entire property, house and shed and garden, and around Michael's car. Luckily there were no other houses near enough to worry about. If Michael had lived in a block of flats with communal air vents, it would already have been too late for decontamination.

The others got out rolls of garbage bags, plastic garden sprayers already filled with disinfectant, boxes of cleaning cloths, and large white plastic drums. Every surface had to be sprayed and wiped down. Hard objects and precious possessions such as jewelry would be sealed in the drums and taken to the Kremlin to be sterilized by high-pressure steam in an autoclave. Everything else would be double-bagged and destroyed in the medical incinerator underneath the BSL4 lab.

Toni got one of the men to help her wipe Michael's black vomit off her suit and spray her. She had to repress an urge to tear the defiled suit off her body.

While the men cleaned up, she looked around, searching for clues as to why this had happened. As she had feared, Michael had stolen the experimental drug because he knew or suspected he had been infected with Madoba-2. But what had he done to expose himself to the virus?

In the shed there was a glass case with an air extractor, rather like an improvised biosafety cabinet. She had hardly looked at it before, because she was concentrating on Michael, but now she saw that there was a dead rabbit in the case. It looked as if it had died of the illness that had infected Michael. Had it come from the laboratory?

Beside it was a water bowl labeled "Joe." That was significant. Laboratory staff rarely named the creatures they worked with. They were kind to the subjects of their experiments, but they did not allow themselves to become attached to animals that were going to be killed. However, Michael had given this creature an identity, and treated it as a pet. Did he feel guilty about his work?

She stepped outside. A police patrol car was drawing

up alongside the biohazard van. Toni had been expecting them. In accordance with the Critical Incident Response Plan that Toni herself had devised, the security
guards at the Kremlin had automatically phoned regional police headquarters at Inverburn to notify them
of a red alert. Now they were coming to find out how
real the crisis was.

Toni had been a police officer herself, all her working life, until two years ago. For most of her career, she
had been a golden girl—promoted rapidly, shown off to
the media as the new style of modern cop, and tipped to
be Scotland's first woman chief constable. Then she had
clashed with her boss over a hot-button issue—racism
in the force. He maintained that police racism was not
institutionalized. She said that officers routinely concealed racist incidents, and that amounted to institu-
tionalization. The row had been leaked to a newspaper,
she had refused to deny what she believed, and she had
been forced to resign.

At the time she had been living with Frank Hackett,
another detective. They had been together eight years,
although they had never married. When she fell out of
favor, he left her. It still hurt.

Two young officers got out of the patrol car, a man
and a woman. Toni knew most local police of her own
generation, and some of the older ones remembered
her late father, Sergeant Antonio Gallo, who had in-
evitably been called Spanish Tony. However, she did not
recognize these two. Over the headset, she said,
"Jonathan, the police have arrived. Would you please
decontaminate and talk to them? Just say we have confirmed the escape of a virus from the lab. They'll call
Jim Kincaid, and I'll brief him when he gets here."

Superintendent Kincaid was responsible for what

they called CBRN—chemical, biological, radiological, and nuclear incidents. He had worked with Toni on her plan. The two of them would implement a careful, low-key response to this incident.

By the time Kincaid arrived, she would like to have some information to give him about Michael Ross. She went into the house. Michael had turned the second bedroom into his study. On a side table were three framed photographs of his mother: as a slim teenager in a tight sweater; as a happy parent, holding a baby that looked like Michael; and in her sixties, with a fat black-and-white cat in her lap.

Toni sat at his desk and read his e-mails, operating the computer keyboard clumsily with her rubber-gloved hands. He had ordered a book called *Animal Ethics* from Amazon. He had also inquired about university courses in moral philosophy. She checked his Internet browser, and found he had recently visited animal-rights Web sites. Clearly, he had become troubled about the morality of his work. But it seemed no one at Oxenford Medical had realized that he was unhappy.

Toni sympathized with him. Every time she saw a beagle or a hamster lying in a cage, deliberately made ill by a disease the scientists were studying, she felt a tug of pity. But then she remembered her father's death. He had suffered a brain tumor in his fifties, and he had died bewildered, humiliated, and in pain. His condition might one day be curable thanks to research on monkey brains. Animal research was a sad necessity, in her opinion.

Michael kept his papers in a cardboard filing box, neatly labeled: "Bills," "Guarantees," "Bank Statements," "Instruction Manuals." Under "Memberships,"

Toni found an acknowledgment of his subscription to an organization called Animals Are Free. The picture was becoming clear.

The work calmed her distress. She had always been good at detective procedures. Being forced out of the police had been a bitter blow. It felt good to use her old skills, and know that she still had the talent.

She found Michael's address book and his appointments diary in a drawer. The diary showed nothing for the last two weeks. As she was opening the address book, a blue flash caught her eye through the window, and she looked out to see a gray Volvo sedan with a police light on its roof. That would be Jim Kincaid.

She went outside and got one of the team to decontaminate her. Then she took off her helmet to talk to the Superintendent. However, the man in the Volvo was not Jim. When his face caught the moonlight, Toni saw that it was Superintendent Frank Hackett—her ex. Her heart sank. Although he was the one who had left, he always acted as if he had been the injured party.

She resolved to be calm, friendly, and businesslike.

He got out of the car and came toward her. She said, "Please don't cross the line—I'll come out." She realized right away she had made an error of tact. He was the police officer and she was the civilian—he would feel that he should be giving orders to her, not the other way around. The frown that crossed his face showed her that he had felt the slight. Trying to be more friendly, she said, "How are you, Frank?"

"What's going on here?"

"A technician from the lab appears to have caught a virus. We've just taken him away in an isolation ambulance. Now we're decontaminating his house. Where's Jim Kincaid?"

"He's on holiday."

"Where?" Toni hoped Jim might be reached and brought back for this emergency.

"Portugal. He and his wife have a wee time-share."

A pity, Toni thought. Kincaid knew about biohazards, but Frank did not.

Reading her mind, Frank said, "Don't worry." He had in his hand a photocopied document an inch thick. "I've got the protocol here." It was the plan Toni had agreed on with Kincaid. Frank had obviously been reading it while waiting. "My first duty is to secure the area." He looked around.

Toni had already secured the area, but she said nothing. Frank needed to assert himself.

He called out to the two uniformed officers in the patrol car. "You two! Move that car to the entrance of the driveway, and don't let anyone by without asking me."

"Good idea," Toni said, though in truth it made no difference to anything.

Frank was referring to the document. "Then we have to make sure no one leaves the scene."

Toni nodded. "There's no one here but my team, all in biohazard suits."

"I don't like this protocol—it puts civilians in charge of a crime scene."

"What makes you think this is a crime scene?"

"Samples of a drug were stolen."

"Not from here."

Frank let that pass. "How did your man catch the virus, anyway? You all wear those suits in the laboratory, don't you?"

"The local health board must figure that out," Toni said, prevaricating. "There's no point in speculation."

"Were there any animals here when you arrived?"

Toni hesitated.

That was enough for Frank, who was a good detective because he did not miss much. "So an animal got out of the lab and infected the technician when he wasn't wearing a suit?"

"I don't know what happened, and I don't want half-baked theories circulating. Could we concentrate for now on public safety?"

"Aye. But you're not just worried about the public. You want to protect the company and your precious Professor Oxenford."

Toni wondered why he said "precious"—but before she could react, she heard a chime from her helmet. "I'm getting a phone call," she said to Frank. "Sorry." She took the headset out of the helmet and put it on. The chime came again; then there was a hiss as the connection was made, and she heard the voice of a security guard on the switchboard at the Kremlin. "Dr. Solomons is calling Ms. Gallo."

Toni said, "Hello?"

The doctor came on the line. "Michael died, Toni."

Toni closed her eyes. "Oh, Ruth, I'm so sorry."

"He would have died even if we'd got to him twenty-four hours earlier. I'm almost certain he had Madoba-2."

Toni's voice was choked by grief. "We did all we could."

"Have you any idea how it happened?"

Toni did not want to say much in front of Frank. "He was troubled about cruelty to animals. And I think he may have been unbalanced by the death of his mother, a year ago."

"Poor boy."

"Ruth, I've got the police here. I'll talk to you later."

"Okay." The connection was broken. Toni took off the headset.

Frank said, "So he died."

"His name was Michael Ross, and he appears to have contracted a virus called Madoba-2."

"What kind of animal was it?"

On the spur of the moment, Toni decided to set a little trap for Frank. "A hamster," she said. "Named Fluffy."

"Could others have become infected?"

"That's the number one question. Michael lived here alone; he had no family and few friends. Anyone who visited him before he got sick would be safe, unless they did something highly intimate, like sharing a hypodermic needle. Anyone who came here when he was showing symptoms would surely have called a doctor. So there's a good chance he has not passed the virus on." Toni was playing it down. If she had been talking to Kincaid, she would have been more candid, for she could have trusted him not to start a scare. But Frank was different. She finished: "But obviously our first priority must be to contact everyone who might have met Michael in the last sixteen days. I've found his address book."

Frank tried a different tack. "I heard you say he was troubled about cruelty to animals. Did he belong to a group?"

"Yes—Animals Are Free."

"How do you know?"

"I've been checking his personal stuff."

"That's a job for the police."

"I agree. But you can't go into the house."

"I could put on a suit."

"It's not just the suit. It's the biohazard training that

you have to undergo before you're allowed to wear one."

Frank was becoming angry again. "Then bring the stuff out here to me."

"Why don't I get one of my team to fax all his papers to you? We could also upload the entire hard drive of his computer."

"I want the originals! What are you hiding in there?"

"Nothing, I promise you. But everything in the house has to be decontaminated, either with disinfectant or by high-pressure steam. Both processes destroy papers and might well damage a computer."

"I'm going to get this protocol changed. I wonder whether the chief constable knows what Kincaid has let you get away with."

Toni felt weary. It was the middle of the night, she had a major crisis to deal with, and she was being forced to pussyfoot around the feelings of a resentful former lover. "Oh, Frank, for God's sake—you might be right, but this is what we've got, so could we try to forget the past and work as a team?"

"Your idea of teamwork is everyone doing what you say."

She laughed. "Fair enough. What do you think should be our next move?"

"I'll inform the health board. They're the lead agency, according to the protocol. Once they've tracked down their designated biohazard consultant, he'll want to convene a meeting here first thing in the morning. Meanwhile, we should start contacting everyone who might have seen Michael Ross. I'll get a couple of detectives phoning every number in that address book. I suggest you question every employee at the Kremlin. It would be useful to have that done by the time we meet with the health board."

"All right." Toni hesitated. She had something she had to ask Frank. His best friend was Carl Osborne, a local television reporter who valued sensation more than accuracy. If Carl got hold of this story, he would start a riot.

She knew that the way to get something from Frank was to be matter-of-fact, not appearing either assertive or needy. "There's a paragraph in the protocol I've got to mention," she began. "It says that no statements should be made to the press without first being discussed by the main interested parties, including the police, the health board, and the company."

"No problem."

"The reason I mention it is that this doesn't need to become a major public scare. The chances are that no one is in danger."

"Good."

"We don't want to hold anything back, but the publicity should be calm and measured. No one needs to panic."

Frank grinned. "You're frightened of tabloid stories about killer hamsters roaming the Highlands."

"You owe me, Frank. I hope you remember."

His face darkened. "I *owe* you?"

She lowered her voice, although there was no one nearby. "You remember Farmer Johnny Kirk." Kirk had been a big-time cocaine importer. Born in the rough Glasgow neighborhood of Garscube Road, he had never seen a farm in his life, but got the nickname from the oversize green rubber boots he wore to ease the pain of the corns on his feet. Frank had put together a case against Farmer Johnny. During the trial, by accident, Toni had come across evidence that would have helped the defense. She had told Frank, but Frank had not informed the court. Johnny was as guilty as sin, and Frank had got a conviction—but if the truth ever came out, Frank's career would be over.

Now Frank said angrily, "Are you threatening to bring that up again if I don't do what you want?"

"No, just reminding you of a time when you needed me to keep quiet about something, and I did."

His attitude changed again. He had been frightened, for a moment, but now he was his old arrogant self. "We all bend the rules from time to time. That's life."

"Yes. And I'm asking you not to leak this story to your friend Carl Osborne, or anyone else in the media."

Frank grinned. "Why, Toni," he said in a tone of mock indignation, "I never do things like that."

7 A.M.

KIT OXENFORD woke early, feeling eager and anxious at the same time. It was a strange sensation.

Today he was going to rob Oxenford Medical.

The idea filled him with excitement. It would be the greatest prank ever. It would be written up in books with titles like *The Perfect Crime.* Even better, it would be revenge on his father. The company would be destroyed, and Stanley Oxenford would be ruined financially. The fact that the old man would never know who had done this to him somehow made it better. It would be a secret gratification that Kit could hug to himself for the rest of his life.

But he was anxious, too. This was unusual. By nature, he was not a worrier. Whatever trouble he was in, he could generally talk his way out. He rarely planned anything.

He had planned today. Perhaps that was his problem.

He lay in bed with his eyes closed, thinking of the obstacles he had to overcome.

First, there was the physical security around the Kremlin: the double row of fencing, the razor wire, the lights, the intruder alarms. Those alarms were protected by tamper switches, shock sensors, and end-of-line circuitry that would detect a short circuit. The alarms were directly connected to regional police headquarters at Inverburn via a phone line that was continuously checked by the system to verify that it was operational.

None of that would protect the place against Kit and his collaborators.

Then there were the guards, watching important areas on closed-circuit television cameras, patrolling the premises hourly. Their TV monitors were fitted with high-security biased switches that would detect equipment substitution, for example if the feed from a camera were replaced by a signal from a videotape player.

Kit had thought of a way around that.

Finally there was the elaborate scheme of access control: the plastic credit-card passes, each bearing a photo of the authorized user plus details of the user's fingerprint embedded in a chip.

Defeating this system would be complicated, but Kit knew how to do it.

His degree was in computer science, and he had been top of his class, but he had an even more important advantage. He had designed the software that controlled the entire security setup at the Kremlin. It was his baby. He had done a terrific job for his ungrateful father, and the system was virtually impenetrable to an outsider, but Kit knew its secrets.

At around midnight tonight, he would walk into the holy of holies, the BSL4 laboratory, the most secure location in Scotland. With him would be his client, a quietly menacing Londoner called Nigel Buchanan, and

two collaborators. Once there, Kit would open the re-
frigerated vault with a simple four-digit code. Then
Nigel would steal samples of Stanley Oxenford's precious new antiviral drug.

They would not keep the samples long. Nigel had a
strict deadline. He had to hand over the samples by ten
o'clock tomorrow morning, Christmas Day. Kit did not
know the reason for the deadline. He did not know who
the customer was, either, but he could guess. It had to be
one of the pharmaceutical multinationals. Having a
sample to analyze would save years of research. The
company would be able to make its own version of the
drug, instead of paying Oxenford millions in licensing
fees.

It was dishonest, of course, but men found excuses
for dishonesty when the stakes were high. Kit could picture the company's distinguished chairman, with his silver hair and pin-striped suit, saying hypocritically, "Can
you assure me categorically that no employee of our
organization broke any laws in obtaining this sample?"

The best part of Kit's plan, he felt, was that the in-
trusion would go unnoticed until long after he and
Nigel had left the Kremlin. Today, Tuesday, was Christmas Eve. Tomorrow and the next day were holidays. At
the earliest, the alarm might be sounded on Friday,
when one or two eager-beaver scientists would show up
for work; but there was a good chance the theft would
not be spotted then or over the weekend, giving Kit and
the gang until Monday of next week to cover their
tracks. It was more time than they needed.

So why was he frightened? The face of Toni Gallo, his
father's security chief, came into his mind. She was a
freckled redhead, very attractive in a muscular sort of
way, though too formidable a personality for Kit's taste.

Was she the reason for his fear? Once before he had underestimated her—with disastrous results.

But his plan was brilliant. "Brilliant," he said aloud, trying to convince himself.

"What is?" said a female voice beside him.

He grunted in surprise. He had forgotten that he was not alone. He opened his eyes. The apartment was pitch-dark.

"What's brilliant?" she repeated.

"The way you dance," he said, improvising. He had met her in a club last night.

"You're not bad yourself," she said in a strong Glasgow accent. "Nifty footwork."

He racked his brains for her name. "Maureen," he said. She must be Catholic, with a name like that. He rolled over and put his arm around her, trying to remember what she looked like. She felt nicely rounded. He liked girls not too thin. She moved toward him willingly. Blond or brunette? he wondered. It might be interestingly kinky to have sex with a girl not knowing what she looked like. He was reaching for her breasts when he remembered what he had to do today, and his amorousness evaporated. "What's the time?" he said.

"Time for a wee shag," Maureen said eagerly.

Kit rolled away from her. The digital clock on the hi-fi said 07:10. "Got to get up," he said. "Busy day." He wanted to be at his father's house in time for lunch. He was going there ostensibly for the Christmas holiday, actually to steal something he needed for tonight's robbery.

"How can you be busy on Christmas Eve?"

"Maybe I'm Santa Claus." He sat on the edge of the bed and switched on the light.

Maureen was disappointed. "Well, this wee elf is

going to have a lie-in, if that's all right with Santa," she said grumpily.

He glanced at her, but she had pulled the duvet over her head. He still did not know what she looked like.

He walked naked to the kitchen and started making coffee.

His loft was divided into two big spaces. There was a living room, with an open kitchen, and a bedroom beyond. The living room was full of electronic gear: a big flat-screen television, an elaborate sound system, and a stack of computers and accessories connected by a jungle of cables. Kit had always enjoyed picking the locks of other people's computer defenses. The only way to become an expert in software security was to be a hacker first.

While he was working for his father, designing and installing protection for the BSL4 laboratory, he had pulled off one of his best scams. With the help of Ronnie Sutherland, then head of security for Oxenford Medical, he had devised a way of skimming money from the company. He had rigged the accounting software so that, in summing a series of suppliers' invoices, the computer simply added 1 percent to the total, then transferred the 1 percent to Ronnie's bank account in a transaction that did not appear on any report. The scam relied on no one checking the computer's arithmetic—and no one had, until one day Toni Gallo saw Ronnie's wife parking a new Mercedes coupe outside Marks & Spencer in Inverburn.

Kit had been astonished and frightened by the dogged persistence with which Toni investigated. There was a discrepancy, and she had to have the explanation. She just never gave up. Worse, when she figured out what was going on, nothing in the world would prevent her from telling the boss, Kit's father. He had pleaded with her not to bring anguish to an old man. He had tried to convince her that Stanley Oxenford in his rage would fire her, not Kit. Finally he had rested a hand lightly on her hip, given her his best naughty-boy grin, and said in a come-to-bed voice, "You and I should be friends, not enemies." None of it had worked.

Kit had not found employment since being fired by his father. Unfortunately, he had continued to gamble. Ronnie had introduced him to an illegal casino where he was able to get credit, doubtless because Kit's father was a famous millionaire scientist. He tried not to think of how much money he now owed: the figure made him sick with fear and self-disgust, and he just wanted to throw himself off the Forth Bridge. But his reward for tonight's work would pay off the entire sum and give him a fresh start.

He took his coffee into the bathroom and looked at himself in the mirror. At one time he had been on the British team for the Winter Olympics, and he had spent every weekend either skiing or training. Then, he had been as lean and fit as a greyhound. Now he saw a little softness in his outline. "You're putting on weight," he said. But he still had thick brown hair that flopped adorably over his forehead. His face looked strained. He tried his Hugh Grant expression, head down bashfully, looking up out of the corners of his blue eyes with a winning smile. Yes, he could still do it. Toni Gallo might be immune, but Maureen had fallen for it only last night.

While shaving, he turned on the bathroom TV and got a local news program. The British Prime Minister had arrived in his Scottish constituency for Christmas. Glasgow Rangers had paid nine million pounds for a striker called Giovanni Santangelo. "There's a good old Scots name," Kit said to himself. The weather was going to continue cold but clear. A fierce blizzard in the Norwegian Sea was drifting south, but was expected to pass to the west of Scotland. Then came a local news story that froze Kit's blood.

He heard the familiar voice of Carl Osborne, a Scottish television celebrity with a reputation for lurid reports. Glancing at the screen, Kit saw the very building he was planning to rob tonight. Osborne was broadcasting from outside the gates of Oxenford Medical. It was still dark, but powerful security lights illuminated the ornate Victorian architecture. "What the hell is this?" Kit said worriedly.

Osborne said, "Scientists experiment with some of the most dangerous viruses in the world right here in Scotland, in the building behind me, dubbed 'Frankenstein's Castle' by local people."

Kit had never heard anyone call it "Frankenstein's Castle." Osborne was making that up. Its nickname was the Kremlin.

"But today, in what seems to some observers to be Nature's retribution for Mankind's meddling, a young technician died of one of these viruses."

Kit put down his razor. This would be woundingly bad publicity for Oxenford Medical, he realized immediately. Normally, he would have gloated at his father's trouble, but today he was more worried about the effect of such publicity on his own plans.

"Michael Ross, thirty-one, was struck down by a virus called Ebola, after the African village where it germinated. This agonizing affliction causes painful, suppurating boils all over the victim's body."

Kit was pretty sure Osborne was getting the facts

wrong, but his audience would not know. This was tabloid television. But would the death of Michael Ross jeopardize Kit's planned robbery?

"Oxenford Medical has always claimed its research poses no threat to local people or the surrounding countryside, but the death of Michael Ross throws that claim into serious doubt."

Osborne was wearing a bulky anorak and a woolly hat, and he looked as if he had not slept much last night. Someone had woken him up in the early hours of the morning with a tip-off, Kit guessed.

"Ross may have been bitten by an animal he stole from the laboratory here and took to his home a few miles away," Osborne went on.

"Oh, no," said Kit. This was getting worse and worse. Surely he was not going to be forced to abandon his grand scheme? It would be too much to bear.

"Did Michael Ross work alone, or was he part of a larger group that may attempt to free more plague-carrying animals from Oxenford Medical's secret laboratories? Do we face the prospect of innocent-seeming dogs and rabbits roaming free over the Scottish landscape, spreading the lethal virus wherever they go? No one here is prepared to say."

Whatever they might or might not say, Kit knew what the people at the Kremlin were doing: upgrading their security as fast as they could. Toni Gallo would be there already, tightening up procedures, checking alarms and cameras, briefing the security guards. It was the worst possible news for Kit. He was enraged. "Why do I have such bad luck?" he said aloud.

"Be that as it may," said Carl Osborne, "Michael Ross appears to have died for love of a hamster named Fluffy." His tone was so tragic that Kit half expected the reporter to wipe a tear from his eye, but Osborne stopped short of that.

The studio anchor, an attractive blonde with carved hair, now said, "Carl, has Oxenford Medical made any comment at all on this extraordinary incident?"

"Yes." Carl looked at a notebook. "They say they are saddened and distressed by the death of Michael Ross, but the indications are that nobody else will be affected by the virus. Nevertheless, they would like to speak to anyone who has seen Ross in the past sixteen days."

"Presumably, people who have been in contact with him may have picked up the virus."

"Yes, and perhaps infected others. So the company's statement that no one else is affected seems more like a pious hope than a scientific prediction."

"A very worrying story," the anchor said to camera. "Carl Osborne with that report. And now football."

In a fury, Kit stabbed at the remote control, trying to turn off the television, but he was too agitated, and kept pressing the wrong buttons. In the end he grabbed the TV cable and yanked the plug out of its socket. He was tempted to throw the set through the window. This was a catastrophe.

Osborne's doomsday forecast about the virus spreading might not be true, but the one sure consequence was that security at the Kremlin would be watertight. Tonight was the worst possible time to try to rob the place. Kit would have to call it off. He was a gambler: if he had a good hand, he was willing to bet the farm, but he knew that when the cards were against him it was best to fold.

At least I won't have to spend Christmas with my father, he thought sourly.

Maybe they could do the job some other time, when

the excitement had died down and security had returned to its normal level. Perhaps the customer could be persuaded to postpone his deadline. Kit shuddered when he thought of his enormous debt remaining unpaid. But there was no point in going ahead when failure was so likely.

He left the bathroom. The clock on the hi-fi said 07:28. It was early to telephone, but this was urgent. He picked up the handset and dialed.

The call was answered immediately. A man's voice said simply, "Yes?"

"This is Kit. Is he in?"

"What do you want?"

"I need to speak to him. It's important."

"He's not up yet."

"Shit." Kit did not want to leave a message. And, on reflection, he did not want Maureen to hear what he had to say. "Tell him I'm coming round," he said. He hung up without waiting for a reply.

7:30 A.M.

TONI GALLO thought she would be out of work by lunchtime.

She looked around her office. She had not been here long. She had only just begun to make the place her own. On the desk was a photograph of her with her mother and her sister, Bella, taken a few years ago when Mother was in good health. Beside it was her battered old dictionary—she had never been able to spell. Just last week she had hung on the wall a picture of herself in her police constable's uniform, taken seventeen years ago, looking young and eager.

She could hardly believe she had already lost this job.

She now knew what Michael Ross had done. He had devised a clever and elaborate way of getting around all her security precautions. He had found the weaknesses and exploited them. There was no one to blame but herself.

She had not known this two hours ago, when she had phoned Stanley Oxenford, chairman and majority shareholder in Oxenford Medical.

She had been dreading the call. She had to give him the worst possible news, and take the blame. She steeled herself for his disappointment, indignation, or perhaps rage.

He had said, "Are you all right?"

She almost cried. She had not anticipated that his first thought would be for her welfare. She did not deserve such kindness. "I'm fine," she said. "We all put on bunny suits before we went into the house."

"But you must be exhausted."

"I snatched an hour's sleep at around five."

"Good," Stanley said, and briskly moved on. "I know Michael Ross. Quiet chap, about thirty, been with us for a few years—an experienced technician. How the hell did this happen?"

"I found a dead rabbit in his garden shed. I think he brought home a laboratory animal and it bit him."

"I doubt it," Stanley said crisply. "More likely he cut himself with a contaminated knife. Even experienced people may get careless. The rabbit is probably a normal pet that starved after Michael fell ill."

Toni wished she could pretend to believe that, but she had to give her boss the facts. "The rabbit was in an improvised biosafety cabinet," she argued.

"I still doubt it. Michael can't have been working alone, in BSL4. Even if his buddy wasn't looking, there are television cameras in every room—he couldn't have stolen a rabbit without being seen on the monitors. Then he had to pass several security guards on the way out—they would have noticed if he were carrying a rabbit. Finally, the scientists working in the lab the following morning would have realized immediately that an animal was missing. They might not be able to tell the difference between one rabbit and another, but they certainly know how many there are in the experiment."

Early though it was, his brain had fired up like the V12 engine in his Ferrari, Toni thought. But he was wrong. "I put all those security barriers in place," she said. "And I'm telling you that no system is perfect."

"You're right, of course." If you gave him good arguments, he could back down alarmingly fast. "I presume we have video footage of the last time Michael was in BSL4?"

"Next thing on my checklist."

"I'll be there at about eight. Have some answers for me then, please."

"One more thing. As soon as the staff begin arriving, rumors will spread. May I tell people that you'll be making an announcement?"

"Good point. I'll speak to everyone in the Great Hall at, say, nine-thirty." The grand entrance hall of the old house was the biggest room in the building, always used for large meetings.

Toni had then summoned Susan Mackintosh, one of the security guards, a pretty girl in her twenties with a boyish haircut and a pierced eyebrow. Susan immediately noticed the picture on the wall. "You look good in a uniform," she said.

"Thanks. I realize you're due to go off duty, but I need a woman for this job."

Susan raised an eyebrow flirtatiously. "I know the feeling."

Toni recalled the company Christmas party, last Friday. Susan had dressed like John Travolta in the movie *Grease*, with slicked hair, drainpipe jeans, and the kind of crepe-soled shoes known in Glasgow as brothel creepers. She had asked Toni to dance. Toni had smiled warmly and said, "I don't think so." A little later, after a few more drinks, Susan had asked her if she slept with men. "Not as much as I'd like," Toni had said.

Toni was flattered that someone so young and pretty was attracted to her, but she pretended not to notice. "I need you to stop all employees as they arrive. Set up a desk in the Great Hall, and don't let them go to their offices or labs until you've spoken to them."

"What should I say?"

"Tell them there's been a virus security breach, and Professor Oxenford is going to give them a full briefing this morning. Be calm and reassuring, but don't go into detail—best leave that to Stanley."

"Okay."

"Then ask them when they last saw Michael Ross. Some will have been asked that question over the phone last night, but only those certified for BSL4, and it does no harm to double-check. If anyone has seen him since he left here on Sunday two weeks ago, tell me immediately."

"Okay."

Toni had a delicate question to ask, and she hesitated, then just came out with it. "Do you think Michael was gay?"

"Not actively."

"Are you sure?"

"Inverburn is a small town. There are two gay pubs, a club, a couple of restaurants, a church . . . I know all those places and I've never seen him in any of them."

"Okay. I hope you don't mind my assuming you'd know, just because . . ."

"It's all right." Susan smiled and gave Toni a direct

look. "You'll have to work harder than that to offend me."

"Thanks."

That was almost two hours ago. Toni had spent most of the time since then viewing video footage of Michael Ross on his last visit to BSL4. She now had the answers Stanley wanted. She was going to tell him what had happened, and then he would probably ask for her resignation.

She recalled her first meeting with Stanley. She had been at the lowest point of her entire life. She was pretending to be a freelance security consultant, but she had no clients. Her partner of eight years, Frank, had left her. And her mother was becoming senile. Toni had felt like Job after he was forsaken by God.

Stanley had summoned her to his office and offered her a short-term contract. He had invented a drug so valuable that he feared he might be the target of industrial espionage. He wanted her to check. She had not told him it was her first real assignment.

After combing the premises for listening devices, she had looked for signs that key employees were living above their means. No one was spying on Oxenford Medical, as it turned out—but, to her dismay, she discovered that Stanley's son, Kit, was stealing from the company.

She was shocked. Kit had struck her as charming and untrustworthy; but what kind of man robs his own father? "The old bugger can afford it. He's got plenty," Kit said carelessly; and Toni knew, from her years with the police, that there was nothing profound about wickedness—criminals were just shallow, greedy people with inadequate excuses.

Kit had tried to persuade her to hush it up. He promised never to do it again if Toni would keep quiet this time. She was tempted: she did not want to tell a recently bereaved man that his son was no good. But to keep quiet would have been dishonest.

So, in the end, and with great trepidation, she had told Stanley everything.

She would never forget the look on his face. He went pale, grimaced, and said, "Aah," as if feeling a sudden internal pain. In that moment, as he struggled to master his profound emotion, she saw both his strength and his sensitivity, and she felt strongly drawn to him.

Telling him the truth had been the right decision. Her integrity had been rewarded. Stanley fired Kit and gave Toni a full-time job. For that, she would always owe him her iron loyalty. She was fiercely determined to repay his trust.

And life had improved. Stanley quickly promoted her from head of security to facilities manager and gave her a raise. She bought a red Porsche.

When she mentioned one day that she had played squash for the national police team, Stanley challenged her to a game on the company court. She beat him, but only just, and they began to play every week. He was very fit, and had a longer reach, but she was twenty years younger, with hair-trigger reflexes. He took a game from her now and again, when her concentration slipped, but in the end she usually won.

And she got to know him better. He played a shrewd game, taking risks that often paid off. He was competitive, but good-humored about losing. Her quick mind was a match for his brain, and she enjoyed the cut-and-thrust. The more she got to know him, the better she liked him. Until, one day, she realized that she did not just like him. It was more than that.

Now she felt that the worst part of losing this job would be not seeing him any longer.

She was about to head down to the Great Hall, to meet him on his way in, when her phone rang.

A woman's voice with a southern English accent said, "This is Odette."

"Hi!" Toni was pleased. Odette Cressy was a detective with the Metropolitan Police in London. They had met on a course at Hendon five years ago. They were the same age. Odette was single and, since Toni had split up with Frank, they had been on holiday together twice. Had they not lived so far apart, they would have been best friends. As it was, they spoke on the phone every couple of weeks.

Odette said, "It's about your virus victim."

"Why would you be interested?" Odette was on the antiterrorist team, Toni knew. "I suppose I shouldn't ask."

"Correct. I'll just say that the name Madoba-2 rang an alarm bell here, and leave you to work it out."

Toni frowned. As a former cop, she could guess what was going on. Odette had intelligence indicating that some group was interested in Madoba-2. A suspect might have mentioned it under interrogation, or the virus had come up in a bugged conversation, or someone whose phone lines were being monitored had typed the name into a computer search engine. Now, anytime a quantity of the virus went astray, the antiterrorist unit would suspect that it had been stolen by fanatics. "I don't think Michael Ross was a terrorist," Toni said. "I think he just became attached to a particular laboratory animal."

"What about his friends?"

"I found his address book, and the Inverburn police are checking the names right now."

"Did you keep a copy?"

It was on her desk. "I can fax it to you right away."

"Thanks—it will save me time." Odette recited a number and Toni wrote it down. "How are you getting on with your handsome boss?"

Toni had not told anyone how she felt about Stanley, but Odette was telepathic. "I don't believe in sex at work—you know that. Anyway, his wife died recently—"

"Eighteen months ago, as I recall."

"Which is not long, after nearly forty years of marriage. And he's devoted to his children and grandchildren, who would probably hate anyone who tried to replace his late wife."

"You know the good thing about sex with an older man? He's so worried about not being young and vigorous that he works twice as hard to please you."

"I'm going to have to take your word for that."

"And what else? Oh, yes, I almost forgot, ha ha: he's rich. Listen, all I'm going to say is this: if you decide you don't want him, I'll have him. Meanwhile, let me know personally if you find out anything new about Michael Ross."

"Of course." Toni hung up and glanced out of the window. Stanley Oxenford's dark blue Ferrari F50 was pulling into the chairman's parking space. She put the copy of Michael's address book into the fax machine and dialed Odette's number.

Then, feeling like a criminal about to be sentenced, she went to meet her boss.

8 A.M.

THE Great Hall was like the nave of a church. It had tall arched windows that let in shafts of sunlight to make patterns on the flagstone floor. The room was spanned by the mighty timbers of an open hammer-beam roof. In the middle of this graced space, incongruously, was a modern oval reception desk with high counters. A uniformed security guard sat on a stool inside the oval.

Stanley Oxenford came through the grand entrance. He was a tall man of sixty with thick gray hair and blue eyes. He did not look the part of a scientist—no bald dome, no stoop, no spectacles. Toni thought he was more like the kind of actor who plays the general in a movie about the Second World War. He dressed well without seeming stuffy. Today he wore a soft gray tweed suit with a waistcoat, a light blue shirt, and—out of respect for the dead, perhaps—a black knitted tie.

Susan Mackintosh had placed a trestle table near the

front door. She spoke to Stanley as he came in. He replied briefly, then turned to Toni. "This is a good idea—buttonholing everyone as they arrive and asking when they last saw Michael."

"Thank you." I've done one thing right, at least, Toni thought.

Stanley went on: "What about staff who are on holiday?"

"Personnel will phone them all this morning."

"Good. Have you found out what happened?"

"Yes. I was right and you were wrong. It was the rabbit."

Despite the tragic circumstances, he smiled. He liked people to challenge him, especially attractive women. "How do you know?"

"From the video footage. Would you like to see it?"

"Yes."

They walked along a wide corridor with oak linen-fold paneling, then turned down a side passage to the central monitoring station, normally called the control room. This was the security center. It had once been a billiards room, but the windows had been bricked up for security, and the ceiling had been lowered to create a hiding place for a snake's nest of cabling. One wall was a bank of television monitors showing key areas of the site, including every room within BSL4. On a long desk were touch screens controlling alarms. Thousands of electronic checkpoints monitored temperature, humidity, and air management systems in all the laboratories—if you held a door open too long, an alarm would sound. A guard in a neat uniform sat at a workstation that gave access to the central security computer.

Stanley said in a surprised tone, "This place has been tidied up since last I was here."

When Toni had taken over security the control room was a mess, littered with dirty coffee cups, old newspapers, broken Biros, and half-empty Tupperware lunch boxes. Now it was clean and tidy, with nothing on the desk except the file the guard was reading. She was pleased Stanley had noticed.

He glanced into the adjacent equipment room, once the gun room, now full of support devices, including the central processing unit for the phone system. It was brightly lit. A thousand cables were clearly labeled with nonremovable, easy-to-read tags, to minimize downtime in case of technical failure. Stanley nodded approval.

This was all to the good, Toni felt; but Stanley already knew she was an efficient organizer. The most important part of her job was making sure nothing dangerous escaped from the BSL4 lab—and in that she had failed.

There were times when she did not know what Stanley was thinking, and this was one. Was he grieving for Michael Ross, fearful for the future of his company, or furious about the security breach? Would he turn his wrath on her, or the dead Michael, or Howard McAlpine? When Toni showed him what Michael had done, would Stanley praise her for having figured it out so quickly, or fire her for letting it happen?

They sat side by side in front of a monitor, and Toni tapped the keyboard to bring up the pictures she wanted him to see. The computer's vast memory stored images for twenty-eight days before erasing them. She was intimately familiar with the program and navigated it with ease.

Sitting beside Stanley, she was absurdly reminded of going to the movies with a boyfriend at the age of fourteen, and allowing him to put his hand up her sweater. The memory embarrassed her, and she felt her neck redden. She hoped Stanley would not notice.

On the monitor, she showed him Michael arriving at the main gate and presenting his pass. "The date and time are on the bottom of the screen," she said. It was fourteen-twenty-seven on the eighth of December. She tapped the keyboard, and the screen showed a green Volkswagen Golf pulling into a parking space. A slight man got out and took a duffel bag from the back of the car. "Watch that bag," Toni said.

"Why?"

"There's a rabbit in it."

"How did he manage that?"

"I guess it's tranquilized, and probably wrapped up tightly. Remember, he's been dealing with laboratory animals for years. He knows how to keep them calm."

The next shot showed Michael presenting his pass again at reception. A pretty Pakistani woman of about forty came into the Great Hall. "That's Monica Ansari," said Stanley.

"She was his buddy. She needed to do some work on tissue cultures, and he was performing the routine weekend check on the animals."

They walked along the corridor Toni and Stanley had taken, but went past the turning for the control room and continued to the door at the end. It looked like all the other doors in the building, with four recessed panels and a brass knob, but it was made of steel. On the wall beside the door was the yellow-and-black warning of the international biohazard symbol.

Dr. Ansari waved a plastic pass in front of a remote card reader, then pressed the forefinger of her left hand to a small screen. There was a pause, while the computer checked that her fingerprint matched the information on the microchip embedded in the smart card. This ensured that lost or stolen cards could not be used by unauthorized persons. While Dr. Ansari waited, she glanced up at the television camera and gave a mock salute. Then the door opened and she stepped through. Michael followed.

Another camera showed them in a small lobby. A row of dials on the wall monitored the air pressure in the lab. The farther you went inside BSL4, the lower the air pressure. This downward gradient ensured that any leakage of air was inward, not outward. From the lobby they went to separate men's and women's changing rooms. "This is when he took the rabbit out of the bag," Toni said. "If his buddy that day had been a man, the plan wouldn't have worked. But he had Monica and, of course, there are no cameras in the changing rooms."

"But damn it, you can't put security cameras in changing rooms," Stanley said. "No one would work here."

"Absolutely," said Toni. "We'll have to think of something else. Watch this."

The next shot came from a camera inside the lab. It showed conventional rabbit racks housed in a clear plastic isolation cover. Toni froze the picture. "Could you explain to me what the scientists are doing in this lab, exactly?"

"Of course. Our new drug is effective against many viruses, but not all. In this experiment it was being tested against Madoba-2, a variant of the Ebola virus that causes a lethal hemorrhagic fever in both rabbits and humans. Two groups of rabbits were challenged with the virus."

"Challenged?"

"Sorry—it's the word we use. It means they were infected. Then one group was injected with the drug."

"What did you find?"

"The drug doesn't defeat Madoba-2 in rabbits. We're a bit disappointed. Almost certainly, it won't cure this type of virus in humans either."

"But you didn't know that sixteen days ago."

"Correct."

"In that case, I think I understand what Michael was trying to do." She touched the keyboard to unfreeze the picture. A figure stepped into shot wearing a light blue plastic space suit with a clear helmet. He stopped by the door to push his feet into rubber overboots. Then he reached up and grabbed a curly yellow air hose hanging from the ceiling. He connected it to an inlet on his belt. As air was pumped in, the suit inflated, until he looked like the Michelin Man.

"This is Michael," Toni said. "He changed faster than Monica, so at the moment he's in there alone."

"It shouldn't happen, but it does," Stanley said. "The two-person rule is observed, but not minute by minute. *Merda*." Stanley often cursed in Italian, having learned a ripe vocabulary from his wife. Toni, who spoke Spanish, usually understood.

On screen Michael went up to the rabbit rack, moving with deliberate slowness in the awkward costume. His back was to the camera and, for a few moments, the pumped-up suit shielded what he was doing. Then he stepped away and dropped something on a stainless-steel laboratory bench.

"Notice anything?" Toni said.

"No."

"Nor did the security guards who were watching the monitors." Toni was defending her staff. If Stanley had not seen what happened, he could hardly blame the guards for missing it, too. "But look again." She went back a couple of minutes and froze the frame as Michael stepped into shot. "One rabbit in that top right-hand cage."

"I see."

"Look harder at Michael. He's got something under his arm."

"Yes—wrapped in blue plastic suit fabric."

She ran the footage forward, stopping again as Michael moved away from the rabbit rack. "How many rabbits in the top right-hand cage?"

"Two, damn it." Stanley looked perplexed. "I thought your theory was that Michael took a rabbit out of the lab. You've shown him bringing one in!"

"A substitute. Otherwise the scientists would have noticed one was missing."

"Then what's his motivation? In order to save one rabbit, he has to condemn another to death!"

"Insofar as he was rational at all, I imagine he felt there was something special about the rabbit he saved."

"For God's sake, one rabbit is the same as another."

"Not to Michael, I suspect."

Stanley nodded. "You're right. Who knows how his mind was working at this point."

Toni ran the video footage forward. "He did his chores as usual, checking the food and water in the cages, making sure the animals were still alive, ticking off his tasks on a checklist. Monica came in, but she went to a side laboratory to work on her tissue cultures, so she could not see him. He went next door, to the larger lab, to take care of the macaque monkeys. Then he came back. Now watch."

Michael disconnected his air hose, as was normal

when moving from one room to another within the lab—the suit contained three or four minutes' worth of fresh air, and when it began to run out the faceplate would fog, warning the wearer. He stepped into a small room containing the vault, a locked refrigerator used for storing live samples of viruses. Being the most secure location in the entire building, it also held all stocks of the priceless antiviral drug. He tapped a combination of digits on its keypad. A security camera inside the refrigerator showed him selecting two doses of the drug, already measured and loaded into disposable syringes.

"The small dose for the rabbit and the large one, presumably, for himself," Toni said. "Like you, he expected the drug to work against Madoba-2. He planned to cure the rabbit and immunize himself."

"The guards could have seen him taking the drug from the vault."

"But they wouldn't find that suspicious. He's authorized to handle these materials."

"They might have noticed that he didn't write anything in the log."

"They might have, but remember that one guard is watching thirty-seven screens, and he's not trained in laboratory practice."

Stanley grunted.

Toni said, "Michael must have figured that the discrepancy wouldn't be noticed until the annual audit, and even then it would be put down to clerical error. He didn't know I was planning a spot check."

On the television screen, Michael closed the vault and returned to the rabbit lab, reconnecting his air hose. "He's finished his chores," Toni explained. "Now he returns to the rabbit racks." Once again, Michael's back concealed what he was doing from the camera. "Here's where he takes his favorite rabbit out of its cage. I think he slips it into its own miniature suit, probably made from parts of an old worn-out one."

Michael turned his left side to the camera. As he walked to the exit, he seemed to have something under his right arm, but it was hard to tell.

Leaving BSL4, everyone had to pass through a chemical shower that decontaminated the suit, then take a regular shower before dressing. "The suit would have protected the rabbit in the chemical shower," Toni said. "My guess is that he then dumped the rabbit suit in the incinerator. The water shower would not have harmed the animal. In the dressing room he put the rabbit in the duffel bag. As he exited the building, the guards saw him carrying the same bag he came in with, and suspected nothing."

Stanley sat back in his seat. "Well, I'm damned," he said. "I would have sworn it was impossible."

"He took the rabbit home. I think it may have bitten him when he injected it with the drug. He injected himself and thought he was safe. But he was wrong."

Stanley looked sad. "Poor boy," he said. "Poor, foolish boy."

"Now you know everything I know," Toni said. She watched him, waiting for the verdict. Was this phase of her life over? Would she be out of work for Christmas?

He gave her a level look. "There's one obvious security precaution we could have taken that would have prevented this."

"I know," she said. "A bag search for everyone entering and leaving BSL4."

"Exactly."

"I've instituted it from this morning."

"Thereby closing the stable door after the horse has bolted."

"I'm sorry," she said. He wanted her to quit, she felt sure. "You pay me to stop this kind of thing happening. I've failed. I expect you'd like me to tender my resignation."

He looked irritated. "If I want to fire you, you'll know soon enough."

She stared at him. Had she been reprieved?

His expression softened. "All right, you're a conscientious person and you feel guilty, even though neither you nor anyone else could have anticipated what happened."

"I could have instituted the bag check."

"I probably would have vetoed it, on the grounds that it would upset staff."

"Oh."

"So I'll tell you this once. Since you came, our security has been tighter than ever before. You're damn good, and I aim to keep you. So, please, no more self-pity."

She suddenly felt weak with relief. "Thank you," she said.

"Now, we've got a busy day ahead—let's get on with it." He went out.

She closed her eyes in relief. She had been forgiven. Thank you, she thought.

8:30 A.M.

MIRANDA OXENFORD ordered a cappuccino Viennoise, with a pyramid of whipped cream on top. At the last moment she asked for a piece of carrot cake as well. She stuffed her change into the pocket of her skirt and carried her breakfast to the table where her thin sister, Olga, was seated with a double espresso and a cigarette. The place was bedecked with paper chains, and a Christmas tree twinkled over the *panini* toaster, but someone with a nice sense of irony had put the Beach Boys on the music system, and they were singing "Surfin' USA."

Miranda often ran into Olga first thing in the morning at this coffee bar in Sauchiehall Street, in the center of Glasgow. They worked nearby: Miranda was managing director of a recruitment agency specializing in IT personnel, and Olga was an advocate. They both liked to take five minutes to gather their thoughts before going into their offices.

They did not look like sisters, Miranda thought, catching a glimpse of her reflection in a mirror. She was short, with curly blond hair, and her figure was, well, cuddly. Olga was tall like Daddy, but she had the same black eyebrows as their late mother, who had been Italian by birth and was always called Mamma Marta. Olga was dressed for work in a dark gray suit and sharply pointed shoes. She could have played the part of Cruella De Vil. She probably terrified juries.

Miranda took off her coat and scarf. She wore a pleated skirt and a sweater embroidered with small flowers. She dressed to charm, not to intimidate. As she sat down, Olga said, "You're working on Christmas Eve?"

"Just for an hour," Miranda replied. "To make sure nothing's left undone over the holiday."

"Same here."

"Have you heard the news? A technician at the Kremlin died of a virus."

"Oh, God, that's going to blight our Christmas."

Olga could seem heartless, but she was not really so, Miranda thought. "It was on the radio. I haven't spoken to Daddy yet, but it seems the poor boy became fond of a lab hamster and took it home."

"What did he do, have sex with it?"

"It probably bit him. He lived alone, so nobody called for help. At least that means he probably didn't pass the virus to anyone else. All the same, it's awful for Daddy. He won't show it, but he's sure to feel responsible."

"He should have gone in for a less hazardous branch of science—something like atomic weapons research."

Miranda smiled. She was especially pleased to see Olga today. She was glad of the chance of a quiet word.

The whole family was about to gather at Steepfall, their father's house, for Christmas. She was bringing her fiancé, Ned Hanley, and she wanted to make sure Olga would be nice to him. But she approached the subject in a roundabout way. "I hope this doesn't spoil the holiday. I've been looking forward to it so much. You know Kit's coming?"

"I'm deeply sensible of the honor our little brother is doing us."

"He wasn't going to come, but I talked him round."

"Daddy will be pleased." Olga spoke with a touch of sarcasm.

"He will, actually," Miranda said reproachfully. "You know it broke his heart to fire Kit."

"I know I've never seen him so angry. I thought he would kill someone."

"Then he cried."

"I didn't see that."

"Nor did I. Lori told me." Lori was Stanley's housekeeper. "But now he wants to forgive and forget."

Olga stubbed her cigarette. "I know. Daddy's magnanimity is boundless. Does Kit have a job yet?"

"No."

"Can't you find him something? It's your field, and he's good."

"Things are quiet—and people know he was sacked by his father."

"Has he stopped gambling?"

"He must have. He promised Daddy he would. And he's got no money."

"Daddy paid his debts, didn't he?"

"I don't think we're supposed to know."

"Come on, Mandy." Olga was using Miranda's childhood name. "How much?"

"You should ask Daddy—or Kit."

"Was it ten thousand pounds?"

Miranda looked away.

"More than that? Twenty?"

Miranda whispered, "Fifty."

"Good God! That little bastard pissed away fifty grand of our inheritance? Wait till I see him."

"Anyway, enough of Kit. You're going to get to know Ned much better this Christmas. I want you to treat him as one of the family."

"Ned should *be* one of the family by now. When are you getting married? You're too old for a long engagement. You've both been married before—it's not as if you have to save up for your trousseau."

This was not the response Miranda was hoping for. She wanted Olga to feel warm toward Ned. "Oh, you know what Ned's like," she said defensively. "He's lost in his own world." Ned was editor of *The Glasgow Review of Books,* a respected cultural-political journal, but he was not practical.

"I don't know how you stand it. I can't abide vacillation."

The conversation was not going the way Miranda wanted. "Believe me, it's a blessed relief after Jasper." Miranda's first husband had been a bully and a tyrant. Ned was the opposite, and that was one of the reasons she loved him. "Ned will never be organized enough to boss me around—half the time he can't remember what day it is."

"Still, you managed perfectly well without a man for five years."

"I did, and I was proud of myself, especially when the economy turned down and they stopped paying me those big bonuses."

"So why do you want another man?"

"Well, you know . . ."

"Sex? Oh, please. Haven't you heard of vibrators?"

Miranda giggled. "It's not the same."

"Indeed it's not. A vibrator is bigger and harder and more reliable and, when you're done with it, you can put it back in the bedside table and forget about it."

Miranda began to feel attacked, as often happened when she talked to her sister. "Ned's very good with Tom," she said. Tom was her eleven-year-old son. "Jasper hardly ever spoke to Tom, except to give him orders. Ned takes an interest in him—asks him questions and listens to the answers."

"Speaking of stepchildren, how does Tom get along with Sophie?" Ned's daughter by his first marriage was fourteen.

"She's coming to Steepfall, too—I'm picking her up later this morning. Tom looks at Sophie the way the Greeks regarded the gods, as supernatural beings who are dangerous unless pacified by constant sacrifices. He's always trying to give her sweets. She'd rather have cigarettes. She's as thin as a stick and prepared to die to stay that way." Miranda looked pointedly at Olga's pack of Marlboro Lights.

"We all have our weaknesses," said Olga. "Have some more carrot cake."

Miranda put down her fork and took a sip of coffee. "Sophie can be difficult, but it's not her fault. Her mother resents me, and the child is bound to pick up that attitude."

"I bet Ned leaves you to deal with the problem."

"I don't mind."

"Now that he's living in your flat, does he pay you rent?"

"He can't afford it. That magazine pays peanuts. And he's still carrying the mortgage on the house his ex lives in. He's not comfortable about being financially dependent, believe you me."

"I can't think why he wouldn't be comfortable. He can have a bonk whenever he feels like it, he's got you to look after his difficult daughter, and he's living rent-free."

Miranda was hurt. "That's a bit harsh."

"You shouldn't have let him move in without committing to a date for the wedding."

The same thought had occurred to Miranda, but she was not going to admit it. "He just thinks everyone needs more time to get used to the idea of his remarriage."

"Who's 'everyone,' then?"

"Well, Sophie, for a start."

"And she reflects her mother's attitudes, you've already admitted. So what you're saying is that Ned won't marry you until his ex gives permission."

"Olga, please take off your advocate's wig when you're talking to me."

"Someone's got to tell you these things."

"You oversimplify everything. I know it's your job, but I'm your sister, not a hostile witness."

"I'm sorry I spoke."

"I'm glad you spoke, because this is just the kind of thing I *don't* want you to say to Ned. He's the man I love, and I want to marry him, so I'm asking you to be nice to him over Christmas."

"I'll do my best," Olga said lightly.

Miranda wanted her sister to understand how important this was. "I need him to feel that he and I can build a new family together, for ourselves and the two children. I'm asking you to help me convince him we can do that."

"All right. Okay."

"If this holiday goes well, I think he'll agree to a date for the wedding."

Olga touched Miranda's hand. "I get the message. I know how much it means to you. I'll be good."

Miranda had made her point. Satisfied, she turned her mind to another area of friction. "I hope things go all right between Daddy and Kit."

"So do I, but there's not much we can do about it."

"Kit called me a few days ago. For some reason, he's dead keen to sleep in the guest cottage at Steepfall."

Olga bridled. "Why should he have the cottage all to himself? That means you and Ned and Hugo and I will all have to squeeze into two poky bedrooms in the old house!"

Miranda had expected Olga to resist this. "I know it's unreasonable, but I said it was okay by me. It was difficult enough to persuade him to come—I didn't want to put an obstacle in the way."

"He's a selfish little bastard. What reason did he give you?"

"I didn't question him."

"Well, I will." Olga took her mobile phone from her briefcase and pressed a number.

"Don't make an issue of this," Miranda pleaded.

"I just want to ask him the question." Speaking into the phone, she said: "Kit—what's this about you sleeping in the cottage? Don't you think it's a bit—" She paused. "Oh. Why not? . . . I see . . . but why don't you—" She stopped abruptly, as if he had hung up on her.

Miranda thought, sadly, that she knew what Kit had said. "What is it?"

Olga put the phone back into her bag. "We don't need to argue about the cottage. He's changed his mind. He's not coming to Steepfall after all."

9 A.M.

OXENFORD MEDICAL was under siege. Reporters, photographers, and television crews massed outside the entrance gates, harassing employees as they arrived for work, crowding around their cars and bicycles, shoving cameras and microphones in their faces, shouting questions. The security guards were trying desperately to separate the media people from the normal traffic, to prevent accidents, but were getting no cooperation from the journalists. To make matters worse, a group of animal-rights protesters had seized the opportunity for some publicity, and were holding a demonstration at the gates, waving banners and singing protest songs. The cameramen were filming the demonstration, having little else to shoot. Toni Gallo watched, feeling angry and helpless.

She was in Stanley Oxenford's office, a large corner room that had been the master bedroom of the house. Stanley worked with the old and the new mingled around him: his computer workstation stood on a scratched wooden table he had had for thirty years, and on a side table was an optical microscope from the sixties that he still liked to use from time to time. The microscope was now surrounded by Christmas cards, one of them from Toni. On the wall, a Victorian engraving of the periodic table of the elements hung beside a photograph of a striking black-haired girl in a wedding dress—his late wife, Marta.

Stanley mentioned his wife often. "As cold as a church, Marta used to say . . . When Marta was alive we went to Italy every other year . . . Marta loved irises." But he had spoken of his feelings about her only once. Toni had said how beautiful Marta looked in the photograph. "The pain fades, but it doesn't go away," Stanley said. "I believe I'll grieve for her every day for the rest of my life." It had made Toni wonder whether anyone would ever love her the way Stanley had loved Marta.

Now Stanley stood beside Toni at the window, their shoulders not quite touching. They watched with dismay as more Volvos and Subarus parked on the grass verge, and the crowd became noisier and more aggressive.

"I'm so sorry about this," Toni said miserably.

"Not your fault."

"I know you said no more self-pity, but I let a rabbit get through my security cordon. Then my bastard ex-partner leaked the story to Carl Osborne, the television reporter."

"I gather you don't get on with your ex."

She had never talked candidly to Stanley about this, but Frank had now intruded into her working life, and she welcomed the chance to explain. "I honestly don't know why Frank hates me. I never rejected him. He left me—and he did it at a moment when I really needed help and support. You'd think he'd punished me enough for whatever I did wrong. But now this."

"I can understand it. You're a standing reproach to him. Every time he sees you, he's reminded of how weak and cowardly he was when you needed him."

Toni had never thought about Frank in quite that way, and now his behavior made a kind of sense. She felt a warm surge of gratitude. Careful not to show too much emotion, she said, "That's perceptive."

He shrugged. "We never forgive those we've wronged."

Toni smiled at the paradox. Stanley was clever about people as well as viruses.

He put a hand on her shoulder lightly, a gesture of reassurance—or was it something more? He rarely made physical contact with his employees. She had felt his touch exactly three times in the year she had known him. He had shaken her hand when he gave her the initial contract, when he took her on the staff, and when he promoted her. At the Christmas party, he had danced with his secretary, Dorothy, a heavy woman with a maternally efficient manner, like an attentive mother duck. He had not danced with anyone else. Toni had wanted to ask him, but she was afraid of making her feelings obvious. Afterward she had wished she were more brash, like Susan Mackintosh.

"Frank may not have leaked the story merely to spite you," Stanley said. "I suspect he would have done it anyway. I imagine Osborne will show his gratitude by reporting favorably on the Inverburn police in general and Superintendent Frank Hackett in particular."

His hand warmed her skin through the silk of her

blouse. Was this a casual gesture, made without thought? She suffered the familiar frustration of not knowing what was on his mind. She wondered if he could feel her bra strap. She hoped he could not tell how much she enjoyed being touched by him.

She was not sure he was right about Frank and Carl Osborne. "It's generous of you to look at it that way," she said. All the same, she resolved that somehow she would make sure the company did not suffer from what Frank had done.

There was a knock at the door and Cynthia Creighton, the company's public-relations officer, came in. Stanley took his hand off Toni's shoulder quickly.

Cynthia was a thin woman of fifty in a tweed skirt and knitted stockings. She was a sincere do-gooder. Toni had once made Stanley laugh by saying Cynthia was the kind of person who made her own granola. Normally hesitant in manner, she was now on the edge of hysteria. Her hair was disheveled, she was breathing hard, and she talked too fast. "Those people *shoved* me," she said. "They're animals! Where are the police?"

"A patrol car is on its way," Toni said. "They should be here in ten or fifteen minutes."

"They should arrest the lot of them."

Toni realized, with a sinking feeling, that Cynthia was not capable of dealing with this crisis. Her main job was to dispense a small charity budget, giving grants to school football teams and sponsored walkers, ensuring that the name of Oxenford Medical appeared frequently in the *Inverburn Courier,* in stories that had nothing to do with viruses or experiments on animals. It was important work, Toni knew, for readers believed the local press, whereas they were skeptical of national newspapers. Consequently, Cynthia's low-key publicity immunized the company against the virulent Fleet Street scare stories that could blight any scientific enterprise. But Cynthia had never dealt with the jackal pack that was the British press in full cry, and she was too distressed to make good decisions.

Stanley was thinking the same thing. "Cynthia, I want you to work with Toni on this," he said. "She has experience of the media from her time with the police."

Cynthia looked relieved and grateful. "Have you?"

"I did a year in the press office—although I never dealt with anything this bad."

"What do you think we should do?"

"Well." Toni did not feel she was qualified to take charge, but this was an emergency, and it seemed she was the best candidate available. She went back to first principles. "There's a simple rule for dealing with the media." It might be too simple for this situation, she thought, but she did not say so. "One, decide what your message is. Two, make sure it's true, so that you'll never have to go back on it. Three, keep saying it over and over again."

"Hmm." Stanley looked skeptical, but he did not seem to have a better suggestion.

Cynthia said, "Don't you think we should apologize?"

"No," Toni said quickly. "It will be interpreted as confirmation that we've been careless. That's not true. Nobody's perfect, but our security is top-notch."

Stanley said, "Is that our message?"

"I don't think so. Too defensive." Toni thought for a moment. "We should start by saying that we're doing work here which is vital for the future of the human race. No, that's too apocalyptic. We're doing medical research that will save lives—that's better. And it has its hazards, but our security is as tight as mortal beings can make it. One thing certain is that many people will die unnecessarily if we *stop*."

"I like that," said Stanley.

"Is it true?" Toni asked.

"No question. Every year a new virus comes out of China and kills thousands. Our drug will save their lives."

Toni nodded. "That's perfect. Simple and telling."

Stanley was still worried. "How will we get the message across?"

"I think you should call a press conference in a couple of hours' time. By midday the news desks will be looking for a fresh angle on the story, so they'll be glad to get something more from us. And most of these people outside will leave once that's happened. They'll know that further developments are unlikely, and they want to go home for Christmas like everyone else."

"I hope you're right," Stanley said. "Cynthia, will you make the arrangements, please?"

Cynthia had not yet recovered her composure. "But what should I do?"

Toni took over. "We'll hold the press conference in the Great Hall. It's the only room big enough, and the chairs are already being set out for Professor Oxenford's address to the staff at half past nine. The first thing you should do is alert the people outside. It will give them something to tell their editors, and might calm them down a bit. Then phone the Press Association and Reuters and ask them to put it on the wire, to inform any of the media who aren't already here."

"Right," Cynthia said uncertainly. "Right." She turned to go. Toni made a mental note to check on her as soon as possible.

As Cynthia left, Dorothy buzzed Stanley and said, "Laurence Mahoney from the United States embassy in London is on line one."

"I remember him," Toni said. "He was here a few months ago. I showed him around." The U.S. military was financing much of Oxenford Medical's research. The Department of Defense was keenly interested in Stanley's new antiviral drug, which promised to be a powerful counter to biological warfare. Stanley had needed to raise money for the prolonged testing process, and the American government had been eager to invest. Mahoney kept an eye on things on behalf of the Defense Department.

"Just a minute, Dorothy." Stanley did not pick up the phone. He said to Toni, "Mahoney is more important to us than all the British media put together. I don't want to talk to him cold. I need to know what line he's taking, so that I can think about how to handle him."

"Do you want me to stall him?"

"Feel him out."

Toni picked up the handset and touched a button. "Hello, Larry, this is Toni Gallo. We met in September. How are you?"

Mahoney was a peevish press officer with a whiny voice that made Toni think of Donald Duck. "I'm worried," he said.

"Tell me why."

"I was hoping to speak to Professor Oxenford," he answered with an edge to his voice.

"And he's keen to talk to you at the first opportunity," Toni said as sincerely as she could manage. "Right now he's with the laboratory director." In fact he was sitting on the edge of his desk, watching her, with an expression on his face that might have been either fond or merely interested. She caught his eye and he looked away. "He'll call you as soon as he has the complete picture—which will certainly be before midday."

"How the hell did you let something like this happen?"

"The young man sneaked a rabbit out of the laboratory in his duffel bag. We've already instituted a compulsory bag search at the entrance to BSL4 to make sure it can't happen again."

"My concern is bad publicity for the American government. We don't want to be blamed for unleashing deadly viruses on the population of Scotland."

"There's no danger of that," Toni said with her fingers crossed.

"Have any of the local reports played up the fact that this research is American-financed?"

"No."

"They'll pick it up sooner or later."

"We should certainly be prepared to answer questions about that."

"The most damaging angle for us—and therefore for you—is the one that says the research is done here because Americans think it's too dangerous to be done in the United States."

"Thanks for the warning. I think we have a very convincing response to that. After all, the drug was invented right here in Scotland by Professor Oxenford, so it's natural it should be tested here."

"I just don't want to get into a situation where the only way to prove our goodwill is to transfer the research to Fort Detrick."

Toni was shocked into silence. Fort Detrick, in the town of Frederick, Maryland, housed the U.S. Army Medical Research Institute of Infectious Diseases. How could the research be transferred there? It would mean the end of the Kremlin. After a long pause, she said, "We're not in that situation, not by a million miles." She wished she could think of a more devastating put-down.

"I sure hope not. Have Stanley call me."

"Thank you, Larry." She hung up and said to Stanley, "They can't transfer your research to Fort Detrick, can they?"

He went pale. "There's certainly no provision in the contract to that effect," he said. "But they are the government of the most powerful country in the world, and they can do anything they want. What would I do—sue them? I'd be in court for the rest of my life, even if I could afford it."

Toni was rocked by seeing Stanley appear vulnerable. He was always the calm, reassuring one who knew how to solve the problem. Now he just looked daunted. She would have liked to give him a comforting hug. "Would they do it?"

"I'm sure the microbiologists at Fort Detrick would prefer to be doing this research themselves, if they had the choice."

"Where would that leave you?"

"Bankrupt."

"What?" Toni was appalled.

"I've invested everything in the new laboratory," Stanley said grimly. "I have a personal overdraft of a million pounds. Our contract with the Department of Defense would cover the cost of the lab over four years. But if they pull the rug now, I've got no way of paying the debts—either the company's or my own."

Toni could hardly take it in. How could Stanley's entire future—and her own—be threatened so suddenly? "But the new drug is worth millions."

"It will be, eventually. I'm sure of the science—that's why I was happy to borrow so much money. But I didn't foresee that the project might be destroyed by mere publicity."

She touched his arm. "And all because a stupid television personality needs a scare story," she said. "I can hardly believe it."

Stanley patted the hand she had rested on his arm, then removed it and stood up. "No point in whining. We've just got to manage our way out of this."

"Yes. You're due to speak to the staff. Are you ready?"

"Yes." They walked out of his office together. "It will be good practice for the press later."

As they passed Dorothy's desk, she held up a hand to stop them. "One moment, please," she said into the phone. She touched a button and spoke to Stanley. "It's the First Minister of Scotland," she said. "Personally," she added, evidently impressed. "He wants a word."

Stanley said to Toni, "Go down to the hall and hold them. I'll be as quick as I can." He went back into his office.

9:30 A.M.

KIT OXENFORD waited more than an hour for Harry McGarry.

McGarry, known as Harry Mac, had been born in Govan, a working-class district of Glasgow. He was raised in a tenement near Ibrox Park, the home of the city's Protestant football team, Rangers. With his profits from drugs, illegal gambling, theft, and prostitution, he had moved—only a mile geographically, but a long way socially—across the Paisley Road to Dumbreck. Now he lived in a large new-built house with a pool.

The place was decorated like an expensive hotel, with reproduction furniture and framed prints on the wall, but no personal touches: no family photographs, no ornaments, no flowers, no pets. Kit waited nervously in the spacious hall, staring at the striped yellow wallpaper and the spindly legs of the occasional tables, watched by a fat bodyguard in a cheap black suit.

Harry Mac's empire covered Scotland and the north

of England. He worked with his daughter, Diana, always called Daisy. The nickname was ironic: she was a violent, sadistic thug.

Harry owned the illegal casino where Kit played. Licensed casinos in Britain suffered under all kinds of petty laws that limited their profits: no house percentage, no table fee, no tipping, no drinking at the tables, and you had to be a member for twenty-four hours before you could play. Harry ignored the laws. Kit liked the louche atmosphere of an illegitimate game.

Most gamblers were stupid, Kit believed; and the people who ran casinos were not much brighter. An intelligent player should always win. In blackjack there was a correct way to play every possible hand—a system called Basic—and he knew it backward. Then, he improved his chances by keeping track of the cards that were dealt from the six-pack deck. Starting with zero, he added one point for every low card—twos, threes, fours, fives, and sixes—and took away one point for every high card—tens, jacks, queens, kings, and aces. (He ignored sevens, eights, and nines.) When the number in his head was positive, the remaining deck contained more high cards than low, so he had a better-than-average chance of drawing a ten. A negative number gave a high probability of drawing a low card. Knowing the odds told him when to bet heavily.

But Kit had suffered a run of bad luck and, when the debt reached fifty thousand pounds, Harry asked for his money.

Kit had gone to his father and begged to be rescued. It was humiliating, of course. When Stanley had fired him, Kit had accused his father bitterly of not caring about him. Now he was admitting the truth: his father did love him, and would do almost anything for him, and Kit knew that perfectly well. His pretense had collapsed ignominiously. But it was worth it. Stanley had paid.

Kit had promised he would never gamble again, and meant it, but the temptation had been too strong. It was madness; it was a disease; it was shameful and humiliating; but it was the most exciting thing in the world, and he could not resist.

Next time his debt reached fifty thousand, he went back to his father, but this time Stanley put his foot down. "I haven't got the money," he said. "I could borrow it, perhaps, but what's the point? You'd lose it and come back for more until we both were broke." Kit had accused him of heartlessness and greed, called him Shylock and Scrooge and fucking Fagin, and sworn never to speak to him again. The words had hurt—he could always hurt his father, he knew that—but Stanley had not changed his mind.

At that point, Kit should have left the country.

He dreamed of going to Italy to live in his mother's hometown of Lucca. The family had visited several times during his childhood, before the grandparents died. It was a pretty walled town, ancient and peaceful, with little squares where you could drink espresso in the shade. He knew some Italian—Mamma Marta had spoken her native tongue to all of them when they were small. He could rent a room in one of the tall old houses and get a job helping people with their computer problems, easy work. He thought he could be happy, living like that.

But, instead, he had tried to win back what he owed.

His debt went up to a quarter of a million.

For that much money, Harry Mac would pursue him to the North Pole. He thought about killing himself, and eyed tall buildings in central Glasgow, wondering if he could get up on the roofs in order to throw himself to his death.

Three weeks ago, he had been summoned to this house. He had felt sick with fear. He was sure they were going to beat him up. When he was shown into the drawing room, with its yellow silk couches, he wondered how they would prevent the blood spoiling the upholstery. "There's a gentleman here wants to ask you a question," Harry had said. Kit could not imagine what question any of Harry's friends would want to ask him, unless it was *Where's the fucking money?*

The gentleman was Nigel Buchanan, a quiet type in his forties wearing expensive casual clothes: a cashmere jacket, dark slacks, and an open-necked shirt. Speaking in a soft London accent, he said, "Can you get me inside the Level Four laboratory at Oxenford Medical?"

There were two other people in the yellow drawing room at the time. One was Daisy, a muscular girl of about twenty-five with a broken nose, bad skin, and a ring through her lower lip. She was wearing leather gloves. The other was Elton, a handsome black man about the same age as Daisy, apparently a sidekick of Nigel's.

Kit was so relieved at not being beaten up that he would have agreed to anything.

Nigel offered him a fee of three hundred thousand pounds for the night's work.

Kit could hardly believe his luck. It would be enough to pay his debts and more. He could leave the country. He could go to Lucca and realize his dream. He felt overjoyed. His problems were solved at a stroke.

Later, Harry had talked about Nigel in reverent tones. A professional thief, Nigel stole only to order, for a prearranged price. "He's the greatest," Harry said. "You're after a painting by Michelangelo? No problem. A nuclear warhead? He'll get it for you—if you can afford it. Remember Shergar, the racehorse that was kidnapped? That was Nigel." He added: "He lives in Liechtenstein," as if Liechtenstein were a more exotic place of residence than Mars.

Kit had spent the next three weeks planning the theft of the antiviral drug. He felt the occasional twinge of remorse as he refined the scheme to rob his father, but mostly he felt a delirious glee at the thought of revenge on the daddy who had fired him, then refused to rescue him from gangsters. It would be a nasty poke in the eye for Toni Gallo, too.

Nigel had gone over the details with him meticulously, questioning everything. Occasionally he would consult with Elton, who was in charge of equipment, especially cars. Kit got the impression that Elton was a valued technical expert who had worked with Nigel before. Daisy was to join them on the raid, ostensibly to provide extra muscle if necessary—though Kit suspected her real purpose was to take £250,000 from him as soon as the fee was in his hands.

Kit suggested they rendezvous at a disused airfield near the Kremlin. Nigel looked at Elton. "That's cool," Elton said. He spoke with a broad London accent: "We could meet the buyer there after—he might want to fly in."

In the end, Nigel had pronounced the plan brilliant, and Kit had glowed with pleasure.

Now, today, Kit had to tell Harry the whole deal was off. He felt wretched: disappointed, depressed, and scared.

At last he was summoned to Harry's presence. Nervous, he followed the bodyguard through the laundry at the back of the house to the pool pavilion. It was built to look like an Edwardian orangery, with glazed tiles in somber colors, the pool itself an unpleasant shade of dark green. Some interior decorator had proposed this, Kit guessed, and Harry had said yes without looking at the plans.

Harry was a stocky man of fifty with the gray skin of a lifelong smoker. He sat at a wrought-iron table, dressed in a purple toweling robe, drinking dark coffee from a small china cup and reading the *Sun*. The newspaper was open at the horoscope. Daisy was in the water, swimming laps tirelessly. Kit was startled to see that she seemed to be naked except for diver's gloves. She always wore gloves.

"I don't need to see you, laddie," Harry said. "I don't want to see you. I don't know anything about you or what you're doing tonight. And I've never met anyone called Nigel Buchanan. Are you catching my drift?" He did not offer Kit a cup of coffee.

The air was hot and humid. Kit was wearing his best suit, a midnight blue mohair, with a white shirt open at the neck. It seemed an effort to breathe, and his skin felt uncomfortably damp under his clothes. He realized he had broken some rule of criminal etiquette by contacting Harry on the day of the robbery, but he had no alternative. "I had to talk to you," Kit said. "Haven't you seen the news?"

"What if I have?"

Kit suppressed a surge of irritation. Men such as Harry could never bring themselves to admit to not knowing something, however trivial. "There's a big flap on at Oxenford Medical," Kit said. "A technician died of a virus."

"What do you want me to do, send flowers?"

"They'll be tightening security. This is the worst possible time to rob the place. It's difficult enough anyway. They have a state-of-the-art alarm system. And the woman in charge is as tough as a rubber steak."

"What a whiner you are."

Kit had not been asked to sit down, so he leaned on the back of a chair, feeling awkward. "We have to call it off."

"Let me explain something to you." Harry took a cigarette from a packet on the table and lit it with a gold lighter. Then he coughed, an old smoker's cough from the depths of his lungs. When the spasm had passed, he spat into the pool and drank some coffee. Then he resumed. "For one thing, I've said it's going to happen. Now you may not realize this, being so well brought up, but when a man says something's going to happen, and then it doesn't, people think he's a wanker."

"Yes, but—"

"Don't even dream of interrupting me."

Kit shut up.

"For another thing, Nigel Buchanan's no drugged-up schoolboy wanting to rob Woolworths in Govan Cross. He's a legend and, more important than that, he's connected with some highly respected people in London. When you're dealing with folk like that, even more you don't want to look like a wanker."

He paused, as if daring Kit to argue. Kit said nothing. How had he got himself involved with these people? He had walked into the wolves' cave, and now he stood paralyzed, waiting to be torn to pieces.

"And for a third thing, you owe me a quarter of a million pounds. No one has ever owed me that much money for so long and still been able to walk without crutches. I trust I'm making myself clear."

Kit nodded silently. He was so scared he felt he might throw up.

"So don't tell me we have to call it off." Harry picked up the *Sun* as if the conversation were over.

Kit forced himself to speak. "I meant postpone it, not call it off," he managed. "We can do it another day, when the fuss has died down."

Harry did not look up. "Ten a.m. on Christmas Day, Nigel said. And I want my money."

"There's no point in doing it if we're going to get caught!" Kit said desperately. Harry did not respond. "Everyone can wait a little longer, can't they?" It was like talking to the wall. "Better late than never."

Harry glanced toward the pool and made a beckoning gesture. Daisy must have been keeping an eye on him, for she immediately climbed out of the pool. She did not take off the gloves. She had powerful shoulders and arms. Her shallow breasts hardly moved as she walked. Kit saw that she had a tattoo over one breast and a nipple ring in the other. When she came closer, he realized she was shaved all over. She had a flat belly and lean thighs, and her pubic mound was prominent. Every detail was visible, not just to Kit but to her father, if he cared to look. Kit felt weird.

Harry did not seem to notice. "Kit wants us to wait for our money, Daisy." He stood up and tightened the belt of his robe. "Explain to him how we feel about that—I'm too tired." He put the newspaper under his arm and walked away.

Daisy grabbed Kit by the lapels of his best suit. "Look," he pleaded. "I just want to make sure this doesn't end in disaster for all of us." Then Daisy jerked him sideways. He lost his balance and would have fallen to the ground, but she took his weight; then she threw him into the pool.

It was a shock but, if the worst thing she did was ruin his suit, he would count himself lucky. Then, as he got his head above the surface, she jumped on him, her knees smashing into his back painfully, so that he cried out and swallowed water as his head went under.

They were at the shallow end. When his feet touched the bottom he struggled to stand upright, but his head was clamped by Daisy's arm, and he was pulled off balance again. She held him facedown under the water.

He held his breath, expecting her to punch him, or something, but she remained still. Needing to breathe, he began to struggle, trying to break her hold, but she was too strong. He became angry, and lashed out feebly with his arms and legs. He felt like a child in a tantrum, flailing helplessly in the grip of its mother.

His need for air became desperate, and he fought down panic as he resisted the urge to open his mouth and gasp. He realized that Daisy had his head under her left arm and was down on one knee with her own head just above the surface. He made himself still, so that his feet floated down. Perhaps she would think he had lost consciousness. His feet touched the bottom. Her grip did not slacken. He got a firm footing, then put all his strength into a sudden upward jerk of his body, to dislodge Daisy's hold. She hardly moved, just tightening her grip on his head. It was like having his skull squeezed by steel pincers.

He opened his eyes underwater. His cheek was pressed against her bony ribs. He twisted his head an inch, opened his mouth, and bit her. He felt her flinch, and her grip weakened a little. He clamped his jaws together, trying to bite all the way through the fold of skin. Then he felt her gloved hand on his face and her fingers pushing into his eyes. Reflexively, he tried to pull away, and involuntarily relaxed his jaws and let her flesh slip from his bite.

Panic overcame him. He could not hold his breath any longer. His body, starved of oxygen, forced him to gasp for air, and water rushed into his lungs. He found himself coughing and vomiting at the same time. After each spasm more water poured down his throat. He realized he would soon die if this went on.

Then she seemed to relent. She jerked his head out of the water. He opened his mouth wide and sucked in blessed pure air. He coughed a jet of water out of his lungs. Then, before he could take a second breath, she shoved his head under again, and instead of air he inhaled water.

Panic turned to something worse. Mad with fear, he thrashed about. Terror gave him strength, and Daisy struggled to hold him, but he could not get his head up. He no longer tried to keep his mouth shut, but let the water flood into him. The sooner he drowned, the sooner the agony would be over.

Daisy pulled his head out again.

He spewed water and drew in a precious gasp of air. Then his head was submerged yet again.

He screamed, but no sound came out. His struggles weakened. He knew Harry had not intended for Daisy to kill him, for then there would be no robbery—but Daisy was not very sane, and it seemed she was going to go too far. Kit decided he was going to die. His eyes were open, showing him only a green blur; then his vision began to darken, as if night were falling.

At last he passed out.

10 A.M.

NED could not drive, so Miranda took the wheel of the Toyota Previa. Her son, Tom, sat behind with his Game Boy. The back row of seats had been folded away to make room for a stack of presents wrapped in red-and-gold paper and tied with green ribbon.

As they pulled away from the Georgian terrace off the Great Western Road where Miranda had her flat, a light snowfall began. There was a blizzard over the sea to the north, but the weather forecasters said it was going to bypass Scotland.

She felt content, driving with the two men in her life, heading for Christmas with her family at her father's house. She was reminded of driving back from university for the holidays, looking forward to home cooking, clean bathrooms, ironed sheets, and that feeling of being loved and cared for.

She headed first for the suburb where Ned's ex-wife

lived. They were to pick up his daughter, Sophie, before driving to Steepfall.

Tom's toy played a descending melody, probably indicating that he had crashed his spaceship or been beheaded by a gladiator. He sighed and said, "I saw an advertisement in a car magazine for these really cool screens that go in the back of the headrests, so the people in the backseat can watch movies and stuff."

"A must-have accessory," said Ned with a smile.

"Sounds expensive," said Miranda.

"They don't cost that much," Tom said.

Miranda looked at him in the driving mirror. "Well, how much?"

"I don't know, just, but they didn't *look* expensive— d'you know what I mean?"

"Why don't you find out the price, and we'll see if we can afford one."

"Okay, great! And if it's too dear for you, I'll ask Grandpa."

Miranda smiled. Catch Grandpa in the right mood and he would give you anything.

Miranda had always hoped Tom would be the one to inherit his grandfather's scientific genius. The jury was still out. His schoolwork was excellent, but not astonishingly so. However, she was not sure what, exactly, her father's talent was. Of course he was a brilliant microbiologist, but he had something more. It was partly the imagination to see the direction in which progress lay, and partly the leadership to inspire a team of scientists to pull together. How could you tell whether an eleven-year-old had that kind of ability? Meanwhile, nothing captured Tom's imagination half as much as a new computer game.

She turned on the radio. A choir was singing a

Christmas carol. Ned said, "If I hear 'Away in a Manger' one more time, I may have to commit suicide by impaling myself on a Christmas tree." Miranda changed the station and got John Lennon singing "War Is Over." Ned groaned and said, "Do you realize that Radio Hell plays Christmas music all the year round? It's a well-known fact."

Miranda laughed. After a minute she found a classical station that was playing a piano trio. "How's this?"

"Haydn—perfect."

Ned was curmudgeonly about popular culture. It was part of his egghead act, like not knowing how to drive. Miranda did not mind: she, too, disliked pop music, soap operas, and cheap reproductions of famous paintings. But she liked carols.

She was fond of Ned's idiosyncrasies, but her conversation with Olga in the coffee bar nagged at her. Was Ned weak? She sometimes wished he were more assertive. Her husband, Jasper, had been too much so. But she sometimes hankered after the kind of sex she had had with Jasper. He had been selfish in bed, taking her roughly, thinking only of his own pleasure—and Miranda, to her shame, had felt liberated, and enjoyed it. The thrill had worn off, eventually, when she got fed up with his being selfish and inconsiderate about everything else. All the same, she wished Ned could be like that just sometimes.

Her thoughts turned to Kit. She was desperately disappointed that he had canceled. She had worked so hard to persuade him to join the family for Christmas. At first he had refused; then he had relented, so she could hardly be surprised that he had changed his mind again. All the same, it was a painful blow, for she badly wanted them all to be together, as they had been most

Christmases before Mamma died. The rift between Daddy and Kit scared her. Coming so soon after Mamma's death, it made the family seem dangerously fragile. And if the family was vulnerable, what could she be sure of?

She turned into a street of old stone-built workers' cottages and pulled up outside a larger house that might have been occupied by an overseer. Ned had lived here with Jennifer until they split up two years ago. Before that they had modernized the place at great expense, and the payments still burdened Ned. Every time Miranda drove past this street, she felt angry about the amount of money Ned was paying Jennifer.

Miranda engaged the hand brake, but left the engine running. She and Tom stayed in the car while Ned walked up the path to the house. Miranda never went inside. Although Ned had left the marital home before he met Miranda, Jennifer was as hostile as if Miranda had been responsible for the breakup. She avoided meeting her, spoke curtly to her on the phone, and—according to the indiscreet Sophie—referred to her as "that fat tart" when speaking to her women friends. Jennifer herself was as thin as a bird, with a nose like a beak.

The door was opened by Sophie, a fourteen-year-old in jeans and a skimpy sweater. Ned kissed her and went inside.

The car radio played one of Dvořák's Hungarian dances. In the backseat, Tom's Game Boy beeped irregularly. Snow blew around the car in flurries. Miranda turned the heater higher. Ned came out of the house, looking annoyed.

He came to Miranda's window. "Jennifer's out," he said. "Sophie hasn't even begun to get ready. Will you come in and help her pack?"

"Oh, Ned, I don't think I should," Miranda said unhappily. She felt uncomfortable about going inside when Jennifer was not there.

Ned looked panicked. "To tell you the truth, I'm not sure what a girl needs."

Miranda could believe that. Ned found it a challenge to pack a case for himself. He had never done it while he was with Jennifer. When he and Miranda were about to take their first holiday together—a trip to the museums of Florence—she had refused, on principle, to do it for him, and he had been forced to learn. However, on subsequent trips—a weekend in London, four days in Vienna—she had checked his luggage, and each time found that he had forgotten something important. To pack for someone else was beyond him.

She sighed and killed the engine. "Tom, you'll have to come, too."

The house was attractively decorated, Miranda thought as she stepped into the hall. Jennifer had a good eye. She had combined plain rustic furniture with colorful fabrics in the way an overseer's house-proud wife might have done a hundred years ago. There were Christmas cards on the mantelpiece, but no tree.

It seemed strange to think that Ned had lived here. He had come home every evening to this house, just as now he came home to Miranda's flat. He had listened to the news on the radio, sat down to dinner, read Russian novels, brushed his teeth automatically, and gone unthinkingly to bed to hold a different woman in his arms.

Sophie was in the living room, lying on a couch in front of the television. She had a pierced navel with a cheap jewel in it. Miranda smelled cigarette smoke. Ned said, "Now, Sophie, Miranda's going to help you get ready, okay, poppet?" There was a pleading note in his voice that made Miranda wince.

"I'm watching a film," Sophie said sulkily.

Miranda knew that Sophie would respond to firmness, not supplication. She picked up the remote control and turned the television off. "Show me your bedroom, please, Sophie," she said briskly.

Sophie looked rebellious.

"Hurry up, we're short of time."

Sophie stood up reluctantly and walked slowly from the room. Miranda followed her upstairs to a messy bedroom decorated with posters of boys with peculiar haircuts and ludicrously baggy jeans.

"We'll be at Steepfall for five days, so you need ten pairs of knickers, for a start."

"I haven't got ten."

Miranda did not believe her, but she said, "Then we'll take what you've got, and you can do laundry."

Sophie stood in the middle of the room, a mutinous expression on her pretty face.

"Come on," Miranda said. "I'm not going to be your maid. Get some knickers out." She stared at the girl.

Sophie was not able to stare her out. She dropped her eyes, turned away, and opened the top drawer of a chest. It was full of underwear.

"Pack five bras," Miranda said.

Sophie began taking items out.

Crisis over, Miranda thought. She opened the door of a closet. "You'll need a couple of frocks for the evenings." She took out a red dress with spaghetti straps, much too sexy for a fourteen-year-old. "This is nice," she lied.

Sophie thawed a little. "It's new."

"We should wrap it so that it doesn't crease. Where do you keep tissue paper?"

"In the kitchen drawer, I think."

"I'll fetch it. You find a couple of clean pairs of jeans."

Miranda went downstairs, feeling that she was beginning to establish the right balance of friendliness and authority with Sophie. Ned and Tom were in the living room, watching TV. Miranda entered the kitchen and called out: "Ned, do you know where tissue paper is kept?"

"I'm sorry. I don't."

"Stupid question," Miranda muttered, and she began opening drawers.

She eventually found some at the back of a cupboard of sewing materials. She had to kneel on the tiled floor to pull the packet from under a box of ribbons. It was an effort to reach into the cupboard, and she felt herself flush. This is ridiculous, she thought. I'm only thirty-five I should be able to bend without effort. I must lose ten pounds. No roast potatoes with the Christmas turkey.

As she took the packet of tissue paper from the cupboard, she heard the back door of the house open, then a woman's footsteps. She looked up to see Jennifer.

"What the hell do you think you're doing?" Jennifer said. She was a small woman, but managed to look formidable, with her high forehead and arched nose. She was smartly dressed in a tailored coat and high-heeled boots.

Miranda got to her feet, panting slightly. To her mortification, she felt perspiration break out on her throat. "I was looking for tissue paper."

"I can see that. I want to know why you're in my house at all."

Ned appeared in the doorway. "Hello, Jenny, I didn't hear you come in."

"Obviously I didn't give you time to sound the alarm," she said sarcastically.

"Sorry," he said, "but I asked Miranda to come in and—"

"Well, don't!" Jennifer interrupted. "I don't want your women here."

She made it sound as if Ned had a harem. In fact he had dated only two women since Jennifer. The first he had seen only once, and the second was Miranda. But it seemed childishly quarrelsome to point that out. Instead, Miranda said, "I was just trying to help Sophie."

"I'll take care of Sophie. Please leave my house."

Ned said, "I'm sorry if we startled you, Jenny, but—"

"Don't bother to apologize. Just get her out of here."

Miranda blushed hotly. No one had ever been so rude to her. "I'd better leave," she said.

"That's right," Jennifer said.

Ned said, "I'll bring Sophie out as soon as I can."

Miranda was as angry with Ned as with Jennifer, though for the moment she was not sure why. She turned toward the hall.

"You can use the back door," Jennifer said.

To her shame, Miranda hesitated. She looked at Jennifer and saw on her face the hint of a smirk. That gave Miranda an ounce of courage. "I don't think so," she said quietly. She went to the front door.

"Tom, come with me," she called.

"Just a minute," he shouted back.

She stepped into the living room. Tom was watching TV. She grabbed his wrist, hauled him to his feet, and dragged him out of the house.

"That hurts!" he protested.

She slammed the front door. "Next time, come when I call."

She felt like crying as she got into the car. Now she had to sit waiting, like a servant, while Ned was in the house with his ex-wife. Had Jennifer actually planned this whole drama as a way of humiliating Miranda? It was possible. Ned had been hopeless. She knew now why she was so cross with him. He had let Jennifer insult her without a word of protest. He just kept apologizing. And for what? If Jennifer had packed a case for her daughter, or even got the girl to do it herself, Miranda would not have had to enter the house. And then, worst of all, Miranda had taken out her anger on her son. She should have shouted at Jennifer, not Tom.

She looked at him in the driving mirror. "Tommy, I'm sorry I hurt your wrist," she said.

"It's okay," he said without looking up from his Game Boy. "I'm sorry I didn't come when you called."

"All forgiven, then," she said. A tear rolled down her cheek, and she quickly wiped it away.

11 A.M.

"VIRUSES kill thousands of people every day," Stanley Oxenford said. "About every ten years, an epidemic of influenza kills around twenty-five thousand people in the United Kingdom. In 1918, flu caused more deaths than the whole of World War One. In the year 2002, three million people died of AIDS, which is caused by human immunodeficiency virus. And viruses are involved in ten percent of cancers."

Toni listened intently, sitting beside him in the Great Hall, under the varnished timbers of the mock-medieval roof. He sounded calm and controlled, but she knew him well enough to recognize the barely audible tremor of strain in his voice. He had been shocked and dismayed by Laurence Mahoney's threat, and the fear that he might lose everything was only just concealed by his unruffled facade.

She watched the faces of the assembled reporters. Would they hear what he was saying and understand the importance of his work? She knew journalists. Some were intelligent, many stupid. A few believed in telling the truth; the majority just wrote the most sensational story they could get away with. She felt indignant that they could hold in their hands the fate of a man such as Stanley. Yet the power of the tabloids was a brutal fact of modern life. If enough of these hacks chose to portray Stanley as a mad scientist in a Frankenstein castle, the Americans might be sufficiently embarrassed to pull the finance.

That would be a tragedy—not just for Stanley, but for the world. True, someone else could finish the testing program for the antiviral drug, but a ruined and bankrupt Stanley would invent no more miracle cures. Toni thought angrily that she would like to slap the dumb faces of the journalists and say, "Wake up—this is about *your* future, too!"

"Viruses are a fact of life, but we don't have to accept that fact passively," Stanley went on. Toni admired the way he spoke. His voice was measured but relaxed. He used this tone when explaining things to younger colleagues. His speech sounded more like a conversation. "Scientists can defeat viruses. Before AIDS, the great killer was smallpox—until a scientist called Edward Jenner invented vaccination in 1796. Now smallpox has disappeared from human society. Similarly, polio has been eliminated in large areas of our world. In time, we will defeat influenza, and AIDS, and even cancer—and it will be done by scientists like us, working in laboratories such as this."

A woman put up a hand and called out, "What are you working on here—exactly?"

Toni said, "Would you mind identifying yourself?"

"Edie McAllan, science correspondent, *Scotland on Sunday.*"

Cynthia Creighton, sitting on the other side of Stanley, made a note.

Stanley said, "We have developed an antiviral drug. That's rare. There are plenty of antibiotic drugs, which kill bacteria, but few that attack viruses."

A man said, "What's the difference?" He added, "Clive Brown, *Daily Record*."

The *Record* was a tabloid. Toni was pleased with the direction the questions were taking. She wanted the press to concentrate on real science. The more they understood, the less likely they were to print damaging rubbish.

Stanley said, "Bacteria, or germs, are tiny creatures that can be seen with a normal microscope. Each of us is host to billions of them. Many are useful, helping us digest food, for example, or dispose of dead skin cells. A few cause illness, and some of those can be treated with antibiotics. Viruses are smaller and simpler than bacteria. You need an electron microscope to see them. A virus cannot reproduce itself—instead, it hijacks the biochemical machinery of a living cell and forces the cell to produce copies of the virus. No known virus is useful to humans. And we have few medicines to combat them. That's why a new antiviral drug is such good news for the human race."

Edie McAllan asked, "What particular viruses is your drug effective against?"

It was another scientific question. Toni began to believe that this press conference would do all that she and Stanley hoped. She quelled her optimism with an effort. She knew, from her experience as a police press officer, that a journalist could ask serious and intelligent questions then go back to the office and write inflammatory garbage. Even if the writer turned in a sensible piece, it might be rewritten by someone ignorant and irresponsible.

Stanley replied, "That's the question we're trying to answer. We're testing the drug against a variety of viruses to determine its range."

Clive Brown said, "Does that include dangerous viruses?"

Stanley said, "Yes. No one is interested in drugs for safe viruses."

The audience laughed. It was a witty answer to a stupid question. But Brown looked annoyed, and Toni's heart sank. A humiliated journalist would stop at nothing to get revenge.

She intervened quickly. "Thank you for that question, Clive," she said, trying to mollify him. "Here at Oxenford Medical we impose the highest possible standards of security in laboratories where special materials are used. In BSL4, which stands for BioSafety Level Four, the alarm system is directly connected with regional police headquarters at Inverburn. There are security guards on duty twenty-four hours a day, and this morning I have doubled the number of guards. As a further precaution, security guards cannot enter BSL4, but monitor the laboratory via closed-circuit television cameras."

Brown was not appeased. "If you've got perfect security, how did the hamster get out?"

Toni was ready for this. "Let me make three points. One, it was not a hamster. You've got that from the police, and it's wrong." She had deliberately given Frank dud information, and he had fallen into her trap, betraying himself as the source of the leaked story. "Please rely on us for the facts about what goes on here. It was a rabbit, and it was not called Fluffy."

They laughed at this, and even Brown smiled.

"Two, the rabbit was smuggled out of the laboratory in a bag, and we have today instituted a compulsory bag search at the entrance to BSL4, to make sure this cannot happen again. Three, I didn't say we had perfect security. I said we set the highest possible standards. That's all human beings can do."

"So you're admitting your laboratory is a danger to innocent members of the Scottish public."

"No. You're safer here than you would be driving on the M8 or taking a flight from Prestwick. Viruses kill many people every day, but only one person has ever died of a virus from our lab, and he was not an innocent member of the public—he was an employee who deliberately broke the rules and knowingly put himself at risk."

On balance it was going well, Toni thought as she looked around for the next question. The television cameras were rolling, the flashguns were popping, and Stanley was coming across as what he was, a brilliant scientist with a strong sense of responsibility. But she was afraid the TV news would throw away the undramatic footage of the press conference in favor of the crowd of youngsters at the gate chanting slogans about animal rights. She wished she could think of something more interesting for the cameramen to point their lenses at.

Frank's friend Carl Osborne spoke up for the first time. He was a good-looking man of about Toni's age with movie-star features. His hair was a shade too yellow to be natural. "Exactly what danger did this rabbit pose to the general public?"

Stanley answered: "The virus is not very infectious across species. In order to infect Michael, we think the rabbit must have bitten him."

"What if the rabbit had got loose?"

Stanley looked out of the window. A light snow was falling. "It would have frozen to death."

"Suppose it had been eaten by another animal. Could a fox have become infected?"

"No. Viruses are adapted to a small number of species, usually one, sometimes two or three. This one does not infect foxes, or any other form of Scottish wildlife, as far as we know. Just humans, macaque monkeys, and certain types of rabbit."

"But Michael could have given the virus to other people."

"By sneezing, yes. This was the possibility that alarmed us most. However, Michael seems not to have seen anyone during the critical period. We have already contacted his colleagues and friends. Nonetheless, we would be grateful if you would use your newspapers and television programs to appeal for anyone who did see him to call us immediately."

"We aren't trying to minimize this," Toni put in hastily. "We are deeply concerned about the incident and, as I've explained, we have already put in stronger security measures. But at the same time we must be careful not to exaggerate." Telling journalists not to exaggerate was a bit like telling lawyers not to be quarrelsome, she thought wryly. "The truth is that the public have not been endangered."

Osborne was not finished. "Suppose Michael Ross had given it to a friend, who had given it to someone else . . . how many people might have died?"

Toni said quickly, "We can't enter into that kind of wild speculation. The virus did not spread. One person died. That's one too many, but it's no reason to start talking about the Four Horsemen of the Apocalypse."

She bit her tongue. That was a stupid phrase to use: someone would probably quote it, out of context, and make it seem as if she had been forecasting doomsday.

Osborne said, "I understand your work is financed by the American army."

"The Department of Defense, yes," Stanley said. "They are naturally interested in ways of combating biological warfare."

"Isn't it true that the Americans have this work done in Scotland because they think it's too dangerous to be done in the United States?"

"On the contrary. A great deal of work of this type goes on in the States, at the Centers for Disease Control in Atlanta, Georgia, and at the U.S. Army Medical Research Institute of Infectious Diseases at Fort Detrick."

"So why was Scotland chosen?"

"Because the drug was invented here at Oxenford Medical."

Toni decided to quit while she was ahead and close the press conference. "I don't want to cut the questioning short, but I know some of you have midday deadlines," she said. "You should all have an information pack, and Cynthia here has extra copies."

"One more question," said Clive Brown of the *Record*. "What's your reaction to the demonstration outside?"

Toni realized she still had not thought of something more interesting for the cameras.

Stanley said, "They offer a simple answer to a complex ethical question. Like most simple answers, theirs is wrong."

It was the right response, but sounded a little hardhearted, so Toni added, "And we hope they don't catch cold."

While the audience was laughing at that, Toni stood up to indicate the conference was over. Then she was struck by inspiration. She beckoned to Cynthia Creighton. Turning her back on the audience, she spoke in a low, urgent voice. "Go down to the canteen, quickly," she said. "Get two or three canteen staff to load up trays with cups of hot coffee and tea, and hand them out to the demonstrators outside the gate."

"What a kind thought," said Cynthia.

Toni was not being kind—in fact she was being cynical—but there was no time to explain that. "It must be done in the next couple of minutes," she said. "Go, go!"

Cynthia hurried away.

Toni turned to Stanley and said, "Well done. You handled that perfectly."

He took a red polka-dotted handkerchief from his jacket pocket and discreetly mopped his face. "I hope it's done the trick."

"We'll know when we see the lunchtime news on television. Now you should slip away; otherwise they'll all be trying to corner you for an exclusive interview." He was under pressure, and she wanted to protect him.

"Good thinking. I need to get home, anyway." He lived in a farmhouse on a cliff five miles from the lab. "I'd like to be there to welcome the family."

That disappointed her. She had been looking forward to reviewing the press conference with him. "Okay," she said. "I'll monitor the reaction."

"At least no one asked me the worst question."

"What was that?"

"The survival rate from Madoba-2."

"What does that mean?"

"No matter how deadly the infection, there are usually some individuals who live through it. Survival rate is a measure of how dangerous it is."

"And what is the survival rate for Madoba-2?"

"Zero," said Stanley.

Toni stared at him. She was glad she had not known that before.

Stanley nodded over her shoulder. "Here comes Osborne."

"I'll head him off at the pass." She moved to intercept the reporter, and Stanley left by a side door. "Hello, Carl. I hope you got everything you needed?"

"I think so. I was wondering what Stanley's first success was."

"He was a member of the team that developed acyclovir."

"Which is?"

"The cream you put on when you get cold sores. The brand name is Zovirax. It's an antiviral drug."

"Really? That's interesting."

Toni did not think Carl was genuinely interested. She wondered what he was really after. She said, "May we rely on you to do a judicious piece that reflects the facts and doesn't exaggerate the danger?"

"You mean will I be talking about the Four Horsemen of the Apocalypse?"

She winced. "Foolish of me to give an example of the kind of hyperbole I was trying to discourage."

"Don't worry. I'm not going to quote you."

"Thanks."

"You shouldn't thank me. I'd use it happily, but my audience wouldn't have the slightest idea what it means." He changed tack. "I've hardly seen you since you split up with Frank. How long ago is it now?"

"He left me at Christmas two years ago."

"How have you been?"

"I've had some bad times, if you want to know the truth. But things are picking up. At least, they were until today."

"We should get together and catch up."

She had no desire to spend time with Osborne, but she politely said, "Sure, why not."

He surprised her by following up quickly. "Would you like to have dinner?"

"Dinner?" she said.

"Yes."

"As in, go out on a date with you?"

"Yes, again."

It was the last thing she had expected. "No!" she said. Then she remembered how dangerous this man could be, and tried to soften her rejection. "I'm sorry, Carl, you took me by surprise. I've known you so long that I just don't think of you that way."

"I might change your thinking." He looked boyishly vulnerable. "Give me a chance."

The answer was still no, but she hesitated for a moment. Carl was handsome, charming, well paid, a local celebrity. Most single women pushing forty would jump at the chance. But she was not even mildly attracted to him. Even if she had not given her heart to Stanley, she would not have been tempted to go out with Carl. Why?

It took her only a second to find the answer. Carl had no integrity. A man who would distort the truth for the sake of a sensational story would be equally dishonest in other areas of life. He was not a monster. There were plenty of men like him, and a few women. But Toni could not contemplate becoming intimate with someone so shallow. How could you kiss, and confess secrets, and lose your inhibitions, and open your body, with someone who could not be trusted? The thought was revolting.

"I'm flattered," she lied. "But no."

He was not ready to give up. "The truth is, I always fancied you, even when you were with Frank. You must have sensed that."

"You used to flirt with me, but you did that with most women."

"It wasn't the same."

"Aren't you seeing that weather girl? I seem to remember a photo in the newspaper."

"Marnie? That was never serious. I did it for publicity, mainly."

He seemed irritated by the reminder, and Toni guessed that Marnie had thrown him over. "I'm sorry to hear that," she said sympathetically.

"Show your compassion in actions, not words. Have dinner with me tonight. I even have a table booked at La Chaumière."

It was a swanky restaurant. He must have made the reservation some time ago—probably for Marnie. "I'm busy tonight."

"You're not still carrying a torch for Frank, are you?"

Toni laughed bitterly. "I did for a while, fool that I am, but I'm over him now. Very over."

"Someone else, then?"

"I'm not seeing anyone."

"But you're interested in someone. It's not the old professor, is it?"

"Don't be ridiculous," Toni said.

"You're not blushing, are you?"

"I hope not, though any woman subjected to this kind of interrogation would be entitled to blush."

"My God, you fancy Stanley Oxenford." Carl was not good at taking rejection, and his face became ugly with resentment. "Of course, Stanley's a widower, isn't he? Children grown up. All that money, and just the two of you to spend it."

"This is really offensive, Carl."

"The truth so often is. You really like highfliers, don't you? First Frank, the fastest-rising detective in the history of the Scottish police. And now a millionaire scientific entrepreneur. You're a starfucker, Toni!"

She had to end this before she lost her temper. "Thank you for coming to the press conference," she said. She held out her hand, and he shook it automatically. "Goodbye." She turned and walked away.

She was shaking with anger. He had made her deepest emotions seem unworthy. She wanted to strangle him, not go out with him. She tried to make herself calm. She had a major professional crisis to deal with, and she could not let her feelings get in the way.

She went to the reception desk near the door and spoke to the supervisor of the security guards, Steve Tremlett. "Stay here until they've all left, and make sure none of them tries to take an unofficial tour." A determined snoop might try to enter high-security areas by "tailgating"—waiting for someone with a pass, then going through the door right behind.

"Leave it to me," Steve said.

Toni began to feel calmer. She put on her coat and went outside. The snow was falling more heavily, but she could see the demonstration. She walked to the guard booth at the gate. Three canteen staff were handing out hot drinks. The protestors had temporarily stopped chanting and waving their banners, and were smiling and chatting instead.

And all the cameras were photographing them.

Everything had gone perfectly, Toni thought. So why did she feel depressed?

She returned to her office. She closed the door and stood still, grateful to be alone for a minute. She had controlled the press conference well, she thought. She had protected her boss from Osborne. And the idea of giving hot drinks to the demonstrators had worked like a charm. It would be unwise to celebrate before seeing the actual coverage, of course, but she felt that every decision she had made had been right.

So why did she feel so down?

Partly it was Osborne. Any encounter with him could leave a person feeling low. But mainly, she realized, it was Stanley. After all she had done for him this morning, he had slipped away with barely a word of thanks. That was what it meant to be the boss, she supposed. And she had long known how important his family was to him. She, by contrast, was just a colleague: valued, liked, respected—but not loved.

The phone rang. She looked at it for a moment, resenting its cheerful warble, not wanting to talk. Then she picked it up.

It was Stanley, calling from his car. "Why don't you drop in at the house in an hour or so? We could watch the news, and learn our fate together."

Her mood lifted instantly. She felt as if the sun had come out. "Of course," she said. "I'd be delighted."

"We might as well be crucified side by side," he said.

"I would consider it an honor."

12 NOON

THE snow became heavier as Miranda drove north. Big white flakes swooped onto the windshield of the Toyota Previa, to be swept aside by the long wipers. She had to slow down as visibility diminished. The snow seemed to soundproof the car, and there was no more than a background swish of tires to compete with the classical music from the radio.

The atmosphere inside was subdued. In the back, Sophie was listening to her own music on headphones, while Tom was lost in the beeping world of Game Boy. Ned was quiet, occasionally conducting the orchestra with one waving forefinger. As he gazed into the snow and listened to Elgar's cello concerto, Miranda watched his tranquil, bearded face, and realized that he had no idea how badly he had let her down.

He sensed her discontent. "I'm sorry about Jennifer's outburst," he said.

Miranda looked in the rearview mirror and saw that

Sophie was nodding her head in time to the music from her iPod. Satisfied that the girl could not hear her, Miranda said, "Jennifer was bloody rude."

"I'm sorry," he said again. He obviously felt no need to explain or apologize for his own role.

She had to destroy his comfortable illusion. "It's not Jennifer's behavior that bothers me," she said. "It's yours."

"I realize it was a mistake to invite you in without warning her."

"It's not that. We all make mistakes."

He looked puzzled and annoyed. "What, then?"

"Oh, Ned! You didn't defend me!"

"I thought you were well able to defend yourself."

"That's not the point! Of course I can look after myself. I don't need mothering. But you should be my champion."

"A knight in shining armor."

"Yes!"

"I thought it was more important to get things calmed down."

"Well, you thought wrong. When the world turns hostile, I don't want you to take a judicious view of the situation—I want you to be on my side."

"I'm afraid I'm not the combative type."

"I know," she said, and they both fell silent.

They were on a narrow road that followed the shore of a sea loch. They passed small farms with a few horses in winter blankets cropping the grass, and drove through villages with white-painted churches and rows of houses along the waterfront. Miranda felt depressed. Even if her family embraced Ned as she had asked them to, did she want to marry such a passive man? She had longed for someone gentle and cultured and bright, but she now realized that she also wanted him to be strong. Was it too much to expect? She thought of her father. He was always kind, rarely angry, never quarrelsome— but no one had ever thought him weak.

Her mood lifted as they approached Steepfall. The house was reached by a long lane that wound through woods. Emerging from the trees, the drive swept around a headland with a sheer drop to the sea.

The garage came into view first. Standing sideways-on to the drive, it was an old cowshed that had been renovated and given three up-and-over doors. Miranda drove past it and along the front of the house.

Seeing the old farmhouse overlooking the beach, its thick stone walls with their small windows and the steep slate roof, she was overwhelmed by a sense of her childhood. She had first come here at the age of five, and every time she returned she became, for a few moments, a little girl in white socks, sitting on the granite doorstep in the sun, playing teacher to a class of three dolls, two guinea pigs in a cage, and a sleepy old dog. The sensation was intense, but fleeting: suddenly she remembered exactly how it had felt to be herself at five, but trying to hold on to the memory was like grabbing at smoke.

Her father's dark blue Ferrari was at the front of the house, where he always left it for Luke, the handyman, to put away. The car was dangerously fast, obscenely curvaceous, and ludicrously expensive for his daily five-mile commute to the laboratory. Parked here on a bleak Scottish cliff top, it was as out of place as a high-heeled courtesan in a muddy farmyard. But he had no yacht, no wine cellar, no racehorse; he did not go skiing in Gstaad or gambling in Monte Carlo. The Ferrari was his only indulgence.

Miranda parked the Toyota. Tom rushed in. Sophie followed more slowly: she had not been here before, though she had met Stanley once, at Olga's birthday party a few months back. Miranda decided to forget about Jennifer for now. She took Ned's hand and they went in together.

They entered, as always, by the kitchen door at the side of the house. There was a lobby, where Wellington boots were kept in a cupboard, then a second door into the spacious kitchen. To Miranda this always felt like coming home. The familiar smells filled her head: roast dinners and ground coffee and apples, and a persistent trace of the French cigarettes Mamma Marta had smoked. No other house had replaced this one as the home of Miranda's soul: not the flat in Camden Town where she had sown her wild oats, nor the modern suburban house where she had been briefly married to Jasper Casson, nor the apartment in Georgian Glasgow in which she had raised Tom, at first alone and now with Ned.

A full-size black standard poodle called Nellie wagged her whole body with joy and licked everyone. Miranda greeted Luke and Lori, the Filipino couple who were preparing lunch. Lori said, "Your father just got home. He's washing."

Miranda told Tom and Sophie to lay the table. She did not want the children to put down roots in front of the TV and stay there all afternoon. "Tom, you can show Sophie where everything is." And having a job to do would help Sophie feel part of the family.

There were several bottles of Miranda's favorite white wine in the fridge. Daddy did not drink much, but Mamma had always had wine, and Daddy made sure there was plenty in the house. Miranda opened a bottle and poured a glass for Ned.

This was a good start, Miranda thought: Sophie happily helping Tom put out knives and forks, and Ned contentedly sipping Sancerre. Perhaps this, rather than the scene with Jennifer, would set the tone for the holiday.

If Ned was going to be part of Miranda's life, he had to love this house and the family that had grown up in it. He had been here before, but he had never brought Sophie and he had never stayed overnight, so this was his first major visit. She so wanted him to have a good time and get on well with everyone.

Miranda's husband, Jasper, had never liked Steepfall. At first he had gone out of his way to charm everyone, but on later visits he had been withdrawn while there and angry after they left. He seemed to dislike Stanley, and complained that he was authoritarian, which was odd, as Stanley rarely told anyone what to do—whereas Marta was so bossy they sometimes called her Mamma Mussolini. Now, with hindsight, Miranda could see that Jasper's hold over her was threatened by the presence of another man who loved her. Jasper did not feel free to bully her while her father was around.

The phone rang. Miranda picked up the extension on the wall by the big fridge. "Hello?"

"Miranda, it's Kit."

She was pleased. "Hello, little brother! How are you?"

"A bit shattered, actually."

"How come?"

"I fell in a swimming pool. Long story. How are things at Steepfall?"

"We're just sitting around drinking Daddy's wine, wishing you were with us."

"Well, I'm coming after all."

"Good!" She decided not to ask what had changed his mind. He would probably just say *long story* again.

"I'll be there in an hour or so. But, listen, can I still have the cottage?"

"I'm sure you can. It's up to Daddy, but I'll talk to him."

As Miranda cradled the handset, her father came in. He wore the waistcoat and trousers of his suit, but he had rolled the cuffs of his shirt. He shook hands with Ned and kissed Miranda and the children. He was looking very trim, Miranda thought. "Are you losing weight?" she asked.

"I've been playing squash. Who was on the phone?"

"That was Kit. He's coming, after all." She watched her father's face, anxious to see his reaction.

"I'll believe it when I see him."

"Oh, Daddy! You might sound more enthusiastic."

He patted her hand. "We all love Kit, but we know what he's like. I hope he shows up, but I'm not counting on it." His tone was light, but Miranda could tell that he was trying to hide an inner hurt.

"He really wants to sleep in the cottage."

"Did he say why?"

"No."

Tom piped up: "He's probably bringing a girl, and doesn't want us all to hear her squeals of delight."

The kitchen went quiet. Miranda was astonished. Where had that come from? Tom was eleven, and never talked about sex. After a moment, they all burst out laughing. Tom looked bashful, and said, "I read that in a book." He was probably trying to seem grown-up in front of Sophie, Miranda decided. He was still a little boy, but not for much longer.

Stanley said, "Anyway, I don't mind where anyone sleeps—you know that." He looked at his watch distractedly. "I have to watch the lunchtime news on television."

Miranda said, "I'm sorry about the technician who died. What made him do it?"

"We all get weird ideas into our heads, but a lonely person has no one to tell him not to be crazy."

The door opened and Olga came in. As always, she entered speaking. "This weather is a nightmare! People are skidding all over the place. Is that wine you're drinking? Let me have some before I explode. Nellie, please don't sniff me there. It's considered vulgar in human society. Hello, Daddy, how are you?"

"Nella merde," he said.

Miranda recognized one of her mother's expressions. It meant "in the shit." Mamma Marta had fondly imagined that if she swore in Italian the children would not understand.

Olga said, "I heard about the guy who died. Is it so bad for you?"

"We'll see when we watch the news."

Olga was followed in by her husband, Hugo, a small man with impish charm. When he kissed Miranda, his lips lingered on her cheek a second too long.

Olga said, "Where shall Hugo put the bags?"

"Upstairs," said Miranda.

"I suppose you've staked your claim to the cottage."

"No, Kit's having it."

"Oh, please!" Olga protested. "That big double bed and a nice bathroom and kitchenette, all for one person, while the four of us share the poky old bathroom upstairs?"

"He particularly asked for it."

"Well, I'm particularly asking for it."

Miranda felt irritated with her sister. "For God's sake, Olga, think of someone other than yourself for a change. You know Kit hasn't been here since . . . that whole mess. I just want to make sure he has a good time."

"So he's getting the best bedroom because he stole from Daddy—is that your logic?"

"You're talking like an advocate again. Save it for your learned friends."

"All right, you two," their father said, sounding just as he had when they were small. "In this case, I think Olga's right. It's selfish of Kit to demand the cottage all to himself. Miranda and Ned can sleep there."

Olga said, "So no one gets what they want."

Miranda sighed. Why was Olga arguing? They all knew their father. Most of the time he would give you anything you wanted, but when he said no it was final. He might be indulgent, but he could not be bullied.

Now he said, "It will teach you not to quarrel."

"No, it won't. You've been imposing these judgments of Solomon for thirty years, and we still haven't learned."

Stanley smiled. "You're right. My approach to child rearing has been wrong all along. Should I start again?"

"Too late."

"Thank God for that."

Miranda just hoped Kit would not be offended enough to turn right around and drive away. The argument was ended by the entrance of Caroline and Craig, the children of Hugo and Olga.

Caroline, seventeen, was carrying a cage containing several white rats. Nellie sniffed it excitedly. Caroline related to animals as a way of avoiding people. It was a phase many girls went through but, Miranda thought, at seventeen she should have got over it.

Craig, fifteen, carried two plastic garbage bags crammed with wrapped gifts. He had Hugo's wicked grin, though he was tall like Olga. He put the bags down, greeted the family perfunctorily, and made a beeline for Sophie. They had met once before, Miranda recalled, at Olga's birthday party. "You got your belly button pierced!" Craig said to Sophie. "Cool! Did it hurt?"

Miranda became aware that there was a stranger in the room. The newcomer, a woman, stood by the door to the hall, so she must have come in by the front entrance. She was tall, with striking good looks: high cheekbones and a curved nose, lush red-blond hair and marvelous green eyes. She wore a brown chalk-stripe suit that was a bit rumpled, and her expert makeup did not quite hide signs of tiredness under her eyes. She was gazing with amusement at the animated scene in the crowded kitchen. Miranda wondered how long she had been watching in silence.

The others began to notice her, and slowly the room fell silent. At last, Stanley turned around. "Ah! Toni!" he said, jumping up from his seat, and Miranda was struck by how pleased he looked. "Kind of you to drop in. Kids, this is my colleague, Antonia Gallo."

The woman smiled as if she thought there was nothing more delightful than a big quarrelsome family. She had a wide, generous smile and full lips. This was the ex-cop who had caught Kit stealing from the company, Miranda realized. Despite that, Stanley seemed to like her.

Stanley introduced them, and Miranda noticed the pride in his tone. "Toni, meet my daughter Olga; her husband, Hugo; and their children, Caroline with the pet rats, and Craig, the tall one. My other daughter, Miranda; her boy, Tom; her fiancé, Ned; and Ned's daughter, Sophie." Toni looked at each member of the family, nodding pleasantly, seeming keenly interested. It was hard to take in eight new names at a time, but Miranda had a feeling Toni would remember them all. "That's Luke peeling carrots and Lori at the stove. Nellie, the lady does not want a chew of your rawhide bone, touched though she is by your generosity."

Toni said, "I'm very glad to meet you all." She sounded as if she meant it, but at the same time she seemed to be under strain.

Miranda said, "You must be having a difficult day. I'm so sorry about the technician who died."

Stanley said, "It was Toni who found him."

"Oh, God!"

Toni nodded. "We're pretty sure he didn't infect anyone else, thank heaven. Now we're just hoping the media won't crucify us."

Stanley looked at his watch. "Excuse us," he said to his family. "We're going to watch the news in my study." He held the door for Toni and they went out.

The children started to chatter again, and Hugo said something to Ned about the Scottish rugby team. Miranda turned to Olga. Their quarrel was forgotten. "Attractive woman," she said musingly.

"Yes," Olga said. "About, what, my age?"

"Thirty-seven, thirty-eight, yes. And Daddy's lost weight."

"I noticed that."

"A shared crisis brings people together."

"Doesn't it just?"

"So what do you think?"

"I think what you think."

Miranda drained her glass of wine. "I thought so."

1 P.M.

TONI was overwhelmed by the scene in the kitchen: adults and children, servants and pets, drinking wine and preparing food and quarreling and laughing at jokes. It had been like walking into a really good party where she knew nobody. She wanted to join in, but she felt excluded. This was Stanley's life, she thought. He and his wife had created this group, this home, this warmth. She admired him for it, and envied his children. They probably had no idea how privileged they were. She had stood there for several minutes, bemused but fascinated. No wonder he was so attached to his family.

It thrilled and dismayed her. She could, if she allowed herself, entertain a fantasy about being part of it, sitting beside Stanley as his wife, loving him and his children, basking in the comfort of their togetherness. But she repressed that dream. It was impossible, and she should not torture herself. The very strength of the family bonds kept her out.

When at last they noticed her, she got a hard look from both daughters, Olga and Miranda. It was a careful scrutiny: detailed, unapologetic, hostile. She had got a similar look from Lori, the cook, though more discreet.

She understood the daughters' reaction. For thirty years Marta had ruled that kitchen. They would have felt disloyal to her had they *not* been hostile. Any woman Stanley liked could turn into a threat. She could disrupt the family. She might change their father's attitudes, turn his affections in new directions. She might bear him children, half-brothers and half-sisters who would care nothing about the history of the original family, would not be bound to them with the unbreakable chains of a shared childhood. She would take some of their inheritance, perhaps all of it. Was Stanley sensing these undercurrents? As she followed him into his study, she felt again the maddening frustration of not knowing what was in his mind.

It was a masculine room, with a Victorian pedestal desk, a bookcase full of weighty microbiology texts, and a worn leather couch in front of a log fire. The dog followed them in and stretched out by the fire like a curly black rug. On the mantelpiece was a framed photograph of a dark-haired teenage girl in tennis whites— the same girl as the bride in the picture on his office wall. Her brief shorts showed long, athletic legs. The heavy eye makeup and the hair band told Toni that the picture had been taken in the sixties. "Was Marta a scientist, too?" Toni asked.

"No. Her degree was in English. When I met her, she was teaching A-level Italian at a high school in Cambridge."

Toni was surprised. She had imagined that Marta

must have shared Stanley's passion for his work. So, she thought, you don't need a doctorate in biology to be married to him. "She was pretty."

"Devastating," Stanley replied. "Beautiful, tall, sexy, foreign, a demon on the court, a heartbreaker off it. I was struck by lightning. Five minutes after I met her, I was in love."

"And she with you?"

"That took longer. She was surrounded by admirers. Men fell like flies. I could never understand why she picked me in the end. She used to say she couldn't resist an egghead."

No mystery there, Toni thought. Marta had liked what Toni liked: Stanley's strength. You knew right away that here was a man who would do what he said and be what he seemed to be, a man you could rely on. He had other attractions, too: he was warm and clever and even well dressed.

She wanted to say *But how do you feel now? Are you still married to her memory?* But Stanley was her boss. She had no right to ask him about his deepest feelings. And there was Marta, on the mantelpiece, wielding her tennis racket like a cudgel.

Sitting on the couch beside Stanley, she tried to put her emotions aside and concentrate on the crisis at hand. "Did you call the U.S. embassy?" she asked him.

"Yes. I got Mahoney calmed down, for the moment, but he'll be watching the news like us."

A lot hung on the next few minutes, Toni thought. The company could be destroyed or saved, Stanley could be bankrupted, she could lose her job, and the world could lose the services of a great scientist. Don't panic, she told herself; be practical. She took a notebook from her shoulder bag. Cynthia Creighton was videotaping the news, back at the office, so Toni would be able to watch it again later, but she would now jot down any immediate thoughts.

The Scottish news came on before the UK bulletin.

The death of Michael Ross was still the top story, but the report was introduced by a newsreader, not Carl Osborne. That was a good sign, Toni thought hopefully. There was no more of Carl's laughably inaccurate science. The virus was correctly named as Madoba-2. The anchor was careful to point out that Michael's death would be investigated by the sheriff at an inquest.

"So far, so good," Stanley murmured.

Toni said, "It looks to me as if a senior news executive watched Carl Osborne's sloppy report over breakfast and came in to the office determined to sharpen up the coverage."

The picture switched to the gates of the Kremlin. "Animal-rights campaigners took advantage of the tragedy to stage a protest outside Oxenford Medical," the anchor said. Toni was pleasantly surprised. That sentence was more favorable than she would have hoped. It implied the demonstrators were cynical media manipulators.

After a brief shot of the demo, the report cut to the Great Hall. Toni heard her own voice, sounding more Scots than she expected, outlining the security system at the laboratory. This was not very effective, she realized: just a voice droning on about alarms and guards. It might have been better to let the cameras film the airlock entrance to BSL4, with its fingerprint recognition system and submarine doors. Pictures were always better than words.

Then there was a shot of Carl Osborne asking, "Exactly what danger did this rabbit pose to the general public?"

Toni leaned forward on the couch. This was the crunch.

They played the interchange between Carl and Stanley, with Carl posing disaster scenarios and Stanley saying how unlikely they were. This was bad, Toni knew. The audience would remember the idea of wildlife becoming infected, even though Stanley had said firmly that it was not possible.

On the screen, Carl said, "But Michael could have given the virus to other people."

Stanley replied gravely, "By sneezing, yes."

Unfortunately, they cut the exchange at that point.

Stanley muttered, "Bloody hell."

"It's not over yet," Toni said. It could get better—or worse.

Toni hoped they would show her hasty intervention, when she had tried to counter the impression of complacency by saying that Oxenford Medical was not trying to downplay the risk. But, instead, there was a shot of Susan Mackintosh on the phone, with a voice-over explaining how the company was calling every employee to check whether they had had contact with Michael Ross. That was all right, Toni thought with relief. The danger was bluntly stated, but the company was shown taking positive action.

The final press conference shot was a close-up of Stanley, looking responsible, saying, "In time, we will defeat influenza, and AIDS, and even cancer—and it will be done by scientists like us, working in laboratories such as this."

"That's good," Toni said.

"Will it outweigh the dialogue with Osborne, about infecting wildlife?"

"I think so. You look so reassuring."

Then there was a shot of the canteen staff giving out steaming hot drinks to the demonstrators in the snow. "Great—they used it!" said Toni.

"I didn't see this," Stanley said. "Whose idea was it?"

"Mine."

Carl Osborne thrust a microphone into the face of a woman employee and said, "These people are demonstrating against your company. Why are you giving them coffee?"

"Because it's cold out here," the woman replied.

Toni and Stanley laughed, delighted with the woman's wit and the positive way it reflected on the company.

The anchor reappeared and said, "The First Minister of Scotland issued a statement this morning, saying, 'I have today spoken to representatives of Oxenford Medical, the Inverburn police, and the Inverburn regional health authority, and I am satisfied that everything possible is being done to ensure that there is no further danger to the public.' And now other news."

Toni said, "My God, I think we saved the day."

"Giving out hot drinks was a great idea—when did you think of that?"

"At the last minute. Let's see what the UK news says."

In the main bulletin, the story of Michael Ross came second, after an earthquake in Russia. The report used some of the same footage, but without Carl Osborne, who was a personality only in Scotland. There was a clip of Stanley saying, "The virus is not very infectious across species. In order to infect Michael, we think the rabbit must have bitten him." There was a low-key statement from the British Environment Minister in London. The report continued the same unhysterical tone of the Scottish news. Toni was hugely relieved.

Stanley said, "It's good to know that not all journalists are like Carl Osborne."

"He asked me to have dinner with him." Toni wondered why she was telling him this.

Stanley looked surprised. *"Ha la faccia peggio del culo!"* he said. "Hell of a nerve."

She laughed. What he had actually said was "His face is worse than his arse," presumably one of Marta's expressions. "He's an attractive man," she said.

"You don't really think so, do you?"

"He's handsome, anyway." She realized she was trying to make him jealous. Don't play games, she told herself.

He said, "What did you say to him?"

"I turned him down, of course."

"I should think so, too." Stanley looked embarrassed and added, "Not that it's any of my business, but he's not worthy of you, not by a light-year." He returned his attention to the television and switched to an all-news channel.

They watched footage of Russian earthquake victims and rescue teams for a couple of minutes. Toni felt foolish for having told Stanley about Osborne, but pleased by his reaction.

The Michael Ross story followed, and once again the tone was coolly factual. Stanley turned off the set. "Well, we escaped crucifixion by TV."

"No newspapers tomorrow, as it's Christmas Day," Toni observed. "By Thursday the story will be old. I think we're in the clear—barring unexpected developments."

"Yes. If we lost another rabbit, we'd be right back in trouble."

"There will be no more security incidents at the lab," Toni said firmly. "I'll make sure of that."

Stanley nodded. "I have to say, you've handled this whole thing extraordinarily well. I'm very grateful to you."

Toni glowed. "We told the truth, and they believed us," she said.

They smiled at each other. It was a moment of happy intimacy. Then the phone rang.

Stanley reached across his desk and picked it up. "Oxenford," he said. "Yes, patch him through here, please. I'm keen to speak to him." He looked up at Toni and mouthed, "Mahoney."

Toni stood up nervously. She and Stanley were convinced they had controlled the publicity well—but would the U.S. government agree? She watched Stanley's face.

He spoke into the phone. "Hello again, Larry, did you watch the news? . . . I'm glad you think so . . . We've avoided the kind of hysterical reaction that you feared . . . You know my facilities director, Antonia Gallo—she handled the press . . . A great job, I agree . . . Absolutely right, we must keep a very tight grip on security from now on . . . yes. Good of you to call. Bye."

Stanley hung up and grinned at Toni. "We're in the clear." Exuberantly, he put his arms around her and hugged her.

She pressed her face into his shoulder. The tweed of his waistcoat was surprisingly soft. She breathed in the warm, faint smell of him, and realized it was a long time since she had been this close to a man. She wrapped her arms around him and hugged him back, feeling her breasts press against his chest.

She would have stayed like that forever, but after a few seconds he gently disengaged, looking bashful. As if to restore propriety, he shook her hand. "All credit to you," he said.

The brief moment of physical contact had aroused her. Oh, God, she thought, I'm wet. How could it happen so quickly?

He said, "Would you like to see the house?"

"I'd love to." Toni was pleased. A man rarely offered to show guests around the house. It was another kind of intimacy.

The two rooms she had already seen, kitchen and study, were at the back, looking onto a yard surrounded by outbuildings. Stanley led Toni to the front of the house and into a dining room with a view of the sea. This part looked like a new extension to the old farmhouse. In a corner was a cabinet of silver cups. "Marta's tennis trophies," Stanley said proudly. "She had a backhand like a rocket launcher."

"How far did she get with her tennis?"

"She qualified for Wimbledon, but never competed because she got pregnant with Olga."

Across the hall, also overlooking the sea, was a drawing room with a Christmas tree. The gifts under the tree spilled across the floor. There was another picture of Marta, a full-length painting of her as a woman of forty, with a fuller figure and a softness around her jawline. It was a warm, pleasant room, but nobody was in it, and Toni guessed the real heart of the house was the kitchen.

The layout was simple: drawing room and dining room at the front, kitchen and study at the back. "There's not much to see upstairs," Stanley said, but he went up anyway, and Toni followed. Was she being shown around her future home? she asked herself. It was a stupid fantasy, and she pushed it aside quickly. He was just being nice.

But he had hugged her.

In the older part of the house, over the study and drawing room, were three small bedrooms and a bathroom. They still bore traces of the children who had grown up in them. There was a poster of the Clash on one wall, an old cricket bat with its grip unraveling in a corner, a complete set of *The Chronicles of Narnia* on a shelf.

In the new extension was a master bedroom suite with a dressing room and a bathroom. The king-size bed was made and the rooms were tidy. Toni felt both excited and uncomfortable to be in Stanley's bedroom. Yet another picture of Marta stood on the bedside table, this one a color photograph taken in her fifties. Her hair was a witchy gray and her face was thin, no doubt by reason of the cancer that had killed her. It was an unflattering photo. Toni thought how much Stanley must still love her, to cherish even this unhappy memento.

She did not know what to expect next. Would he make a move, with his wife watching from the bedside table and his children downstairs? She felt it was not his style. He might be thinking of it, but he would not jump a woman so suddenly. He would feel that etiquette demanded he woo her in the normal way. To hell with dinner and a movie, she wanted to say; just grab me, for God's sake. But she kept silent, and after showing her the marble bathroom, he led the way back downstairs.

The tour was a privilege, of course, and should have drawn her closer to Stanley; but in fact she felt excluded, as if she had looked in through a window at a family sitting at their table, absorbed in one another and self-sufficient. She felt a sense of anticlimax.

In the hall, the big poodle nudged Stanley with her nose. "Nellie wants to go outside," he said. He looked out of the little window beside the door. "The snow has stopped—shall we get a breath of air?"

"Sure."

Toni put on her parka and Stanley picked up an old blue anorak. They stepped outside to find the world painted white. Toni's Porsche Boxster stood beside Stanley's Ferrari F50 and two other cars, each topped with snow, like iced cakes. The dog headed for the cliff, evidently taking a habitual route. Stanley and Toni followed. Toni realized that the dog bore a distinct resemblance to the late Marta, with her curly black hair.

Their feet displaced the powdery snow to reveal tough seaside grass beneath. They crossed a long lawn. A few stunted trees grew at angles, blown slantwise by the tireless wind. They met two of the children coming back from the cliff: the older boy with the attractive grin and the sulky girl with the pierced navel. Toni remembered their names: Craig and Sophie. When Stanley had introduced everyone, in the kitchen, she had memorized every detail eagerly. Craig was working hard to charm Sophie, Toni could see, but the girl walked along with her arms crossed, looking at the ground. Toni envied the simplicity of the choices they faced. They were young and single, at the beginning of adulthood, with nothing to do but embrace the adventure of life. She wanted to tell Sophie not to play hard to get. Take love while you can, she thought; it may not always come to you so easily.

"What are your Christmas plans?" Stanley asked.

"About as different from yours as could be. I'm going

to a health spa with some friends, all singles or childless couples, for a grown-up Christmas. No turkey, no crackers, no stockings, no Santa. Just gentle pampering and adult conversation."

"It sounds wonderful. I thought you usually had your mother."

"I have done for the past few years. But this Christmas my sister, Bella, is taking her—somewhat to my surprise."

"Surprise?"

Toni made a wry face. "Bella has three children, and she feels that excuses her from other responsibilities. I'm not sure that's fair, but I love my sister, so I accept it."

"Do you want to have children, one day?"

She caught her breath. It was a deeply intimate question. She wondered what answer he would prefer to hear. She did not know, so she told the truth. "Maybe. It was the one thing my sister always wanted. The desire for babies dominated her life. I'm not like that. I envy you your family—they obviously love and respect you and like being with you. But I don't necessarily want to sacrifice everything else in life in order to become a parent."

"I'm not sure you have to sacrifice everything," Stanley said.

You didn't, Toni thought, but what about Marta's chance at Wimbledon? But she said something else. "And you? You could start another family."

"Oh, no," he said quickly. "My children would be most put out."

Toni felt a little disappointed that he was so decisive about that.

They reached the cliff. To the left, the headland

sloped down to a beach, now carpeted with snow. To the right, the ground dropped sheer into the sea. On that side, the edge was barred by a stout wooden fence four feet high, big enough to deter small children without obstructing the view. They both leaned on the fence and looked at the waves a hundred feet below. There was a long, deep swell, rising and falling like the chest of a sleeping giant. "What a lovely spot," Toni said.

"Four hours ago I thought I was going to lose it."

"Your home?"

He nodded. "I had to pledge the place as security for my overdraft. If I go bust, the bank takes the house."

"But your family . . ."

"They would be heartbroken. And now, since Marta went, they're all I really care about."

"All?" she said.

He shrugged. "In the end, yes."

She looked at him. His expression was serious but unsentimental. Why was he telling her this? As a message, Toni assumed. It was not true that his children were all he cared about—he was profoundly involved in his work. But he wanted her to understand how important the family's unity was to him. Having seen them together in the kitchen, she could understand it. But why had he chosen this moment to say so? Perhaps he was afraid he might have given her a wrong impression.

She needed to know the truth. An awful lot had happened in the last few hours, but all of it was ambiguous. He had touched her, hugged her, shown her his house, and asked her if she wanted children. Did it mean anything, or not? She had to know. She said, "You're telling me you'd never do anything to jeopardize what I saw in your kitchen, the togetherness of your family."

"Yes. They all draw their strength from it, whether they realize it or not."

She faced him and looked directly into his eyes. "And that's so important to you that you would never start another family."

"Yes."

The message was clear, Toni thought. He liked her, but he was not going to take it any farther. The hug in the study had been a spontaneous expression of triumph, the tour of the house an unguarded moment of intimacy; and now he was pulling back. Reason had prevailed. She felt tears come to her eyes. Horrified that she might be showing her emotions, she turned away, saying, "This wind . . ."

She was saved by young Tom, who came running through the snow, calling, "Grandpa! Grandpa! Uncle Kit's here!"

They went with the boy back to the house, not speaking, both embarrassed.

A fresh double row of tire tracks led to a black Peugeot coupe. It was not much of a car, but it looked stylish—just right for Kit, Toni thought sourly. She did not want to meet him. She would not have relished the prospect at the best of times, and right now she was too bruised to face an abrasive encounter. But her shoulder bag was in the house, so she was obliged to follow Stanley inside.

Kit was in the kitchen, being welcomed by his family—like the prodigal son, Toni thought. Miranda hugged him, Olga kissed him, Luke and Lori beamed, and Nellie barked for his attention. Toni stood at the kitchen door and watched Stanley greet his son. Kit looked wary. Stanley seemed both pleased and grieved, in the way he did when he spoke of Marta. Kit held out a hand to shake, but his father embraced him. "I'm very glad you came, my boy," Stanley said. "Very glad indeed."

Kit said, "I'd better get my bag from the car. I'm in the cottage, yeah?"

Miranda looked nervous and said, "No, you're upstairs."

"But—"

Olga overrode him. "Don't make a fuss—Daddy has decided, and it's his house."

Toni saw a flash of pure rage in Kit's eyes, but he covered up quickly. "Whatever," he said. He was trying to give the impression that it was no big deal, but that flash said otherwise, and Toni wondered what secret project he had that made him so keen to sleep outside the main house tonight.

She slipped into Stanley's study. The memory of that hug came back to her in force. That was the closest she was going to get to making love to him, she thought. She wiped her eyes on her sleeve.

Her notebook and bag lay on his antique desk, where she had left them. She slid the notebook into the bag, slung the bag over her shoulder, and returned to the hall.

Looking into the kitchen, she saw Stanley saying something to the cook. She waved to him. He interrupted his conversation and came over. "Toni, thanks for everything."

"Happy Christmas."

"To you, too." She went out quickly.

Kit was outside, opening the boot of his car. Glancing into it, Toni saw a couple of gray boxes, computer equipment of some kind. Kit was an IT specialist, but what did he need to bring with him for Christmas at his father's house?

She hoped to pass him without speaking but, as she was opening her car door, he looked up and caught her eye. "Happy Christmas, Kit," she said politely.

He lifted a small suitcase from the boot and slammed the lid. "Get lost, bitch," he said, and he walked into the house.

2 P.M.

CRAIG was thrilled to see Sophie again. He had been captivated by her at his mother's birthday party. She was pretty in a dark-eyed, dark-haired way and, although she was small and slight, her body was softly rounded—but it was not her looks that had bewitched him; it was her attitude. She did not give a damn, and that fascinated him. Nothing impressed her: not Grandpa's Ferrari F50, nor Craig's football skills—he played for Scotland in the under-sixteens—nor the fact that his mother was a QC. Sophie wore what she liked, she ignored "No Smoking" signs, and if someone was boring her, she would walk away in midsentence. At the party, she had been fighting with her father about getting her navel pierced—which he flatly forbade—and here she was with a stud in it.

It made her difficult to get on with. Showing her around Steepfall, Craig found that nothing pleased her. It seemed that silence was as near as she got to praise.

Otherwise, she would utter an abbreviated put-down: "Gross," or "Dumb," or "So weird." But she did not walk away, so he knew he was not boring her.

He took her to the barn. It was the oldest building on the property, built in the eighteenth century. Grandpa had put in heating, lighting, and plumbing, but you could still see the original timber framing. The ground floor was a playroom with a billiards table, a bar football game, and a big TV. "This is an okay place to hang out," he said.

"Quite cool," she said—the most enthusiasm she had yet shown. She pointed to a raised platform. "What's that?"

"A stage."

"Why do you need a stage?"

"My mother and Aunt Miranda used to do plays when they were girls. They once produced *Antony and Cleopatra* with a cast of four in this barn."

"Strange."

Craig pointed to two camp beds. "Tom and I are sleeping here," he said. "Come upstairs. I'll show you your bedroom."

A ladder led to the hayloft. There was no wall, just a handrail for safety. Two single beds were neatly made up. The only furniture was a coat rail for hanging clothes and a cheval mirror. Caroline's suitcase was on the floor, open.

"It's not very private," Sophie said.

Craig had noticed that. The sleeping arrangements seemed to him to be full of promise. His older sister, Caroline, and his young cousin, Tom, would be around, of course, but nevertheless he was enjoying a vague but exciting feeling that all kinds of things might happen. "Here." He unfolded an old concertina screen. "You can undress behind this if you're shy."

Her dark eyes sparked resentment. "I'm not *shy*," she said, as if the suggestion were insulting.

He found her flash of anger strangely thrilling. "Just asking," he said. He sat on one of the beds. "It's quite comfortable—better than our camp beds."

She shrugged.

In his fantasy, she would now sit on the bed beside him. In one version, she pushed him backward, pretending to fight with him, and having started out wrestling they ended up kissing. In another scenario, she would take his hand and tell him how much his friendship meant to her, and then she would kiss him. But now, in real life, she was neither playful nor sentimental. She turned away and looked around the bare hayloft with an expression of distaste, and he knew that kissing was not on her mind. She sang quietly: "I'm dreaming of a shite Christmas."

"The bathroom's underneath here, at the back of the stage. There's no bath, but the shower works all right."

"How luxurious." She got up from the bed and went down the ladder, still singing her obscene adaptation of Bing Crosby's Christmas classic.

Well, he thought, we've only been here a couple of hours, and I've got five whole days to win her around.

He followed her down. There was one more thing that might get her excited. "I've got something else to show you." He led the way outside.

They stepped into a big square yard with one building on each of its four sides: the main house, the guest cottage, the barn they had just left, and the three-car garage. Craig led Sophie around the house to the front door, avoiding the kitchen, where they might be given chores. When they stepped inside, he saw that there were snowflakes caught in her gleaming dark hair. He stopped and stared, transfixed.

She said, "What?"

"Snow in your hair," he said. "It looks beautiful."

She shook her head impatiently, and the flakes disappeared. "You're bizarre," she said.

Okay, he thought, so you don't like compliments.

He led her up the stairs. In the old part of the house were three small bedrooms and an old-fashioned bathroom. Grandpa's suite was in the new extension. Craig tapped on the door, in case Grandpa was inside. There was no reply, and he went in.

He walked quickly through the bedroom, past the big double bed, into the dressing room beyond. He opened a closet door and pushed aside a row of suits, pinstripes and tweeds and checks, mostly gray and blue. He got down on his knees, reached into the closet, and shoved at the back wall. A panel two feet square swung open on a hinge. Craig crawled through it.

Sophie followed.

Craig reached back through the gap, pulled the closet door shut, then closed the panel. Fumbling in the dark, he found a switch and turned on the light, a single unshaded bulb hanging from a roof beam.

They were in an attic. There was a big old sofa with stuffing bursting out of holes in the upholstery. Beside it a stack of moldering photograph albums stood on the floorboards. There were several cardboard boxes and tea chests, which Craig had found, on earlier visits, to contain his mother's school reports, novels by Enid Blyton inscribed in a childish hand "This book belongs to Miranda Oxenford age 9½," and a collection of ugly ashtrays, bowls, and vases that must have been either unwanted gifts or ill-judged purchases. Sophie ran her fingers over the strings of a dusty guitar: it was out of tune.

"You can smoke up here," Craig said. Empty cigarette packets of forgotten brands—Woodbines, Players, Senior Service—made him think this might have been where his mother began her addiction. There were also wrappers from chocolate bars: perhaps plump Aunt Miranda was responsible for those. And he presumed Uncle Kit had amassed the collection of magazines with titles such as *Men Only, Panty Play,* and *Barely Legal.*

Craig hoped Sophie would not notice the magazines, but they caught her eye immediately. She picked one up. "Wow, get this, porn!" she said, suddenly more animated than she had been all morning. She sat on the sofa and began to leaf through it.

Craig looked away. He had been through all the magazines, though he was ready to deny it. Porn was a boy thing, and strictly private. But Sophie was reading *Hustler* right in front of him, scrutinizing the pages as if she had to take an exam on it.

To distract her, he said, "This whole part of the house used to be the dairy, when the place was a farm. Grandpa turned the dairy into the kitchen, but the roof was too high, so he just put a ceiling in and used this space for storage."

She did not even look up from the magazine. "Every one of these women is shaved!" she said, embarrassing him further. "So creepy."

"You can see into the kitchen," he persisted. "Over here, where the flue from the Aga comes up through the ceiling." He lay flat and looked through a wide gap between the boards and a metal shaft. He could see the entire kitchen: the hall door at the far end, the long scrubbed-pine table, the cupboards on both sides, the side doors into the dining room and the laundry, the cooking range at this end, and two doors on either side of the range, one leading to a big walk-in larder and the other leading to the boot lobby and the side entrance. Most of the family were around the table. Craig's sister, Caroline, was feeding her rats, Miranda was pouring wine, Ned was reading the *Guardian,* Lori was poaching a whole salmon in a long fish kettle. "I think Aunt Miranda's getting drunk," Craig said.

That caught Sophie's interest. She dropped the magazine and lay beside Craig to look. "Can't they see us?" she said quietly.

He studied her as she stared through the gap. Her hair was pushed behind her ears. The skin of her cheek looked unbearably soft. "Have a look, next time you're in the kitchen," he said. "You'll see that there's a ceiling light right behind the gap which makes it difficult to make out, even when you know it's there."

"So, like, nobody knows you're here?"

"Well, everyone knows there's an attic. And watch out for Nellie. She'll look up and cock her head, listening, as soon as you move. She knows you're here—and anyone watching her may catch on."

"Still, this is pretty cool. Look at my father. He's pretending to read the paper, but he keeps making eyes at Miranda. Yech." She rolled on her side, propped herself on her elbow, and fished a packet of cigarettes out of her jeans pocket. "Want one?"

Craig shook his head. "You can't smoke if you're serious about football."

"How can you be serious about football? It's a game!"

"Sports are more fun if you're good at them."

"Yeah, you're right." She blew out smoke. He watched her lips. "That's probably why I don't like sports. I'm such a spastic."

Craig realized he had broken through some kind of barrier. She was talking to him at last. And what she said was quite intelligent. "What are you good at?" he asked.

"Not much."

He hesitated, then blurted out, "Once, at a party, a girl told me I was a good kisser." He held his breath. He needed to break the ice with her somehow—but was this too soon?

"Oh?" She seemed interested in an academic way. "What do you do?"

"I could show you."

A look of panic crossed her face. "No way!" She held up a hand, as if to ward him off, although he had not moved.

He realized he had been too impetuous. He could have kicked himself. "Don't worry," he said, smiling to hide his disappointment. "I won't do anything you don't want, I promise."

"It's just that I've got this boyfriend."

"Oh, I see."

"Yeah. But don't tell anyone."

"What's he like?"

"My boyfriend? He's a student." She looked away, screwing up her eyes against the smoke from her cigarette.

"At Glasgow University?"

"Yes. He's nineteen. He thinks I'm seventeen."

Craig was not sure whether to believe her. "What's he studying?"

"Who cares? Something boring. Law, I think."

Craig looked through the gap again. Lori was sprinkling chopped parsley over a steaming bowl of potatoes. Suddenly he felt hungry. "Lunch is ready," he said. "I'll show you the other way out."

He went to the end of the attic and opened a large door. A narrow ledge overhung a drop of fifteen feet to the ground. Above the door, on the outside of the building, was a pulley: that was how the sofa and tea chests had been brought up. Sophie said, "I can't jump from here."

"No need." Craig brushed snow off the ledge with his hands, then walked along it to the end and stepped two feet down on to a lean-to roof over the boot lobby. "Easy."

Looking anxious, Sophie followed in his footsteps. When she reached the end of the ledge, he offered her his hand. She took it, gripping unnecessarily hard. He handed her down onto the lean-to roof.

He stepped back up on the ledge to close the big door, then returned to Sophie's side. They went cautiously down the slippery roof. Craig lay on his front and slid over the edge, then dropped the short distance to the ground.

Sophie followed suit. When she was lying on the roof with her legs dangling over the edge, Craig reached up with both hands, held her by the waist, and lifted her down. She was light.

"Thanks," she said. She looked triumphant, as if she had come successfully through a trying experience.

It wasn't that difficult, Craig thought as they went into the house for lunch. Perhaps she's not as confident as she pretends.

3 P.M.

THE Kremlin looked pretty. Snow clung to its gargoyles and crochets, doorcases and window ledges, outlining the Victorian ornamentation in white. Toni parked and went inside. The place was quiet. Most people had gone home, for fear of getting caught in the snow—not that people needed much of an excuse to leave early on Christmas Eve.

She felt hurt and sensitive. She had been in an emotional car crash. But she had to put thoughts of love firmly out of her mind. Later, perhaps, when she lay alone in bed tonight, she would brood over the things Stanley had said and done; but now she had work to do.

She had scored a triumphant success—that was why Stanley had hugged her—but all the same a worry nagged at her. Stanley's words repeated in her brain: *If we lost another rabbit, we'd be right back in trouble.* It was true. Another incident of the same kind would bring the story back to life but ten times worse. No amount of public-relations work could keep the lid on it. *There will be no more security incidents at the lab,* she had told him. *I'll make sure of that.* Now she had to make her words come true.

She went to her office. The only threat that she could imagine was from the animal rights activists. The death of Michael Ross might inspire others to attempt to "liberate" laboratory animals. Alternatively, Michael might have been working with activists who had another plan. He might even have given them the kind of inside information that could help them defeat the Kremlin's security.

She dialed regional police headquarters in Inverburn and asked for Detective-Superintendent Frank Hackett, her ex. "Got away with it, didn't you?" he said. "Luck of the devil. You should have been crucified."

"We told the truth, Frank. Honesty is the best policy—you know that."

"You didn't tell me the truth. A hamster called Fluffy! You made me look a fool."

"It was unkind, I admit. But you shouldn't have leaked the story to Carl. Shall we call it quits?"

"What do you want?"

"Do you think anyone else was involved with Michael Ross in stealing the rabbit?"

"No opinion."

"I gave you his address book. I presume you've been checking his contacts. What about the people in Animals Are Free, for example—are they peaceful protestors, or might they do something more dangerous?"

"My investigation is not yet complete."

"Come on, Frank, I'm just looking for a little guidance. How worried should I be about the possibility of another incident?"

"I'm afraid I can't help you."

"Frank, we loved one another once. We were partners for eight years. Does it have to be like this?"

"Are you using our past relationship to persuade me to give you confidential information?"

"No. To hell with the information. I can get it elsewhere. I just don't want to be treated as an enemy by someone I used to love. Is there a law that says we can't be nice to one another?"

There was a click, then a dial tone. He had hung up.

She sighed. Would he ever come around? She wished he would get another girlfriend. That might calm him down.

She dialed Odette Cressy, her friend at Scotland Yard. "I saw you on the news," Odette said.

"How did I look?"

"Authoritative." Odette giggled. "Like you would *never* go to a nightclub in a see-through dress. But I know better."

"Just don't tell anyone the truth."

"Anyway, your Madoba-2 incident appears to have no connections with . . . my kind of interest." She meant terrorism.

"Good," Toni said. "But tell me something—speaking purely theoretically."

"Of course."

"Terrorists could get samples of a virus such as Ebola relatively easily by going to a hospital somewhere in central Africa where the only security is a nineteen-year-old cop slouching in the lobby smoking cigarettes. So why would they attempt the extraordinarily difficult task of robbing a high-security laboratory?"

"Two reasons. One, they simply don't know how easy

it is to get Ebola in Africa. Two, Madoba-2 is not the same as Ebola. It's worse."

Toni remembered what Stanley had told her, and shuddered. "Zero survival rate."

"Exactly."

"What about Animals Are Free? Did you check them out?"

"Of course. They're harmless. The worst they're likely to do is block a road."

"That's great news. I just want to make sure there's not another incident of the same kind."

"It looks unlikely from my end."

"Thanks, Odette. You're a friend, and that's a rare thing."

"You sound a bit low."

"Oh, my ex is being difficult."

"Is that all? You're used to him. Did something happen with the professor?"

Toni could never fool Odette, even over the phone. "He told me his family is the most important thing in the world to him, and he would never do anything to upset them."

"Bastard."

"When you find a man who isn't a bastard, ask him if he's got a brother."

"What are you doing for Christmas?"

"Going to a spa. Massage, facials, manicures, long walks."

"On your own?"

Toni smiled. "It's nice of you to worry about me, but I'm not that sad."

"Who are you going with?"

"A whole crowd. Bonnie Grant, an old friend—we were at university together, the only two girls in the engineering faculty. She's recently divorced. Charles and

Damien, you know them. And two couples you haven't met."

"The gay boys will cheer you up."

"You're right." When Charlie and Damien let their hair down, they could make Toni laugh until she cried. "What about you?"

"Not sure. You know how I hate to plan ahead."

"Well, enjoy spontaneity."

"Happy Christmas."

They hung up, and Toni summoned Steve Tremlett, the guard supervisor.

She had taken a chance with Steve. He had been a pal of Ronnie Sutherland, the former head of security who had conspired with Kit Oxenford. There was no evidence Steve had known about the fraud. But Toni had feared he might resent her for firing his friend. She had decided to give him the benefit of the doubt, and had made him supervisor. He had rewarded her trust with loyalty and efficiency.

He arrived within a minute. He was a small, neat man of thirty-five with receding fair hair cut in the brutally short style that was fashionable. He carried a cardboard folder. Toni pointed to a chair and he sat down.

"The police don't think Michael Ross was working with others," she said.

"I had him down as a loner."

"All the same, we have to have this place buttoned up tight tonight."

"No problem."

"Let's make doubly sure of that. You have the duty roster there?"

Steve handed over a sheet of paper. Normally there were three security guards on duty overnight and on weekends and holidays. One sat in the gatehouse, one in reception, and one in the control room, watching the monitors. In case they needed to step away from their stations, they carried phones that were cordless extensions to the house network. Every hour, the guard from reception made a tour of the main building, and the guard from the gatehouse walked around the outside. At first, Toni had thought three was too few for such a high-security operation, but the sophisticated technology was the real security, and the human beings merely backup. All the same, she had doubled the guard for this Christmas holiday, so that there would be two people at each of the three stations, and they would patrol every half hour.

"I see you're working tonight."

"I need the overtime."

"All right." Security guards regularly worked twelve-hour shifts, and it was not very unusual for them to do twenty-four hours, when staff were short or, as tonight, in an emergency. "Let me check your emergency call list."

Steve passed her a laminated sheet from the folder. It listed the agencies he was to phone in case of fire, flood, power cut, computer crash, phone system faults, and other problems.

Toni said, "I want you to ring each of these in the next hour. Just ask them if the number will be operational over Christmas."

"Very good."

She handed back the sheet. "Don't hesitate to call the police at Inverburn if you're the least worried about anything."

He nodded. "My brother-in-law Jack is on duty tonight, as it happens. My missus has taken the children over to their place for Christmas."

"How many people will there be at headquarters tonight, do you know?"

"On the night shift? An inspector, two sergeants, and six constables. And there'll be a duty superintendent on call."

It was a small complement, but there would be nothing much to do once the pubs had closed and the drunks had gone home. "You don't happen to know who the duty super is?"

"Yes. It's your Frank."

Toni did not comment. "I'll have my mobile phone with me day and night, and I don't expect to be anywhere out of range. I want you to call me the minute anything unusual happens, regardless of the time, okay?"

"Of course."

"I don't mind being woken up in the middle of the night." She would be sleeping alone, but she did not say that to Steve, who might have considered it an embarrassing confidence.

"I understand," he said, and perhaps he did.

"That's all. I'll be leaving in a few minutes." She checked her watch; it was almost four. "Happy Christmas, Steve."

"To you, too."

Steve left. Twilight was falling, and Toni could see her own reflection in the window. She looked rumpled and weary. She closed down her computer and locked her filing cabinet.

She needed to get going. She had to return home and change, then drive to the spa, which was fifty miles away. The sooner she hit the road, the better: the forecast said the weather would not get worse, but forecasts could be wrong.

She was reluctant to leave the Kremlin. Its security

was her job. She had taken every precaution she could think of, but she hated to hand over responsibility.

She forced herself to stand up. Her job was facilities director, not security guard. If she had done everything possible to safeguard the place, she could leave. If not, she was incompetent and should resign.

Besides, she knew the real reason she wanted to stay. As soon as she turned her back on the job, she would have to think about Stanley.

She shouldered her bag and left the building.

The snow was falling more heavily.

4 P.M.

KIT was furious about the sleeping arrangements.

He sat in the living room with his father, his nephew Tom, his brother-in-law, Hugo, and Miranda's fiancé, Ned. Mamma Marta looked down on them from her portrait on the wall. Kit always felt she looked impatient in that picture, as if she could hardly wait to get out of her ball gown, put on an apron, and start making lasagne.

The women of the family were preparing tomorrow's Christmas dinner, and the older children were in the barn. The men were watching a movie on TV. The hero, played by John Wayne, was a narrow-minded bully, a bit like Harry Mac, Kit thought. He found it hard to follow the plot. He was too tense.

He had *specifically* told Miranda he needed to be in the cottage. She had been so sentimental about his joining the family for Christmas, she had practically gone down on her knees to plead with him to come. But, after he had agreed to do what she wanted, she had failed to fulfill the one condition he had made. Typical woman.

The old man was not sentimental, though. He was about as softhearted as a Glasgow policeman on a Saturday night. He had obviously overruled Miranda, with Olga's encouragement. Kit thought his sisters ought to have been called Goneril and Regan, after the predatory daughters of King Lear.

Kit had to leave Steepfall tonight and come back tomorrow morning without anyone knowing he had been away. If he had been sleeping in the cottage, it would have been easier. He could have pretended to go to bed, turned off the lights, then sneaked away quietly. He had already moved his car to the garage forecourt, away from the house, so that no one would hear the engine starting. He would be back by midmorning, before anyone would expect him to be up, and could have slipped quietly back into the cottage and gone innocently to bed.

Now it would be much more difficult. His room was in the creaky old part of the main house, next to Olga and Hugo. He would have to wait until everyone had retired. When the house was quiet, he would have to creep out of his room, tiptoe down the stairs, and leave the house in total silence. If someone should open a door—Olga, for instance, crossing the landing to go to the bathroom—what would he say? "I'm just going to get some fresh air." In the middle of the night, in the snow? And what would he do in the morning? It was almost certain that someone would see him coming in. He would have to say he had been for a walk, or a drive. And then, later, when the police were asking questions, would anyone remember his uncharacteristic early morning stroll?

He tried to put that worry out of his mind. He had a more immediate problem. He had to steal the smart card his father used to enter BSL4.

He could have bought any number of such cards from a security supplier, but smart cards came from the manufacturer embedded with a site code that ensured they would work at only one location. Cards bought from a supplier would have the wrong code for the Kremlin.

Nigel Buchanan had questioned him persistently about stealing the card. "Where does your father keep it?"

"In his jacket pocket, usually."

"And if it's not there?"

"In his wallet, or his briefcase, I expect."

"How can you take it without being seen?"

"It's a big house. I'll do it when he's in the bath, or out for a walk."

"Won't he notice it's gone?"

"Not until he needs to use it, which won't be until Friday at the earliest. By then I'll have put it back."

"Can you be sure?"

At that point Elton had interrupted. In his broad south London accent he had said, "Bloody hell, Nige! We're counting on Kit to get us into a heavily guarded high-security laboratory. We're in trouble if he can't nick something off his own fuckin' father."

Stanley's card would have the right site code, but the chip in it would contain Stanley's fingerprint data, not Kit's. However, he had thought of a way around that.

The movie was building to a climax. John Wayne was about to start shooting people. This was a good moment for Kit to make a clandestine move.

He got up, grunted something about the bathroom,

and went out. From the hall, he glanced into the kitchen. Olga was stuffing a huge turkey while Miranda cleaned brussels sprouts. Along one wall were two doors, one to the laundry and the other to the dining room. As he looked, Lori came out of the laundry carrying a folded tablecloth and took it into the dining room.

Kit stepped into his father's study and closed the door.

The likeliest place for the smart card was in one of the pockets of his father's suit coat, as he had told Nigel. He had expected to find the jacket either on the hook behind the door or draped over the back of the desk chair; but he saw immediately that it was not in the room.

He decided to check some other possibilities while he was here. It was risky—anyone might come in, and what would he say? But he had to take chances. The alternative was no robbery, no three hundred thousand pounds, no ticket to Lucca—and, worst of all, the debt to Harry Mac unpaid. He remembered what Daisy had done to him that morning, and shuddered.

The old man's briefcase was on the floor beside the desk. Kit went through it quickly. It contained a file of scatter graphs, all meaningless to Kit; today's *Times* with the crossword not quite finished; half a bar of chocolate; and the small leather notebook in which his father made lists of things he had to do. Old people always had lists, Kit had noticed. Why were they so terrified of forgetting something?

The top of the pedestal desk was tidy, and Kit could not see a card or anything that might contain one: just a small stack of files, a pencil jar, and a book entitled *Seventh Report of the International Committee on Taxonomy of Viruses.*

He started opening the drawers. His breath came fast and he felt his heartbeat speed up. But if he were caught, what would they do—call the police? He told himself he had nothing to lose, and carried on; but his hands were unsteady.

His father had been using this desk for thirty years, and the accumulation of useless objects was staggering: souvenir key rings, dried-up pens, an old-fashioned printing calculator, stationery with out-of-date phone codes, ink bottles, manuals for obsolete software—how long was it since anyone had used PlanPerfect? But there was no smart card.

Kit left the room. No one had seen him go in, and no one saw him go out.

He went quietly up the stairs. His father was not an untidy man, and rarely lost things: he would not have carelessly left his wallet in some unlikely place such as the boot cupboard. The only remaining possibility was the bedroom.

Kit went inside and closed the door.

His mother's presence was gradually disappearing. Last time he was here, her possessions were still scattered around: a leather writing case, a silver brush set that had belonged to her mother, a photograph of Stanley in an antique frame. Those had gone. But the curtains and the upholstery were the same, done in a bold blue-and-white fabric that was typical of his mother's dramatic taste.

On either side of the bed were a pair of Victorian commode chests made of heavy mahogany, used as bedside tables. His father had always slept on the right of the big double bed. Kit opened the drawers on that side. He found a flashlight, presumably for power cuts, and a volume of Proust, presumably for insomnia. He checked the drawers on his mother's side of the bed, but they were empty.

The suite was arranged as three rooms: first the bedroom, then the dressing room, then the bathroom. Kit went into the dressing room, a square space lined with closets, some painted white, some with mirrored doors. Outside it was twilight, but he could see well enough for what he needed to do, so he did not switch on the lights.

He opened the door of his father's suit cupboard. There on a hanger was the jacket of the suit Stanley was wearing today. Kit reached into the inside pocket and drew out a large black leather wallet, old and worn. It contained a small wad of banknotes and a row of plastic cards. One was a smart card for the Kremlin.

"Bingo," Kit said softly.

The bedroom door opened.

Kit had not closed the door to the dressing room, and he was able to look through the doorway and see his sister Miranda step into the bedroom, carrying an orange plastic laundry basket.

Kit was in her line of sight, standing at the open door of the suit cupboard, but she did not immediately spot him in the twilight, and he quickly moved behind the dressing room door. If he peeked around the side of the door, he could see her reflected in the big mirror on the bedroom wall.

She switched the lights on and began to strip the bed. She and Olga were obviously doing some of Lori's chores. Kit decided he would just have to wait.

He suffered a moment of self-dislike. Here he was, acting like an intruder in the house of his family. He was stealing from his father and hiding from his sister. How had it got like this?

He knew the answer. His father had let him down.

Just when he needed help, Stanley had said no. That was the cause of everything.

Well, he would leave them all behind. He would not even tell them where he was going. He would make a new life in a different country. He would disappear into the small-town routine of Lucca, eating tomatoes and pasta, drinking Tuscan wine, playing pinochle for low stakes in the evenings. He would be like a background figure in a big painting, the passerby who does not look at the dying martyr. He would be at peace.

Miranda began to make up the bed with fresh sheets, and at that moment Hugo came in.

He had changed into a red pullover and green corduroy trousers, and he looked like a Christmas elf. He closed the door behind him. Kit frowned. Did Hugo have secrets to discuss with his wife's sister?

Miranda said, "Hugo, what do you want?" She sounded wary.

Hugo gave her a conspiratorial grin, but he said, "I just thought I'd give you a hand." He went to the opposite side of the bed and started tucking in the sheet.

Kit was standing behind the dressing room door with his father's wallet in one hand and a smart card for the Kremlin in the other, but he could not move without risking discovery.

Miranda tossed a clean pillowcase across the bed. "Here," she said.

Hugo stuffed a pillow into it. Together they arranged the bedcover. "It seems ages since we've seen you," Hugo said. "I miss you."

"Don't talk rubbish," Miranda said coolly.

Kit was puzzled but fascinated. What was going on here?

Miranda smoothed the cover. Hugo came around the

end of the bed. She picked up her laundry basket and held it in front of her like a shield. Hugo gave his impish grin and said, "How about a kiss, for old times' sake?"

Kit was mystified. What old times was Hugo talking about? He had been married to Olga for nearly twenty years. Had he kissed Miranda when she was fourteen?

"Stop that; right now," Miranda said firmly.

Hugo grasped the laundry basket and pushed. The backs of Miranda's legs came up against the edge of the bed. Involuntarily, she sat down. She released the basket and used her hands to balance herself. Hugo tossed the basket aside, bent over her, and pushed her back, kneeling on the bed with his legs either side of her. Kit was flabbergasted. He had guessed that Hugo might be something of a Lothario, just from his generally flirtatious manner with attractive women; but he had never imagined him with Miranda.

Hugo pushed up her loose, pleated skirt. She had heavy hips and thighs. She was wearing lacy black knickers and a garter belt, and for Kit this was the most astonishing revelation yet.

"Get off me now," she said.

Kit did not know what to do. This was none of his business, so he was not inclined to interfere; but he could hardly stand here and watch. Even if he turned away, he could not help hearing what was going on. Could he sneak past them while they were wrestling? No, the room was too small. He remembered the panel at the back of the closet that led to the attic, but he could not get to the closet without risking being seen. In the end he just stood paralyzed, looking on.

"Just a quickie," Hugo said. "No one will know."

Miranda drew back her right arm and swung at

Hugo's face, hitting him square on the cheek with a mighty slap. Then she lifted her knee sharply, making contact somewhere in the area of his groin. She twisted, threw him off, and jumped to her feet.

Hugo remained lying on the bed. "That hurt!" he protested.

"Good," she said. "Now listen to me. Never do anything like that again."

He zipped his fly and stood up. "Why not? What will you do—tell Ned?"

"I ought to tell him, but I haven't got the courage. I slept with you once, when I was lonely and depressed, and I've regretted it bitterly ever since."

So that was it, Kit thought—Miranda slept with Olga's husband. He was shocked. He was not surprised by Hugo's behavior—shagging the wife's sister on the side was the kind of cozy setup many men would like. But Miranda was prissily moral about such things. Kit would have said that she would not sleep with *anyone's* husband, let alone her sister's.

Miranda went on: "It was the most shameful thing I've done in my life, and I don't want Ned to find out about it, ever."

"So what are you threatening to do? Tell Olga?"

"She would divorce you and never speak to me again. It would explode this family."

It might not be that bad, Kit thought; but Miranda was always anxious about keeping the family together.

"That leaves you a bit helpless, doesn't it?" Hugo said, looking pleased. "Since we can't be enemies, why don't you just kiss me nicely and be friends?"

Miranda's voice went cold. "Because you disgust me."

"Ah, well." Hugo sounded resigned, but unashamed.

"Hate me, then. I still adore you." He gave his most charming smile and left the room, limping slightly.

As the door slammed, Miranda said, "You fucking bastard."

Kit had never heard her swear like that.

She picked up her laundry basket; then, instead of going out as he expected, she turned toward him. She must have fresh towels for the bathroom, he realized. There was no time to move. In three steps she reached the entrance to the dressing room and turned on the lights.

Kit was just able to slip the smart card into his trousers pocket. An instant later she saw him. She gave a squeal of shock. "Kit! What are you doing there? You gave me a fright!" She went white, and added, "You must have heard everything."

"Sorry." He shrugged. "I didn't want to."

Her complexion changed from pale to flushed. "You won't tell, will you?"

"Of course not."

"I'm serious, Kit. You must never tell. It would be awful. It could ruin two marriages."

"I know, I know."

She saw the wallet in his hand. "What are you up to?"

He hesitated; then he was inspired. "I needed cash." He showed her the banknotes in the wallet.

"Oh, Kit!" She was distressed, not judgmental. "Why do you always want easy money?"

He bit back an indignant retort. She believed his cover story—that was the main thing. He said nothing and tried to look ashamed.

She went on: "Olga always says you'd rather steal a shilling than earn an honest pound."

"All right, don't rub it in."

"You mustn't pilfer from Daddy's wallet—it's awful!"

"I'm a bit desperate."

"I'll give you money!" She put down the laundry basket. There were two pockets in the front of her skirt. She reached into one and pulled out a crumple of notes. She extracted two fifties, smoothed them out, and gave them to Kit. "Just ask me—I'll never turn you down."

"Thanks, Mandy," he said, using her childhood name.

"But you must never steal from Daddy."

"Okay."

"And, for pity's sake, don't ever tell anyone about me and Hugo."

"I promise," he said.

5 P.M.

TONI had been sleeping heavily for an hour when her alarm clock woke her.

She found that she was lying on the bed fully dressed. She had been too tired even to take off her jacket and shoes. But the nap had refreshed her. She was used to odd hours, from working night shifts on the police force, and she could fall asleep anywhere and wake up instantly.

She lived on one floor of a subdivided Victorian house. She had a bedroom, a living room, a small kitchen, and a bathroom. Inverburn was a ferry port, but she could not see the sea. She was not very fond of her home: it was the place to which she had fled when she broke up with Frank, and it had no happy memories. She had been here two years, but she still regarded it as temporary.

She got up. She stripped off the business suit she had been wearing for two days and a night, and dumped it in the dry-cleaning basket. With a robe on over her underwear, she moved rapidly around the flat, packing a case for five nights at a health spa. She had planned to pack last night and leave at midday today, so she had some catching up to do.

She could hardly wait to get to the spa. It was just what she needed. Her woes would be massaged away; she would sweat out toxins in the sauna; she would have her nails painted and her hair cut and her eyelashes curled. Best of all, she would play games and tell stories with a group of old friends, and forget her troubles.

Her mother should be at Bella's place by now. Mother was an intelligent woman who was losing her mind. She had been a high school math teacher, and had always been able to help Toni with her studies, even when Toni was in the final year of her engineering degree. Now she could not check her change in a shop. Toni loved her intensely and was deeply saddened by her decline.

Bella was a bit slapdash. She cleaned the house when the mood took her, cooked when she felt hungry, and sometimes forgot to send her children to school. Her husband, Bernie, was a hairdresser, but worked infrequently because of some vague chest ailment. "The doctor's signed me off for another four weeks," he would usually say in response to the routine inquiry "How are you?"

Toni hoped Mother would be all right at Bella's place. Bella was an amiable slattern, and Mother never seemed to mind her ways. Mother had always been happy to visit the windy Glasgow council estate and eat undercooked fries with her grandchildren. But she was now in the early stages of senility. Would she be as philosophical as ever about Bella's haphazard housekeeping? Would Bella be able to cope with Mother's increasing waywardness?

Once when Toni had let slip an irritated remark about Bella, Mother had said crisply, "She doesn't try as hard as you—that's why she's happier." Mother's conversation had become tactless, but her remarks could be painfully accurate.

After Toni had packed, she washed her hair, then took a bath to soak away two days of tension. She fell asleep in the tub. She woke with a start, but only a minute or so had passed—the water was still hot. She got out and dried herself vigorously.

Looking in the full-length mirror, she thought, I've got everything I had twenty years ago—it's all just three inches lower. One of the good things about Frank, at least in the early days, had been the pleasure he took in her body. "You've got great tits," he would say. She thought they were too large for her frame, but he worshipped them. "I've never seen a pussy this color," he once told her as he lay between her legs. "It's like a ginger biscuit." She wondered how long it would be before someone else marveled at the color of her pubic hair.

She dressed in tan jeans and a dark green sweater. As she was closing her suitcase, the phone rang. It was her sister. "Hi, Bella," said Toni. "How's Mother?"

"She's not here."

"What? You were supposed to pick her up at one o'clock!"

"I know, but Bernie had the car and I couldn't get away."

"And you still haven't left?" Toni looked at her watch. It was half past five. She pictured Mother at the home, sitting in the lobby in her coat and hat, with her suitcase beside the chair, hour after hour, and she felt cross. "What are you thinking of?"

"The thing is, the weather's turned bad."

"It's snowing all over Scotland, but not heavily."

"Well, Bernie doesn't want me to drive sixty miles in the dark."

"You wouldn't have had to drive in the dark if you'd picked her up when you promised!"

"Oh, dear, you're getting angry. I knew this would happen."

"I'm not angry—" Toni paused. Her sister had caught her before with this trick. In a moment they would be talking about Toni managing her anger, instead of Bella breaking a promise. "Never mind how I feel," Toni said. "What about Mother? Don't you think she must be disappointed?"

"Of course, but I can't help the weather."

"What are you going to do?"

"There isn't anything I can do."

"So you're going to leave her in the home over Christmas?"

"Unless you have her. You're only ten miles away."

"Bella, I'm booked into a spa! Seven friends are expecting me to join them for five days. I've paid four hundred pounds' deposit and I'm looking forward to a rest."

"That sounds a bit selfish."

"Just a minute. I've had Mother the last three Christmases, but I'm selfish?"

"You don't know how hard it is with three children and a husband too ill to work. You've got plenty of money and only yourself to worry about."

And I'm not stupid enough to marry a layabout and have three children by him, Toni thought, but she did not say it. There was no point in arguing with Bella. Her way of life was its own punishment. "So you're asking me to cancel my holiday, drive to the home, pick up Mother, and look after her over Christmas."

"It's up to you," Bella said in a tone of elevated piety. "You must do what your conscience tells you."

"Thanks for that helpful advice." Toni's conscience said she should be with their mother, and Bella knew that. Toni could not let Mother spend Christmas in an institution, alone in her room, or eating tasteless turkey and lukewarm sprouts in the canteen, or receiving a cheap present in gaudy wrapping from the home's caretaker dressed as Santa Claus. Toni did not even need to think about it. "All right, I'll go and fetch her now."

"I'm just sorry you couldn't do it more graciously," said her sister.

"Oh, fuck off, Bella," said Toni, and she hung up the phone.

Feeling depressed, she called the spa and canceled her reservation. Then she asked to speak to one of her party. After a delay, it was Charlie who came to the phone. He had a Lancashire accent. "Where are you?" he said. "We're all in the Jacuzzi—you're missing the fun!"

"I can't come," she said miserably, and she explained.

Charlie was outraged. "It's not fair on you," he said. "You need a break."

"I know, but I can't bear to think of her on her own in that place when others are with their families."

"Plus you've had a few problems at work today."

"Yes. It's very sad, but I think Oxenford Medical has come through it all right—provided nothing else happens."

"I saw you on the telly."

"How did I look?"

"Gorgeous—but I fancied your boss."

"Me, too, but he's got three grown-up children he doesn't want to upset, so I think he's a lost cause."

"By heck, you have had a bad day."

"I'm sorry to let you all down."

"It won't be the same without you."

"I'll have to hang up, Charlie—I'd better fetch Mother as soon as possible. Happy Christmas." She cradled the handset and sat staring at the phone. "What a miserable life," she said aloud. "What a miserable bloody life."

6 P.M.

CRAIG'S relationship with Sophie was advancing very slowly.

He had spent all afternoon with her. He had beaten her at table tennis and lost at pool. They had agreed about music—they both liked guitar bands better than drum-and-bass. They both read horror fiction, though she loved Stephen King and he preferred Anne Rice. He told her about his parents' marriage, which was stormy but passionate, and she told him about Ned and Jennifer's divorce, which was rancorous.

But she gave him no encouragement. She did not casually touch his arm, or look intently at his face when he talked to her, or bring into the conversation romantic topics such as dating and necking. Instead, she talked of a world that excluded him, a world of nightclubs—how did she get in, at fourteen?—and friends who took drugs and boys who had motorcycles.

As dinner approached, he began to feel desperate.

He did not want to spend five days pursuing her for the sake of one kiss at the end. His idea was to win her over on the first day and spend the holiday *really* getting to know her. Clearly this was not her timetable. He needed a shortcut to her heart.

She seemed to consider him beneath her romantic notice. All this talk of older people implied that he was just a kid, even though he was older than Sophie by a year and seven months. He had to find some way to prove he was as mature and sophisticated as she.

Sophie would not be the first girl he had kissed. He had dated Caroline Stratton from tenth grade at his school for six weeks, but although she was pretty he had been bored. Lindy Riley, the plump sister of a footballing friend, had been more exciting, and had let him do several things he had never done before, but then she had switched her affections to the keyboard player in a Glasgow rock band. And there were several other girls he had kissed once or twice.

But this felt different. After meeting Sophie at his mother's birthday party, he had thought about her every day for four months. He had downloaded one of the photographs his father had taken at the party, showing Craig gesturing with his hands and Sophie laughing. He used it as the screen saver on his computer. He still looked at other girls, but always comparing them with Sophie, thinking that by comparison this one was too pale, that one too fat, another simply plain-looking, and all of them tediously conventional. He did not mind that she was difficult—he was used to difficult women: his mother was one. There was just something about Sophie that stabbed him in the heart.

At six o'clock, slumped on the couch in the barn, he

decided he had watched as much MTV as he needed for one day. "Want to go over to the house?" he asked her.

"What for?"

"They'll all be sitting around the kitchen table."

"So?"

Well, Craig thought, it's sort of nice. The kitchen is warm, and you can smell dinner cooking, and my dad tells funny stories, and Aunt Miranda pours wine, and it just feels good. But he knew that would not impress Sophie, so he said, "There might be drinks."

She stood up. "Good. I want a cocktail."

Dream on, Craig thought. Grandpa was not going to serve hard liquor to a fourteen-year-old. If they were having champagne, she might get half a glass. But Craig did not disillusion her. They put on coats and went out.

It was now full dark, but the yard was brightly lit by lamps mounted on the walls of the surrounding buildings. Snow swirled thickly in the air, and the ground was slippery underfoot. They crossed to the main house and approached the back door. Just before they went in, Craig glanced around the corner of the house and saw Grandpa's Ferrari, still parked at the front, the snow now two inches thick on the sweeping arc of its rear spoiler. Luke must have been too busy to put it away.

Craig said, "Last time I was here, Grandpa let me drive his car into the garage."

"You can't drive," Sophie said skeptically.

"I haven't got a license, but that doesn't mean I can't handle a car." He was exaggerating. He had driven his father's Mercedes station wagon a couple of times, once on a beach and once on a disused airstrip, but never on a regular road.

"All right, then, park it now," Sophie said.

Craig knew he should ask permission. But if he said so, it would sound as if he were trying to back out. Anyway, Grandpa might say no; then Craig would have lost the chance to prove his point to Sophie. So he said, "All right, then."

The car was unlocked, and the key was in the ignition.

Sophie leaned against the wall of the house by the back door, arms folded, her stance saying, *Okay, show me.* Craig was not going to let her get away with that. "Why don't you come with me?" he said. "Or are you scared?"

They both got into the car.

It was not easy. The seats were low slung, almost on a level with the doorsills, and Craig had to put one leg in, then slide his backside across the flat armrest. He slammed the door.

The gearshift was severely utilitarian, just an upright aluminum rod with a knob on the end. Craig checked that it was in neutral, then turned the ignition key. The car started with a roar like a 747.

Craig half hoped the noise would bring Luke running out of the house, arms raised in protest. However, the Ferrari was at the front door, and the family were in the kitchen, at the back of the house, overlooking the yard. The thunder of the car did not penetrate the thick stone walls of the old farmhouse.

The whole car seemed to tremble, as if in an earthquake, as the big engine turned over with lazy potency. Craig's body felt the vibrations through the black leather seat. "This is cool!" Sophie said excitedly.

Craig switched on the headlights. Two cones of light reached out from the front of the car, stretching across the garden, filled with snowflakes. He rested his hand on the knob of the gearshift, touched the clutch pedal with his foot, then looked behind. The driveway went back in a straight line to the garage before turning to curve around the cliff top.

"Come on, then," said Sophie. "Drive it."

Craig put on a casual air to conceal his reluctance. "Relax," he said. He released the hand brake. "Enjoy the ride." He depressed the clutch, then moved the stick through the open-gate Ferrari gearshift into reverse. He touched the accelerator pedal as gently as he could. The engine snarled menacingly. He released the clutch a millimeter at a time. The car began to creep backward.

He held the steering wheel lightly, not moving it to either side, and the car went in a straight line. With the clutch fully out, he touched the throttle again. The car shot backward, passing the garage. Sophie let out a scream of fear. Craig transferred his foot from the accelerator to the brake. The car skidded on the snow but, to Craig's relief, it did not waver from its straight line. As it came to a halt he remembered, at the last minute, to engage the clutch and prevent a stall.

He felt pleased with himself. He had kept control, just. Better yet, Sophie had been scared, while he appeared calm. Maybe she would stop acting so superior.

The garage stood at a right angle to the house, and now its doors were ahead and to the left of the Ferrari. Kit's car, a black Peugeot coupe, was parked in front of the garage block at its far end. Craig found a remote control under the Ferrari's dashboard and clicked. The farthermost of three garage doors swung up and over.

The concrete apron in front of the garage was covered with a smooth layer of snow. There were a clump of bushes at the near corner of the building and a large tree on the far side of the apron. Craig simply had to avoid those and slot the car into its bay.

More confident now, he moved the gearshift into the notch for first gear, touched the accelerator, then released the clutch. The car moved forward. He turned the steering wheel, which was heavy at low speed, not being power-assisted. The car obediently turned left. He depressed the throttle another millimeter, and it picked up speed, just enough to feel exciting. He swung right, aiming for the open door, but he was going too fast. He touched the brake.

That was his mistake.

The car was moving quickly on snow with its front wheels turning right. As soon as the brakes bit, the rear wheels lost traction. Instead of continuing to turn right into the open garage door, the car slid sideways across the snow. Craig knew what was happening, but had no idea what to do about it. He spun the steering wheel farther to the right, but that made the skid worse, and the car drifted inexorably over the slippery surface, like a boat blown by a gale. Craig stamped on the brake and the clutch at the same time, but it made no difference.

The garage building slid away to the right of the windshield. Craig thought he would crash into Kit's Peugeot, but to his blissful relief the Ferrari missed the other car by several inches. Losing momentum, it slowed down. For a moment he thought he had got away with it. But, just before the car came to a complete stop, its front nearside wing touched the big tree.

"That was great!" Sophie said.

"No, it bloody was not." Craig put the stick in neutral and released the clutch, then sprang out of the car. He walked around to the front. The impact had felt gentle but, to his dismay, he saw by the light of the lamps on the garage wall a large, unmistakable dimple in the gleaming blue wing. "Shit," he said miserably.

Sophie got out and looked. "It's not a very big dent," she said.

"Don't talk bollocks." The size did not matter. The bodywork was damaged and Craig was responsible. He felt a sensation of nausea deep in his stomach. What a Christmas present for Grandpa.

"They might not notice it," Sophie said.

"Of course they'll bloody notice it," he said angrily. "Grandpa will see it as soon as he looks at the car."

"Well, that might not be for a while. He's not likely to go out in this weather."

"What difference does that make?" Craig said impatiently. He knew he was sounding petulant, but he hardly cared. "I'll have to own up."

"Better if you're not here when the shit hits the fan."

"I don't see—" He paused. He did see. If he confessed now, Christmas would be blighted. Mamma Marta would have said, *There will be a bordello,* by which she meant uproar. If he said nothing, but confessed later, perhaps there would be less fuss. Anyway, the prospect of postponing discovery for a few days was tempting.

"I'll have to put it in the garage," he said, thinking aloud.

"Park it with the dented side right up against the wall," Sophie suggested. "That way, it won't be noticed by anyone just walking past."

Sophie's idea was beginning to make sense, Craig thought. There were two other cars in the garage: a massive Toyota Land Cruiser Amazon off-road car with four-wheel drive, which Grandpa used in weather like this; and Luke's old Ford Mondeo, in which he drove himself and Lori between this house and their cottage a mile away. Luke would certainly enter the garage this evening to get his car and drive home. If the weather got worse, he might borrow the big Land Cruiser and leave his Ford here. Either way, he had to enter the garage. But if the Ferrari were hard up against the wall, the dent would not be visible.

The engine was still running. Craig sat in the driver's seat. He engaged first gear and drove slowly forward. Sophie ran into the garage and stood in the car's headlights. As it entered the garage, she used her hands to show Craig how close he was to the wall.

On his first attempt he was no closer than eighteen inches from the wall. That was not good enough. He had to try again. He looked nervously in the rearview mirror, but no one else was around. He was grateful for the cold weather that kept everyone indoors in the warm.

On his third attempt he managed to position the car four or five inches off the wall. He got out and looked. It was impossible to see the dent from any angle.

He closed the door; then he and Sophie headed for the kitchen. Craig felt jangled and guilty, but Sophie was in high spirits. "That was awesome," she said.

Craig realized he had impressed her at last.

7 P.M.

KIT set up his computer in the box room, a small space that could be reached only by going through his bedroom. He plugged in his laptop, a fingerprint scanner, and a smart-card reader-writer he had bought second-hand for £270 on eBay.

This room had always been his lair. When he was small, they had had only the three bedrooms: Mamma and Daddy in the main room, Olga and Miranda in the second room, and Kit in a cot in this box room off the girls' room. After the extension was built, and Olga went off to university, Kit had the bedroom as well as the box room, but this had remained his den.

It was still furnished as a schoolboy's study, with a cheap desk, a bookshelf, a small TV set, and a seat known as the sleepchair, which unfolded into a small single bed and had often been used by school friends coming to stay. Sitting at the desk, he thought wistfully of the tedious hours of homework he had done here, geography and biology, medieval kings and irregular verbs, *Hail, Caesar!* He had learned so much, and forgotten it all.

He took the pass he had stolen from his father and slid it into the reader-writer. Its top stuck out of the slot, clearly showing the printed words "Oxenford Medical." He hoped no one would come into the room. They were all in the kitchen. Lori was making *osso bucco* according to Mamma Marta's famous recipe—Kit could smell the oregano. Daddy had opened a bottle of champagne. By now they would be telling stories that began "Do you remember when . . . ?"

The chip in the card contained details of his father's fingerprint. It was not a simple image, for that was too easy to fake—a photograph of the finger could fool a normal scanner. Rather, Kit had built a device that measured twenty-five points of the fingerprint, using minute electrical differences between ridges and valleys. He had also written a program that stored these details in code. At his apartment he had several prototypes of the fingerprint scanner and he had, naturally, kept a copy of the software he had created.

Now he set his laptop to read the smart card. The only danger was that someone at Oxenford Medical—Toni Gallo, perhaps—might have modified the software so that Kit's program would no longer work; for example, by requiring an access code before the card could be read. It was unlikely that anyone would have gone to such trouble and expense to guard against a possibility that must have seemed fanciful—but it was conceivable. And he had not told Nigel about this potential snag.

He waited a few anxious seconds, watching the screen.

At last it shimmered and displayed a page of code: Stanley's fingerprint details. Kit sighed with relief and saved the file.

His niece Caroline walked in, carrying a rat.

She was dressed younger than her age, in a flower-patterned dress and white stockings. The rat had white fur and pink eyes. Caroline sat on the sleepchair, stroking her pet.

Kit suppressed a curse. He could hardly tell her that he was doing something secret and would prefer to be alone. But he could not continue while she sat there.

She had always been a nuisance. From an early age she had hero-worshipped her young uncle Kit. As a boy he had quickly wearied of this and become fed up with the way she followed him around. But she was hard to shake off.

He tried to be nice. "How's the rat?" he said.

"His name is Leonard," she replied in a tone of mild reproof.

"Leonard. Where did you get him?"

"Paradise Pets in Sauchiehall Street." She let the rat go, and it ran up her arm and perched on her shoulder.

Kit thought the girl was insane, carrying a rat around as if it were a baby. Caroline looked like her mother, Olga, with long dark hair and heavy black eyebrows, but where Olga was dryly severe, Caroline was as wet as a rainy February. She was only seventeen; she might grow out of it.

He hoped she was too wrapped up in herself and her pet to notice the card sticking up out of the reader and the words "Oxenford Medical" printed along its top. Even she would realize he was not supposed to have a pass for the Kremlin nine months after he was fired.

"What are you doing?" she asked him.

"Work. I need to finish this today." He longed to snatch the telltale card out of the reader, but he feared that would only call her attention to it.

"I won't bother you, just carry on."

"Nothing happening downstairs?"

"Mummy and Aunt Miranda are stuffing the stockings in the drawing room, so I've been chucked out."

"Ah." He turned back to the computer and switched the software into "Read" mode. His next step should be to scan his own fingerprint, but he could not let her see that. She might not grasp the significance herself, but she could easily mention it to someone who would. He pretended to study the screen, racking his brains for a way to get rid of her. After a minute he was inspired. He faked a sneeze.

"Bless you," she said.

"Thanks." He sneezed again. "You know, I think poor dear Leonard is doing this to me."

"How could he?" she said indignantly.

"I'm slightly allergic, and this room is so small."

She stood up. "We don't want to make people sneeze, do we, Lennie?" She went out.

Kit closed the door gratefully behind her, then sat down and pressed the forefinger of his right hand to the glass of the scanner. The program scrutinized his fingerprint and encoded the details. Kit saved the file.

Finally, he uploaded his own fingerprint details to the smart card, overwriting his father's. No one else could have done this, unless they had copies of Kit's own software, plus a stolen smart card with the correct site code. If he were devising the system anew he still would not bother to make the cards nonrewritable. Nevertheless, Toni Gallo might have. He looked anxiously at the screen, half-expecting an error message saying "YOU DO NOT HAVE ACCESS."

No such message appeared. Toni had not outsmarted him this time. He reread the data from the chip, to make sure the procedure had been successful. It had: the card now carried Kit's fingerprint details, not Stanley's. "Yes!" he said aloud, mutedly triumphant.

He removed the card from the machine and put it in his pocket. It would now give him access to BSL4. When he waved the card at the reader, and pressed his finger to the touch screen, the computer would read the data on the card and compare it with the fingerprint, find they matched, and unlock the door.

After he returned from the lab, he would reverse the process, erasing his own fingerprint data from the chip and reinstating Stanley's, before he replaced the card in his father's wallet sometime tomorrow. The computer at the Kremlin would record that Stanley Oxenford had entered BSL4 in the early hours of 25 December. Stanley would protest that he had been at home in bed, and Toni Gallo would tell the police that no one else could have used Stanley's card because of the fingerprint check. "Sweet," he said aloud. It pleased him to think how baffled they would all be.

Some biometric security systems matched the fingerprint with data stored on a central computer. If the Kremlin had used that configuration, Kit would have needed access to the database. But employees had an irrational aversion to the thought of their personal details being stored on company computers. Scientists in particular often read the *Guardian* and became finicky about their civil rights. Kit had chosen to store the fingerprint record on the smart card, rather than the central database, to make the new security setup more acceptable to the staff. He had not anticipated that one day he would be trying to defeat his own scheme.

He felt satisfied. Stage One was complete. He had a working pass for BSL4. But, before he could use it, he had to get inside the Kremlin.

He took his phone from his pocket. The number he dialed was the mobile of Hamish McKinnon, one of the security guards on duty at the Kremlin tonight. Hamish was the company dope dealer, supplying marijuana to the younger scientists and Ecstasy to the secretaries for their weekends. He did not deal in heroin or crack, knowing that a serious addict was sure to betray him sooner or later. Kit had asked Hamish to be his inside man tonight, confident that Hamish would not dare to spill the beans, having his own secrets to conceal.

"It's me," Kit said when Hamish answered. "Can you talk?"

"And a happy Christmas to you too, Ian, you old bugger," Hamish said cheerily. "Just a tick, I'm going to step outside . . . That's better."

"Everything all right?"

Hamish's voice became serious. "Aye, but she's doubled the guard, so I've got Willie Crawford with me."

"Where are you stationed?"

"In the gatehouse."

"Perfect. Is everything quiet?"

"Like a graveyard."

"How many guards in total?"

"Six. Two here, two at reception, and two in the control room."

"Okay. We can cope with that. Let me know if anything unusual happens."

"Okay."

Kit ended the call and dialed a number that gave him access to the telephone system computer at the Kremlin. The number was used by Hibernian Telecom, the company that had installed the phones, for remote diagnosis of faults. Kit had worked closely with Hibernian, because the alarms he had installed used phone lines. He knew the number and the access code. Once again, he had a moment of tension, worrying that the number or the code might have been changed in the nine months since he had left. But they had not.

His mobile phone was linked to his laptop by a wireless connection that worked over distances of fifty feet or so—even through walls, which might be useful later. Now he used the laptop to access the central processing unit of the Kremlin's phone system. The system had tamper detectors—but they did not register an alarm if the company's own phone line and code were used.

First he closed down every phone on the site except the one on the desk in reception.

Next, he diverted all calls into and out of the Kremlin to his mobile. He had already programmed his laptop to recognize the numbers likeliest to come up, such as Toni Gallo's. He would be able to answer the calls himself, or play recorded messages to the callers, or even redirect calls and eavesdrop on the conversations.

Finally, he caused every phone in the building to ring for five seconds. That was just to get the attention of the security guards.

Then he disconnected and sat on the edge of his chair, waiting.

He was fairly sure what would happen next. The guards had a list of people to call in the event of different emergencies. Their first action now should be to call the phone company.

He did not have to wait long. His mobile rang. He left it, watching his laptop. After a moment, a message appeared on the screen saying: "Kremlin calls Toni."

That was not what he had expected. They should have called Hibernian first. Nevertheless, he was prepared. Quickly, he activated a recorded message. The security guard who was trying to reach Toni Gallo heard a female voice saying that the mobile he was calling might be switched off or out of range, and advising him to try later. The guard hung up.

Kit's phone rang again almost immediately. Kit hoped the guards would now be calling the phone company, but once again he was disappointed. The screen said "Kremlin calls RPHQ." The guards were ringing regional police headquarters at Inverburn. Kit was happy for the police to be informed. He redirected the call to the correct number and listened in.

"This is Steven Tremlett, security guard supervisor at Oxenford Medical, calling to report an unusual incident."

"What's the incident, Mr. Tremlett?"

"No big emergency, but we have a problem with our phone lines, and I'm not sure the alarms will work."

"I'll log it. Can you get your phones fixed?"

"I'll call out a repair crew, but God knows when they'll get here, being Christmas Eve."

"Do you want a patrol to call?"

"It wouldn't do any harm, if they've not much on."

Kit hoped the police would pay a visit to the Kremlin. It would add conviction to his cover.

The policeman said, "They'll be busy later, when the pubs chuck out, but it's quiet the noo."

"Right. Tell them I'll give them a cup of tea."

They hung up. Kit's mobile rang a third time and the

screen said: "Kremlin calls Hibernian." At last, he thought with relief. This was the one he had been waiting for. He touched a button and said into his phone, "Hibernian Telecom, can I help you?"

Steve's voice said, "This is Oxenford Medical. We have a problem with our phone system."

Kit exaggerated his Scots accent to disguise his voice. "Would that be Greenmantle Road, Inverburn?"

"Aye."

"What's the problem?"

"All the phones are out except this one. The place is empty, of course, but the thing is, the alarm system uses the phone lines, and we need to be sure that's working properly."

At that point, Kit's father walked into the room.

Kit froze, paralyzed with fear and terror, as if he were a child again. Stanley looked at the computer and the mobile phone and raised his eyebrows. Kit pulled himself together. He was no longer a kid frightened of a reprimand. Trying to make himself calm, he said into the phone, "Let me call you back in two minutes." He touched the keyboard of his laptop, and the screen went dark.

"Working?" his father said.

"Something I have to finish."

"At Christmas?"

"I said I would deliver this piece of software by December the twenty-fourth."

"By now your customer will have gone home, like all sensible folk."

"But his computer will show that I e-mailed the program to him before midnight on Christmas Eve, so he won't be able to say I was late."

Stanley smiled and nodded. "Well, I'm glad you're

being conscientious." He stood silent for several seconds, obviously having something else to say. A typical scientist, he thought nothing of long pauses in conversation. The important thing was precision.

Kit waited, trying to hide his frantic impatience. Then his mobile rang.

"Shit," he said. "Sorry," he said to his father. He checked his screen. This was not a diverted Kremlin call, but one directly to his mobile from Hamish McKinnon, the security guard. He could not ignore it. He pressed the phone hard to his ear, so that the voice of the caller would not leak out to be heard by his father. "Yes?"

Hamish said excitedly, "All the phones here have gone kaput!"

"Okay, that's expected. It's part of the program."

"You said to tell you if anything unusual—"

"Yes, and you were right to ring me, but I have to hang up now. Thank you." He ended the call.

His father spoke. "Is our quarrel really behind us now?"

Kit resented this kind of talk. It suggested that the two disputants must be equally guilty. But he was desperate to get back on the phone, so he said, "I think so, yes."

"I know you think you've been unjustly treated," his father said, reading his mind. "I don't see your logic, but I accept that you believe it. And I, too, feel that I was unfairly done by. But we have to try to forget that, and be friends again."

"So says Miranda."

"And I'm just not sure you have put it behind you. I sense you holding something back."

Kit tried to keep his face wooden so that his guilt

would not show. "I'm doing my best," he said. "It's not easy."

Stanley seemed satisfied. "Well, I can't ask any more of you than that," he said. He put his hand on Kit's shoulder, bent down, and kissed the top of his head. "I came to tell you supper's almost ready."

"I'm nearly done. I'll come down in five minutes."

"Good." Stanley went out.

Kit slumped in his chair. He was shaking with a mixture of shame and relief. His father was shrewd, and suffered no illusions—yet Kit had survived the interrogation. But it had been ghastly while it lasted.

When his hands were steady enough, he dialed the Kremlin again.

The phone was picked up immediately. Steve Tremlett's voice said, "Oxenford Medical."

"Hibernian Telecom here." Kit remembered to change his voice. He had not known Tremlett well, and nine months had passed since he had left Oxenford Medical, so it was unlikely Steve would remember his voice; but he was not going to take the chance. "I can't access your central processing unit."

"I'm not surprised. That line must be down also. You'll have to send someone."

This was what Kit wanted, but he was careful not to sound eager. "It's going to be difficult to get a repair crew out to you at Christmas."

"Don't give me that." Steve's voice betrayed a touch of anger. "You guarantee to attend to any fault within four hours, every day of the year. That's the service we pay you for. It's now seven-fifty-five p.m., and I'm logging this call."

"All right, keep your shirt on. I'll get a crew to you as soon as possible."

"Give me a time estimate, please."

"I'll do my best to get them to you by midnight."

"Thank you, we'll be waiting." Steve hung up.

Kit put down his mobile. He was perspiring. He wiped his face with his sleeve. So far, it had all gone perfectly.

8:30 P.M.

STANLEY dropped his bombshell during dinner.

Miranda felt mellow. The *osso bucco* was hearty and satisfying, and her father had opened two bottles of Brunello di Montepulciano to go with it. Kit was restless, dashing upstairs every time his mobile rang, but everyone else was relaxed. The four kids ate quickly, then retired to the barn to watch a DVD movie called *Scream 2*, leaving six adults around the table in the dining room: Miranda and Ned, Olga and Hugo, Daddy at the head and Kit at the foot. Lori served coffee while Luke loaded the dishwasher in the kitchen.

Then Stanley said, "How would you all feel if I started dating again?"

Everyone went quiet. Even Lori reacted: she stopped pouring coffee and stood still, staring at him in shock.

Miranda had guessed, but all the same it was disquieting to hear him come right out and say it. She said, "I suppose we're talking about Toni Gallo."

He looked startled and said, "No."

Olga said, "Oh, poo."

Miranda did not believe him, either, but she refrained from contradicting him.

"Anyway, I'm not talking about anyone in particular, I'm discussing a general principle," he went on. "Mamma Marta has been dead for a year and a half, may she rest in peace. For almost four decades she was the only woman in my life. But I'm sixty, and I probably have another twenty or thirty years to live. I may not want to spend them alone."

Lori shot him a hurt look. He was not alone, she wanted to say; he had her and Luke.

Olga said bad-temperedly, "So why consult us? You don't need our permission to sleep with your secretary or anyone else."

"I'm not asking permission. I want to know how you would feel *if* it happened. And it won't be my secretary, by the way. Dorothy is very happily married."

Miranda spoke, mainly to prevent Olga saying something harsh. "I think we'd find it hard, Daddy, to see you with another woman in this house. But we want you to be happy, and I believe we'd do our best to welcome someone you loved."

He gave her a wry look. "Not exactly a ringing endorsement, but thank you for trying to be positive."

Olga said, "You won't get that much from me. For God's sake, what are we supposed to say to you? Are you thinking of marrying this woman? Would you have more children?"

"I'm not thinking of marrying anyone," he said tetchily. Olga was irritating him by refusing to argue on his terms. Mamma had always been able to get under his skin in exactly the same way. He added, "But I'm not ruling anything out."

"It's outrageous," Olga stormed. "When I was a child I hardly saw you. You were always at the lab. Mamma and I were at home with baby Mandy from seven-thirty in the morning until nine at night. We were a one-parent family, and it was all for your career, so that you could invent narrow-spectrum antibiotics and an ulcer drug and an anticholesterol pill, and become famous and rich. Well, I want a reward for my sacrifice."

"You had a very expensive education," Stanley said.

"It's not enough. I want my children to inherit the money you made, and I don't want them to share it with a litter of brats bred by some tart who knows nothing except how to take advantage of a widower."

Miranda let out a cry of protest.

Hugo, embarrassed, said, "Don't beat about the bush, Olga dear. Say what's on your mind."

Stanley's expression darkened, and he said, "I wasn't planning to date *some tart.*"

Olga saw that she had gone too far. She said, "I didn't mean that last part." For her, that amounted to an apology.

Kit said flippantly, "It won't be much different. Mamma was tall, athletic, nonintellectual, and Italian. Toni Gallo is tall, athletic, nonintellectual, and Spanish. I wonder if she cooks."

"Don't be stupid," Olga told him. "The difference is that for the last forty years Toni hasn't been part of this family, so she's not one of us. She's an outsider."

Kit bridled. "Don't call me stupid, Olga. At least I can see what's under my nose."

Miranda's heart missed a beat. What was he talking about?

The same question occurred to Olga. "What's under my nose that I can't see?"

Miranda glanced surreptitiously at Ned. She feared that later he might ask her what Kit meant. He often picked up on such things.

Kit backed off. "Oh, stop cross-examining me. You're a pain in the arse."

"Aren't you concerned about your financial future?" Olga said to Kit. "Your inheritance is threatened as much as mine. Have you got so much money that you don't care?"

Kit laughed humorlessly. "Yeah, right."

Miranda said to Olga, "Aren't you being a bit mercenary?"

"Well, Daddy did ask."

Stanley said, "I thought you might feel badly about your mother's being replaced by someone new. It never occurred to me that your main concern would be my will."

Miranda felt hurt for her father. But she was more worried about Kit and what he might say. As a child, he had never been good at keeping secrets. She and Olga had been obliged to keep everything from him. If they trusted him with a confidence, he would blurt it out to Mamma in five minutes. Now he knew Miranda's darkest secret. He was no longer a child, but on the other hand he had never really grown up. This was dangerous. Her heart beat like a tom-tom. Perhaps if she took part in the conversation she had a chance of controlling it. She addressed Olga. "The important thing is to keep the family together. Whatever Daddy decides, we mustn't let it break us up."

"Don't lecture me about the family," Olga said angrily. "Talk to your brother."

Kit said, "Get off my case!"

Stanley said, "I don't want to rake all that up again."

Olga persisted. "But he's the one who has come closest to destroying the family."

"Fuck you, Olga," Kit said.

"Easy," Stanley said firmly. "We can have a passionate discussion without descending to insults and obscenity."

"Come on, Daddy," Olga said. She was furious, because she had been called mercenary, and she needed to counterattack. "What could be more threatening to the family than one of us who steals from another?"

Kit was red with shame and fury. "I'll tell you," he said.

Miranda knew what was coming. Terrified, she stretched out her arm toward Kit with her hand upright in a *Halt* sign. "Kit, calm down, please," she said frantically.

He was not listening. "I'll tell you what could be more threatening to the family."

Miranda shouted at him: "Just shut up!"

Stanley realized there was a subtext of which he was ignorant, and he frowned with puzzlement. "What are you two talking about?"

Kit said, "I'm talking about someone—"

Miranda stood up. "No!"

"—someone who sleeps—"

Miranda snatched up a glass of water and threw it in Kit's face.

There was a sudden hush.

Kit wiped his face with his napkin. With everyone watching him in shocked silence, he said, ". . . sleeps with her sister's husband."

Olga was bewildered. "This makes no sense. I never slept with Jasper—or Ned."

Miranda held her head in her hands.

"I didn't mean you," Kit said.

Olga looked at Miranda. Miranda looked away.

Lori, still standing there with the coffeepot, gave a gasp of sudden, shocked comprehension.

Stanley said, "Good God! I never imagined that."

Miranda looked at Ned. He was horrified. He said, "Did you?"

She did not reply.

Olga turned to Hugo. "You and my sister?"

He tried his bad-boy grin. Olga swung her arm and slapped his face. The blow had a solid sound, more like a punch. "Ow!" he cried, and rocked back in his chair.

Olga said, "You lousy, lying . . ." She searched for words. "You worm. You pig. You bloody bastard, you rotten sod." She turned to Miranda. "And you!"

Miranda could not meet her eye. She looked down at the table. A small cup of coffee was in front of her. The cup was fine white china with a blue stripe, Mamma's favorite set.

"How could you?" Olga said to her. "How could you?"

Miranda would try to explain, one day; but anything she said now would sound like an excuse. So she just shook her head.

Olga stood up and walked out of the room.

Hugo looked sheepish. "I'd better . . ." He followed her.

Stanley suddenly realized that Lori was standing there listening to every word. Belatedly, he said, "Lori, you'd better help Luke in the kitchen."

She started as if awakened. "Yes, Professor Oxenford."

Stanley looked at Kit. "That was brutal." Anger made his voice shake.

"Oh, that's right, blame me," Kit said petulantly. "I didn't sleep with Hugo, did I?" He threw down his napkin and left.

Ned was mortified. "Um, excuse me," he said, and he went out.

Only Miranda and her father were left in the room. Stanley got up and came to her side. He put his hand on her shoulder. "They'll all calm down about it, eventually," he said. "This is bad, but it will pass."

She turned to him and pressed her face into the soft tweed of his waistcoat. "Oh, Daddy, I'm sorry," she said, and she began to cry.

9:30 P.M.

THE weather was getting worse. Toni's drive to the old folks' home had been protracted, but the return journey was even slower. There was a thin layer of snow on the road, beaten hard by car tires, frozen too solid to turn into slush. Nervous drivers went at a crawl, delaying everyone else. Toni's red Porsche Boxster was the perfect car for overtaking sluggards, but it was not at its best in slippery conditions, and there was little she could do to shorten her journey.

Mother sat contentedly beside her, wearing a green wool coat and a felt hat. She was not in the least angry with Bella. Toni was disappointed by this, and was ashamed of feeling so. Deep inside, she wanted Mother to be furious with Bella, as Toni herself had been. It would have vindicated her. But Mother seemed to think it was Toni's fault she had been kept waiting so long. Toni had said irritably, "You do realize that Bella was supposed to pick you up hours ago."

"Yes, dear, but your sister's got a family to take care of."

"And I've got a responsible job."

"I know. It's your substitute for children."

"So it's okay for Bella to let you down, but not for me."

"That's right, dear."

Toni tried to follow Mother's example and be magnanimous. But she kept thinking of her friends at the spa, sitting in the Jacuzzi, or acting charades, or drinking coffee by a big log fire. Charles and Damien would become more hilariously camp as the evening progressed and they relaxed. Michael would tell stories about his Irish mother, a legendary spitfire in her hometown of Liverpool. Bonnie would reminisce about college days, the scrapes she and Toni had got into as the only two females in an engineering department of three hundred students. They would all be having so much fun, while Toni drove through the snow with her mother.

She told herself to stop being pathetic. I'm a grown-up, she thought, and grown-ups have responsibilities. Besides, Mother might not be alive for many more years, so I should enjoy having her with me while I can.

She found it harder to look on the bright side when she thought about Stanley. She had felt so close to him this morning, and now the gulf between them was bigger than the Grand Canyon. She asked herself constantly whether she had pushed him too hard. Had she made him choose between his family and her? Perhaps if she had backed off he would not have felt forced into a decision. But she had not exactly thrown herself at him, and a woman had to give a man a little encouragement, otherwise he might never speak at all.

There was no point in regrets, she told herself. She had lost him, and that was that.

Up ahead she saw the lights of a petrol station. "Do you need the toilet, Mother?" she said.

"Yes, please."

Toni slowed down and pulled onto the forecourt. She topped up her tank, then took her mother inside. Mother went to the ladies' room while Toni paid. As Toni returned to the car, her mobile phone rang. Thinking it might be the Kremlin calling, she snatched the phone up hurriedly. "Toni Gallo."

"This is Stanley Oxenford."

"Oh." She was taken aback. She had not been expecting this.

"Perhaps I'm phoning at an inconvenient time," he said politely.

"No, no, no," she said quickly, sliding behind the wheel. "I imagined the call was from the Kremlin, and I was worried that something might have gone wrong there." She closed the car door.

"Everything's fine, as far as I know. How's your spa?"

"I'm not there." She told him what had happened.

"How terribly disappointing," he said.

Her heart was beating faster, for no very good reason. "What about you—is everything all right?" She was wondering why he had phoned. At the same time, she watched the brightly lit pay booth. It would be a while before her mother emerged.

"Family dinner ended in an upset. It's not exactly unknown—we do have rows sometimes."

"What was it about?"

"I probably shouldn't tell you."

Then why have you phoned me? she thought. It was extraordinary for Stanley to make a pointless call. He was usually so focused that she sensed he had in front of him a list of topics he needed to cover.

"In brief, Kit revealed that Miranda had slept with Hugo—her sister's husband."

"Good God!" Toni pictured each of them: handsome, malicious Kit; plump, pretty Miranda; Hugo, a pint-size charmer; and the formidable Olga. It was a ripe tale, but what was more surprising was that Stanley should repeat it to her, Toni. Once again, he was treating her as if they were intimate friends. But she mistrusted that impression. If she allowed her hopes to rise, he would crush her again. All the same, she did not want to end the conversation. "How do you feel about it?" she said.

"Well, Hugo has always been a bit flaky. Olga knows him by now, after almost twenty years of marriage. She's humiliated, and mad as hell—in fact I can hear her yelling at this very moment—but I think she'll forgive him. Miranda explained the circumstances to me. She didn't have an affair with Hugo, just slept with him once, when she was depressed after the breakup of her marriage; and she's been feeling ashamed of herself ever since. I think eventually Olga will forgive her, too. It's Kit who bothers me." His voice became sad. "I always wanted my son to be courageous and principled, and grow into an upright man who could be respected by everyone; but he's sly and weak."

Toni realized, in a flash of revelation, that Stanley was talking to her as he would have talked to Marta. After a row such as this, the two of them would have gone to bed and discussed the role of each of their children. He was missing his wife and making Toni a substitute. But this thought no longer enthralled her. Quite the reverse: she was resentful. He had no right to use her in this way. She felt exploited. And she really ought to make sure her mother was all right in the petrol station toilet.

She was about to tell him so when he said, "But I shouldn't burden you with all this. I called to say something else."

That was more like Stanley, she thought. And Mother would be okay for a few minutes more.

He went on, "After Christmas, will you have dinner with me one evening?"

What now? she thought. She said, "Of course." What did this mean?

"You know how I disapprove of men who make romantic advances towards their employees. It puts the employee in such a difficult position—she's bound to feel that if she refuses, she may suffer in her career."

"I have no such fears," she said, a bit stiffly. Was he saying that this invitation was not a romantic advance, so she did not need to worry? She found herself short of breath, and strove to sound normal. "I'd be delighted to have dinner with you."

"I've been thinking about our conversation this morning, on the cliff."

So have I, she thought.

He went on: "I said something to you then that I've been regretting ever since."

"What . . ." She could hardly breathe. "What was that?"

"That I could never start another family."

"You didn't mean it?"

"I said it because I had become . . . frightened. Strange, isn't it? At my time of life, to be scared."

"Scared of what?"

There was a long pause; then he said, "Of my feelings."

Toni almost dropped the phone. She felt a flush spread from her throat to her face. "Feelings," she repeated.

"If this conversation is embarrassing you dreadfully, you just have to say so, and I'll never refer to it again."

"Go on."

"When you told me that Osborne had asked you out, I realized you wouldn't be single forever, probably not much longer. If I'm making a complete fool of myself, please tell me right away, and put me out of my misery."

"No—" Toni swallowed. He was finding this extraordinarily difficult, she realized. It must be forty years since he had spoken this way to a woman. She ought to help him. She should make it clear that she was not offended. "No, you're not making a fool of yourself, not at all."

"I thought this morning that perhaps you might feel warmly toward me, and that's what scared me. Am I right to tell you all this? I wish I could see your face."

"I'm very glad," she said in a low voice. "I'm very happy."

"Really?"

"Yes."

"When can I see you? I want to talk some more."

"I'm with my mother. We're at a petrol station. She's just coming out of the toilet. I can see her now." Toni got out of the car, still holding the phone to her ear. "Let's talk tomorrow morning."

"Don't hang up yet. There's so much to say."

Toni waved at her mother and called: "Over here!" Mother saw her and turned. Toni opened the passenger door and helped her in, saying, "I'm just finishing off this phone call."

Stanley said, "Where are you?"

She closed the door on Mother. "Only about ten miles from Inverburn, but progress is painfully slow."

"I want us to meet tomorrow. We've both got family

obligations, but we're entitled to some time to ourselves."

"We'll work something out." She opened the driver's door. "I must go—Mother's getting cold."

"Goodbye," he said. "Call me anytime you feel like it. Anytime."

"Goodbye." She flipped the phone shut and got into the car.

"That's a big smile," Mother said. "You've cheered up. Who was on the phone—someone nice?"

"Yes," Toni said. "Someone very nice indeed."

10:30 P.M.

KIT waited in his room, impatient for everyone to settle down for the night. He needed to get away as soon as possible, but everything would be ruined if someone heard him leave, so he forced himself to linger.

He sat at the old desk in the box room. His laptop was still plugged in, to conserve the battery: he would need it later tonight. His mobile phone was in his pocket.

He had dealt with three calls to and from the Kremlin. Two had been harmless personal calls to guards, and he had let them through. The third had been a call from the Kremlin to Steepfall. Kit guessed that Steve Tremlett, having failed to reach Toni Gallo, might have wanted to let Stanley know about the problem with the phones. He had played a recorded message saying there was a fault on the line.

While he waited, he listened restlessly to the sounds of the house. He could hear Olga and Hugo having a row in the next bedroom to his, Olga firing questions and assertions like a pistol, Hugo by turns abject, pleading, persuading, bantering, and abject again. Downstairs, Luke and Lori clattered pots and crockery in the kitchen for half an hour; then the front door slammed as they left to go to their house a mile away. The children were in the barn, and Miranda and Ned had presumably gone to the guest cottage. Stanley was the last to bed. He had gone into his study, closed the door, and made a phone call—you could tell when someone was on the phone elsewhere in the house, because a "busy" light appeared on all the extensions. After a while Kit heard him climb the stairs and close his bedroom door. Olga and Hugo both went to the bathroom, and afterward they were quiet; either reconciled or exhausted. The dog, Nellie, would be in the kitchen, lying next to the Aga, the warmest place in the house.

Kit waited a little longer, giving them all a chance to go to sleep.

He felt vindicated by the family squabble earlier. Miranda's peccadillo proved that he was not the only sinner in the family. They blamed him for revealing a secret, but it was better to have these things out in the open. Why should his transgressions be blown up out of all proportion and hers discreetly hidden away? Let them be angry. He had enjoyed seeing Olga smack Hugo. My old sister packs a punch, he thought with amusement.

He wondered if he dared leave yet. He was ready. He had taken off his distinctive signet ring, and had replaced his stylish Armani wristwatch with a nondescript Swatch. He was dressed in jeans and a warm black sweater; he would carry his boots and put them on downstairs.

He stood up—then heard the back door slam. He cursed with frustration. Someone had come in—one or two of the kids, probably, raiding the fridge. He waited to hear the door again, indicating that they had left; but instead footsteps mounted the stairs.

A moment later he heard his bedroom door open. The footsteps crossed the outer room and Miranda came into the box room. She wore Wellington boots and a Barbour over her nightdress, and she was carrying a sheet and a duvet. Without speaking, she went to the sleepchair and unfolded it.

Kit was irate. "For God's sake, what do you want?"

"I'm sleeping here," she replied calmly.

"You can't!" he said, panicking.

"I don't see why not."

"You're supposed to be in the cottage."

"I've had a row with Ned, thanks to your dinnertime revelation, you sneaking little shit."

"I don't want you here!"

"I don't give a damn what you want."

Kit tried to stay calm. He watched with dismay as Miranda made up a bed on the sleepchair. How was he going to steal out of his bedroom, with her in here where she could hear everything? She was upset, she might not go to sleep for hours. And then, in the morning, she was sure to get up before he returned and notice his absence. His alibi was collapsing.

He had to go now. He would pretend to be even angrier than he really was. "Fuck you," he said. He unplugged his laptop and closed the lid. "I'm not staying here with you." He stepped into the bedroom.

"Where are you going?"

Out of her sight, he picked up his boots. "I'm going to watch TV in the drawing room."

"Keep the volume low." She slammed the door between the two rooms.

Kit went out.

He tiptoed across the dark landing and down the stairs. The woodwork creaked, but this house shifted constantly, and no one took any notice of odd noises. A faint light from the porch lamp came through a small window beside the front door and made halos around the hat stand, the newel post at the foot of the stairs, and the stack of directories on the telephone table. Nellie came out of the kitchen and stood by the door, wagging her tail, hoping with irrepressible canine optimism to be taken for a walk.

Kit sat on the stairs and put his boots on, listening for the sound of a door opening above him. This was a dangerous moment, and he felt a shiver of fear as he fumbled with his laces. People were always walking around in the middle of the night: Olga might want a drink of water, Caroline could come over from the barn looking for a headache pill, Stanley might be struck by scientific inspiration and go to his computer.

He tied his bootlaces and put on his black Puffa jacket. He was almost out.

If someone saw him now, he would simply go. No one would stop him. The problem would arise tomorrow. Knowing he had left, they might guess where he had gone, and his whole plan was that no one should understand what had happened.

He shoved Nellie away from the door and opened it. The house was never locked: Stanley believed that intruders were unlikely in this lonely spot, and anyway the dog was the best burglar alarm.

Kit stepped outside. It was bitterly cold, and the snow was falling heavily. He pushed Nellie's nose back inside and closed the door behind himself with a soft click.

The lights around the house were left on all night, but despite them he could hardly see the garage. The snow was several inches thick on the ground. In a minute his socks and the cuffs of his jeans were soaked. He wished he had worn Wellingtons.

His car was on the far side of the garage, a duvet of snow on its roof. He hoped it would start. He got in, putting his laptop on the passenger seat beside him, so that he could deal quickly with calls to and from the Kremlin. He turned the key in the ignition. The car coughed and spluttered but, after a few seconds, the engine turned over.

Kit hoped no one had heard it.

The snow was so heavy it was blinding. He was obliged to switch on his headlights, and pray that no one was looking out of a window.

He pulled away. The car slid alarmingly on the thick snow. He crept forward, careful not to turn the steering wheel suddenly. He coaxed the car onto the drive, maneuvered cautiously around the headland and into the woods, and followed the lane all the way to the main road.

Here the snow was not virgin. There were tire tracks in both directions. He turned north, heading away from the Kremlin, and drove in the tracks. After ten minutes he turned onto a side road that wound over hills. There were no tire tracks here, and he slowed even more, wishing he had four-wheel drive.

At last he saw a sign that read "Inverburn School of Flying." He turned into an entry. Double wire gates stood open. He drove in. His headlights picked out a hangar and a control tower.

The place appeared deserted. For a moment, Kit half-hoped the others would not show up and he could call off the whole thing. The thought of suddenly ending this terrible tension was so appealing that his spirits sank and he began to feel depressed. Pull yourself together, he thought. Tonight will be the end of all your troubles.

The hangar door stood partly open. Kit drove slowly in. There were no planes inside—the airfield operated only in the summer months—but he immediately saw a light-colored Bentley Continental that he recognized as Nigel Buchanan's. Beside it stood a van marked "Hibernian Telecom."

The others were not in sight, but a faint light came from the stairwell. Carrying his laptop, Kit followed the stairs up to the control tower.

Nigel sat at the desk, wearing a pink roll-neck sweater and a sports jacket, looking calm, holding a mobile phone to his ear. Elton leaned against the wall, dressed in a tan trench coat with the collar turned up. He had a big canvas bag at his feet. Daisy slumped on a chair, heavy boots on the windowsill. She wore tight-fitting gloves of light tan suede that looked incongruously ladylike.

Nigel spoke into the phone in his soft London voice. "It's snowing quite heavily here, but the forecast says the worst of the storm will pass us by . . . Yeah, you will be able to fly tomorrow morning, no problem . . . We'll be here well before ten . . . I'll be in the control tower, I'll talk to you as you come in . . . There won't be any trouble, so long as you've got the money, all of it, in fifties, as agreed."

The talk of money gave Kit a shiver of excitement.

Three hundred thousand pounds, in his hands, in twelve hours and a few minutes. True, he would have to give most of it to Daisy immediately, but he would keep fifty thousand. He wondered how much room fifty grand in fifty-pound notes would take up. Could he keep it in his pockets? He should have brought a briefcase . . .

"Thank *you,*" Nigel was saying. "Goodbye." He turned around. "What-ho, Kit. You're bang on time."

Kit said, "Who was on the phone—our buyer?"

"His pilot. He'll be arriving by helicopter."

Kit frowned. "What will his flight plan say?"

"That he's taking off from Aberdeen and landing in London. No one will know that he made an unscheduled stop at the Inverburn Flying School."

"Good."

"I'm glad you approve," Nigel said with a touch of sarcasm. Kit constantly questioned him about his areas of responsibility, worried that Nigel, though experienced, was not as educated or as intelligent as he. Nigel answered his questions with an affectation of amusement, obviously feeling that Kit, as an amateur, ought to trust him.

Elton said, "Let's get dragged up, shall we?" He took from his bag four sets of overalls with "Hibernian Telecom" printed on the back. They all climbed into them.

Kit said to Daisy, "The gloves look odd with the overalls."

"Too bad," she said.

Kit stared at her for a few moments, then dropped his gaze. She was trouble, and he wished she were not coming tonight. He was scared of her, but he also hated her, and he was determined to put her down, both to establish his authority and by way of revenge for what she had done to him that morning. There was going to be a clash before long, and he both feared it and longed for it.

Next, Elton handed out faked identity cards that said "Hibernian Telecom Field Maintenance Team." Kit's card bore a photograph of an older man who looked nothing like him. The man in the picture had black hair that grew halfway over his ears in a style that had never been fashionable in Kit's lifetime, plus a heavy Zapata mustache and glasses.

Elton reached into his bag yet again and handed Kit a black wig, a black mustache, and a pair of heavy-framed glasses with tinted lenses. He also gave him a hand mirror and a small tube of glue. Kit glued the mustache to his upper lip and put on the wig. His own hair was mid-brown and cut fashionably short. Looking in the mirror, he was satisfied that the disguise altered his appearance radically. Elton had done a good job.

Kit trusted Elton. His humor covered a ruthless efficiency. He would do whatever was necessary to finish the job, Kit thought.

Tonight Kit planned to avoid anyone among the guards who had been employed at the Kremlin when he was there. However, if he had to speak to any of them, he felt confident they would not recognize him. He had taken off his distinctive jewelry, and he would change his voice.

Elton also had disguises for Nigel, Daisy, and himself. They were not known to anyone at the Kremlin, so they were in no danger of being recognized immediately; but later the security guards would describe the intruders to the police, and the disguises would ensure that those descriptions bore no relation to their actual faces.

Nigel also had a wig, Kit saw. Nigel's own hair was sandy-colored and short, but his wig was midgray and chin-length, making the casually elegant Londoner look like an aging Beatle. He also had glasses with unfashionably large frames.

Daisy had a long blond wig over her shaved head. Tinted contact lenses turned her eyes from brown to bright blue. She was even more hideous than usual. Kit had often wondered about her sex life. He had once met someone who claimed to have slept with her, but all the man would say about it was "I've still got the bruises." As Kit looked, she removed the steel rings that pierced her eyebrow, her nose, and her lower lip. She looked only a little less weird.

Elton's own disguise was the most subtle. All he had was a set of false teeth that gave him an overbite—but he looked completely different. The handsome dude had gone, and in his place was a nerd.

Finally, he gave them all baseball caps with "Hibernian Telecom" printed on them. "Most of those security cameras are placed high," he explained. "A cap with a long peak will make sure they don't get a good shot of your face."

They were ready. There was a moment of silence while they looked at one another. Then Nigel said, "Showtime."

They left the control tower and went down the stairs to the hangar. Elton got into the driving seat of the van. Daisy jumped in next to him. Nigel took the third seat. There was no more room in the front: Kit would have to sit on the floor in the back with the tools.

As he stared at them, wondering what to do, Daisy edged close to Elton and put a hand on his knee. "Do you fancy blondes?" she said.

He stared ahead expressionlessly. "I'm married."

She moved her hand up his thigh. "I bet you fancy a white girl, for a change, though, don't you?"

"I'm married to a white girl." He took hold of her wrist and moved her hand off his leg.

Kit decided this was the moment to deal with her. With his heart in his mouth, he said, "Daisy, get in the back of the van."

"Fuck off," she replied.

"I'm not asking you. I'm telling you. Get in the back."

"Try and make me."

"Okay, I will."

"Go ahead," she said with a grin. "I'm looking forward to this."

"The operation is off," Kit said. He was breathing hard, out of fear, but he made his voice calm. "Sorry, Nigel. Good night, all." He walked away from the van on shaky legs.

He got into his own car, started the engine, turned on the headlights, and waited.

He could see into the front of the van. They were arguing. Daisy was waving her arms. After a minute, Nigel got out of the van and held the door. Still Daisy argued. Nigel went around to the back and opened the rear doors, then returned to the front.

At last, Daisy got out. She stood staring malevolently at Kit. Nigel spoke to her again. Finally she got in the back of the van and slammed the doors.

Kit returned to the van and got into the front. Elton pulled away, drove out of the garage, and stopped. Nigel closed the big hangar door and got into the van. Elton muttered, "I hope they're right about the weather forecast. Look at this fucking snow." They headed out through the gate.

Kit's mobile rang. He lifted the lid of his laptop. On the screen he read: "Toni calling Kremlin."

11:30 P.M.

TONI'S mother had fallen asleep the moment they pulled out of the petrol station. Toni had stopped the car, reclined the seat, and made a pillow with a scarf. Mother slept like a baby. Toni found it odd, to be looking after her mother the way she would take care of a child. It made her feel old.

But nothing could depress her spirits after her conversation with Stanley. In his characteristic restrained style, he had declared his feelings. She hugged the knowledge to herself as she drove through the snow, mile after slow mile, to Inverburn.

Mother was fast asleep when they reached the outskirts of the town. There were still revelers about. The traffic kept the town roads clear of snow, and Toni was able to drive without feeling that at any moment the car might slide out of control. She took the opportunity to call the Kremlin, just to check in.

The call was answered by Steve Tremlett. "Oxenford Medical."

"This is Toni. How are things?"

"Hi, Toni. We have a slight problem, but we're dealing with it."

Toni felt a chill. "What problem?"

"Most of the phones are out. Only this one works, at reception."

"How did that happen?"

"No idea. The snow, probably."

Toni shook her head, perplexed. "That phone system cost hundreds of thousands of pounds. It shouldn't break down because of bad weather. Can we get it fixed?"

"Yes. I've called out a crew from Hibernian Telecom. They should be here in the next few minutes."

"What about the alarms?"

"I don't know whether they're functional or not."

"Damn. Have you told the police?"

"Yes. A patrol car dropped in earlier. The officers had a bit of a look around, didn't see anything untoward. They've left now, gone to arrest Yuletide drunks in town."

A man staggered into the road in front of Toni's car, and she swerved to avoid him. "I can see why," she said.

There was a pause. "Where are you?"

"Inverburn."

"I thought you were going to a health farm."

"I was, but a family problem cropped up. Let me know what the repairmen find, okay? Call me on the mobile number."

"Sure."

Toni hung up. "Hell," she said to herself. First Mother, now this.

She wound her way through the web of residential streets that climbed the hillside overlooking the harbor. When she reached her building, she parked, but did not get out.

She had to go to the Kremlin.

If she had been at the spa, there would have been no question of her coming back—it was too far away. But she was here in Inverburn. The journey would take a while, in this weather—an hour, at least, instead of the usual ten or fifteen minutes—but it was perfectly possible. The only problem was Mother.

Toni closed her eyes. Was it really necessary for her to go? Even if Michael Ross had been working with Animals Are Free, it seemed unlikely that they could be behind the failure of the phone system. It could not easily be sabotaged. On the other hand, she would have said yesterday that it was impossible to smuggle a rabbit out of BSL4.

She sighed. There was only one decision she could make. Bottom line, the security of the laboratories was her responsibility, and she could not stay at home and go to bed while something strange was going on at Oxenford Medical.

Mother could not be left alone, and Toni could not ask neighbors to look after her at this hour. Mother would just have to come along to the Kremlin.

As she put the gearshift into first, a man got out of a light-colored Jaguar sedan parked a few cars farther along the curb. There was something familiar about him, she thought, and she hesitated to pull away. He walked along the pavement toward her. By his gait she judged that he was slightly tipsy, but in control. He came to her window and she recognized Carl Osborne, the television reporter. He was carrying a small bundle.

She put the gearshift back into neutral and wound down the window. "Hello, Carl," she said. "What are you doing here?"

"Waiting for you. I was ready to give up."

Mother woke up and said, "Hello, is this your boyfriend?"

"This is Carl Osborne, and he's not my boyfriend."

With her usual tactless accuracy, Mother said, "Perhaps he'd like to be."

Toni turned to Carl, who was grinning. "This is my mother, Kathleen Gallo."

"A privilege to meet you, Mrs. Gallo."

"Why were you waiting for me?" Toni asked him.

"I brought you a present," he said, and he showed her what was in his hand. It was a puppy. "Merry Christmas," he said, and tipped it into her lap.

"Carl, for God's sake, don't be ridiculous!" She picked up the furry bundle and tried to give it back.

He stepped away and held up his hands. "He's yours!"

The little dog was soft and warm in her hands, and part of her wanted to hold it close, but she knew she had to get rid of it. She got out of the car. "I don't want a pet," she said firmly. "I'm a single woman with a demanding job and an elderly mother, and I can't give a dog the care and attention it needs."

"You'll find a way. What are you going to call him? Carl is a nice name."

She looked at the pup. It was an English sheepdog, white with gray patches, about eight weeks old. She could hold it in one hand, just. It licked her with a rough tongue and gave her an appealing look. She hardened her heart.

She walked to his car and put the puppy gently down

on the front seat. "You name him," she said. "I've got too much on my plate."

"Well, think about it," he said, looking disappointed. "I'll keep him tonight, and call you tomorrow."

She got back into her car. "Don't call me, please." She put the stick into first.

"You're a hard woman," he said as she pulled away.

For some reason, that jibe got to her. I'm not hard, she thought. Unexpected tears came to her eyes. I've had to deal with the death of Michael Ross, and a rabid pack of reporters, and I've been called a bitch by Kit Oxenford, and my sister has let me down, and I've canceled the holiday I was looking forward to. I take responsibility for myself and for Mother and for the Kremlin, and I can't manage a puppy as well, and that's flat.

Then she remembered Stanley, and she realized she did not care a hoot what Carl Osborne said.

She rubbed her eyes with the back of her hand and peered ahead into the swirling snowflakes. Turning out of her Victorian street, she headed for the main road out of town.

Mother said, "Carl seems nice."

"He's not very nice, actually, Mother. In fact he's shallow and dishonest."

"Nobody's perfect. There can't be many eligible men of your age."

"Almost none."

"You don't want to end up alone."

Toni smiled to herself. "Somehow I don't think I will."

The traffic thinned out as she left the town center, and the snow lay thick on the road. Maneuvering carefully through a series of roundabouts, she noticed a car close on her tail. Looking in the rearview mirror, she identified it as a light-colored Jaguar sedan.

Carl Osborne was following her.

She pulled over, and he stopped right behind her.

She got out and went to his window. "What now?"

"I'm a reporter, Toni," he said. "It's almost midnight on Christmas Eve, and you're looking after your elderly mother, yet you're in your car and you seem to be heading for the Kremlin. This has to be a story."

"Oh, shit," said Toni.

CHRISTMAS DAY

MIDNIGHT

THE Kremlin looked like something from a fairy tale, with snow falling thickly around its floodlit roofs and towers. As the van with "Hibernian Telecom" on its side approached the main gate, Kit had a momentary fancy that he was the Black Knight riding up to besiege the place.

He felt relieved to get here. The storm was turning into a full-scale blizzard, contrary to the forecast, and the journey from the airfield had taken longer than expected. The delay made him fearful. Every minute that passed made it more likely that snags would threaten his elaborate plan.

The phone call from Toni Gallo worried him. He had put her through to Steve Tremlett, fearing that if he played her a fault message she might drive to the Kremlin to find out what was going on. But, having listened in to the conversation, Kit thought she might do that anyway. It was lousy bad luck that she was in Inverburn, instead of at a spa fifty miles away.

The first of the two barriers lifted, and Elton moved the van forward and drew level with the gatehouse. There were two guards in the booth, as Kit expected. Elton wound down the window. A guard leaned out and said, "We're glad to see you laddies."

Kit did not know the man but, recalling his conversation with Hamish, he realized it must be Willie Crawford. Looking past him, Kit saw Hamish himself.

Willie said, "It's good of you to come out at Christmas."

"All part of the job," Elton said.

"Three of you, is it?"

"Plus Goldilocks in the back."

A low snarl came from behind. "Watch your mouth, shitface."

Kit suppressed a groan. How could they squabble at such a crucial moment?

Nigel murmured, "Knock it off, you two."

Willie did not appear to have heard the exchange. He said, "I need to see identification for everyone, please."

They all took out their faked cards. Elton had based them on Kit's recollection of what the Hibernian Telecom pass looked like. The phone system rarely broke down, so Kit had figured no guard was likely to remember what a genuine pass looked like. Now, with a security guard scrutinizing the cards as if they were dubious fifty-pound notes, Kit held his breath.

Willie wrote down the name from each card. Then he handed them all back without comment. Kit looked away and allowed himself to breathe again.

"Drive to the main entrance," Willie said. "You'll be all right if you stay between the lampposts." The road ahead was invisible, covered with snow. "At reception you'll find a Mr. Tremlett, who can tell you where to go."

The second barrier lifted, and Elton pulled forward. They were inside.

Kit felt sick with fear. He had broken the law before, with the scam that got him fired, but that had not felt like crime—it was more like cheating at cards, something he had done since he was eleven years old. This was a straightforward burglary, and he could go to jail. He swallowed hard and tried to concentrate. He thought of the enormous sum he owed Harry Mac. He remembered the blind terror he had felt this morning, when Daisy held his head under water and he thought he was dying. He had to go through with this.

Nigel said quietly to Elton, "Try not to aggravate Daisy."

"It was just a joke," Elton said defensively.

"She's got no sense of humor."

If Daisy heard, she did not respond.

Elton parked at the main entrance and they got out. Kit carried his laptop. Nigel and Daisy took tool boxes from the back of the van. Elton had an expensive-looking burgundy leather briefcase, very slim with a brass catch—typical of his taste, but a bit odd for a telephone repairman, Kit thought.

They passed between the stone lions of the porch and entered the Great Hall. Low security lights intensified the churchlike look of the Victorian architecture: the mullioned windows, the pointed arches, and the serried timbers of the roof. The dimness made no difference to the security cameras, which—Kit knew—worked by infrared light.

At the modern reception desk in the middle of the hall were two more guards. One was an attractive young woman Kit did not recognize, and the other was Steve Tremlett. Kit hung back, not wanting Steve to look at him too closely. "You'll want to access the central processing unit," Steve said.

Nigel answered, "That's the place to start."

Steve raised his eyebrows at the London accent, but made no comment. "Susan will show you the way—I need to stay by the phone."

Susan had short hair and a pierced eyebrow. She wore a shirt with epaulettes, a tie, dark serge uniform trousers, and black lace-up shoes. She gave them a friendly smile and led them along a corridor paneled in dark wood.

A weird calm seemed to descend on Kit. He was inside, being escorted by a security guard, about to rob the place. He felt fatalistic. The cards had been dealt, and he had placed his bet, so there was nothing to do now but play out his hand, win or lose.

They entered the control room.

The place was cleaner and tidier than Kit remembered, with all cables neatly stowed and logbooks in a row on a shelf. He presumed that was Toni's influence. Here also there were two guards instead of one. They sat at the long desk, watching the monitors. Susan introduced them as Don and Stu. Don was a dark-skinned south Indian with a thick Glasgow accent, and Stu was a freckled redhead. Kit did not recognize either one. An extra guard was no big deal, Kit told himself: just another pair of eyes to shield things from, another brain to be distracted, another person to be lulled into apathy.

Susan opened the door to the equipment room. "The CPU is in there."

A moment later Kit was inside the inner sanctum. Just like that! he thought, although it had taken weeks of preparation. Here were the computers and other devices that ran not just the phone system but also the lighting, the security cameras, and the alarms. Even to get this far was a triumph.

He said to Susan, "Thanks very much—we'll take it from here."

"If there's anything you need, come to reception," she said, and she left.

Kit put his laptop on a shelf and connected it to the security computer. He pulled over a chair and turned his laptop so that the screen could not be seen by someone standing in the doorway. He felt Daisy's eyes on him, suspicious and malevolent. "Go into the next room," he said to her. "Keep an eye on the guards."

She glared resentfully at him for a moment, then did as he said.

Kit took a deep breath. He knew exactly what he had to do. He needed to work fast, but carefully.

First, he accessed the program that controlled the video feed from thirty-seven closed-circuit television cameras. He looked at the entrance to BSL4, which appeared normal. He checked the reception desk and saw Steve there, but not Susan. Scanning the input from other cameras, he located Susan patrolling elsewhere in the building. He noted the time.

The computer's massive memory stored the camera images for four weeks before overwriting them. Kit knew his way around the program, for he had installed it. He located the video from the cameras in BSL4 this time last night. He checked the feed, random sampling footage, to make sure no crazy scientist had been working in the lab in the middle of the night; but all the images showed empty rooms. Good.

Nigel and Elton watched him in tense silence.

He then fed last night's images into the monitors the guards were currently watching.

Now someone could walk around BSL4 doing anything he liked without their knowing.

The monitors were fitted with biased switches that would detect equipment substitution, for example if the feed came from a separate videotape deck. However, this footage was not coming from an outside source, but direct from the computer's memory—so it did not trigger the alarm.

Kit stepped into the main control room. Daisy was slumped in a chair, wearing her leather jacket over the Hibernian Telecom overalls. Kit studied the bank of screens. All appeared normal. The dark-skinned guard, Don, looked at him with an inquiring expression. As a cover, Kit said, "Are any of the phones in here working?"

"None," said Don.

Along the bottom edge of each screen was a line of text giving the time and date. The time was the same on the screens that showed yesterday's footage—Kit had made sure of that. But yesterday's footage showed yesterday's date.

Kit was betting that no one ever looked at that date. The guards scanned the screens for activity; they did not read text that told them what they already knew.

He hoped he was right.

Don was wondering why the telephone repairman was so interested in the television monitors. "Something we can do for you?" he said in a challenging tone.

Daisy grunted and stirred in her chair, like a dog sensing tension among the humans.

Kit's mobile phone rang.

He stepped back into the equipment room. The message on the screen of his laptop said: "Kremlin calling Toni." He guessed that Steve wanted to let Toni know that the repair team had arrived. He decided to put the call through: it might reassure Toni and discourage her from coming here. He touched a key, then listened in on his mobile.

"This is Toni Gallo." She was in her car; Kit could hear the engine.

"Steve here, at the Kremlin. The maintenance team from Hibernian Telecom have arrived."

"Have they fixed the problem?"

"They've just started work. I hope I didn't wake you."

"No, I'm not in bed. I'm on my way to you."

Kit cursed. It was what he had been afraid of.

"There's really no need," Steve told Toni.

Kit thought: That's right!

"Probably not," she replied. "But I'll feel more comfortable."

Kit thought: When will you get here?

Steve had the same thought. "Where are you now?"

"I'm only a few miles away, but the roads are terrible, and I can't go faster than fifteen or twenty miles an hour."

"Are you in your Porsche?"

"Yes."

"This is Scotland. You should have bought a Land Rover."

"I should have bought a bloody tank."

Come on, Kit thought, how long?

Toni answered his question. "It's going to take me at least half an hour, maybe an hour."

They hung up, and Kit cursed under his breath.

He told himself that a visit by Toni would not be fatal. There would be nothing to warn her that a robbery was going on. Nothing should seem amiss for several days. It would appear only that there had been a problem with the phone system, and a repair team had fixed it. Not until the scientists returned to work would anyone realize that BSL4 had been burgled.

The main danger was that Toni might see through Kit's disguise. He looked completely different, he had removed his distinctive jewelry, and he could easily alter his voice, making it more Scots; but she was a sharp-nosed bitch and he could not afford to take any chances. If she showed up, he would keep out of her way as much as possible, and let Nigel do the talking. All the same, the risk of something going wrong would increase tenfold.

But there was nothing he could do about it, except hurry.

His next task was to get Nigel into the lab without any of the guards seeing. The main problem here was the patrols. Once an hour, a guard from reception made a tour of the building. The patrol followed a prescribed route, and took twenty minutes. Having passed the entrance to BSL4, the guard would not come back for an hour.

Kit had seen Susan patrolling a few minutes ago, when he connected his laptop to the surveillance program. Now he checked the feed from reception and saw her sitting with Steve at the desk, her circuit done. Kit checked his watch. He had a comfortable thirty minutes before she went on patrol again.

Kit had dealt with the cameras in the high-security lab, but there was still one outside the door, showing the entrance to BSL4. He called up yesterday's feed and ran the footage at double fast-forward. He needed a clear half hour, with no one passing across the screen. He stopped at the point where the patrolling guard appeared. Beginning when the guard left the picture, he fed yesterday's images into the monitor in the next room. Don and Stu should see nothing but an empty corridor for the next hour, or until Kit returned the system to normal. The screen would show the wrong time as well as the wrong date, but once again Kit was gambling that the guards would not notice.

He looked at Nigel. "Let's go."

Elton stayed in the equipment room to make sure no one interfered with the laptop.

Passing through the control room, Kit said to Daisy, "We're going to get the nanometer from the van. You stay here." There was no such thing as a nanometer, but Don and Stu would not know that.

Daisy grunted and looked away. She was not much good at acting the part. Kit hoped the guards would simply assume she was bad-tempered.

Kit and Nigel walked quickly to BSL4. Kit waved his father's smart card in front of the scanner, then pressed the forefinger of his left hand to the screen. He waited while the central computer compared the information from the screen with that on the card. He noticed that Nigel was carrying Elton's smart burgundy leather briefcase.

The light over the door remained stubbornly red. Nigel looked at Kit anxiously. Kit told himself this had to work. The chip contained the encoded details of his own fingerprint—he had checked. What could go wrong?

Then a woman's voice behind them said, "I'm afraid you can't go in there."

Kit and Nigel turned. Susan was standing behind them. She appeared friendly but anxious. She should have been at reception, Kit thought in a panic. She was not due to patrol for another thirty minutes . . .

Unless Toni Gallo had doubled the patrols as well as doubling the guard.

There was a chime like a doorbell. All three of them looked at the light over the door. It turned green, and the heavy door swung slowly open on motorized hinges.

Susan said, "How did you open the door?" Her voice betrayed fear now.

Involuntarily, Kit looked down at the stolen card in his hand.

Susan followed his gaze. "You're not supposed to have a pass!" she said incredulously.

Nigel moved toward her.

She turned on her heel and ran.

Nigel went after her, but he was twice her age. He'll never catch her, Kit thought. He let out a shout of rage: how could everything go so wrong, so quickly?

Then Daisy emerged from the passage leading to the control room.

Kit would not have thought he would ever be glad to see her ugly face.

She seemed unsurprised at the scene that confronted her: the guard running toward her, Nigel following, Kit frozen to the spot. Kit realized that she must have been watching the monitors in the control room. She would have seen Susan leave the reception desk and walk toward BSL4. She had realized the danger and moved to deal with it.

Susan saw Daisy and hesitated, then ran on, apparently determined to push past.

The hint of a smile touched Daisy's lips. She drew back her arm and smashed her gloved fist into Susan's face. The blow made a sickening sound, like a melon dropped on a tiled floor. Susan collapsed as if she had run into a wall. Daisy rubbed her knuckles, looking pleased.

Susan got to her knees. Sobs bubbled through the blood covering her nose and mouth. Daisy took from the pocket of her jacket a flexible blackjack about nine inches long and made, Kit guessed, of steel ball bearings in a leather case. She raised her arm.

Kit shouted: "No!"

Daisy hit Susan over the head with the blackjack. The guard collapsed soundlessly.

Kit yelled: "Leave her!"

Daisy raised her arm to hit Susan again, but Nigel stepped forward and grabbed Daisy's wrist. "No need to kill her," he said.

Daisy stepped back reluctantly.

"You mad cow!" Kit cried. "We'll all be guilty of murder!"

Daisy looked at the light brown glove on her right hand. There was blood on the knuckles. She licked it off thoughtfully.

Kit stared at the unconscious woman on the floor. The sight of her crumpled body was sickening. "This wasn't supposed to happen!" he said in alarm. "Now what are we going to do with her?"

Daisy straightened her blond wig. "Tie her up and hide her somewhere."

Kit's brain began to come back on line after the shock of sudden violence. "Right," he said. "We'll put her inside BSL4. The guards aren't allowed in there."

Nigel said to Daisy, "Drag her inside. I'll find something to tie her up with." He stepped into a side office.

Kit's mobile phone rang. He ignored it.

Kit used his card to reopen the door, which had closed automatically. Daisy picked up a red fire extinguisher and used it to prop the door open. Kit said, "You can't do that. It will set off the alarm." He removed the extinguisher.

Daisy looked skeptical. "The alarm goes off if you prop a door open?"

"Yes!" Kit said impatiently. "There are air management systems here. I know, I put the alarms in myself. Now shut up and do as you're told!"

Daisy got her arms around Susan's chest and pulled her along the carpet. Nigel emerged from the office with a long power lead. They all passed into BSL4. The door closed behind them.

They were in a small lobby leading to the changing rooms. Daisy propped Susan against the wall underneath a pass-through autoclave that permitted sterilized items to be removed from the lab. Nigel tied her hands and feet with the electrical lead.

Kit's phone stopped ringing.

The three of them went outside. No pass was needed to exit: the door opened at the push of a green button set into the wall.

Kit was trying desperately to think ahead. His entire plan was ruined. There was no possibility now that the theft would remain undiscovered. "Susan will be missed quite soon," he said, making himself keep calm. "Don and Stuart will notice that she's disappeared off the monitors. And even if they don't, Steve will be alerted when she fails to return from her patrol. Either way, we don't have time to get into the laboratory and out again before they raise the alarm. Shit, it's all gone wrong!"

"Calm down," Nigel said. "We can handle this, so long as you don't panic. We just have to deal with the other guards, like we dealt with her."

Kit's phone rang again. He could not tell who was calling without his computer. "It's probably Toni Gallo," he said. "What do we do if she shows up? We can't pretend nothing's wrong if all the guards are tied up!"

"We'll just deal with her as and when she arrives."

Kit's phone kept ringing.

12:30 A.M.

TONI was driving at ten miles an hour, leaning forward over the steering wheel to peer into the blinding snowfall, trying to see the road. Her headlights did nothing but illuminate a cloud of big, soft snowflakes that seemed to fill the universe. She had been staring so long that her eyelids hurt, as if she had got soap in her eyes.

Her mobile became a hands-free car phone when slotted into a cradle on the dashboard of the Porsche. She had dialed the Kremlin, and now she listened as it rang out unanswered.

"I don't think anyone's there," Mother said.

The repairmen must have downed the entire system, Toni thought. Were the alarms working? What if something serious went wrong while the lines were down? Feeling troubled and frustrated, she touched a button to end the call.

"Where are we?" Mother asked.

"Good question." Toni was familiar with this road

but she could hardly see it. She seemed to have been driving forever. She glanced to the side from time to time, looking for landmarks. She thought she recognized a stone cottage with a distinctive wrought-iron gate. It was only a couple of miles from the Kremlin, she recalled. That cheered her up. "We'll be there in fifteen minutes, Mother," she said.

She looked in the rearview mirror and saw the headlights that had been with her since Inverburn: the pest Carl Osborne in his Jaguar, doggedly following her at the same sluggard pace. On another day she would have enjoyed losing him.

Was she wasting her time? Nothing would please her more than to reach the Kremlin and find everything calm: the phones repaired, the alarms working, the guards bored and sleepy. Then she could go home and go to bed and think about seeing Stanley tomorrow.

At least she would enjoy the look on Carl Osborne's face when he realized he had driven for hours in the snow, at Christmas, in the middle of the night, to cover the story of a telephone fault.

She seemed to be on a straight stretch, and she chanced speeding up. But it was not straight for long, and almost immediately she came to a right-hand bend. She could not use the brakes, for fear of skidding, so she changed down a gear to slow the car, then held her foot steady on the throttle as she turned. The tail of the Porsche wanted to break free—she could feel it—but the wide rear tires held their grip.

Headlights appeared coming toward her, and for a welcome change she could make out a hundred yards of road between the two cars. There was not much to see: snow eight or nine inches thick on the ground, a drystone wall on her left, a white hill on her right.

The oncoming car was traveling quite fast, she noted nervously.

She recalled this stretch of road. It was a long, wide bend that turned through ninety degrees around the foot of the hill. She held her line through the curve.

But the other car did not.

She saw it drift across the carriageway to the crown of the road, and she thought, Fool, you braked into the turn, and your back slipped away.

In the next instant, she realized with horror that the car was heading straight for her.

It crossed the middle of the road and came at her broadside. It was a hot hatch with four men in it. They were laughing and, in the split second for which she could see them, she divined that they were young merry-makers too drunk to realize the danger they were in. "Look out!" she screamed uselessly.

The front of the Porsche was about to smash into the side of the skidding hatchback. Toni acted reflexively. Without thinking about it, she jerked her steering wheel to the left. The nose of her car turned. Almost simultaneously, she pushed down the accelerator pedal. The car leaped forward and skidded. For an instant the hatchback was alongside her, inches away.

The Porsche was angled left and sliding forward. Toni swung the wheel right to correct the skid, and applied a featherlight touch to the throttle. The car straightened up and the tires gripped.

She thought the hatchback would hit her rear wing; then she thought it would miss by a hair; then there was a clang, loud but superficial-sounding, and she realized her bumper had been hit.

It was not much of a blow, but it destabilized the Porsche, and the rear swung left, out of control again.

Toni desperately tugged the steering wheel to the left, turning into the skid; but, before her corrective action could take effect, the car hit the drystone wall at the side of the road. There was a terrific bang and the sound of breaking glass; then the car came to a stop.

Toni looked worriedly at her mother. She was staring ahead, mouth open, bewildered—but unharmed. Toni felt a moment of relief—then she thought of Osborne.

She looked fearfully in the rearview mirror, thinking the hatchback must smash into Osborne's Jaguar. She could see the red rear lights of the hatch and the white headlights of the Jag. The hatchback fishtailed; the Jag swung hard over to the side of the road; the hatchback straightened up and went by.

The Jaguar came to a stop, and the car full of drunk boys went on into the night. They were probably still laughing.

Mother said in a shaky voice, "I heard a bang—did that car hit us?"

"Yes," Toni said. "We had a lucky escape."

"I think you should drive more carefully," said Mother.

12:35 A.M.

KIT was fighting down panic. His brilliant plan had collapsed in ruins. Now there was no way the robbery would go undetected until the staff returned to work after the holiday. At most, it might remain a secret until six o'clock this morning, when the next shift of security guards arrived. But if Toni Gallo were still on her way here, the time left was even shorter.

If his plan had worked, there would have been no violence. Even now, he thought with helpless frustration, it had not been strictly necessary. The guard Susan could have been captured and tied up without injury. Unfortunately, Daisy could not resist an opportunity for brutality. Kit hoped desperately that the other guards could be rounded up without further nauseating scenes of bloodshed.

Now, as they ran to the control room, both Nigel and Daisy drew guns.

Kit was horrified. "We agreed no weapons!" he protested.

238

"Good thing we ignored you," Nigel replied.

They came to the door. Kit stared aghast at the guns. They were small automatic pistols with fat grips. "This makes it armed robbery—you realize that."

"Only if we're caught." Nigel turned the handle and kicked the door open.

Daisy burst into the room, yelling at the top of her voice: "On the floor! Now! Both of you!"

There was only a moment's hesitation, while the two security guards went from shock and bewilderment to fear; then they threw themselves down.

Kit felt powerless. He had intended to enter the room first and say, *Please stay calm and do as you're told. Then you won't get hurt.* But he had lost control. There was nothing he could do now but string along and try to make sure nothing else went wrong.

Elton appeared in the doorway of the equipment room. He took in the scene in an instant.

Daisy screamed at the guards: "Facedown, hands behind your backs, eyes closed! Quick, quick, or I'll shoot you in the balls!"

They did as she said but, even so, she kicked Don in the face with a heavy boot. He cried out and flinched away, but remained prone.

Kit placed himself in front of Daisy. "Enough!" he shouted.

Elton shook his head in amazement. "She's loony fucking tunes."

The gleeful malevolence on Daisy's face frightened Kit, but he forced himself to stare at her. He had too much at stake to let her ruin everything. "Listen to me!" he shouted. "You're not in the lab yet, and you won't ever get there at this rate. If you want to be empty-handed when we meet the client at ten, just carry on the way you are." She turned away from his pointing finger, but he went after her. "No more brutality!"

Nigel backed him. "Ease up, Daisy," he said. "Do as he says. See if you can tie these two up without kicking their heads in."

Kit said, "We'll put them in the same place as the girl."

Daisy tied their hands with electrical cable; then she and Nigel herded them out at gunpoint. Elton stayed behind, watching the monitors, keeping an eye on Steve in reception. Kit followed the prisoners to BSL4 and opened the door. They put Don and Stu on the floor next to Susan and tied their feet. Don was bleeding from a nasty cut on his forehead. Susan seemed conscious but groggy.

"One left," said Kit as they stepped outside. "Steve, in the Great Hall. And no unnecessary violence!"

Daisy gave a grunt of disgust.

Nigel said, "Kit, try not to say any more in front of the guards about the client and our ten o'clock rendezvous. If you tell them too much, we may have to kill them."

Kit realized, aghast, what he had done. He felt like a fool.

His phone rang.

"That might be Toni," he said. "Let me check." He ran back to the equipment room. His laptop screen said, "Toni calling Kremlin." He transferred the call to the phone on the desk at reception and listened in.

"Hi, Steve, this is Toni. Any news?"

"The repair crew are still here."

"Everything all right otherwise?"

With the phone to his ear, Kit stepped into the control room and stood behind Elton to watch Steve on the monitor. "Yeah, I think so. Susan Mackintosh should have finished her patrol by now, but maybe she went to the ladies' room."

Kit cursed.

Toni said anxiously, "How late is she?"

On the monitor, in black-and-white, Steve checked his wristwatch. "Five minutes."

"Give her another five minutes. Then go and look for her."

"Okay. Where are you?"

"Not far away, but I've had an accident. A car full of drunks clipped the rear end of the Porsche."

Kit thought, I wish they'd killed you.

Steve said, "Are you okay?"

"Fine, but my car's damaged. Fortunately, another car was following me, and he's giving me a lift."

And who the hell was that? "Shit," Kit said aloud. "Her and some fellow."

"When will you be here?"

"Twenty minutes, maybe thirty."

Kit's knees went weak. He staggered and sat in one of the guards' chairs. Twenty minutes—thirty at the most! It took twenty minutes to get suited up for BSL4!

Toni said goodbye and hung up the phone.

Kit ran across the control room and out into the corridor. "She'll be here in twenty or thirty minutes," he said. "And there's someone with her. I don't know who. We have to move fast."

They ran along the corridor. Daisy, going first, burst into the Great Hall and yelled: "On the floor—now!"

Kit and Nigel ran in after her and stopped abruptly. The room was empty. "Shit," said Kit.

Steve had been at the desk twenty seconds ago. He could not have gone far. Kit looked around the half-dark room, at the chairs for waiting visitors, the coffee table with science magazines, the rack of leaflets about Oxenford Medical's work, the display case with models of complex molecules. He stared up into the dimly lit skeleton of the hammer-beam roof, as if Steve might be hiding among the timber ribs.

Nigel and Daisy ran along radiating corridors, opening doors.

Kit's eye was caught by two stick figures, male and female, on a door: the toilets. He ran across the hall. There was a short corridor leading to separate men's and ladies' rooms. Kit went into the men's room.

It appeared empty. "Mr. Tremlett?" He pushed open all the cubicle doors. No one was there.

As he stepped out, he saw Steve returning to the reception desk. The guard must have been in the ladies' room—searching for Susan, Kit realized.

Steve turned around, hearing Kit. "Looking for me?"

"Yes." Kit realized he could not apprehend Steve without help. Kit was younger, and athletic, but Steve was a fit man in his thirties, and might not give up without a fight. "Something I need to ask you," Kit said, playing for time. He made his accent more Scots than was natural, to make sure Steve did not find his voice familiar.

Steve lifted the flap and entered the oval of the desk. "And what would that be?"

"Just a minute." Kit turned away and shouted after Nigel and Daisy. "Hey! Back in here!"

Steve looked troubled. "What's going on? You lot aren't supposed to be wandering around the building."

"I'll explain in a minute."

Steve looked hard at him and frowned. "Have you been here before?"

Kit swallowed. "No, never."

"There's something familiar about you."

Kit's mouth went dry and he found it hard to speak. "I work with the emergency team." Where were the others?

"I don't like this." Steve picked up the phone on the desk.

Where were Nigel and Daisy? Kit shouted again: "Get back in here, you two!"

Steve dialed, and the mobile in Kit's pocket rang. Steve heard it. He frowned, thinking; then a look of shocked understanding came over his face. "You messed with the phones!"

Kit said, "Stay calm, and you won't get hurt." As soon as the words were out of his mouth, he realized his mistake: he had confirmed Steve's suspicions.

Steve acted quickly. He leaped nimbly over the desk and ran for the door.

Kit yelled: "Stop!"

Steve stumbled, fell, and got up again.

Daisy came running into the hall, saw Steve, and turned toward the main door, heading him off.

Steve saw that he could not make it to the door and turned instead into the corridor leading to BSL4.

Daisy and Kit ran after him.

Steve sprinted down the long corridor. There was an exit toward the rear of the building, Kit recalled. If Steve made it outside, they might never catch him.

Daisy was well ahead of Kit, arms pumping like a sprinter, and Kit recalled her powerful shoulders in the swimming pool; but Steve was running like a hare, and pulling away from them. He was going to escape.

Then, as Steve drew level with the door leading to the control room, Elton stepped into the corridor in front of him. Steve was going too fast to take evasive action. Elton stuck out a foot and tripped Steve, who went flying.

As Steve hit the ground, facedown, Elton fell on him, with both knees in the small of his back, and pushed the barrel of a pistol into his cheek. "Don't move, and you won't get shot in the face," he said. His voice was calm but convincing.

Steve lay still.

Elton stood, keeping the gun pointed at Steve. "That's the way to do it," he said to Daisy. "No blood."

She looked scornful.

Nigel came running up. "What happened?"

"Never mind!" Kit shouted. "We're out of time!"

"What about the two guards in the gatehouse?" Nigel said.

"Forget them! They don't know what's happened here, and they're not likely to find out—they stay out there all night." He pointed at Elton. "Get my laptop from the equipment room and wait for us in the van." He turned to Daisy. "Bring Steve, tie him up in BSL4, then get into the van. We have to go into the laboratory—now!"

12:45 A.M.

IN the barn, Sophie had produced a bottle of vodka.

Craig's mother had ordered lights out at midnight, but she had not come back to check, so the youngsters were sitting in front of the television set, watching an old horror movie. Craig's dopey sister, Caroline, stroked a white rat and pretended she thought the film was silly. His little cousin, Tom, was pigging out on chocolates and trying to stay awake. Sexy Sophie smoked cigarettes and said nothing. Craig was alternately worrying about the dented Ferrari and watching for a chance to kiss Sophie. Somehow the setting was not romantic enough. But would it get any better?

The vodka surprised him. He had thought her talk of cocktails was just showing off. But she went up the ladder to the hayloft bedroom, where her bag was, and came back down with a half bottle of Smirnoff in her hand. "Who wants some?" she said.

They all did.

The only glasses they had were plastic tumblers decorated with pictures of Pooh and Tigger and Eeyore. There was a fridge with soft drinks and ice. Tom and Caroline mixed their vodka with Coca-Cola. Craig, not sure what to do, copied Sophie and drank it straight with ice. The taste was bitter, but he liked the warm glow as it went down his throat.

The movie was going through a dull patch. Craig said to Sophie, "Do you know what you're getting for Christmas?"

"Two decks and a mixer, so I can deejay. You?"

"Snowboarding holiday. Some guys I know are going to Val d'Isère at Easter, but it's expensive. I've asked for the money. So you want to be a deejay?"

"I think I'd be good at it."

"Is that, like, your career plan?"

"Dunno." Sophie looked scornful. "What's your 'career plan'?"

"Can't make up my mind. I'd love to play football professionally. But then you're finished before you're forty. And anyway, I might not be good enough. I'd really like to be a scientist like Grandpa."

"A bit boring."

"No! He discovers fantastic new drugs, he's his own boss, he makes piles of money, and he drives a Ferrari F50—what's boring?"

She shrugged. "I wouldn't mind the car." She giggled. "Except for the dent."

The thought of the damage he had done to his grandfather's car no longer depressed Craig. He was feeling pleasantly relaxed and carefree. He toyed with the idea of kissing Sophie right now, ignoring the others. What held him back was the thought that she might reject him in front of his sister, which would be humiliating.

He wished he understood girls. No one ever told you anything. His father probably knew all there was to know. Women seemed to take to Hugo instantly, but Craig could not figure out why, and when he asked, his father just laughed. In a rare moment of intimacy with his mother, he had asked her what attracted girls to a man. "Kindness," she had said. That was obviously rubbish. When waitresses and shop assistants responded to his father, grinning at him, blushing, walking away with a distinct wiggle, it was not because they thought he would be kind to them, for God's sake. But what was it? All Craig's friends had surefire theories about sex appeal, and they were all different. One believed that girls liked a guy to be masterful and tell them what to do; another said that if you ignored them they would flock around you; others claimed girls were interested only in an athletic physique, or good looks, or money. Craig was sure they were all wrong, but he had no hypothesis of his own.

Sophie drained her glass. "Another?"

They all had another.

Craig began to realize that the movie was, in fact, hilarious. "That castle is so obviously made of plywood," he said with a chuckle.

Sophie said, "And they all have sixties eye makeup and hairstyles, even though it's set in the Middle Ages."

Caroline suddenly said, "Oh, God, I'm so sleepy." She got to her feet, climbed the ladder with some difficulty, and disappeared.

Craig thought, One down, one to go. Maybe the scene could turn romantic after all.

The old witch in the story had to bathe in the blood of a virgin to make herself young again. The bathtub scene was a hilarious combination of titillation and gross-out, and both Craig and Sophie giggled helplessly.

"I'm going to be sick," said Tom.

"Oh, no!" Craig sprang to his feet. He felt dizzy for a second, then recovered. "Bathroom, quick," he said. He took Tom's arm and led him there.

Tom started to throw up a fatal second before he reached the toilet.

Craig ignored the mess on the floor and guided him to the bowl. Tom puked some more. Craig held the boy's shoulders and tried not to breathe. There goes the romantic atmosphere, he thought.

Sophie came to the door. "Is he all right?"

"Yeah." Craig put on the air of a snooty schoolteacher. "An injudicious combination of chocolates, vodka, and virgin's blood."

Sophie laughed. Then, to Craig's surprise, she grabbed a length of toilet roll, got down on her knees, and began to clean the tiled floor.

Tom straightened up.

"All done?" Craig asked him.

Tom nodded.

"Sure?"

"Sure."

Craig flushed the toilet. "Now clean your teeth."

"Why?"

"So you won't smell so bad."

Tom brushed his teeth.

Sophie threw a wad of paper into the toilet and took some more.

Craig led Tom out of the bathroom to his camp bed on the floor. "Get undressed," he said. He opened Tom's small suitcase and found a pair of Spider-Man pajamas. Tom put them on and climbed into bed. Craig folded his clothes.

"I'm sorry I heaved," Tom said.

"It happens to the best of us," Craig said. "Forget it." He pulled the blanket up to Tom's chin. "Sweet dreams."

He returned to the bathroom. Sophie had cleaned up with surprising efficiency, and she was pouring disinfectant into the bowl. Craig washed his hands, and she stood beside him at the sink and did the same. It felt comradely.

In a low, amused voice, Sophie said, "When you told him to brush his teeth, he asked why."

Craig grinned at her in the mirror. "Like, he wasn't planning to kiss anyone tonight, so why bother?"

"Right."

She looked the most beautiful she had all day, Craig thought as she smiled at him in the mirror, her dark eyes sparkling with amusement. He took a towel and handed her one end. They both dried their hands. Craig pulled the towel, drawing her to him, and kissed her lips.

She kissed him back. He parted his lips a little, and let her feel the tip of his tongue. She seemed tentative, unsure how to respond. Could it be that, for all her talk, she had not done much kissing?

He murmured, "Shall we go back to the couch? I never like snogging in the bog."

She giggled and led the way out.

Craig thought, I'm not this witty when I'm sober.

He sat close to Sophie on the couch and put his arm around her. They watched the film for a minute; then he kissed her again.

12:55 A.M.

AN airtight submarine door led from the changing room into the biohazard zone. Kit turned the four-spoked wheel and opened the door. He had been inside the laboratory before it was commissioned, when there were no dangerous viruses present, but he had never entered a live BSL4 facility—he was not trained. Feeling that he was taking his life in his hands, he stepped through the doorway into the shower room. Nigel followed him, carrying Elton's burgundy briefcase. Elton and Daisy were waiting outside in the van.

Kit closed the door behind them. The doors were electronically linked so that the next would not open until the last was shut. His ears popped. Air pressure was reduced in stages as you entered BSL4, so that any air leaks were inward, preventing the escape of dangerous agents.

They passed through another doorway, into a room where blue plastic space suits hung from hooks. Kit

250

took off his shoes. "Find one your size and get into it," he said to Nigel. "We've got to shortcut the safety precautions."

"I don't like the sound of that."

Kit did not either, but they had no choice. "The normal procedure is too long," he said. "You have to take off all your clothes, including underwear, even your jewelry, then put on surgical scrubs, before you suit up." He took a suit off a hook and began to climb into it. "Coming out takes even longer. You have to shower in your suit, first with a decontamination solution, then with water, on a predetermined cycle that takes five minutes. Then you take off the suit and your scrubs and shower naked for five minutes. You clean your nails, blow your nose, clear your throat and spit. Then you get dressed. If we do all that, half the Inverburn police could be here by the time we get out. We'll skip the showers, take off our suits, and run."

Nigel was appalled. "How dangerous is it?"

"Like driving your car at a hundred and thirty miles an hour—it might kill you, but it probably won't, so long as you don't make a habit of it. Hurry up, get a damn suit on." Kit closed his helmet. The plastic faceplate gave slightly distorted vision. He closed the diagonal zip across the front of the suit, then helped Nigel.

He decided they could do without the usual surgical gloves. He used a roll of duct tape to attach the suit gauntlets to the rigid circular wrists of Nigel's suit, then got Nigel to do the same for him.

From the suit room they stepped into the decontamination shower, a cubicle with spray faucets on all sides as well as above. They felt a further drop in air pressure—twenty-five or fifty pascals from one room to the next, Kit recalled. From the shower they entered the lab proper.

Kit suffered a moment of pure fear. There was something in the air here that could kill him. All his glib talk about shortcutting safety precautions and driving at a hundred and thirty now seemed foolhardy. I could die, he thought. I could catch a disease and suffer a hemorrhage so bad the blood would come out of my ears and eyes and my penis. What am I doing here? How could I be so stupid?

He breathed slowly and made himself calm. You're not exposed to the atmosphere here in the lab; you'll be breathing pure air from outside, he told himself. No virus can penetrate this suit. You're a lot safer from infection than you would be in economy class on a packed 747 to Orlando. Get a grip.

Curly yellow air hoses dangled from the ceiling. Kit grabbed one and connected it to the inlet on Nigel's belt and saw Nigel's suit begin to inflate. He did the same for himself and heard the inward rush of air. His terror abated.

A row of rubber boots stood by the door, but Kit ignored them. Their main purpose was to protect the feet of the suits and prevent them wearing out.

He surveyed the lab, getting his bearings, trying to forget the danger and concentrate on what he had to do. The place had a shiny look due to the epoxy paint used to make the walls airtight. Microscopes and computer workstations stood on stainless-steel benches. There was a fax machine for sending your notes out— paper could not be taken into the showers or passed through the autoclaves. Kit noted fridges for storing samples, biosafety cabinets for handling hazardous materials, and a rack of rabbit cages under a clear plastic cover. The red light over the door would flash when the phone rang, as it was difficult to hear inside the suits.

The blue light would warn of an emergency. Closed-circuit television cameras covered every corner of the room.

Kit pointed to a door. "I think the vault is through there." He crossed the room, his air hose extending as he moved. He opened the door on a room no bigger than a closet, containing an upright refrigerator with a keypad combination lock. The LED keys were scrambled, so that the order of numbers in the squares was different every time. This made it impossible to figure out the code by watching someone's fingers. But Kit had installed the lock, so he knew the combination—unless it had been changed.

He keyed the numbers and pulled the handle.

The door opened.

Nigel looked over his shoulder.

Measured doses of the precious antiviral drug were kept in disposable syringes, ready for use. The syringes were packaged in small cardboard boxes. Kit pointed to the shelf. He raised his voice so that Nigel could hear him through the suit. "This is the drug."

Nigel said, "I don't want the drug."

Kit wondered if he had misheard. "What?" he shouted.

"I don't want the drug."

Kit was astounded. "What are you talking about? Why are we here?"

Nigel did not respond.

On the second shelf were samples of various viruses ready to be used to infect laboratory animals. Nigel looked carefully at the labels, then selected a sample of Madoba-2.

Kit said, "What the hell do you want that for?"

Without answering, Nigel took all the remaining

samples of the same virus from the shelf, twelve boxes altogether.

One was enough to kill someone. Twelve could start an epidemic. Kit would have been reluctant to touch the boxes, even wearing a biohazard suit. But what was Nigel up to?

Kit said, "I thought you were working for one of the pharmaceutical giants."

"I know."

Nigel could afford to pay Kit three hundred thousand pounds for tonight's work. Kit did not know what Elton and Daisy were getting but, even if it were a smaller fee, Nigel had to be spending something like half a million. To make that worth his while, he must be getting a million from the customer, maybe two. The drug was worth that, easily. But who would pay a million pounds for a sample of a deadly virus?

As soon as Kit asked himself the question, he knew the answer.

Nigel carried the sample boxes across the laboratory and placed them in a biosafety cabinet.

A biosafety cabinet was a glass case with a slot at the front through which the scientist could put his arms in order to perform experiments. A pump ensured that the flow of air ran from outside the cabinet to inside. A perfect seal was not considered necessary when the scientist was wearing a suit.

Next, Nigel opened the burgundy leather briefcase. The top was lined with blue plastic cooler packs. Virus samples needed to be kept at low temperatures, Kit knew. The bottom half of the briefcase was filled with white polystyrene chips of the kind used to package delicate objects. Lying on the chips, like a precious jewel, was an ordinary perfume spray bottle, empty. Kit recognized the bottle. It was a brand called Diablerie. His sister Olga used it.

Nigel put the bottle in the cabinet. It misted over with condensation. "They told me to turn on the air extractor," he said. "Where's the switch?"

"Wait!" Kit said. "What are you doing? You have to tell me!"

Nigel found the switch and turned it on. "The customer wants the product in deliverable form," he said with an air of indulgent patience. "I'm transferring the samples to the bottle here, in the cabinet, because it's dangerous to do it anywhere else." He took the top off the perfume bottle, then opened a sample box. Inside was a clear Pyrex vial with graduation marks printed in white on its side. Working awkwardly with his gauntleted hands, Nigel unscrewed the cap of the vial and poured the liquid into the Diablerie bottle. He recapped the vial and picked up another one.

Kit said, "The people you're selling this to—do you know what they want it for?"

"I can guess."

"It will kill people—hundreds, maybe thousands!"

"I know."

The perfume spray was the perfect delivery mechanism. It was a simple means of creating an aerosol. Filled with the colorless liquid that contained the virus, it looked completely innocent, and would pass unnoticed through all security checks. A woman could take it out of her handbag in any public place and look quite innocent as she filled the air with the vapor that would be fatal to everyone who inhaled it. She would kill herself, too—as terrorists often did. She would slaughter more people than any suicide bomber. Horrified, Kit said, "You're talking about mass murder!"

"Yes." Nigel turned to look at Kit. His blue eyes were intimidating even through two faceplates. "And you're in it, now, and as guilty as anyone, so shut your mouth and let me concentrate."

Kit groaned. Nigel was right. Kit had never thought to be involved in anything more than theft. He had been horrified when Daisy blackjacked Susan. This was a thousand times worse—and there was nothing Kit could do. If he tried to stop the heist now, Nigel would probably kill him—and if things went wrong, and the virus was not delivered to the customer, Harry Mc-Garry would have him killed for not paying his debt. He had to follow it through to the end and pick up his payment. Otherwise he was dead.

He also had to make sure Nigel handled the virus properly; otherwise he was dead anyway.

With his arms inside the biosafety cabinet, Nigel emptied the contents of all the sample vials into the perfume bottle, then replaced the spray top. Kit knew that the outside of the bottle was now undoubtedly contaminated—but someone seemed to have told Nigel this, for he put the bottle into the pass-out tank, which was full of decontamination fluid, and removed it from the other side. He wiped the bottle dry, then took two Ziploc food bags from the briefcase. He put the perfume bottle into one, sealed the bag, then put the bagged bottle into the second. Finally he put the double-bagged bottle back into the briefcase and closed the lid.

"We're done," he said.

They left the lab, Nigel carrying the briefcase. They passed through the decontamination shower without using it—there was no time. In the suit room they climbed out of the cumbersome plastic space suits and put their shoes back on. Kit kept well away from Nigel's suit—the gloves were sure to be contaminated with minute traces of the virus.

They moved through the normal shower, again without using it, through the changing room, and into the lobby. The four security guards were tied up and propped against the wall.

Kit checked his watch. It was thirty minutes since he had eavesdropped on Toni Gallo's conversation with Steve. "I hope Toni isn't here."

"If she is, we'll neutralize her."

"She's an ex-cop—she won't be as easy to deal with as these guards. And she might recognize me, even in this disguise."

He pressed the green button that opened the door. He and Nigel ran down the corridor and into the Great Hall. To Kit's monumental relief, it was empty: Toni Gallo had not yet arrived. We made it, he thought. But she could get here at any second.

The van was outside the main door, its engine running. Elton was at the wheel, Daisy in the back. Nigel jumped in, and Kit followed him, shouting: "Go! Go! Go!"

Elton roared off before Kit got the door shut.

The snow lay thick on the ground. The van immediately skidded and slewed sideways, but Elton got it back under control. They stopped at the gate.

Willie Crawford leaned out. "All fixed?" he said.

Elton wound down the window. "Not quite," he said. "We need some parts. We'll be back."

"It's going to take you a while, in this weather," the guard said conversationally.

Kit muffled a grunt of impatience. From the back, Daisy said in a low voice, "Shall I shoot the bastard?"

Elton said calmly, "We'll be as quick as we can." Then he closed the window.

After a moment the barrier lifted, and they pulled out.

As they did so, headlights flashed. A car was approaching from the south. Kit made it out to be a light-colored Jaguar sedan.

Elton turned north and roared away from the Kremlin.

Kit looked in the mirror and watched the headlights of the car. It turned into the gates of the Kremlin.

Toni Gallo, Kit thought. A minute too late.

1:15 A.M.

TONI was in the passenger seat beside Carl Osborne when he braked to a halt alongside the gatehouse of the Kremlin. Her mother was in the back.

She handed Carl her pass and her mother's pension book. "Give these to the guard with your press card," she said. All visitors had to show identification.

Carl slid the window down and handed over the documents.

Looking across him, Toni saw Hamish McKinnon. "Hi, Hamish, it's me," she called. "I've got two visitors with me."

"Hello, Ms. Gallo," said the guard. "Is that lady in the back holding a dog?"

"Don't ask," she said.

Hamish copied the names and handed back the press card and the pension book. "You'll find Steve in reception."

"Are the phones working?"

"Not yet. The repair crew just left to fetch a spare part." He lifted the barrier, and Carl drove in.

Toni suppressed a wave of irritation at Hibernian Telecom. On a night such as this, they really should carry all the parts they might need. The weather was continuing to get worse, and the roads might soon be impassable. She doubted they would be back before morning.

This spoiled a little plan she had. She had been hoping to phone Stanley in the morning and tell him that there had been a minor problem at the Kremlin overnight but she had solved it—then make arrangements to meet him later in the day. Now it seemed her report might not be so satisfactory.

Carl pulled up at the main entrance. "Wait here," Toni said, and sprang out before he could argue. She did not want him in the building if she could avoid it. She ran up the steps between the stone lions and pushed through the door. She was surprised to see no one at the reception desk.

She hesitated. One of the guards might be on patrol, but they should not both have gone. They could be anywhere in the building—and the door was unguarded.

She headed for the control room. The monitors would show where the guards were.

She was astonished to find the control room empty.

Her heart seemed to go cold. This was very bad. Four guards missing—this was not just a divergence from procedure. Something was wrong.

She looked again at the monitors. They all showed empty rooms. If four guards were in the building, one of them should appear on a monitor within seconds. But there was no movement anywhere.

Then something caught her eye. She looked more closely at the feed from BSL4.

The dateline said December 24. She checked her watch. It was after one o'clock in the morning. Today was Christmas Day, December 25. She was looking at old pictures. Someone had tampered with the feed.

She sat at the workstation and accessed the program. In three minutes she established that all the monitors covering BSL4 were showing yesterday's footage. She corrected them and looked at the screens.

In the lobby outside the changing rooms, four people were sitting on the floor. She stared at the monitor, horrified. Please, God, she thought, don't let them be dead.

One moved.

She looked more closely. They were guards, all in dark uniforms; and their hands were behind their backs, as if they were tied up.

"No, no!" she said aloud.

But there was no escaping from the dismal conclusion that the Kremlin had been raided.

She felt doomed. First Michael Ross, now this. Where had she gone wrong? She had done all she could to make this place secure—and she had failed utterly. She had let Stanley down.

She turned for the door, her first instinct being to rush to BSL4 and untie the captives. Then her police training reasserted itself. Stop, assess the situation, plan the response. Whoever had done this could still be in the building, though her guess was that the villains were the Hibernian Telecom repairmen who had just left. What was her most important task? To make sure she was not the only person who knew about this.

She picked up the phone on the desk. It was dead, of course. The fault in the phone system was probably part of whatever was going on. She took her mobile from her pocket and called the police. "This is Toni Gallo, in charge of security at Oxenford Medical. There's been an incident here. Four of my security guards have been attacked."

"Are the perpetrators still on the premises?"

"I don't think so, but I can't be sure."

"Anyone injured?"

"I don't know. As soon as I get off the phone, I'll check—but I wanted to tell you first."

"We'll try to get a patrol car to you—though the roads are terrible." He sounded like an unsure young constable.

Toni tried to impress him with a sense of urgency. "This could be a biohazard incident. A young man died yesterday of a virus that escaped from here."

"We'll do our best."

"I believe Frank Hackett is on duty tonight. I don't suppose he's in the building?"

"He's on call."

"I strongly recommend you phone him at home and wake him up and tell him about this."

"I've made a note of your suggestion."

"We have a fault on the phones here, probably caused by the intruders. Please take my mobile number." She read it out. "Ask Frank to call right away."

"I've got the message."

"May I ask your name?"

"P.C. David Reid."

"Thank you, Constable Reid. We'll be waiting for your patrol car." Toni hung up. She felt sure the constable had not grasped the importance of her call, but he would surely pass the information to a superior. Anyway, she did not have time to argue. She hurried out of the control room and ran along the corridor to BSL4. She swiped her pass through the card reader, held her fingertip to the scanner, and went in.

There were Steve, Susan, Don, and Stu, in a row against the wall, bound hand and foot. Susan looked as if she had walked into a tree: her nose was swollen and there was blood on her chin and chest. Don had a nasty abrasion on his forehead.

Toni knelt down and began to untie them. "What the hell happened here?" she said.

1:30 A.M.

THE Hibernian Telecom van was plowing through snow a foot deep. Elton drove at ten miles an hour in high gear to keep from skidding. Thick snowflakes bombarded the vehicle. They formed two wedges at the bottom of the windshield, and they grew steadily, so that the wipers described an ever smaller arc, until Elton could no longer see out and had to stop the van to clear the snow away.

Kit was distraught. He had thought himself involved in a heist that would do no real harm. His father would lose money, but on the other hand Kit would be enabled to repay Harry Mac, a debt that his father should have paid anyway, so there was no real injustice. But the reality was different. There could be only one reason for buying Madoba-2. Someone wanted to kill large numbers of people. Kit had never thought to be guilty of this.

He wondered who Nigel's customer represented:

Japanese fanatics, Muslim fundamentalists, an IRA splinter group, suicidal Palestinians, or a group of paranoid Americans with high-powered rifles living in remote mountain cabins in Montana. It hardly mattered. Whoever got the virus would use it, and crowds of people would die bleeding from their eyes.

But what could he do? If he tried to abort the heist and take the virus samples back to the lab, Nigel would kill him, or let Daisy do it. He thought of opening the van door and jumping out. It was going slowly enough. He might disappear into the blizzard before they could catch him. But then they would still have the virus, and he would still owe Harry a quarter of a million pounds.

He had to see this through to the end. Maybe, when it was all over, he could send an anonymous message to the police, naming Nigel and Daisy, and hope that the virus could be traced before it was used. Or maybe he would be wiser to stick to his plan and vanish. No one would want to start a plague in Lucca.

Maybe the virus would be released on his plane to Italy, and he would pay the penalty himself. There would be justice.

Peering ahead through the snowstorm, he saw an illuminated sign that read "Motel." Elton turned off the road. There was a light over the door, and eight or nine cars in the car park. The place was open. Kit wondered who would spend Christmas at a motel. Hindus, perhaps, and stranded businessmen, and illicit lovers.

Elton pulled up next to a Vauxhall Astra station wagon. "The idea was to ditch the van here," he said. "It's too easily identifiable. We're supposed to go back to the airstrip in that Astra. But I don't know if we're going to make it."

From the back, Daisy said, "You stupid prick, why didn't you bring a Land Rover?"

"Because the Astra is one of the most popular and least noticeable cars in Britain, and the forecast said no snow, you ugly cow."

"Knock it off, you two," Nigel said calmly. He pulled off his wig and glasses. "Take off your disguises. We don't know how soon those guards will be giving descriptions to the police."

The others followed suit.

Elton said, "We could stay here, take rooms, wait it out."

"Dangerous," Nigel replied. "We're only a few miles from the lab."

"If we can't move, the police can't either. As soon as the weather eases, we take off."

"We have an appointment to meet our customer."

"He's not going to fly his helicopter in this muck."

"True."

Kit's mobile rang. He checked his laptop. It was a regular call, not one diverted from the Kremlin system. He picked it up. "Yeah?"

"It's me." Kit recognized the voice of Hamish McKinnon. "I'm on my mobile. I've got to be quick, while Willie's in the toilet."

"What's happening?"

"She arrived just after you left."

"I saw the car."

"She found the other guards tied up and called the police."

"Can they get there, in this weather?"

"They said they'd try. She just came up to the gatehouse and told us to expect them. When they'll get here— Sorry, gotta go." He hung up.

Kit pocketed his phone. "Toni Gallo has found the guards," he announced. "She's called the police, and they're on their way."

"That settles it," Nigel said. "Let's get in the Astra."

1:45 A.M.

AS Craig slipped his hand under the hem of Sophie's sweater, he heard steps. He broke the clinch and looked around.

His sister was coming down from the hayloft in her nightdress. "I feel a bit strange," she said, and crossed the room to the bathroom.

Thwarted, Craig turned his attention to the film on TV. The old witch, transformed into a beautiful girl, was seducing a handsome knight.

Caroline emerged, saying, "That bathroom smells of puke." She climbed the ladder and went back to bed.

"No privacy here," Sophie said in a low voice.

"Like trying to make love in Glasgow Central Station," Craig said, but he kissed her again. This time, she opened her lips and her tongue met his. He was so pleased that he moaned with delight.

He put his hand all the way up inside her sweater and felt her breast. It was small and warm. She was wearing a thin cotton bra. He squeezed gently, and she gave an involuntary groan of pleasure.

Tom's voice piped: "Will you two stop grunting? I can't sleep!"

They stopped kissing. Craig took his hand out from under her sweater. He was ready to explode with frustration. "I'm sorry about this," he murmured.

Sophie said, "Why don't we go somewhere else?"

"Like, where?"

"How about that attic you showed me earlier?"

Craig was thrilled. They would be completely alone, and no one would disturb them. "Brilliant," he said, and he stood up.

They put on coats and boots, and Sophie pulled on a pink woolly hat with a bobble. It made her look cute and innocent. "A bundle of joy," Craig said.

"What is?"

"You are."

She smiled. Earlier, she would have called him "so boring" for saying something like that. Their relationship had changed. Maybe it was the vodka. But Craig thought the turning point had come in the bathroom, when they had dealt with Tom together. Perhaps Tom, by being a helpless child, had forced them to act like adults. After that, it was hard to revert to being sulky and cool.

Craig would never have guessed that the way to a girl's heart might be cleaning up puke.

He opened the barn door. A cold wind blew a flurry of snow over them like confetti. Craig stepped out quickly, held the door for Sophie, then closed it.

Steepfall looked impossibly romantic. Snow covered the steeply sloping roof, lay in great mounds on the window-sills, and filled the courtyard to the depth of a foot. The lanterns on the surrounding walls had halos of golden light filled with dancing snowflakes. Snow encrusted a wheelbarrow, a stack of firewood, and a garden hose, transforming them into ice sculptures.

Sophie's eyes were wide. "It's a Christmas card," she said.

Craig took her hand. They crossed the courtyard with high steps, like wading birds. They rounded the corner of the house and came to the back door. Craig brushed a layer of snow off the top of a trash can. He stood on it and heaved himself up onto the low roof of the boot lobby.

He looked back. Sophie was hesitating. "Here!" he hissed. He held out his hand.

She grasped it and pulled herself up onto the can. With his other hand, Craig grabbed the edge of the sloping roof, to steady himself, then helped her up beside him. For a moment they lay side by side in the snow, like lovers in bed. Then Craig got to his feet.

He stepped onto the ledge that ran below the loft door, kicked off most of the snow, and opened the big door. Then he returned to Sophie.

She got to her hands and knees but, when she tried to stand, her rubber boots slipped and she fell. She looked scared.

"Hold on to me," Craig said, and pulled her to her feet. What they were doing was not very dangerous, and she was making more of it than she should, but he did not mind, for it gave him a chance to be strong and protective.

Still holding her hand, Craig stood on the ledge. She stepped up beside him and grabbed him around the waist. He would have liked to linger there, with her clinging to him so hard; but he went on, walking sideways along the ledge to the open door, then helped her inside.

He closed the door behind them and turned on the light. This was perfect, Craig thought excitedly. They were alone, in the middle of the night, and nobody would come in to disturb them. They could do anything they liked.

He lay down and looked through the hole in the floor into the kitchen. A single light burned over the door to the boot room. Nellie lay in front of the Aga, head up, ears cocked, listening: she knew he was there. "Go back to sleep," he murmured. Whether she heard him or not, the dog put her head down and closed her eyes.

Sophie was sitting on the old couch, shivering. "My feet are freezing."

"You've got snow in your boots." He knelt in front of her and pulled her Wellingtons off. Her socks were soaked. He took those off, too. Her small white feet felt as if they had been in the fridge. He tried to warm them with his hands. Then, inspired, he unbuttoned his coat, lifted his sweater, and pressed the soles of her feet to his bare chest.

She said, "Oh, my God, that feels so good."

She had often said that to him in his fantasies, he reflected, but not in quite the same circumstances.

2 A.M.

TONI sat in the control room, watching the monitors.

Steve and the guards had related everything that had happened, from when the "repair crew" entered the Great Hall up to the moment that two of them emerged from the BSL4 lab, passed through the little lobby, and vanished—one carrying a slim burgundy leather briefcase. Don had told her, while Steve gave him first aid, how one of the men had tried to stop the violence. The words he had shouted were burned into Toni's brain: *If you want to be empty-handed when we meet the client at ten, just carry on the way you are.*

Clearly, they had come here to steal something from the laboratory, and they had taken it away in that briefcase. Toni had a dreadful feeling she knew what it was.

She was running the BSL4 footage from 12:55 to 1:15. Although the monitors had not shown these images at the time, the computer had stored them. Now she was watching two men inside the lab, wearing biohazard suits.

She gasped when she saw one of them open the door to the little room that contained the vault. He tapped numbers into the keypad—he knew the code! He opened the fridge door; then the other man began to remove samples.

Toni froze the playback.

The camera was placed above the door, and looked over the man's shoulder into the refrigerator. His hands were full of small white boxes. Toni's fingers played over the keyboard, and the black-and-white picture on the monitor was enlarged. She could see the international biohazard symbol on the boxes. He was stealing virus samples. She zoomed in further and ran the image-enhancement program. Slowly, the words on one of the boxes became clear: "Madoba-2."

It was what she had feared, but the confirmation hit her like the cold wind of death. She sat staring at the screen, frozen with dread, her heart sounding in her chest like a funeral bell. Madoba-2 was the most deadly virus imaginable, an infectious agent so terrible that it had to be guarded by multiple layers of security and touched only by highly trained staff in isolation clothing. And it was now in the hands of a gang of thieves who were carrying it around in a damn briefcase.

Their car might crash; they could panic and throw the briefcase away; the virus might fall into the possession of people who did not know what it was—the risks were horrendous. And even if they did not release it by accident, their "client" would do so deliberately. Someone was planning to use the virus to murder people in hundreds and thousands, perhaps to cause a plague that might mow down entire populations.

And they had obtained the murder weapon from her.

In despair, she restarted the footage, and watched with horror while one of the intruders emptied the contents of the vials into a perfume spray marked "Diablerie." That was obviously the delivery mechanism. The ordinary-looking perfume bottle was now a weapon of mass destruction. She watched him carefully double-bag it and place it in the briefcase, bedded in polystyrene packing chips.

She had seen enough. She knew what needed to be done. The police had to gear up for a massive operation—and fast. If they moved quickly, they could still catch the thieves before the virus was handed over to the buyer.

She returned the monitors to their default position and left the control room.

The security guards were in the Great Hall, sitting on the couches normally reserved for visitors, drinking tea, thinking the crisis was over. Toni decided to take a few seconds to regain control. "We have important work to do," she said briskly. "Stu, go to the control room and resume your duties, please. Steve, get behind the desk. Don, stay where you are." Don had a makeshift dressing over the cut on his forehead.

Susan Mackintosh, who had been blackjacked, was lying on a couch used by waiting visitors. The blood had been washed from her face but she was severely bruised. Toni knelt beside her and kissed her forehead. "Poor you," she said. "How do you feel?"

"Pretty groggy."

"I'm so sorry this happened."

Susan smiled weakly. "It was worth it for the kiss."

Toni patted her shoulder. "You're recovering already."

Her mother was sitting next to Don. "That nice boy Steven made me a cup of tea," she said. The puppy sat on spread-out newspaper at her feet. She fed it a piece of biscuit.

"Thanks, Steve," Toni said.

Mother said, "He'd make a nice boyfriend for you."

"He's married," Toni replied.

"That doesn't seem to make much difference, nowadays."

"It does to me." Toni turned to Steve. "Where's Carl Osborne?"

"Men's room."

Toni nodded and took out her phone. It was time to call the police.

She recalled what Steve Tremlett had told her about the duty staff at Inverburn regional headquarters tonight: an inspector, two sergeants, and six constables, plus a superintendent on call. It was nowhere near enough to deal with a crisis of this magnitude. She knew what she would do, if she were in charge. She would call in twenty or thirty officers. She would commandeer snowplows, set up roadblocks, and ready a squad of armed officers to make the arrest. And she would do it fast.

She felt invigorated. The horror of what had happened began to fade from her mind as she concentrated on what had to be done. Action always bucked her up, and police work was the best sort of action.

She got David Reid again. When she identified herself, he said, "We sent you a car, but they turned back. The weather—"

She was horrified. She had thought a police car was on its way. "Are you serious?" she said, raising her voice.

"Have you looked at the roads? There are abandoned cars everywhere. No point in a patrol getting stuck in the snow."

"Christ! What kind of wimps are the police recruiting nowadays?"

"There's no need for that kind of talk, madam."

Toni got herself under control. "You're right. I'm sorry." She recalled, from her training, that when the police response to a crisis went badly amiss, it was often due to wrong identification of the hazard in the first few minutes, when someone inexperienced like P.C. Reid was dealing with the initial report. Her first task was to make sure he had the key information to pass to his superior. "Here's the situation. One: the thieves stole a significant quantity of a virus called Madoba-2 which is lethal to humans, so this is a biohazard emergency."

"Biohazard," he said, obviously writing it down.

"Two: the perpetrators are three men—two white and one black—and a white woman. They're driving a van marked 'Hibernian Telecom.' "

"Can you give me fuller descriptions?"

"I'll get the guard supervisor to call you with that information in a minute—he saw them. I didn't. Three: we have two injured people here, one who has been coshed and the other kicked in the head."

"How serious would you say the injuries are?"

She thought she had already told him that, but he seemed to be asking questions from a list. "The guard who has been coshed should see a doctor."

"Right."

"Four: the intruders were armed."

"What sort of weapons?"

Toni turned to Steve, who was a gun buff. "Did you get a look at their firearms?"

Steve nodded. "Nine-millimeter Browning automatic pistols, all three of them—the kind that take a thirteen-round magazine. They looked like ex-army stock to me." Toni repeated the description to Reid.

"Armed robbery, then," he said.

"Yes—but the important thing is that they can't be far away, and that van is easy to identify. If we move quickly, we can catch them."

"Nobody can move quickly tonight."

"Obviously you need snowplows."

"The police force doesn't have snowplows."

"There must be several in the area; we have to clear the roads most winters."

"Clearing snow from roads is not a police function; it's a local authority responsibility."

Toni was ready to scream with frustration, but she bit her tongue. "Is Frank Hackett there?"

"Superintendent Hackett is not available."

She knew that Frank was on call—Steve had told her. "If you won't wake him up, I will," she said. She broke the connection and dialed his home number. He was a conscientious officer; he would be sleeping by the phone.

He picked it up. "Hackett."

"Toni. Oxenford Medical has been robbed of a quantity of Madoba-2, the virus that killed Michael Ross."

"How did you let that happen?"

It was the question she was asking herself, but it stung when it came from him. She retorted, "If you're so smart, figure out how to catch the thieves before they get away."

"Didn't we send a car out to you an hour ago?"

"It never got here. Your tough coppers saw the snow and got scared."

"Well, if we're stuck, so are our suspects."

"You're not stuck, Frank. You can get here with a snowplow."

"I don't have a snowplow."

"The local council has several—phone them up."

There was a long pause. "I don't think so," he said at last.

Toni could have killed him. Frank enjoyed using his authority negatively. It made him feel powerful. He especially liked defying her—she had always been too assertive for him. How had she lived with him for so long? She curbed the retort that was on the tip of her tongue and said, "What's your thinking, Frank?"

"I can't send unarmed men chasing after a gang with guns. We'll need to assemble our firearms-trained officers, take them to the armory, and get them kitted out with Kevlar vests, guns, and ammunition. That's going to take a couple of hours."

"Meanwhile the thieves are getting away with a virus that could kill thousands!"

"I'll put out an alert for the van."

"They might switch cars. They could have an off-road Jeep parked somewhere."

"They still won't get far."

"What if they have a helicopter?"

"Toni, curb your imagination. There are no thieves with helicopters in Scotland."

These were not local hooligans running off with jewelry or banknotes—but Frank had never really understood biohazards. "Frank, use *your* imagination. These people want to start a plague!"

"Don't tell me how to do the job. You're not a cop anymore."

"Frank—" She stopped. He had broken the connection. "Frank, you're a dumb bastard," she said into the dead phone; then she hung up.

Had he always been this bad? It seemed to her that

when they were living together he was more reasonable. Perhaps she had been a good influence on him. He had certainly been willing to learn from her. She recalled the case of Dick Buchan, a multiple rapist who had refused to tell Frank where the bodies were despite hours of intimidation, shouting, and threats of violence. Toni talked quietly to him about his mother and broke him in twenty minutes. After that, Frank had asked her advice about every major interrogation. But since they split up, he seemed to have regressed.

She frowned at her phone, racking her brains. How was she going to put a bomb under Frank? She had something over him—the Farmer Johnny Kirk story. If the worse came to the worst, she could use that to blackmail him. But first there was one more call she could try. She scrolled through the memory of her mobile and found the home number of Odette Cressy, her friend at Scotland Yard.

The phone was answered after a long wait. "This is Toni," she said. "I'm sorry to wake you."

Odette spoke to someone else. "Sorry, sweetheart, it's work."

Toni was surprised. "I didn't expect you to be with someone."

"It's just Santa Claus. What's new?"

Toni told her.

Odette said, "Jesus Christ, this is what we were afraid of."

"I can't believe I let it happen."

"Is there anything that might give us a hint about when and how they plan to use it?"

"Two things," Toni said. "One: they didn't just steal the stuff—they poured it into a perfume sprayer. It's ready to use. The virus can be released in any crowded place—at a cinema, on a plane, in Harrods. No one would know it was happening."

"A perfume spray?"

"Diablerie."

"Well done—at least we know what we're looking for. What else?"

"A guard heard them talk about meeting the client at ten."

"At ten. They're working fast."

"Exactly. If they deliver the stuff to their customer by ten o'clock this morning, it could be in London tonight. They could release it in the Albert Hall tomorrow."

"Good work, Toni. My God, I wish you'd never left the police."

Toni began to feel more cheerful. "Thanks."

"Anything else?"

"They turned north when they left here—I saw their van. But there's a blizzard, and the roads are becoming impassable. So they probably aren't far from where I'm standing."

"That means we have a chance of catching them before they deliver the goods."

"Yes—but I haven't been able to persuade the local police of the urgency."

"Leave that to me. Terrorism comes under the Cabinet Office. Your hometown boys are about to get a phone call from Number Ten Downing Street. What do you need—helicopters? HMS *Gannet* is an hour away from you."

"Put them on standby. I don't think helicopters can fly in this blizzard and, if they could, the crew wouldn't be able to see what's on the ground. What I need is a snowplow. They should clear the road from Inverburn to here, and the police should make this their base. Then they can start looking for the fugitives."

"I'll make sure it happens. Keep calling me, okay?"

"Thanks, Odette." Toni hung up.

She turned around. Carl Osborne stood immediately behind her, making notes.

2:30 A.M.

ELTON drove the Vauxhall Astra station wagon slowly, plowing through more than a foot of soft, fresh snow. Nigel sat beside him, clutching the burgundy leather briefcase with its deadly contents. Kit was in the back with Daisy. He kept glancing over Nigel's shoulder at the briefcase, imagining a car crash in which the briefcase was crushed and the bottle smashed, and the liquid was sprayed into the air like poisoned champagne to kill them all.

He was maddened with impatience as their speed dropped to bicycle pace. He wanted to get to the airfield as fast as possible and put the briefcase in a safe place. Every minute they spent on the open road was dangerous.

But he was not sure they would get there. After leaving the car park of the Dew Drop Inn, they had not seen another moving vehicle. Every mile or so, they passed an abandoned car or truck, some at the side of the road and some right in the middle. One was a police Range Rover on its side.

Suddenly a man stepped into the headlights, waving frantically. He wore a business suit and tie, and had no coat or hat. Elton glanced at Nigel, who murmured, "Don't even dream of stopping." Elton drove straight at the man, who dived out of the way at the last moment. As they swept by, Kit glimpsed a woman in a cocktail dress, hugging a thin shawl around her shoulders, standing beside a big Bentley, looking desperate.

They passed the turning for Steepfall, and Kit wished he were a boy again, lying in bed at his father's house, knowing nothing about viruses or computers or the odds at blackjack.

The snow became so heavy that little was visible through the windshield but whiteness. Elton was almost blind, steering by guesswork, optimism, and glances out of the side windows. Their speed dropped to the pace of a run, then a brisk walk. Kit longed for a more suitable car. In his father's Toyota Land Cruiser Amazon, parked only a tantalizing couple of miles from where they were right now, they would have had a better chance.

On a hill, the tires began to slip in the snow. The car gradually lost forward momentum. It came to a stop and then, to Kit's horror, began to slide back. Elton tried braking, but that only made the skid faster. He turned the steering wheel. The back swerved left. Elton spun the wheel in the opposite direction, and the car came to rest slewed at an angle across the road.

Nigel cursed.

Daisy leaned forward and said to Elton, "What did you do that for, you pillock?"

Elton said, "Get out and push, Daisy."

"Screw you."

"I mean it," he said. "The brow of the hill is only a few yards away. I could make it, if someone would give the car a push."

Nigel said, "We'll all push."

Nigel, Daisy, and Kit got out. The cold was bitter, and the snowflakes stung Kit's eyes. They got behind the car and leaned on it. Only Daisy had gloves. The metal was bitingly cold on Kit's bare hands. Elton let the clutch out slowly, and they took the strain. Kit's feet were soaking wet in seconds. But the tires bit. Elton pulled away from them and drove to the top of the hill.

They trudged up the slope, slipping in the snow, panting with the effort, shivering. Were they going to do this on every hill for the next ten miles?

The same thought had occurred to Nigel. When they got back into the car, he said to Elton, "Is this car going to get us there?"

"We might be all right on this road," Elton said. "But there's three or four miles of country lane before you get to the airfield."

Kit made up his mind. He said, "I know where there's a sport-utility vehicle with four-wheel drive—a Toyota Land Cruiser."

Daisy said, "We could get stuck in that—remember the police Range Rover we passed?"

Nigel said, "It has to be better than an Astra. Where is this car?"

"At my father's house. To be exact, it's in his garage, the door to which is not quite visible from the house."

"How far?"

"A mile back along this road, then another mile down a side turning."

"What are you suggesting?"

"We park in the woods near the house, borrow the Land Cruiser, and drive to the airfield. Afterward, Elton brings the Land Cruiser back and takes the Astra."

"By then it will be daylight. What if someone sees him putting the car back in your father's garage?"

"I don't know. I'll have to make up a story, but it can't be worse than getting stuck here."

Nigel said, "Has anyone got a better idea?"

No one did.

Elton turned the car around and went back down the hill in low gear. After a few minutes, Kit said, "Take that side road."

Elton pulled up. "No way," he said. "Look at the snow down that lane—it's eighteen inches thick, and there's been no traffic on it for hours. We won't get fifty yards."

Kit had the panicky feeling he got when losing at blackjack, that a higher power was dealing him all the wrong cards.

Nigel said, "How far are we from your father's house?"

"A bit—" Kit swallowed. "A bit less than a mile."

Daisy said, "It's a long way in this fucking weather."

"The alternative," Nigel said, "is to wait here until a vehicle comes along, then hijack it."

"We'll wait a bloody long time," Elton said. "We haven't seen a moving car on this road since we left the laboratory."

Kit said, "You three could wait here while I go and get the Land Cruiser."

Nigel shook his head. "Something might happen to you. You could get stuck in the snow, and we wouldn't be able to find you. Better to stay together."

There was another reason, Kit guessed: Nigel did not trust Kit alone. He probably feared that Kit might have second thoughts and call the police. Nothing was further from Kit's mind—but Nigel might not feel sure of that.

There was a long silence. They sat still, reluctant to leave the warmth that blasted from the car's heater. Then Elton turned off the engine and they got out.

Nigel held on tightly to the briefcase. That was the reason they were all going through this. Kit was carrying his laptop. He might still need to intercept calls to and from the Kremlin. Elton found a flashlight in the glove compartment and gave it to Kit. "You're leading the way," he said.

Without further discussion, Kit headed off, plowing through snow up to his knees. He heard grunts and curses from the others, but he did not look back. They would keep up with him or get left behind.

It was painfully cold. None of them was dressed for this. They had expected to be indoors or in cars. Nigel had a sports jacket, Elton a raincoat, and Daisy a leather jacket. Kit was the most warmly dressed, in his Puffa jacket. Kit wore Timberlands and Daisy had motorcycle boots, but Nigel and Elton wore ordinary shoes.

Soon Kit was shivering. His hands hurt, though he tried to keep them stuffed in his coat pockets. The snow soaked his jeans up to the knees and melted into his boots. His ears and his nose seemed frozen.

The familiar lane, along which he had walked and bicycled a thousand times in his boyhood, was buried out of sight, and he quickly began to feel confused about where he was. This was Scottish moorland, and no hedge or wall marked the edge of the road, as it would have in other parts of Britain. The land on either side was uncultivated, and no one had ever seen any reason to fence it off.

He felt he might have veered from the road. He stopped, and with his bare hands dug down into the snow.

"What now?" Nigel said bad-temperedly.

"Just a minute." Kit found frozen turf. That meant he had strayed from the paved road. But which way? He blew on his icy hands, trying to warm them. The land to his right seemed to slope up. He guessed the road was that way. He trudged a few yards in that direction, then dug down again. This time he found tarmac. "This way," he said with more confidence than he felt.

In time, the melted snow that had soaked his jeans and socks began to freeze again, so that he had ice next to his skin. When they had been walking for half an hour, he had a feeling he was going around in a circle. His sense of direction failed. On a normal night, the lights outside the house should have been visible in the distance, but tonight nothing shone through the snowfall to give him a beacon. There was no sound or smell of the sea: it might have been fifty miles away. He realized that if they got lost they would die of exposure. He felt truly frightened.

The others followed him in exhausted silence. Even Daisy stopped bitching. They were breathless and shivering, and had no energy to complain.

At last Kit sensed a deeper darkness around him. The snow seemed to fall less heavily. He almost bumped into the thick trunk of a big tree. He had reached the woods near the house. He felt so relieved that he wanted to kneel down and give thanks. From this point on, he could find the way.

As he followed the winding track through the trees, he could hear someone's teeth chattering like a drumroll. He hoped it was Daisy.

He had lost all feeling in his fingers and toes, but he could still move his legs. The snow was not quite so thick on the ground, here in the shelter of the trees, and he was able to walk faster. A faint glow ahead told him he was approaching the lights of the house. At last he emerged from the woods. He headed for the light and came to the garage.

The big doors were closed, but there was a side door that was never locked. Kit found it and went inside. The other three followed. "Thank God," Elton said grimly. "I thought I was going to die in sodding Scotland."

Kit shone his flashlight. Here was his father's blue Ferrari, voluptuously curved, parked very close to the wall. Next to it was Luke's dirty white Ford Mondeo. That was surprising: Luke normally drove himself and Lori home in it at the end of the evening. Had they stayed the night, or . . . ?

He shone his flashlight at the far end of the garage, where the Toyota Land Cruiser Amazon was usually parked.

The bay was empty.

Kit felt like crying.

He realized immediately what had happened. Luke and Lori lived in a cottage at the end of a rough road more than a mile away. Because of the weather, Stanley had let them take the four-wheel-drive car. They had left behind the Ford, which was no better in the snow than the Astra.

"Oh, shit," said Kit.

Nigel said, "Where's the Toyota?"

"It's not here," Kit said. "Jesus Christ, now we're in trouble."

3:30 A.M.

CARL OSBORNE was speaking into his mobile phone. "Is anyone on the news desk yet? Good—put me through."

Toni crossed the Great Hall to where Carl sat. "Wait, please."

He put his hand over the phone. "What?"

"Please hang up and listen to me. Just for a moment."

He said into the phone: "Get ready to do a voice record—I'll get back to you in a couple of minutes." He pressed the HANG-UP button and looked expectantly at Toni.

She felt desperate. Carl could do untold damage with a scaremongering report. She hated to plead, but she had to try to stop him. "This could finish me," she said. "I let Michael Ross steal a rabbit, and now I've allowed a gang to get away with samples of the virus itself."

"Sorry, Toni, but it's a tough old world."

"This could ruin the company, too," she persisted. She was being more candid than she liked, but she had to do it. "Bad publicity might frighten our . . . investors."

Carl did not miss a trick. "You mean the Americans."

"It doesn't matter who. The point is that the company could be destroyed." And so could Stanley, she thought, but she did not say it. She was trying to sound reasonable and unemotional, but her voice was close to cracking. "They don't deserve it!"

"You mean your beloved Professor Oxenford doesn't deserve it."

"All he's doing is trying to find cures for human illnesses, for Christ's sake!"

"And make money at the same time."

"As you do, when you bring the truth to the Scottish television audience."

He stared at her, not sure if she was being sarcastic. Then he shook his head. "A story is a story. Besides, it's sure to come out. If I don't do it, someone else will."

"I know." She looked out of the windows of the Great Hall. The weather showed no sign of easing. At best, there might be some improvement with daylight. "Just give me three hours," she said. "File at seven."

"What difference will that make?"

Possibly none at all, she thought, but it was her only chance. "Maybe by then we'll be able to say that the police have caught the gang, or at least that they're on the trail and expect to arrest them at any moment." Perhaps the company, and Stanley, could survive the crisis if it were resolved quickly.

"No deal. Someone else could get the story in the meantime. As soon as the police know, it's out there. I can't take that risk." He dialed.

Toni stared at him. The truth was bad enough. Seen through the distorting lens of tabloid television, the story would be catastrophic.

"Record this," Carl said into his mobile. "You can run it with a still photo of me holding a phone. Ready?"

Toni wanted to kill him.

"I'm speaking from the premises of Oxenford Medical, where the second biosecurity incident in two days has hit this Scottish pharmaceutical company."

Could she stop him? She had to try. She looked around. Steve was behind the desk. Susan was lying down, looking pale, but Don was upright. Her mother was asleep. So was the puppy. She had two men to help her.

"Excuse me," she said to Carl.

He tried to ignore her. "Samples of a deadly virus, Madoba-2—"

Toni put her hand over his phone. "I'm sorry. You can't use that here."

He turned away and tried to continue. "Samples of a deadly—"

She crowded him and again put her hand between his phone and his mouth. "Steve! Don! Over here, now!"

Carl said into the phone, "They're trying to stop me filing a report. Are you recording this?"

Toni spoke loud enough for the phone to pick up her words. "Mobile phones may interfere with delicate electronic equipment operating in the laboratories, so they may not be used here." It was untrue, but it would serve as a pretext. "Please turn it off."

He held it away from her and said loudly, "Get off me!"

Toni nodded at Steve, who snatched the phone from Carl's hand and turned it off.

"You can't do this!" Carl said.

"Of course I can. You're a visitor here, and I'm in charge of security."

"Bullshit—security has nothing to do with it."

"Say what you like. I make the rules."

"Then I'll go outside."

"You'll freeze to death."

"You can't stop me leaving."

Toni shrugged. "True. But I'm not giving you back your phone."

"You're stealing it."

"Confiscating it for security reasons. We'll mail it to you."

"I'll find a pay phone."

"Good luck." There was not a public phone within five miles.

Carl pulled on his coat and went out. Toni and Steve watched him through the windows. He got into his car and started the engine. He got out again and scraped several inches of snow off the windshield. The wipers began to operate. Carl got in and pulled away.

Steve said, "He left the dog behind."

The snowfall had eased a little. Toni cursed under her breath. Surely the weather was not going to improve just at the wrong moment?

A mound of snow grew in front of the Jaguar as it climbed the rise. A hundred yards from the gate, it stopped.

Steve smiled. "I didn't think he'd get far."

The car's interior light came on. Toni frowned, worried.

Steve said, "Maybe he's going to sulk out there, engine turning over, heater on full blast, until he runs out of petrol."

Toni peered through the snowstorm, trying to see better.

"What's he doing?" Steve said. "Looks like he's talking to himself."

Toni realized what was happening, and her heart sank. "Shit," she said. "He is talking—but not to himself."

"What?"

"He has another phone in the car. He's a reporter. He has backup equipment. Hell, I never thought of that."

"Shall I run out there and stop him?"

"Too late now. By the time you get there, he'll have said enough. Damn." Nothing was going right. She felt like giving up, walking away and finding a darkened room and lying down and closing her eyes. But instead she pulled herself together. "When he comes back in, just sneak outside and see whether he's left the keys in the ignition. If he has, take them—then at least he won't be able to phone again."

"Okay."

Her mobile rang and she picked up. "Toni Gallo."

"This is Odette." She sounded shaken.

"What's happened?"

"Fresh intelligence. A terrorist group called Scimitar has been actively shopping for Madoba-2."

"Scimitar? An Arab group?"

"Sounds like it, though we're not sure—the name might be intentionally misleading. But we think your thieves are working for them."

"My God. Do you know anything else?"

"They aim to release it tomorrow, Boxing Day, at a major public location somewhere in Britain."

Toni gasped. She and Odette had speculated that this might be so, but the confirmation was shocking. People stayed at home on Christmas Day, then went out on Boxing Day. All over Britain, families would go to soccer matches, horse races, cinemas and theaters and bowling alleys. Many would catch flights to ski resorts and Caribbean beaches. The opportunities were endless. "But where?" Toni said. "What event?"

"We don't know. So we have to stop these thieves. The local police are on their way to you with a snowplow."

"That's great!" Toni's spirits lifted. If the thieves could be caught, everything would change. Not only would the virus be recaptured and the danger averted, but Oxenford Medical would not look so bad in the press, and Stanley would be saved.

Odette went on: "I've also alerted your neighboring police forces, plus Glasgow; but Inverburn is where the action will be, I think. The guy in charge there is called Frank Hackett. The name rang a bell—he's not your ex, is he?"

"Yes. That was part of the problem. He likes to say no to me."

"Well, you'll find him a chastened man. He's had a phone call from the Chancellor of the Duchy of Lancaster. Sounds comical, doesn't it? But he's in charge of the Cabinet Office briefing room, which we call COBRA. In other words, he's the antiterrorism supremo. Your ex must have jumped out of his bed as if it was on fire."

"Don't waste your sympathy, he doesn't deserve it."

"Since then, he's heard from my boss, another life-enhancing experience. The poor sod is on his way to you with a snowplow."

"I'd rather have the snowplow without Frank."

"He's had a hard time. Be nice to him."

"Yeah, right," said Toni.

3:45 A.M.

DAISY was shivering so much she could hardly hold the ladder. Elton climbed the rungs, grasping a pair of garden shears in one frozen hand. The exterior lamps shone through the filter of falling snow. Kit watched from the garage door, his teeth chattering. Nigel was in the garage, arms wrapped around the burgundy leather briefcase.

The ladder was propped up against the side of Steepfall. Telephone wires emerged at the corner of the house and ran at roof height to the garage. From there, Kit knew, they connected with an underground pipe that ran to the main road. Severing the cables here would cut off the entire property from telephone contact. It was just a precaution, but Nigel had insisted, and Kit had found a ladder and shears in the garage.

Kit felt as if he were in a nightmare. He had known that tonight's work would be dangerous, but in his worst moments he had never anticipated that he would be standing outside his family home while a gangster cut the phone lines and a master thief clutched a case containing a virus that could kill them all.

Elton took his left hand off the ladder, balancing cautiously, and held the shears in both hands. He leaned forward, caught a cable between the blades, pressed the handles together, and dropped the shears.

They landed points-down in the snow six inches from Daisy, who let out a yell of shock.

"Hush!" Kit said in a stage whisper.

"He could have killed me!" Daisy protested.

"You'll wake everyone!"

Elton came down the ladder, retrieved the shears, and climbed up again.

They had to go to Luke and Lori's cottage and take the Toyota Land Cruiser, but Kit knew they could not go immediately. They were nearly falling down with exhaustion. Worse, Kit was not sure he could find Luke's place. He had almost lost his way looking for Steepfall. The snow was falling as hard as ever. If they tried to go on now, they would get lost or die of exposure or both. They had to wait until the blizzard eased, or until daylight gave them a better chance of finding their way. And, to make absolutely sure no one could find out that they were here, they were cutting off the phones.

This time, Elton succeeded in snipping the lines. As he came down the ladder, Kit picked up the loose cable ends, twisted them into a bundle, and draped them against the garage wall where they were less conspicuous.

Elton carried the ladder into the garage and dropped it. It clanged on the concrete floor. "Try not to make so much noise!" Kit said.

Nigel looked around the bare stone walls of the converted stable. "We can't stay here."

Kit said, "Better in here than out there."

"We're cold and wet and there's no heat. We could die."

Elton said, "Bloody right."

"We'll run the engines of the cars," Kit said. "That will warm the place."

"Don't be stupid," Elton said. "The fumes will kill us long before the heat warms us."

"We could drive the Ford outside and sit in it."

Daisy said, "Fuck that. I want a cup of tea and hot food and a dram. I'm going in the house."

"No!" The thought of these three in his family home filled Kit with horror. It would be like taking mad dogs home. And what about the briefcase with its virulent contents? How could he let them carry that into the kitchen?

Elton said, "I'm with her. Let's go into the house."

Kit wished bitterly that he had not told them how to cut off the phones. "But how would I explain you?"

"They'll all be asleep."

"And if it's still snowing when they get up?"

Nigel said, "Here's what you say. You don't know us. You met us on the road. Our car is stuck in a snowdrift a couple of miles away. You took pity on us and brought us back here."

"They aren't supposed to know I've left the house!"

"Say you went out for a drink."

Elton said, "Or to meet a girl."

Daisy said, "How old are you, anyway? You need to ask Daddy before you can go out at night?"

It infuriated Kit to be condescended to by a thug like Daisy. "It's a question of what they'll believe, you brain-dead gorgon. Who would be daft enough to go out in a snowstorm and drive miles for a drink, when there's plenty of booze in the house anyway?"

She retorted, "Someone daft enough to lose a quarter of a million pounds at blackjack."

"You'll think of a plausible story, Kit," said Nigel. "Let's get inside, before our fucking feet drop off."

"You left your disguises in the van. My family will see your real faces."

"It doesn't matter. We're just unfortunate stranded motorists. There'll be hundreds like us. It will be on the news. Your family won't connect us with the people who robbed the laboratory."

"I don't like it," Kit said. He was scared of defying these three criminals, but desperate enough to do it. "I'm not taking you into the house."

"We're not asking your permission," Nigel said contemptuously. "If you don't show us the way, we'll find it ourselves."

What they did not understand, Kit thought despairingly, was that his family were all very smart. Nigel, Elton, and Daisy would have difficulty fooling them. "You don't *look* like a group of innocent people who got stranded."

"What do you mean?" Nigel said.

"You're not the average Scots family," Kit told him. "You're a Londoner, Elton's black, and Daisy's a bloody psychopath. My sisters may notice that."

"We'll just be polite and not say much."

"Say nothing at all would be the best plan. Any rough stuff and the game will be up."

"Of course. We want them to think we're harmless."

"Especially Daisy." Kit turned to her. "You keep your hands to yourself."

Nigel backed Kit. "Yeah, Daisy, try not to give the bloody game away. Act like a girl, just for a couple of hours, okay?"

She said, "Yeah, yeah," and turned away.

Kit realized that at some point in the argument he had given in. "Shit," he said. "Just remember that you need me to show you where the Land Cruiser is. If any harm comes to my family, you can forget it."

With a fatalistic feeling that he was helpless to stop himself hurtling toward disaster, he led them around the house to the back door. It was unlocked, as always. As he opened it, he said, "All right, Nellie, it's me," so that the dog would not bark.

When he entered the boot lobby, warm air washed over him like a blessing. Behind him, he heard Elton say, "Oh, God, that's better."

Kit turned and hissed, "Keep your voices down, please!" He felt like a schoolteacher trying to quiet heedless children in a museum. "The longer they stay asleep, the easier it will be for us—don't you see that?" He led them through the lobby and into the kitchen. "Be nice, Nellie," he said quietly. "These are friends."

Nigel patted Nellie, and the dog wagged her tail. They took off their wet coats. Nigel stood the briefcase on the kitchen table and said, "Put the kettle on, Kit."

Kit put down his laptop and turned on the small TV set on the kitchen counter. He found a news channel, then filled the kettle.

A pretty newsreader said, "An unexpected change in the prevailing wind has brought a surprise blizzard to most of Scotland."

Daisy said, "You can say that again."

The newsreader spoke in a seductive voice, as if inviting the viewer back to her place for a nightcap. "In some parts, more than twelve inches of snow fell in as many hours."

"I'll give you twelve inches in some parts," said Elton.

They were relaxing, Kit saw with trepidation. He felt even more tense than before.

The newsreader told of car accidents, blocked roads, and abandoned vehicles. "To hell with all that," Kit said irately. "When's it going to stop?"

"Make the tea, Kit," said Nigel.

Kit put out mugs, a sugar bowl, and a jug of milk. Nigel, Daisy, and Elton sat around the scrubbed-pine table, just like family. The kettle boiled. Kit made a pot of tea and a *cafetière* of coffee.

The television picture changed, and a weather forecaster appeared in front of a chart. They all went quiet. "Tomorrow morning the blizzard will die away as quickly as it came," he said.

"Yes!" Nigel said triumphantly.

"The thaw will follow before midday."

"Be precise!" Nigel said in exasperation. "What time before midday?"

"We can still make it," Elton said. He poured tea and added milk and sugar.

Kit shared his optimism. "We should leave at first light," he said. Seeing the way ahead cheered him up.

"I hope we can," Nigel said.

Elton sipped his tea. "By the cringe, that's better. Lazarus must have felt like this when he was raised from the dead."

Daisy stood up. She opened the door to the dining room and peered into the gloom. "What room is this?"

Kit said, "Where do you think you're going?"

"I need a shot of booze in this tea." She turned on the light and went in. A moment later, she made a triumphant noise, and Kit heard her opening the cocktail cabinet.

Kit's father walked into the kitchen from the hall,

wearing gray pajamas and a black cashmere dressing gown. "Good morning," he said. "What's all this?"

"Hello, Daddy," Kit said. "Let me explain."

Daisy came in from the dining room holding a full bottle of Glenmorangie in her gloved hand.

Stanley raised his eyebrows at her. "Do you want a glass of whisky?" he said.

"No, thanks," she replied. "I've got a whole bottle here."

4:15 A.M.

TONI called Stanley at home as soon as she had a spare moment. There was nothing he could do, but he would want to know what was happening. And she did not want him to learn about the break-in from the news.

It was a conversation she dreaded. She had to tell him that she was responsible for a catastrophe that could ruin his life. How would he feel about her after that?

She dialed his number and got the "disconnected" tone. His phone must be out of order. Perhaps the snow had brought down the lines. She was relieved not to have to give him the dreadful news.

He did not carry a mobile, but there was a phone in his Ferrari. She dialed that and left a message. "Stanley, this is Toni. Bad news—a break-in at the lab. Please call my mobile as soon as you can." He might not get the message until it was too late, but at least she had tried.

She stared impatiently out of the windows of the

Great Hall. Where were the police with their snow-plow? They would be coming from the south, from Inverburn, on the main road. She guessed that the plow traveled at about fifteen miles per hour, depending on the depth of snow it had to clear. The trip should take twenty or thirty minutes. It should be here by now. Come on, come on!

She hoped it would leave here almost immediately, and get on the northward track of the Hibernian Telecom van. The van would be easy to spot, with the name in large white letters on a dark background.

But the thieves might have thought of that, she realized suddenly. They had probably planned to switch vehicles soon after leaving the Kremlin. That was how she would have done it. She would have picked a nondescript car, something like a Ford Fiesta that looked like a dozen other models, and left it in a car park, outside a supermarket or a railway station. The thieves would drive straight to the car park and be in a completely different vehicle a few minutes after leaving the scene of the crime.

The thought dismayed her. How then would the police identify the thieves? They would have to check every car and see whether the occupants were three men and a woman.

She wondered agitatedly whether there was anything she could do to hurry the process. Assuming the gang had switched vehicles somewhere near here, what were the possibilities? They needed a location where a vehicle might be parked for several hours without attracting attention. There were no railway stations or supermarkets in the vicinity. What was there? She went to the reception desk and got a notepad and ballpoint pen. She made a list:

- *Inverburn Golf Club*
- *Dew Drop Inn*
- *Happy Eater*
- *Greenfingers Garden Centre*
- *Scottish Smoked Fish Products*
- *Williams Press (Printing & Publishing)*

She did not want Carl Osborne to know what she was doing. Carl had returned from his car to the warmth of the hall, and was listening to everything. Unknown to him, he could no longer phone from the car—Steve had sneaked out and taken the keys from the ignition—but all the same, Toni was taking no chances.

She spoke quietly to Steve. "We're going to do some detective work." She tore her sheet of paper into two and gave half to Steve. "Ring these places. Everything's closed, of course, but you should find a caretaker or security guard. Tell them we've had a robbery, but don't say what's missing. Say the getaway vehicle may have been abandoned on their premises. Ask if they can see a Hibernian Telecom van outside."

Steve nodded. "Smart thinking—maybe we can get on their trail and give the police a head start."

"Exactly. But don't use the desk phone, I don't want Carl to hear. Go to the far end of the hall, where he can't eavesdrop. Use the mobile you took from him."

Toni moved well away from Carl and took out her mobile. She called information and got the number for the golf club. She dialed and waited. The phone rang for more than a minute. Then a sleepy voice answered: "Yes? Golf club. Hello?"

Toni introduced herself and told the story. "I'm trying to locate a van with 'Hibernian Telecom' on its side. Is it in your car park?"

"Oh, I get you, the getaway vehicle, aye."

Her heart missed a beat. "It's there?"

"No, at least it wasn't when I came on duty. There's a couple of cars here, mind you, left by gentlemen who found themselves reluctant to drive by the end of lunch yesterday—do you know what I mean?"

"When did you come on duty?"

"Seven o'clock in the evening."

"Could a van have parked there since then? Perhaps at about two o'clock this morning?"

"Well, maybe . . . I've no way of telling."

"Could you have a look?"

"Aye, I could look!" He spoke as if it were an idea of startling originality. "Hold the line. I'll just be a minute." There was a knock as he put the phone down.

Toni waited. Footsteps receded and returned.

"No, I don't think there's a van out there."

"Okay."

"The cars are all covered in snow, mind you, so you can't see them properly. I'm not even sure which is mine!"

"Yes, thank you."

"But a van, you see, would be higher than the rest, wouldn't it? So it would stand out. No, there's no van there."

"You've been very helpful. I appreciate it."

"What did they steal?"

Toni pretended not to hear the question, and hung up. Steve was talking and clearly had not yet struck gold. She dialed the Dew Drop Inn.

The phone was answered by a cheerful young man. "Vincent speaking, how may I help you?"

Toni thought he sounded like the kind of hotel employee who seems eager to please until you actually ask for something. She went through her routine again.

"There are lots of vehicles in our car park—we're open over Christmas," Vincent told her. "I'm looking at the closed-circuit television monitor, but I don't see a van. Unfortunately, the camera doesn't cover the entire car park."

"Would you mind going to the window and having a good look? It's really important."

"I'm quite busy, actually."

At this time of night? Toni did not voice the thought. She adopted a sweetly considerate tone and said, "It will save the police making a trip to interview you, you see."

That worked. He did not want his quiet night shift disrupted by squad cars and detectives. "Just hold on." He went away and came back.

"Yes, it's here," he said.

"Really?" Toni was incredulous. It seemed a long time since she had enjoyed a piece of luck.

"Ford Transit van, blue, with 'Hibernian Telecom' in large white letters on the side. It can't have been there long, because it's not under as much snow as the rest of the cars—that's how come I can see the lettering."

"That's tremendously helpful, thank you. I don't suppose you noticed whether another car is missing—possibly the car they left in?"

"No, sorry."

"Okay—thanks again!" She hung up and looked across at Steve. "I've found the getaway vehicle!"

He nodded toward the window. "And the snow-plow's here."

4:30 A.M.

DAISY drained her cup of tea and filled it up again with whisky.

Kit felt unbearably tense. Nigel and Elton might be able to keep up the pretense of being innocent travelers accidentally stranded, but Daisy was hopeless. She looked like a gangster and acted like a hooligan.

When she put the bottle down on the kitchen table, Stanley picked it up. "Don't get drunk. There's a good girl," he said mildly. He stoppered the bottle.

Daisy was not used to people telling her what to do. Mostly they were too frightened. She looked at Stanley as if she was ready to kill him. He was elegantly vulnerable in his gray pajamas and black robe. Kit waited for the explosion.

"A little whisky makes you feel better, but a lot makes you feel worse," Stanley said. He put the bottle in a cupboard. "My father used to say that, and he was fond of whisky."

Daisy was suppressing her rage. The effort was visible to Kit. He feared what might happen if she should lose it. Then the tension was broken by his sister Miranda, who came in wearing a pink nightgown with a flower pattern.

Stanley said, "Hello, my dear, you're up early."

"I couldn't sleep. I've been on the sleepchair in Kit's old study. Don't ask why." She looked at the strangers. "It's early for Christmas visitors."

"This is my daughter Miranda," Stanley said. "Mandy, meet Nigel, Elton, and Daisy."

A few minutes ago, Kit had introduced them to his father and, before he realized his mistake, he had given their real names.

Miranda nodded to them. "Did Santa bring you?" she said brightly.

Kit explained. "Their car died on the main road near our turnoff. I picked them up. Then my car gave out, too, and we walked the rest of the way here." Would she believe it? And would she ask about the burgundy leather briefcase that stood on the kitchen table like a bomb?

She questioned a different aspect of the story. "I didn't know you'd left the house—where on earth did you go, in the middle of the night, in this weather?"

"Oh, you know." Kit had thought about how he would respond to this question, and now he put on a sheepish grin. "Couldn't sleep, felt lonely, went to look up an old girlfriend in Inverburn."

"Which one? Most of the young women in Inverburn are old girlfriends of yours."

"I don't think you know her." He thought of a name quickly. "Lisa Fremont." He almost bit his tongue. She was a character in a Hitchcock movie.

Miranda did not react to the name. "Was she pleased to see you?"

"She wasn't in."

Miranda turned away and picked up the coffeepot.

Kit wondered whether she believed him. The story he had made up was not really good enough. However, Miranda could not possibly guess *why* he was lying. She would assume he was involved with a woman he didn't want people to know about—probably someone's wife.

While Miranda was pouring coffee, Stanley addressed Nigel. "Where are you from? You don't sound Scots." It seemed like small talk, but Kit knew his father was probing.

Nigel answered in the same relaxed tone. "I live in Surrey, work in London. My office is in Canary Wharf."

"You're in the financial world."

"I source high-tech systems for third-world countries, mainly the Middle East. A young oil sheik wants his own discotheque and doesn't know where to buy the gear, so he comes to me and I solve his problem." It sounded pat.

Miranda brought her coffee to the table and sat opposite Daisy. "What nice gloves," she said. Daisy was wearing expensive-looking light brown suede gloves that were soaking wet. "Why don't you dry them?"

Kit tensed. Any conversation with Daisy was hazardous.

Daisy gave a hostile look, but Miranda did not see it, and persisted. "You need to stuff them, so they'll keep their shape," she said. She took a roll of paper towel from the counter. "Here, use this."

"I'm fine," Daisy muttered angrily.

Miranda raised her eyebrows in surprise. "Have I said something to offend you?"

Kit thought, Oh, God, here it comes.

Nigel stepped in. "Don't be daft, Daisy. You don't want to spoil your gloves." There was an edge of insistence in his voice, making the words sound more like an order than a suggestion. He was as worried as Kit. "Do what the lady says, she's being nice to you."

Once again, Kit waited for the explosion. But, to his surprise, Daisy took off her gloves. Kit was astonished to see that she had small, neat hands. He had never noticed that. The rest of her was brutish: the black eye makeup, the broken nose, the zippered jacket, the boots. But her hands were beautiful, and she obviously knew it, for they were well manicured, with clean nails and a pale pink nail varnish. Kit was bemused. Somewhere inside that monster there was an ordinary girl, he realized. What had happened to her? She had been brought up by Harry Mac—that was what.

Miranda helped her stuff the wet gloves with paper towels. "How are you three connected?" she asked Daisy. Her tone was conventionally polite, as if she were making conversation at a dinner party, but she was probing. Like Stanley, she had no idea how dangerous it was.

Daisy looked panicked. She made Kit think of a schoolgirl being questioned on homework she had forgotten to do. Kit wanted to fill the awkward silence, but it would look odd if he answered for her. After a moment, Nigel spoke. "Daisy's father is an old friend of mine."

That was fine, Kit thought, though Miranda would wonder why Daisy could not have said it herself.

Nigel added, "And Elton works for me."

Miranda smiled at Elton. "Right-hand man?"

"Driver," he replied brusquely. Kit reflected that it was a good thing Nigel was personable—he had to supply enough charm for the three of them.

Stanley said, "Well, I'm sorry the weather has turned out so poorly for your Christmas in Scotland."

Nigel smiled. "If I'd wanted to sunbathe, I would have gone to Barbados."

"You and Daisy's father must be good friends, to spend Christmas together."

Nigel nodded. "We go way back."

It seemed obvious to Kit that Nigel was lying. Was that because he knew the truth? Or was it apparent to Stanley and Miranda, too? Kit could not sit still any longer: the strain was unbearable. He jumped up. "I'm hungry," he said. "Dad, is it okay if I scramble some eggs for everyone?"

"Of course."

"I'll give you a hand," Miranda said. She put sliced bread in the toaster.

Stanley said, "Anyway, I hope the weather improves soon. When were you planning to return to London?"

Kit got a pack of bacon out of the fridge. Was his father suspicious, or merely curious?

"Heading back on Boxing Day," Nigel said.

"A short Christmas visit," Stanley commented, still gently challenging the story.

Nigel shrugged. "Work to do, you know."

"You may have to stay longer than you anticipated. I can't see them clearing the roads by tomorrow."

The thought seemed to make Nigel anxious. He pushed up the sleeve of his pink sweater and looked at his watch.

Kit realized he needed to do something to show he

was not in league with Nigel and the other two. As he began to make breakfast, he resolved not to defend or excuse the strangers. On the contrary, he should question Nigel skeptically, as if he mistrusted the story. He might deflect suspicion from himself by pretending that he, too, was dubious about the strangers.

Before he could put his resolution into practice, Elton suddenly became talkative. "How about your Christmas, Professor?" he said. Kit had introduced his father as Professor Oxenford. "Got your family all around you, it seems. What, two children?"

"Three."

"With husbands and wives, of course."

"My daughters have partners. Kit's single."

"And grandchildren?"

"Yes."

"How many? If you don't mind me asking."

"I don't mind in the least. I have three grandchildren."

"Are all the grandkids here?"

"Yes, and another youngster."

"That's nice for you and Mrs. Oxenford."

"My wife died eighteen months ago, sadly."

"Sorry to hear that."

"Thank you."

What was this interrogation about? Kit asked himself. Elton was smiling and leaning forward, as if his questions were motivated by nothing more than friendly curiosity, but Kit could see that it was a charade, and he wondered anxiously whether that was just as obvious to his father.

Elton had not finished. "This must be a big house, to sleep, what, ten of you?"

"We have some outbuildings."

"Oh, handy." He looked out of the window, although the snow made it difficult to see anything. "Guest cottages, like."

"There's a cottage and a barn."

"Very useful. And staff quarters, I presume."

"Our staff have a cottage a mile or so away. I doubt if we'll see them today."

"Oh. Shame." Elton lapsed into silence again— having carefully established exactly how many people were on the property.

Kit wondered if anyone else had noticed that.

5 A.M.

THE snowplow was a Mercedes truck with a blade hooked to its front attachment plate. It had "Inverburn Plant Hire" on its side and flashing orange lights on its roof, but to Toni it looked like a winged chariot from heaven.

The blade was angled to push the snow to the side of the road. The plow quickly cleared the drive from the gatehouse to the main entrance of the Kremlin, its blade lifting automatically to clear speed bumps. By the time it stopped at the main entrance, Toni had her coat on, ready to go. It was four hours since the thieves had left—but if they had got stuck in the snow, they could still be caught.

The plow was followed by three police cars and an ambulance. The ambulance crew came in first. They took Susan out on a stretcher, though she said she could walk. Don refused to go. "If a Scotsman went to hospital every time he got a kick in the head, the doctors could never cope," he said.

Frank came in wearing a dark suit with a white shirt and a tie. He had even found time to shave, probably in the car. Toni saw the grim expression on his face and realized with dismay that he was spoiling for a fight. No doubt he resented being forced by his superiors to do what Toni wanted. She told herself to be patient and avoid a showdown.

Toni's mother looked up from petting the puppy and said, "Hello, Frank! This is a surprise. Are you and Toni getting back together?"

"Not today," he muttered.

"Shame."

Frank was followed by two detectives carrying large briefcases—a crime-scene team, Toni presumed. Frank nodded to Toni and shook hands with Carl Osborne, but spoke to Steve. "You're the guard supervisor?"

"Aye. Steve Tremlett. You're Frank Hackett. I've met you before."

"I gather four guards were assaulted."

"Me and three others, aye."

"Did all the assaults take place in the same location?"

What was Frank doing? Toni wondered impatiently. Why was he asking trivial questions when they needed to get going right away?

Steve answered, "Susan was attacked in the corridor. I was tripped up in about the same place. Don and Stu were held at gunpoint and tied up in the control room."

"Show me both places, please."

Toni was astonished. "We need to go after these people, Frank. Why don't you leave this to your team?"

"Don't tell me how to do the job," he replied. He looked pleased that she had given him an opportunity to put her down. She groaned inwardly. This was not the time to rerun their domestic conflicts. He turned back to Steve and said, "Lead the way."

Toni suppressed a curse and followed along. So did Carl Osborne.

The detectives put crime-scene tape across the corridor where Steve had been tripped up and Susan had been blackjacked. Then they went to the control room, where Stu was watching the monitors. Frank taped the doorway.

Steve said, "All four of us were tied up and taken inside the BSL4 facility. Not the laboratory itself, just the lobby."

"Which is where I found them," Toni added. "But that was four hours ago—and the perpetrators are getting farther away every minute."

"We'll take a look at that location."

"No, you won't," Toni said. "It's a restricted area. You can see it on monitor nineteen."

"If it's not the actual laboratory, I presume there's no danger."

He was right, but Toni was not going to let him waste more time. "No one is allowed past the door without biohazard training. That's the protocol."

"Hell with your protocol. I'm in charge here."

Toni realized she had inadvertently done what she had vowed to avoid: gone head-to-head with Frank. She tried to sidestep the issue. "I'll take you to the door."

They went to the entrance. Frank looked at the card reader, then said to Steve, "I'm ordering you to give me your pass."

Steve said, "I don't have a pass. Security guards aren't allowed in."

Frank turned to Toni. "Do you have a pass?"

"I've done biohazard training."

"Give me your pass."

She handed it over. Frank waved it at the scanner, then pushed the door. It remained locked. He pointed at the small screen on the wall. "What's that?"

"A fingerprint reader. The pass won't work without the correct fingerprint. It's a system we installed to prevent foolish people getting in with stolen cards."

"It didn't stop the thieves tonight, did it?" Having scored a point, Frank turned on his heel.

Toni followed him. Back in the Great Hall there were two men in yellow high-visibility jackets and rubber boots, smoking. Toni thought at first that they were snowplow operators, but when Frank began to brief them she realized they were police officers. "You check every vehicle you pass," he said. "Radio in the registration number, and we'll find out whether it's stolen or rented. Tell us if there's anyone in the cars. You know what we're looking for—three men and a woman. Whatever you do, don't approach the occupants. These laddies have guns, and you don't, so you're strictly reconnaissance. There's an armed response unit on its way. If we can locate the perpetrators, we'll send them in. Is that clear?"

The two men nodded.

"Go north and take the first turnoff. I think they headed east."

Toni knew that was wrong. She was reluctant to confront Frank again, but she could not let the reconnaissance team go the wrong way. He would be furious, but she had to do it. She said, "The thieves didn't head east."

Frank ignored her. "That takes you to the main road for Glasgow."

Toni said again, "The perpetrators didn't go that way."

The two constables watched the exchange with interest, looking from Frank to Toni and back like spectators at a tennis match.

Frank reddened. "No one asked your opinion, Toni."

"They didn't take that route," she persisted. "They continued north."

"I suppose you reached that conclusion by feminine intuition?"

One of the constables laughed.

Why do you lead with your chin? Toni thought. She said calmly, "The getaway vehicle is in the car park of the Dew Drop Inn, on this road five miles north."

Frank turned redder, embarrassed because she knew something he did not. "And how did you acquire this information?"

"Detective work." I was a better cop than you, and I still am, she thought; but she kept the thought to herself. "I phoned around. Better than intuition." You asked for that, you bastard.

The constable laughed again, then smothered it when Frank glared at him.

Toni added, "The thieves might be at the motel, but more likely they switched cars there and drove on."

Frank suppressed his fury. "Go to the motel," he said to the two constables. "I'll give you further orders when you're on the road. On your way."

They hurried out. At last, Toni thought.

Frank summoned a plainclothes detective from one of the cars and told him to follow the snowplow to the motel, check out the van, and find out whether anyone there had seen anything.

Toni turned her mind to the next step. She wanted to stay in close touch with the police operation. But she had no car. And Mother was still here.

She saw Carl Osborne talking quietly to Frank. Carl pointed at his Jaguar, still stuck halfway up the drive. Frank nodded, and said something to a uniformed officer, who went outside and spoke to the snowplow driver. They were going to free Carl's car, Toni guessed.

Toni addressed Carl. "You're going with the snowplow."

He looked smug. "It's a free country."

"Don't forget to take the puppy."

"I was planning to leave him with you."

"I'm coming with you."

"You're out of your mind."

"I need to get to Stanley's house. It's on this road, five miles beyond the Dew Drop Inn. You can leave me and Mother there." After she had briefed Stanley, she could borrow a car from him, leave Mother at Steepfall, and follow the snowplow.

"You want me to take your mother, too?" Carl said incredulously.

"Yes."

"Forget it."

Toni nodded. "Let me know if you change your mind."

He frowned, suspicious of her ready acceptance of his refusal; but he said no more, and put on his coat.

Steve Tremlett opened his mouth to speak, but Toni discreetly flapped her hand at him in a "Keep quiet" gesture.

Carl went to the door.

Toni said, "Don't forget the puppy."

He picked up the dog and went out to his car.

Toni watched through the windows as the convoy moved off. The snowplow cleared the pile in front of Carl's Jaguar, then climbed the slope to the gatehouse.

One police car followed. Carl sat in his car for a moment, then got out again and returned to the Great Hall.

"Where are my keys?" he said angrily.

Toni smiled sweetly. "Have you changed your mind about taking me?"

Steve jingled the bunch of keys in his pocket.

Carl made a sour face. "Get in the damn car," he said.

5:30 A.M.

MIRANDA felt uneasy about the weird threesome of Nigel, Elton, and Daisy. Were they what they claimed to be? Something about them made her wish she were not wearing her nightdress.

She had had a bad night. Lying uncomfortably on the sleepchair in Kit's old study, she had drifted in and out of consciousness, dreaming of her stupid, shameful affair with Hugo, and waking to feel resentful of Ned for failing to stand up for her once again. He should have been angry with Kit for betraying the secret, but instead he just said that secrets always come out sooner or later. They had acted out a rerun of the quarrel in the car earlier that day. Miranda had hoped this holiday would be the occasion for her family to accept Ned, but she was beginning to think it might be the moment when she rejected him. He was just too weak.

When she heard voices downstairs, she had been relieved, for it meant she could get up. Now she felt perturbed. Did Nigel have no wife, family, or even girl-friend who wanted to see him at Christmas? What about Elton? She was pretty sure Nigel and Elton were not a gay couple: Nigel had looked at her nightdress with the speculative eyes of a man who would like to see underneath it.

Daisy would seem weird in any company. She was the right age to be Elton's girlfriend, but they seemed to dislike each other. So what was she doing with Nigel and his driver?

Nigel was not a friend of Daisy's family, Miranda decided. There was no warmth between them. They were more like people who had to work together even though they did not get on very well. But if they were colleagues, why lie about it?

Her father looked strained, too. She wondered if he was also having suspicious thoughts.

The kitchen filled with delicious smells: frying bacon, fresh coffee, and toast. Cooking was one of the things Kit did well, Miranda mused: his food was always attractively presented. He could make a dish of spaghetti look like a royal feast. Appearances were important to her brother. He could not hold down a job or keep his bank account in credit, but he was always well dressed and drove a cool car, no matter how hard up he was. In his father's eyes, he combined frivolous achievements with grave weaknesses. The only time Stanley had been happy about Kit was when he was in the Winter Olympics.

Now Kit handed each of them a plate with crisp bacon, slices of fresh tomato, scrambled eggs sprinkled with chopped herbs, and triangles of hot buttered toast. The tension in the room eased a little. Perhaps, Miranda thought, that was what Kit had been aiming at. She was not really hungry, but she took a forkful of eggs. He had flavored them with a little Parmesan cheese, and they tasted delightfully tangy.

Kit made conversation. "So, Daisy, what do you do for a living?" He gave her his winning smile. Miranda knew he was only being polite. Kit liked pretty girls, and Daisy was anything but that.

She took a long time to reply. "I work with my father," she said.

"And what's his line?"

"His line?"

"I mean, what type of business does he do?"

She seemed baffled by the question.

Nigel laughed and said, "My old friend Harry has so many things going, it's hard to say what he does."

Kit surprised Miranda by being insistent. In a challenging tone he said to Daisy, "Well, give us an example of one of the things he does, then."

She brightened and, as if struck by inspiration, said, "He's into property." She seemed to be repeating something she had heard.

"Sounds as if he likes owning things."

"Property development."

"I'm never sure what that means, 'property development.' "

It was not like Kit to question people aggressively, Miranda thought. Perhaps he, too, found the guests' account of themselves hard to believe. She felt relieved. This proved that they were strangers. Miranda had feared in the back of her mind that Kit was involved in some kind of shady business with them. You never knew, with him.

There was impatience in Nigel's voice as he said, "Harry buys an old tobacco warehouse, applies for planning permission to turn it into luxury flats, then sells it to a builder at a profit."

Once again, Miranda realized, Nigel was answering for Daisy. Kit seemed to have the same thought, for he said, "And how exactly do you help your father with this work, Daisy? I should think you'd be a good saleswoman."

Daisy looked as if she would be better at evicting sitting tenants. She gave Kit a hostile glare. "I do different things," she said, then tilted up her chin, as if defying him to find fault with her answer.

"And I'm sure you do them with charm and efficiency," Kit said.

Kit's flattery was becoming sarcastic, Miranda thought anxiously. Daisy was not subtle, but she might know when she was being insulted.

The tension spoiled Miranda's breakfast. She had to talk to her father about this. She swallowed, coughed, and pretended to have something stuck in her throat. Coughing, she got up from the table. "Sorry," she spluttered.

Her father snatched up a glass and filled it at the tap.

Still coughing, Miranda left the room. As she intended, her father followed her into the hall. She closed the kitchen door and motioned him into his study. She coughed again, for effect, as they went in.

He offered her the glass, and she waved it away. "I was pretending," she said. "I wanted to talk to you. What do you think about our guests?"

He put the glass down on the green leather top of his desk. "A weird bunch. I wondered if they were shady friends of Kit's, until he started questioning the girl."

"Me, too. They're lying about something, though."

"But what? If they're planning to rob us, they're getting off to a slow start."

"I don't know, but I feel threatened."

"Do you want me to call the police?"

"That might be an overreaction. But I wish *someone* knew these people were in our house."

"Well, let's think—who can we phone?"

"How about Uncle Norman?" Her father's brother, a university librarian, lived in Edinburgh. They loved each other in a distant way, content to meet about once a year.

"Yes. Norman will understand. I'll tell him what's happened, and ask him to phone me in an hour and make sure we're all right."

"Perfect."

Stanley picked up the phone on his desk and put it to his ear. He frowned, replaced the handset, and picked it up again. "No dial tone," he said.

Miranda felt a stab of fear. "Now I *really* want us to call someone."

He tapped the keyboard of his computer. "No e-mail, either. It's probably the weather. Heavy snow sometimes brings down the lines."

"All the same . . ."

"Where's your mobile phone?"

"In the cottage. Don't you have one?"

"Only in the Ferrari."

"Olga must have one."

"No need to wake her." Stanley glanced out of the window. "I'll just throw on a coat over my pajamas and go to the garage."

"Where are the keys?"

"Key cupboard."

The key cupboard was on the wall in the boot lobby. "I'll fetch them for you."

They stepped into the hall. Stanley went to the front door and found his boots. Miranda put her hand on the knob of the kitchen door, then hesitated. She could hear Olga's voice coming from the kitchen. Miranda had not spoken to her sister since the moment last night when Kit had treacherously blurted out the secret. What would she say to Olga, or Olga to her?

She opened the door. Olga was leaning against the kitchen counter, wearing a black silk wrap that reminded Miranda of an advocate's gown. Nigel, Elton, and Daisy sat at the table like a panel. Kit stood behind them, hovering anxiously. Olga was in full courtroom mode, interrogating the strangers across the table. She said to Nigel, "What on earth were you doing out so late?" He might have been a delinquent teenager.

Miranda noticed a rectangular bulge in the pocket of the silk robe: Olga never went anywhere without her phone. Miranda was going to turn and tell her father not to bother to put his boots on, but she was arrested by Olga's performance.

Nigel frowned with disapproval, but answered all the same. "We were on our way to Glasgow."

"Where had you been? There's not much north of here."

"A big country house."

"We probably know the owners. Who are they?"

"Name of Robinson."

Miranda watched, waiting for an opportunity to quietly borrow Olga's phone.

"Robinson doesn't ring a bell. Almost as common as Smith and Brown. What was the occasion?"

"A party."

Olga raised her dark eyebrows. "You come to Scotland to spend Christmas with your old friend. Then you and his daughter go off to a party and leave the poor man alone?"

"He wasn't feeling too well."

Olga turned the spotlight on Daisy. "What sort of a daughter are you, to leave your sick father at home on Christmas Eve?"

Daisy stared back in mute anger. Miranda suddenly feared that Daisy could be violent. Kit seemed to have the same thought, for he said, "Take it easy, Olga."

Olga ignored him. "Well?" she said to Daisy. "Haven't you got anything to say for yourself?"

Daisy picked up her gloves. For some reason, Miranda found that ominous. Daisy put the gloves on, then said, "I don't have to answer your questions."

"I think you do." Olga looked back at Nigel. "You're three complete strangers, sitting in my father's kitchen, filling yourselves with his food, and the story you tell is highly implausible. I think you need to explain yourselves."

Kit said anxiously, "Olga, is this really necessary? They're just people who got stranded—"

"Are you sure?" she said. She turned her gaze back to Nigel.

Nigel had seemed relaxed, but now anger showed as he said, "I don't like being interrogated."

"If you don't like it, you can leave," Olga said. "But if you want to stay in my father's house, you need to tell a better story than this farrago."

"We can't leave," Elton said indignantly. "Look out the window. It's a fucking blizzard."

"Please don't use that word in this house. My mother

always forbade obscenities, except in foreign languages, and we've kept her rule since her death." Olga reached for the coffeepot, then pointed to the burgundy briefcase on the table. "What's this?"

"It's mine," Nigel said.

"Well, we don't keep luggage on the table." She reached out and picked it up. "Not much in it—ow!" She yelled because Nigel had grabbed her arm. "That hurts!" she cried.

Nigel's mask of urbanity had gone. He spoke quietly but distinctly. "Put the case down. Now."

Stanley appeared beside Miranda in a coat, gloves, and boots. "What the hell do you think you're doing?" he said to Nigel. "Take your hands off my daughter!"

Nellie barked loudly. With a quick movement, Elton reached down and grabbed the dog's collar.

Olga stubbornly kept hold of the briefcase.

Kit said, "Put the case down, Olga."

Daisy grabbed the case. Olga tried to keep hold of it, and somehow the case flew open. Polystyrene packing chips scattered all over the kitchen table. Kit gave a shout of fear, and Miranda wondered momentarily what he was so frightened of. Out of the case fell a perfume bottle in two Ziploc bags.

With her free hand, Olga slapped Nigel's face.

Nigel slapped her back. Everyone shouted at once. Stanley gave a grunt of rage, pushed past Miranda, and strode toward Nigel. Miranda shouted: "No—"

Daisy stood in Stanley's way. He tried to push her aside. There was a blur of movement, and Stanley cried out and fell back, bleeding from his mouth.

Then, suddenly, both Nigel and Daisy were holding guns.

Everyone went quiet except Nellie, who was barking

frantically. Elton twisted her collar, throttling her, until she shut up. The room was silent.

Olga said, "Who the hell are you people?"

Stanley looked at the perfume spray on the table and said fearfully, "Why is that bottle double-bagged?"

Miranda slipped out through the door.

5:45 A.M.

KIT stared in fear at the Diablerie bottle on the kitchen table. But the glass had not smashed; the top had not fallen off; the double plastic bags had stayed intact. The lethal fluid remained safely inside its fragile container.

But now that Nigel and Daisy had pulled guns, they could no longer pretend to be innocent victims of the storm. As soon as the news from the laboratory got out, they would be connected with the theft of the virus.

Nigel, Daisy, and Elton might escape, but Kit was in a different position. There was no doubt who he was. Even if he escaped today, he would be a fugitive from justice for the rest of his life.

He thought furiously, trying to devise a way out.

Then, as everyone stood frozen, staring at the vicious little dark gray pistols, Nigel moved his gun a fraction of an inch, mistrustfully pointing it at Kit, and Kit was seized by inspiration.

There was still no reason why the family should sus-

pect *him,* he realized. He might have been deceived by
the three fugitives. His story that they were total
strangers still stood up.

But how could he make that clear?

Slowly, he raised his hands in the traditional gesture
of surrender.

Everyone looked at him. There was a moment when
he thought the gang themselves would betray him. A
frown passed over Nigel's brow. Elton looked openly
startled. Daisy sneered.

Kit said, "Dad, I'm so sorry I brought these people
into the house. I had no idea . . ."

His father gave him a long look, then nodded. "Not
your fault," he said. "You can't turn strangers away in a
blizzard. There was no way you could have known"—
he turned and gave Nigel a look of scorching contempt—
"just what *kind* of people they are."

Nigel got it immediately and jumped in to back up
Kit's pretense. "I'm sorry to return your hospitality this
way . . . Kit, is it? Yes . . . You saved our lives in the
snow. Now we're pointing guns at you. This old world
never was fair."

Elton's expression cleared as he grasped the decep-
tion.

Nigel went on: "If your bossy sister hadn't poked her
nose in, we might have left peacefully, and you would
never have found out what bad people we are. But she
would insist."

Daisy finally understood, and turned away with a
scornful expression.

It occurred to Kit that Nigel and the gang might just
kill his family. They were willing to steal a virus that
would slaughter thousands, so why would they hesitate
to gun down the Oxenfords? It was different, of course:

the notion of killing thousands with a virus was a bit abstract, whereas shooting adults and children in cold blood would be more difficult. But they might do it if they had to. They might kill Kit, too, he realized with a shudder. Fortunately, they still needed him. He knew the way to Luke's cottage and the Toyota Land Cruiser. They would never find it without him. He resolved to remind Nigel of that at the first opportunity.

"What's in that bottle is worth a lot of money, you see," Nigel finished.

To reinforce the simulation, Kit said, "What is it?"

"Never you mind," said Nigel.

Kit's mobile phone rang.

He did not know what to do. The caller was probably Hamish. There must have been some development at the Kremlin that the inside man thought Kit needed to know about. But how could he speak to Hamish without betraying himself to his family? He stood paralyzed, while everyone listened to his ring tone playing Beethoven's ninth symphony.

Nigel solved the problem. "Give me that," he said.

Kit handed over his phone, and Nigel answered it. "Yes, this is Kit," he said, in a fair imitation of a Scots accent.

The person at the other end seemed to believe him, for there was a silence while Nigel listened.

"Got it," he said. "Thanks." He hung up and pocketed the phone. "Someone wanting to warn you about three dangerous desperadoes in the neighborhood," he said. "Apparently the police are coming after them with a snowplow."

CRAIG could not figure Sophie out. One minute she was painfully shy, the next bold to the point of embarrassment. She let him put his hands inside her sweater, and even unfastened her bra when he fumbled with the hooks; and he thought he would die of pleasure when he held both her breasts in his hands—but then she refused to let him look at them in the candlelight. He got even more excited when she unbuttoned his jeans, as if she had been doing this sort of thing for years; but she did not seem to know what to do next. Craig wondered whether there was some code of behavior that he did not know about. Or was she just as inexperienced as he? She was getting better at kissing, anyway. At first she had been hesitant, as if not really sure whether she really wanted to do it; but after a couple of hours' practice she was enthusiastic.

Craig felt like a sailor in a storm. All night he had ridden waves of hope and despair, desire and disappointment, anxiety and delight. At one moment she had whispered, "You're so nice. I'm not nice. I'm vile." And then, when he kissed her again, her face was wet with tears. What are you supposed to do, he wondered, when a girl starts crying while you've got your hand inside her panties? He had started to withdraw his hand, feeling that must be what she wanted, but she grabbed his wrist and held him there. "I think you're nice," he said, but that sounded feeble, so he added: "I think you're wonderful."

Although he felt bewildered, he was also intensely happy. He had never felt so close to a girl. He was bursting with love and tenderness and joy. When he heard the noise from the kitchen, they were talking about how far to go.

She said, "Do you want to go the whole way?"

"Do you?"

"I do if you do."

Craig nodded. "I really want to."

"Have you got condoms?"

"Yes." He fumbled in his jeans pocket and took out the little packet.

"So you planned this?"

"I didn't have a plan." It was half-true: he hadn't had much of a plan. "I was hoping, though. Ever since I met you I've been thinking about, well, seeing you again, and so on. And all day today . . ."

"You were so persistent."

"I just wanted to be with you like this."

It was not very eloquent, but it seemed to be what she wanted to hear. "All right, then. Let's do it."

"Are you sure?"

"Yes. Now. Quickly."

"Good."

"Oh, my God, what's that?"

Craig had been aware of people in the kitchen below. He had vaguely heard the murmur of voices. Then someone had clattered a saucepan, and he had smelled bacon. He was not sure what the time was, but it seemed early for breakfast. However, he had taken no notice, confident that no one would interrupt them here in the attic. Now the sounds could not be ignored. First he heard Grandpa shout—an unusual event in itself. Nellie started barking like a fiend; there was a scream that sounded remarkably like Craig's mother; then several male voices yelled at once.

Sophie said in a frightened voice, "Is this normal?"

"No," he replied. "They have arguments, but not shouting matches."

"What's going on?"

He hesitated. Part of him wanted to forget the noise and act as if he and Sophie were in a universe of their own, lying on the old sofa under their coats. He could have ignored an earthquake to concentrate on her soft skin and hot breath and moist lips. But another part of him felt that the interruption was not entirely unwelcome. They had done almost everything: it might even be nice to postpone the ultimate, so that there was something else to look forward to, a further delight to anticipate.

Below them, the kitchen went quiet as suddenly as it had burst into sound.

"Strange," he said.

"It's spooky."

Sophie sounded frightened, and that made up Craig's mind. He kissed her lips once more, then stood up. He pulled up his jeans and stepped across the attic to the hole in the floor. He lay down and looked through the gap in the floorboards.

He saw his mother, standing up with her mouth open, looking shocked and frightened. Grandpa was wiping blood off his chin. Uncle Kit had his hands in the air. Three strangers were in the room. At first he thought they were all men; then he realized one was an ugly girl with a shaved head. The young black man was holding Nellie's collar, twisting it hard. The older man and the girl held guns.

Craig murmured, "Bloody hell, what's happening down there?"

Sophie lay beside him. After a moment she gasped. "Are those things guns?" she whispered.

"Yes."

"Oh, my God, we're in trouble."

Craig thought. "We have to call the police. Where's your phone?"

"I left it in the barn."

"Damn."

"Oh, God, what can we do?"

"Think. Think. A phone. We need a phone." Craig hesitated.

He was frightened. He really wanted to lie still and shut his eyes tightly. He might have done that, were it not for the girl beside him. He did not know all the rules, but he knew that a man was supposed to show courage when a girl was frightened, especially when they were lovers, or nearly. And if he was not feeling brave, he had to pretend.

Where was the nearest phone? "There's an extension beside Grandpa's bed."

Sophie said, "I can't do anything. I'm too scared."

"You'd better stay here."

"Okay."

Craig stood up. He buttoned his jeans and buckled the belt, then went to the low door. He took a breath, then opened it. He crawled into Grandpa's suit cupboard, pushed at the door, and emerged into the dressing room.

The lights were on. Grandpa's dark brown brogue-style shoes were side by side on the carpet, and the blue shirt he had been wearing yesterday lay on top of a pile of clothes in the linen basket. Craig stepped into the bedroom. The bed was unmade, as if Grandpa had just got out of it. On the bedside table was a copy of *Scientific American* magazine, open—and the phone.

Craig had never dialed 999 in his life. What were you supposed to say? He had seen people do it on television. You had to give your name and location, he thought. Then what? "There are men with guns in our kitchen." It sounded melodramatic—but probably all 999 calls were dramatic.

He picked up the phone. There was no dial tone.

He put his finger on the cradle and jiggled it, then listened again. Nothing.

He replaced the handset. Why were the phones out? Was it just a fault—or had the strangers cut the wires?

Did Grandpa have a mobile? Craig pulled open the bedside drawer. Inside he saw a flashlight and a book, but no phone. Then he remembered: Grandpa had a phone in his car, but did not carry a mobile.

He heard a sound from the dressing room. Sophie poked her head out of the suit cupboard, looking frightened. "Someone's coming!" she hissed. A moment later, Craig heard a heavy footstep on the landing.

He darted into the dressing room. Sophie ducked back into the attic. Craig fell on his knees and crawled through the suit cupboard just as he heard the bedroom door open. He had no time to close the cupboard door. He wriggled through the low door, then quickly turned and closed it softly behind him.

Sophie whispered, "The older man told the girl to search the house. He called her Daisy."

"I heard her boots on the landing."

"Did you get through to the police?"

He shook his head. "The phone's dead."

"No!"

He heard Daisy's heavy tread in the dressing room. She would see the open cupboard door. Would she spot the low door behind the suits? Only if she looked carefully.

Craig listened. Was she staring into the open cupboard at this minute? He felt shaky. Daisy was not big—an inch or two shorter than he was, he guessed—but she looked absolutely terrifying.

The silence dragged out. He thought he heard her

step into the bathroom. After a shorter pause, her boots crossed the dressing room and faded away. The bedroom door slammed.

"Oh, God, I'm so scared," Sophie said.

"Me, too," said Craig.

MIRANDA was in Olga's bedroom with Hugo.

When she left the kitchen she had not known what to do. She could not go outside—she was in her nightdress and bare feet. She had raced up the stairs with the thought of locking herself in the bathroom, but realized almost at once that that would be useless. She stood on the landing, dithering. She was so frightened that she wanted to vomit. She had to call the police—that was the priority.

Olga had her mobile in the pocket of her negligee—but Hugo probably had his own.

Frightened though she was, Miranda had hesitated for a split second outside the door. The last thing she wanted was to be in a bedroom with Hugo. Then she heard someone step out of the kitchen into the hall. Quickly, she opened Hugo's door, slid inside, and closed it quietly.

Hugo was standing at the window, looking out. He was naked, and had his back to the door. "Would you look at this bloody weather?" he said, obviously thinking his wife had come back.

Miranda was momentarily arrested by his casual tone. Obviously Olga and Hugo had made up their quarrel, after yelling at each other half the night. Had Olga already forgiven her husband for having sex with her sister? It seemed quick—but perhaps they had had this row before, about other women. Miranda had often wondered about Olga's deal with her flirtatious husband, but Olga had never spoken of it. Maybe they had a script: infidelity, discovery, quarrel, reconciliation, then back to infidelity.

"It's me," Miranda said.

He spun around, startled, then smiled. "And in *déshabillé*—what a lovely surprise! Let's get into bed, quick."

She heard heavy footsteps on the stairs, and at the same time noticed that Hugo's belly was much bigger than when she had gone to bed with him—he looked like a little round gnome—and she wondered how she could have found him attractive. "You have to phone the police right now," she said. "Where's your mobile?"

"Just here," he said, pointing to the bedside table. "What on earth is wrong?"

"People with guns in the kitchen—dial 999, quickly!"

"Who are they?"

"Never bloody mind!" She heard heavy footsteps on the landing. She stood frozen, terrified that the door would burst open, but the steps went by. Her voice became a kind of low scream. "They're probably looking for me. Get on with it!"

Hugo came out of shock. He snatched up his phone, dropped it on the floor, picked it up, and jabbed at the ON button. "Damn thing takes forever!" he said in frustration. "Did you say *guns*?"

"Yes!"

"How did the people get in?"

"Said they were stranded—what is the matter with that phone?"

"Searching," he said. "Come on, come on!"

Miranda heard the footsteps outside again. This time she was ready. She flung herself on the floor and slid sideways under the double bed just as the door flew open.

She closed her eyes and tried to make herself small. Feeling foolish, she opened her eyes again. She saw Hugo's bare feet, with hairy ankles, and a pair of black motorcycle boots with steel-tipped toes. She heard Hugo say, "Hello, gorgeous, who are you?"

His charm did not work on Daisy. She said, "Give me that phone."

"I was just—"

"Now, you fat fool."

"Here, take it."

"Now come with me."

"Let me put something on."

"Don't worry. I'm not going to bite your little cock off."

Miranda saw Hugo's feet step away from Daisy. She moved quickly toward him; then there was the sound of a blow, and he let out a cry. Both pairs of feet moved toward the door together. They passed out of Miranda's sight, and a moment later she heard them going down the stairs.

Miranda said to herself, "Oh, God, what do I do now?"

6 A.M.

CRAIG and Sophie lay side by side on the floorboards of the attic, looking down through the hole into the kitchen, as Craig's father was dragged naked into the room by Daisy.

Craig was shocked and disturbed. It was a scene from a nightmare, or an old painting of sinners being dragged down into hell. He could hardly grasp that this humiliated, helpless figure was his *father,* the master of the house, the only person with the nerve to stand up to his domineering mother, the man who had ruled Craig for all fifteen years of his life. He felt disoriented and weightless, as if gravity had been switched off and he did not know which way was down.

Sophie began to cry softly. "This is awful," she whispered. "We're all going to be murdered."

The need to comfort her gave Craig strength. He put his arm around her narrow shoulders. She was trembling. "It is awful, but we're not dead yet," he said. "We can get help."

"How?"

"Where is your phone, exactly?"

"I left it in the barn, upstairs by the bed. I think I dropped it into my suitcase when I changed."

"We have to go there and use it to call the police."

"What if those terrible people see us?"

"We'll stay away from the kitchen windows."

"We can't—the barn door is right opposite!"

She was right, Craig knew, but they had to take the risk. "They probably won't look out."

"But what if they do?"

"You can hardly see across the backyard anyway, in this snow."

"They're bound to spot us!"

He did not know what else to tell her. "We have to try."

"I can't do it. Let's just stay here."

It was tempting, but Craig knew that if he hid himself and did nothing to help his family, he would feel ashamed. "You can stay, if you like, while I go to the barn."

"No—don't leave me alone!"

He had guessed she might say that. "Then you'll have to come with me."

"I don't want to."

He squeezed her shoulders and kissed her cheek. "Come on. Be brave."

She wiped her nose on her sleeve. "I'll try."

He stood up and put on his boots and coat. Sophie sat motionless, watching him in the candlelight. Trying to walk softly, for fear of being heard below, he found her rubber boots, then knelt down and put them on her small feet. She cooperated passively, stunned by shock. He gently pulled her upright and helped her on with her anorak. He zipped it up at the front, pulled the hood over her head, then brushed her hair back with his hand. The hood gave her a gamine look, and for a fleeting moment he thought how pretty she was.

He opened the big loft door. A freezing wind blew a dense flurry of snow into the attic. The lamp over the back door spread a small half circle of light, showing the snow lying thicker than ever on the ground. The trashcan lid looked like Ali Baba's hat.

There were two windows at this end of the house, one from the pantry and the other from the boot lobby. The sinister strangers were in the kitchen. If he was very unlucky, one of them might step into the pantry or the boot lobby at just the wrong moment, and spot him— but he thought the odds were in his favor.

"Come on," he said.

Sophie stood beside him and looked down. "You go first."

He leaned out. There was a light in the boot lobby, but not in the pantry. Would anyone see him? On his own he might have been terrified, but Sophie's fear made him braver. He swept the snow off the ledge with his hand, then walked along it to the lean-to roof of the boot lobby. He swept a section of the roof clear, then stood upright and reached out to her. He held her hand as she inched along the edge. "You're doing fine," he said softly. It was not difficult—the ledge was a foot wide—but she was shaky. At last she stepped down to the lean-to roof. "Well done," Craig said.

Then she slipped.

Her feet skidded from under her. Craig still had hold of her hand, but he could not keep her upright, and she sat down with a thud that must have reverberated below. She landed awkwardly and tipped over backward, sliding down the icy slates on her bottom.

Craig grabbed at her and grasped a handful of anorak. He tugged, trying to arrest her slide, but his feet were on the same slippery surface, and all that happened was that she drew him along with her. He skated down the roof after her, struggling to remain upright and trying to slow her down.

When her feet hit the gutter at the lip of the roof, she came to a halt; but her bottom was half off the sloping side edge. She tilted sideways. Craig tightened his grip on her coat and pulled, drawing her toward him and safety—then he slipped again. He let go of her coat, waving his arms to stay upright.

Sophie screamed and fell off the roof.

She dropped ten feet and landed in soft new snow behind the trash can.

Craig leaned over the edge. Little light fell in that dark corner, and he could hardly see her. "Are you all right?" he said. There was no reply. Had she been knocked unconscious? "Sophie!"

"I'm okay," she said miserably.

The back door opened.

Quickly, Craig lowered himself to a sitting position.

A man stepped out. Craig could just see a head of short dark hair. He glanced over the side. The extra light spilling from the open door made Sophie just visible. Her pink anorak disappeared into the snow, but her dark jeans showed. She lay still. He could not see her face.

A voice from inside called, "Elton! Who's out there?"

Elton waved a flashlight from side to side, but the

beam showed nothing but snowflakes. Craig flattened himself on the roof.

Elton turned to the right, away from Sophie, and walked a few steps into the storm, shining his flashlight in front of him.

Craig pressed himself to the roof, hoping Elton would not glance up. Then he realized that the loft door was still wide open. If Elton happened to shine his flashlight that way, he could not fail to see it and investigate—which would be disastrous. Moving slowly, Craig crawled up the lean-to roof. As soon as he could reach, he got hold of the lower edge of the door and gently pushed it. It swung slowly through an arc. Craig gave it a final shove and released it, then quickly lay down again. The door closed with an audible click.

Elton turned. Craig lay still. He saw the beam of the flashlight play over the gable end of the house and the loft door.

The voice came from inside again. "Elton?"

The flashlight beam moved off. "I can't see nothing," Elton shouted back irritably.

Craig risked moving his head to look. Elton was walking the other way, toward Sophie. He stopped at the trash can. If he peeked around the angle of the lobby and shone his flashlight into the corner, he would see her. When that happened, Craig decided, he would dive off the roof onto Elton's head. He would probably get beaten up, but Sophie might escape.

After a long moment, Elton turned away. "Nothing out here but fucking snow," he called out, and he stepped back inside the house and slammed the door.

Craig groaned with relief. He found he was shaking. He tried to make himself calm. Thinking about Sophie helped. He jumped off the roof and landed beside her. Bending down, he said, "Did you hurt yourself?"

She sat up. "No, but I'm so scared."

"Okay. Can you stand up?"

"Are you sure he's gone?"

"I saw him go in and close the door. They must have heard your scream, or maybe the bump as you slipped on the roof—but in this storm they probably aren't sure it was anything."

"Oh, God, I hope so." She struggled to her feet.

Craig frowned, thinking. The gang were obviously alert. If he and Sophie went directly across the yard to the barn, they could be seen by someone looking out of the kitchen windows. They would do better to strike out into the garden, circle around the guest cottage, and approach the barn from behind. They would still risk being seen going in through the door, but the round-about route would minimize their exposure. "This way," he said. He took her hand, and she followed him willingly enough.

They felt the wind blowing more fiercely. The storm was coming in off the sea. Away from the shelter of the house, the snow no longer fell in swirling flurries, but pelted down in hard, slanting lines, stinging their faces and getting into their eyes.

When Craig could no longer see the house, he turned at a right angle. Their progress was slow. The snow lay two feet deep, making it tiring to walk. He could not see the cottage. Measuring his steps, Craig walked what he guessed was the width of the yard. Now completely blind, he figured he must have drawn level with the barn, and he turned again. He counted the paces until he should have bumped up against its wooden end wall.

But there was nothing.

He felt sure he could not have gone wrong. He had been meticulous. He walked another five paces. He feared they might be lost, but he did not want Sophie to know that. Suppressing a feeling of panic, he turned again, heading back toward the main house. The complete darkness meant that Sophie could not see his face so, fortunately, she did not know how scared he was.

They had been outside less than five minutes, but already his feet and hands were agonizingly cold. Craig realized they were in serious danger. If they could not find shelter, they would freeze to death.

Sophie was not stupid. "Where are we?"

Craig made himself sound more confident than he felt. "Just coming up to the barn. A few steps more."

He should not have made such a rash prediction. After ten more steps they were still in blackness.

He figured he must have walked farther away from the buildings than he had at first reckoned. Therefore his return leg had been too short. He swung right again. Now he had turned so many times that he was no longer sure of his angles. He trudged ten more strides and stopped.

"Are we lost?" Sophie said in a small voice.

"We can't be far from the barn!" Craig said angrily. "We only went a few steps into the garden."

She put her arms around him and hugged him. "It's not your fault."

He knew it was, but he was grateful to her anyway.

"We could shout," she suggested. "Caroline and Tom might hear us and shout back."

"Those people in the kitchen might hear us, too."

"That would be better than freezing."

She was right, but Craig did not want to admit it.

How was it possible to get lost in just a few yards? He refused to believe it.

He hugged her, but felt despair. He had thought himself superior to Sophie, because she was more frightened than he, and he had felt very manly for a few moments, protecting her; but now he had got them both lost. Some man, he thought, some protector. Her boyfriend the law student would have done better, if he existed.

From the corner of his eye, he saw a light.

He turned in that direction, and it was gone. His eyes registered nothing but blackness. Wishful thinking?

Sophie sensed his tension. "What?"

"I thought I saw a light." When he turned his face to her, the light seemed to reappear in the corner of his eye. But when he looked up again it was gone.

He vaguely remembered something from biology about peripheral vision registering things invisible to direct sight. There was a reason for it, that had to do with the blind spot on the retina. He turned to Sophie again. The light reappeared. This time he did not turn toward it, but concentrated on what he could make out without moving his eyes. The light flickered, but it was there.

He turned toward it, and it was gone again; but he knew its direction. "This way."

They plowed through the snow. The light did not immediately reappear, and Craig wondered if he had suffered a hallucination, like the mirage of an oasis seen in the desert. Then it flickered into sight and immediately disappeared again.

"I saw it!" Sophie cried.

They trudged on. Two seconds later, it came back into view, and this time it stayed. Craig felt a rush of relief, and realized that for a few moments back there he really had thought he was going to die and take Sophie with him.

When they came closer to the light, he saw that it was the one over the back door. They had walked around in a circle, and now they were back where they had started.

6:15 A.M.

MIRANDA lay still for a long time. She was terrified that Daisy would return, but unable to do anything about it. In her mind, Daisy came stomping into the room in her motorcycle boots, knelt on the floor, and looked under the bed. Miranda could see Daisy's brutish face—the shaved skull and the broken nose and the dark eyes that looked bruised by the black eyeliner. The vision of that face was so scary that sometimes Miranda just squeezed her eyes shut as tightly as she could, until she saw fireworks on the back of her eyelids.

In the end it was the thought of Tom that made her move. Somehow she had to protect her eleven-year-old son. But how? There was nothing she could do alone. She would be willing to put her body between the gang and the children, but it would be pointless: she would be thrown aside like a sack of potatoes. Civilized people were no good at violence—that was what made them civilized.

The answer was the same as before. She had to find a phone and get help.

That meant she had to go to the guest cottage. She had to crawl out from under the bed, leave the bedroom, and creep downstairs, hoping she would not be heard by the gang in the kitchen, praying that one of them would not step into the hall and see her. She needed to grab a coat and boots, for she was barefoot and naked but for a cotton nightdress, and she knew she could not go three yards, dressed as she was, in a blizzard with the snow two feet deep. Then she had to make her way around the house, staying well away from the windows, to the cottage, and get the phone she had left in her handbag on the floor by the door.

She tried to summon her nerve. What was she frightened of? The tension, she thought: the strain was petrifying. But it would not be for long. Half a minute to go down the stairs; a minute to put on coat and boots; two minutes, perhaps three, to tramp through the snow to the cottage. Less than five minutes, that was all.

She began to feel resentful. How dared they make her scared to walk around her own father's house? Indignation gave her courage.

Shaking, she slid out from under the bed. The bedroom door was open. She peeped out, saw that all was clear, and stepped onto the landing. She could hear voices from the kitchen. She looked down.

There was a hat stand at the foot of the stairs. Most of the family's coats and boots were kept in a walk-in closet in the boot lobby by the back door, but Daddy always left his in the hall, and she could see his old blue anorak hanging from the stand, and below it the leather-lined rubber boots that kept his feet warm while he walked Nellie. They should be enough to keep her from freezing to death while she plowed through the snow to the cottage. It would take her only a few seconds to slip them on and sneak out through the front door.

If she had the guts.

She started to tiptoe down the stairs.

The voices from the kitchen became louder. There was an argument going on. She heard Nigel say, "Well, bloody well look again, then!" Did that mean someone was going to search the house? She turned and ran back, going up the stairs two at a time. As she reached the landing, she heard heavy boots in the hall—Daisy.

It was no good hiding under the bed again. If Daisy was being sent back for a second search, she was bound to look harder this time. Miranda stepped into her father's bedroom. There was one place she could hide: the attic. When she was ten years old, she had made it her den. All the children had, at different times.

The door of the suit cupboard stood open.

She heard Daisy's steps on the landing.

She fell to her knees, crawled inside, and opened the low door that led to the attic. Then she turned and closed the cupboard door behind her. She backed into the attic and closed the low door.

She realized immediately that she had made an error that might be fatal. Daisy had searched the house a quarter of an hour or so ago. She must have seen the door of the suit cupboard standing open. Would she now remember that, and realize that someone must have closed it subsequently? And would she be smart enough to guess why?

Miranda heard footsteps in the dressing room. She held her breath as Daisy walked to the bathroom and back. She heard the sound of cupboard doors being flung open. She bit her thumb to keep from screaming with fear. There was a brushing sound as Daisy rummaged among suits and shirts. The low door was hard to see, unless you got down on your knees and looked under the hanging clothes. Would Daisy be so thorough?

There was a long moment of quiet.

Then Daisy's footsteps receded through the bedroom.

Miranda felt so relieved that she wanted to cry. She stopped herself: she had to be brave. What was happening in the kitchen? She remembered the hole in the floor. She crawled slowly across to take a look.

HUGO looked so pathetic that Kit almost felt sorry for him. He was a short man, and pudgy. He had fatty breasts with hairy nipples and a belly that hung over his genitals. The thin legs below his round body made him look like an ill-designed doll. He seemed all the more tragic by contrast with his usual self. He was normally poised and self-assured, dressed in natty suits that flattered his figure, and he flirted with the confidence of a matinee idol. Now he looked foolish and mortified.

The family were crowded together at one end of the kitchen, by the pantry door, away from any exits: Kit himself, his sister Olga in her black silk wrap, their father with swollen lips where Daisy had punched him, and Olga's husband, the naked Hugo. Stanley was sitting down, holding Nellie, stroking her to keep her calm, afraid she would be shot if she attacked the strangers. Nigel and Elton stood on the other side of the table, and Daisy was searching the upstairs.

Hugo stepped forward. "There are towels and things in the laundry," he said. The laundry was off the kitchen, on the same side as the dining room. "Let me get something to wrap around me."

Daisy heard this as she returned from her search. She picked up a tea towel. "Try this," she said, and flicked it at his crotch. Kit remembered, from school shower room horseplay, how that could sting. Hugo let out an involuntary yelp. He turned around, and she flicked it again, catching him on the backside. He skipped away, into the corner, and Daisy laughed. Hugo was completely humiliated.

It was unpleasant to see, and Kit felt slightly sick.

"Stop playing around," Nigel said angrily. "I want to know where the other sister is—Miranda. She must have slipped out. Where did she go?"

Daisy said, "I've looked all over the house twice. She's not in the building."

"She could be hiding."

"And she could be the invisible fucking woman, but I can't find her."

Kit knew where she was. A minute ago he had seen Nellie cock her head and lift one black ear. Someone had entered the attic, and it had to be Miranda. Kit wondered if his father had noticed Nellie's reaction. Miranda was no great threat, up there with no phone, wearing only a nightdress. Still Kit wondered if there was a way he could warn Nigel about her.

Elton said, "Maybe she went outside. That noise we heard was probably her."

Nigel's reply betrayed exasperation. "So how come you didn't see her when you went to look?"

"Because it's bloody dark!" Elton was becoming irritated by Nigel's hectoring tone.

Kit guessed the noise outside had been some of the kids, fooling around. There had been a thud, then a scream, as if a person or animal had hit the back door. A deer might have bumped into the door, but deer did not scream, they made a mooing sound like cattle. A large bird could conceivably have been blown against the door by the storm, and might have made a noise like a scream. However, Kit thought the likeliest culprit was Miranda's son, young Tom. He was eleven, just the right age for creeping around at night, playing commandos.

If Tom had looked through the window and seen the guns, what would he do? First he would search for his mother, but he would not find her. Then he would wake his sister, perhaps, or Ned. Either way, Nigel had little time to spare. He needed to capture the rest of the family before anyone made a phone call. But there was nothing Kit could do without blowing his cover, so he sat tight and kept his mouth shut.

"She was only wearing a nightdress," Nigel said. "She can't have gone far."

Elton said, "Well, I'll go and check the outbuildings, shall I?"

"Wait a minute." Nigel frowned, thinking. "We've searched every room in the house, yeah?"

Daisy said, "Aye, like I told you."

"We've taken mobile phones from three of them—Kit, the naked gnome, and the snotty sister. And we're sure there are no others in the house."

"Aye." Daisy had checked for phones when she was searching.

"Then we'd better check the other buildings."

"Right," Elton said. "There's a cottage, a barn, and a garage, the old man said."

"Check the garage first—there will be phones in the cars. Then the cottage and the barn. Round up the rest of the family and bring them here. Make sure you get all their phones. We'll just keep them all under guard here for an hour or two. Then we'll run."

It was not a bad plan, Kit thought. When all the family was in one place, with no phones, there would be nothing they could do. No one was going to come to the door on Christmas morning—no milkman, no postman, no delivery van from Tesco or Majestic Wine—so there was no danger of any outsider becoming suspicious. The gang could sit tight and wait for daylight.

Elton put on his jacket and looked out of the window, peering into the snow. Following his gaze, Kit noticed that the cottage and barn across the courtyard were barely visible through the snow by the light of the outside lamps. There was still no letup.

Daisy said, "I'll check the garage if Elton goes to the cottage."

Elton said, "We'd better get on with it. Someone might be calling the police right now."

Daisy pocketed her gun and zipped up her leather jacket.

Nigel said, "Before you go, let's shut this lot up someplace where they can't cause trouble."

That was when Hugo jumped Nigel.

Everyone was taken totally by surprise. Kit had written Hugo off, as had the gang. But he leaped forward with furious energy, punching Nigel in the face again and again with both fists. He had chosen his moment well, for Daisy had put her weapon away, and Elton had never drawn his, so Nigel was the only one with a gun in his hand, and he was so busy trying to dodge blows that he could not use it.

Nigel staggered back, bumping against the kitchen counter. Hugo went at him like a fiend, thumping his face and body, screaming something incomprehensible.

In a few seconds he landed a lot of blows, but Nigel did not drop the gun.

Elton was the quickest to react. He grabbed Hugo and tried to pull him off. Being naked, Hugo was hard to grasp and, for a moment, Elton could not get a grip, his hands sliding off Hugo's moving shoulders.

Stanley released Nellie, who was barking furiously, and the dog flung herself on Elton, biting his legs. She was an old dog, and had a soft mouth, but she was a distraction.

Daisy reached for her gun. The barrel seemed to catch on her pocket lining as she tried to draw it out. Then Olga picked up a plate and threw it across the room at her. Daisy dodged, and the plate hit her glancingly on the shoulder.

Kit stepped forward to grab Hugo, then stopped himself.

The last thing he wanted was for the family to overwhelm the gang. Although he was shocked by the true purpose of the theft he had organized, his own survival was uppermost in his mind. It was less than twenty-four hours since Daisy had almost killed him in the swimming pool, and he knew that if he failed to repay her father, he faced an end every bit as painful as death from the virus in the perfume bottle. He would intervene on Nigel's side, against his own family, if he had to—but did he have to? He still wanted to maintain the fiction that he had never seen Nigel before tonight. So he stood helplessly looking on as contrary impulses clashed within him.

Elton put both arms around Hugo in a powerful bear hug. Hugo struggled gamely, but he was smaller and less fit, and could not shake Elton off. Elton lifted Hugo's feet off the ground and stepped back, pulling him away from Nigel.

Daisy kicked Nellie accurately in the ribs with a heavy boot, and the dog whimpered and fled to the corner of the room.

Nigel was bleeding from his nose and mouth, and there were angry red marks around his eyes. He glared malevolently at Hugo and raised his right hand, which still grasped the gun.

Olga took a step forward, shouting: "No!"

Instantly, Nigel swung his arm and pointed the gun at her.

Stanley grabbed her and held her back, saying at the same time, "Don't shoot. Please don't shoot."

Nigel kept the gun pointed at Olga and said, "Daisy, have you still got that sap?" Looking pleased, Daisy took out her blackjack. Nigel nodded toward Hugo. "Hurt this bastard."

Seeing what was coming, Hugo began to struggle, but Elton tightened his hold.

Daisy drew back her right arm and smashed the blackjack into Hugo's face. It hit his cheekbone with a sickening crunch. He made a noise between a shout and a scream. Daisy hit him again, and blood spurted from his mouth and ran down his bare chest. With a spiteful grin, Daisy eyed his genitals, then kicked him in the groin. She hit him with the blackjack again, this time on the top of his head, and he fell unconscious. But that made no difference to Daisy. She hit him full on the nose, then kicked him again.

Olga let out a wail of grief and rage, broke free of her father's grasp, and threw herself at Daisy.

Daisy swung the blackjack at her, but Olga was too close, and the blow whistled behind her head.

Elton dropped Hugo, who slumped on the tiled floor, and made a grab for Olga.

Olga got her hands on Daisy's face and scratched.

Nigel had his gun pointed at Olga but he hesitated to shoot, no doubt fearing that he would hit Elton or Daisy, both of whom were struggling with Olga.

Stanley turned to the stovetop and picked up the heavy frying pan in which Kit had scrambled a dozen eggs. He raised it high in the air, then brought it down on Nigel, aiming at the man's head. At the last instant Nigel saw it coming, and dodged. The pan hit his right shoulder. He cried out in pain, and the gun flew from his hand.

Stanley tried to catch the gun, but missed. It landed on the kitchen table, an inch from the perfume bottle. It bounced onto the seat of a pine chair, rolled over, and dropped to the floor at Kit's feet.

Kit bent down and picked it up.

Nigel and Stanley looked at him. Sensing the dramatic change, Olga, Daisy, and Elton stopped fighting and turned to look at Kit holding the gun.

Kit hesitated, torn in half by the agony of the decision.

They all stared at him for a long moment of stillness.

At last he turned the gun around, holding it by the barrel, and gave it back to Nigel.

6:30 A.M.

CRAIG and Sophie found the barn at last.

They had waited a few minutes by the back door, hesitating, then realized they would freeze to death if they stayed there indefinitely. Screwing up their courage, they had crossed the yard directly, heads bent, praying that no one would look out of the kitchen windows. The twenty paces from one side to the other seemed to take forever through the thick snow. Then they followed the front wall of the barn, always in full view from the kitchen. Craig did not dare to look in that direction: he was too frightened of what he might see. When at last they reached the door, he took one swift glance. In the dark he could not see the building itself, just the lighted windows. The snow further obscured his view, and he could see only vague figures moving in the kitchen. There was no sign that anyone had glanced out at the wrong moment.

He pulled the big door open. They stepped inside,

and he closed it gratefully. Warm air washed over him. He was shivering, and Sophie's teeth were chattering like castanets. She threw off her snow-covered anorak and sat on one of the big hospital-style radiators. Craig would have liked to take a minute to warm himself, but there was no time for that—he had to get help fast.

The place was dimly lit by a night-light next to the camp bed where Tom lay. Craig looked closely at the boy, wondering whether to wake him. He seemed to have recovered from Sophie's vodka, and was sleeping peacefully in his Spider-Man pajamas.

Craig's eye was caught by something on the floor beside the pillow. It was a photograph. Craig picked it up and held it in the light. It appeared to have been taken at his mother's birthday party, and showed Tom with Sophie, her arm around his shoulders. Craig smiled to himself. I'm not the only one who was captivated by her that afternoon, he thought. He put the picture back, saying nothing to Sophie.

There was no point in waking Tom, he decided. There was nothing the boy could do, and he would only be terrified. He was better off asleep.

Craig went quickly up the ladder that led to the hayloft bedroom. On one of the narrow beds he could make out the heap of blankets that covered his sister, Caroline. She seemed fast asleep. Like Tom, she was better off that way. If she woke up and found out what was going on, she would have hysterics. He would try not to wake her.

The second bed had not been slept in. On the floor next to it he could see the shape of an open suitcase. Sophie said she had dropped her phone on top of her clothes. Craig crossed the room, moving cautiously in the near-dark. As he bent down, he heard, very near to him, the soft rustle and squeak of something alive, and he grunted a startled curse, his heart hammering in his chest; then he realized it was Caroline's damn rats moving in their cage. He pushed the cage aside and began to search Sophie's case.

Working by touch, he rummaged in the contents. On top was a plastic shopping bag containing a gift-wrapped parcel. Otherwise it was mostly clothes, neatly folded: someone had helped Sophie pack, he guessed, for he did not take her to be a tidy person. He was momentarily distracted by a silky bra; then his hand closed over the oblong shape of a mobile phone. He flipped its lid, but no lights came on. He could not see well enough to find the ON-OFF switch.

He hurried back down the ladder with the phone in his hand. There was a standard lamp by the bookshelf. He turned it on and held Sophie's phone under the light. He found the POWER button and pressed it, but nothing happened. He could have cried with frustration. "I can't get the bloody thing to come on!" he whispered.

She held out her hand, still sitting on the radiator, and he gave her the phone. She pressed the same button, frowned, pressed it again, then jabbed at it repeatedly. At last she said, "The battery has run down."

"Shit! Where's the charger?"

"I don't know."

"In your suitcase?"

"I don't think so."

Craig became exasperated. "How can you *possibly* not know where your phone charger is?"

Sophie's voice went small. "I think I left it at home."

"Jesus Christ!" Craig controlled his temper with an effort. He wanted to tell her she was a stupid fool, but that would not help. He was silent for a moment. The memory of kissing her came back to him, and he could not be angry. His rage evaporated, and he put his arms around her. "All right," he said. "Never mind."

She rested her head on his chest. "I'm sorry."

"Let's think of something else."

"There must be more phones, or a charger we can use."

He shook his head. "Caroline and I don't carry mobiles—my mother won't let us have them. She doesn't go to the toilet without hers, but she says we don't need them."

"Tom hasn't got one. Miranda thinks he's too young."

"Hell."

"Wait!" She pulled away from him. "Wasn't there one in your grandfather's car?"

Craig snapped his fingers. "The Ferrari—right! And I left the keys in. All we have to do is get to the garage, and we can phone the police."

"You mean we have to go outside again?"

"You can stay here."

"No, I want to come."

"You wouldn't be alone—Tom and Caroline are here."

"I want to be with you."

Craig tried not to show how pleased he was. "You'd better get your coat on again, then."

Sophie came off the radiator. Craig picked her coat up from the floor and helped her into it. She looked up at him, and he tried an encouraging smile. "Ready?"

A trace of her old spirit came back. "Yeah. Like, what can happen? We could be murdered—that's all. Let's go."

They went outside. It was still pitch-dark, and the snowfall was heavy, bursts of stinging pellets rather than clouds of butterflies. Once again, Craig looked nervously across the yard to the house, but he could see no more than before, which meant the strangers in the kitchen were unlikely to see him. He took Sophie's hand. Steering by the courtyard lights, he led her to the end of the barn, away from the house, then crossed the yard to the garage.

The side door was unlocked, as always. It was as cold inside as out. There were no windows, so Craig risked switching on the lights.

Grandpa's Ferrari was where Craig had left it, parked close to the wall to hide the dent. Like a flash, he remembered the shame and fear he had felt twelve hours ago, after he had crashed into the tree. It seemed strange now that he had been so anxious and afraid about something as trivial as a dent in a car. He recalled how eager he had been to impress Sophie and get her to like him. It was not long ago, but it seemed far in the past.

Also in the garage was Luke's Ford Mondeo. The Toyota Land Cruiser had gone: Luke must have borrowed it last night.

He went to the Ferrari and pulled the door handle. It would not open. He tried again, but the door was locked. "Fuck," he said feelingly.

"What's the matter?" Sophie said.

"The car's locked."

"Oh, no!"

He looked inside. "And the keys have gone."

"How did that happen?"

Craig banged his fist on the car roof in frustration. "Luke must have noticed that the car was unlocked last night, when he was leaving. He must have removed the keys from the ignition, locked the car, and taken the keys back to the house for Grandpa."

"What about the other car?"

Craig opened the door of the Ford and looked inside. "No phone."

"Can we get the Ferrari keys back?"

Craig made a face. "Maybe."

"Where are they kept?"

"In the key box, on the wall of the boot lobby."

"At the back of the kitchen?"

Craig nodded grimly. "Just about two yards from those people with guns."

6:45 A.M.

THE snowplow moved slowly along the two-lane road in the dark. Carl Osborne's Jaguar followed it. Toni was at the wheel of the Jag, peering ahead as the wipers struggled to clear away the thickly falling snow. The view through the windshield did not change. Straight ahead were the flashing lights of the snowplow; on her near side was the bank of snow freshly shoveled up by the blade; on the off side, virgin snow lay across the road and over the moors as far as the car's headlights reached.

Mother was asleep in the back with the puppy on her lap. Beside Toni, Carl was quiet, dozing or sulking. He had told Toni that he hated other people driving his car, but she had insisted, and he had been forced to yield, as she had the keys.

"You just never give an inch, do you?" he had muttered before sinking into silence.

"That's why I was such a good cop," she replied.

From the back, Mother said, "It's why you haven't got a husband."

That was more than an hour ago. Now Toni was struggling to stay awake, fighting the hypnotic sway of the wipers, the warmth from the heater, and the monotony of the view. She almost wished she had let Carl drive. But she needed to stay in control.

They had found the getaway vehicle at the Dew Drop Inn. It contained wigs, false mustaches, and plain-lensed spectacles, obviously disguise materials; but no clues as to where the gang might be headed. The police car had stayed there while the officers questioned Vincent, the young hotel employee Toni had spoken to on the phone. The snowplow continued north, on Frank's instructions.

For once, Toni agreed with Frank. It made sense for the gang to switch cars at a location that was on their route, rather than delay their getaway with a diversion. Of course, there was always the possibility that they had foreseen how the police would think and deliberately chosen a location that would mislead pursuers. But in Toni's experience villains were not that subtle. Once they had the swag in their hands, they wanted to get away as fast as they could.

The snowplow did not stop when it passed stationary vehicles. There were two police officers in the cab with the driver, but they were under strict instructions to observe only, for they were not armed, and the gang were. Some of the cars were abandoned, others had one or two people inside, but so far none contained three men and a woman. Most of the occupied cars started up and fell in behind the snowplow, following the track it cleared. There was now a small convoy behind the Jaguar.

Toni was beginning to feel pessimistic. She had hoped by now to have spotted the gang. After all, by the time the thieves had left the Dew Drop Inn, the roads had been all but impassable. How far could they have got?

Could they have some kind of hideout nearby? It seemed improbable. Thieves did not like to go to earth close to the scene of the crime—quite the opposite. As the convoy moved north, Toni worried more and more that her guess was wrong, and the thieves might have driven south.

She spotted a familiar direction sign saying "Beach," and realized they must be near Steepfall. Now she had to put the second part of her plan into operation. She had to go to the house and brief Stanley.

She was dreading it. Her job was to prevent this kind of thing happening. She had done several things right: her vigilance had ensured that the theft was discovered sooner rather than later; she had forced the police to take the biohazard seriously and give chase; and Stanley had to be impressed by the way she had reached him in a blizzard. But she wanted to be able to tell him that the perpetrators had been caught and the emergency was over. Instead, she was going to report her own failure. It would not be the joyous reunion she had anticipated.

Frank was at the Kremlin. Using Osborne's car phone, Toni dialed his mobile.

Frank's voice came out of the Jaguar's speakers. "Detective-Superintendent Hackett."

"Toni here. The snowplow is approaching the turnoff for Stanley Oxenford's house. I'd like to brief him on what's happened."

"You don't need my permission."

"I can't get him on the phone, but the house is only a mile down a side road—"

"Forget it. I've got an armed response team here now, bristling with firepower and itching to go. I'm not going to delay finding the gang."

"It will take the snowplow five or six minutes to clear the lane—and you'll get me out of your hair. And my mother."

"Tempting though that is, I'm not willing to hold up the search for five minutes."

"Stanley may be able to assist the investigation in some way. After all, he is the victim."

"The answer's no," Frank said, and he hung up.

Osborne had heard both sides of the conversation. "This is my car," he said. "I'm not going to Steepfall—I want to stay with the snowplow. I might miss something."

"You can stay with it. You'll leave me and my mother at the house and follow the plow back to the main road. When I've briefed Stanley, I'll borrow a car and catch you up."

"Well, Frank has nixed that scheme."

"I haven't played my ace yet." She dialed Frank again.

This time, his answer was abrupt. "What?"

"Remember Farmer Johnny."

"Go to hell."

"I'm using a hands-free phone, and Carl Osborne is beside me, listening to us both. Where did you tell me to go, again?"

"Pick up the fucking phone."

Toni detached the handset from its cradle and put it to her ear, so that Carl could not hear Frank. "Call the snowplow driver, Frank, please."

"You bitch, you've always held the Farmer Johnny case over my head. You know he was guilty."

"Everyone knows that. But only you and I know what you did to get a conviction."

"You wouldn't tell Carl."

"He's listening to everything I say."

Frank's voice took on a sanctimonious note. "I suppose there's no point in talking to you about loyalty."

"Not since the moment you told Carl about Fluffy the hamster."

That shot went home. Frank began to sound defensive. "Carl wouldn't do the Farmer Johnny story. He's a mate."

"Your trust is deeply touching—him being a journalist, and all."

There was a long silence.

Toni said, "Make up your mind, Frank—the turning is just ahead. Either the snowplow diverts, or I spend the next hour briefing Carl on Farmer Johnny."

There was a click and a hum as Frank hung up.

Toni cradled the phone.

Carl said, "What was that all about?"

"If we drive past the next left turn, I'll tell you."

A few moments later, the snowplow turned onto the side road leading to Steepfall.

7 A.M.

HUGO lay bleeding on the tiled floor, unconscious but breathing.

Olga was weeping. Her chest heaved as she was racked with uncontrollable sobbing. She was close to hysterics.

Stanley Oxenford was gray with shock. He looked like a man who has been told he is dying. He stared at Kit, his face showing despair and bewilderment and suppressed rage. His expression said, *How could you do this to us?* Kit tried not to look at him.

Kit was in a rage. Everything was going wrong. His family now knew he was in league with the thieves, and there was no way they would lie about it, which meant the police would eventually know the whole story. He was doomed to a life on the run from the law. He could hardly contain his anger.

He was also afraid. The virus sample in its perfume

bottle lay on the kitchen table, protected only by two transparent plastic bags. Kit's fear heated his wrath.

Nigel ordered Stanley and Olga to lie facedown beside Hugo, threatening them with his gun. He was so angry at the beating he had taken from Hugo that he might have welcomed an excuse to pull the trigger. Kit would not have tried to stop him. The way he felt, he could have killed someone himself.

Elton searched out improvised ropes—appliance cords, a length of clothesline, and a ball of twine.

Daisy tied up Olga, the unconscious Hugo, and Stanley, binding their feet together and their hands behind their backs. She pulled the cords tight, so that they cut into the flesh, and yanked at the knots to make sure there was no looseness. Her face wore the ugly little smile she showed when she was hurting people.

Kit said to Nigel, "I need my phone."

Nigel said, "Why?"

Kit said, "In case there's a call to the Kremlin that I need to intercept."

Nigel hesitated.

Kit said, "For Christ's sake, I gave you your gun!"

Nigel shrugged and handed over the phone.

"How can you do this, Kit?" Olga said, as Daisy knelt on their father's back. "How can you watch your family being treated this way?"

"It's not my fault!" he rejoined angrily. "If you'd behaved decently to me, none of this would have happened."

"Not your fault?" his father said in bewilderment.

"First you fired me. Then you refused to help me financially, so I ended up owing money to gangsters."

"I fired you because you stole!"

"I'm your son—you should have forgiven me!"

"I *did* forgive you."

"Too late."

"Oh, God."

"I was forced into this!"

Stanley spoke in a voice of authoritative contempt that was familiar to Kit from childhood: "No one is forced into something like this."

Kit hated that tone: it used to be a sign that he had done something particularly stupid. "You don't understand."

"I fear I understand all too well."

That was just typical of him, Kit thought. He always thought he knew best. Well, he looked pretty stupid now, with Daisy tying his hands behind his back.

"What is this about, anyway?" Stanley said.

"Shut your gob," Daisy said.

He ignored her. "What in God's name are you up to with these people, Kit? And what's in the perfume bottle?"

"I said shut up!" Daisy kicked Stanley in the face.

He grunted with pain, and blood came out of his mouth.

That will teach you, Kit thought with savage satisfaction.

Nigel said, "Turn on the TV, Kit. Let's see when this bloody snow is going to stop."

They watched advertisements: January sales, summer holidays, cheap loans. Elton took Nellie by the collar and shut her in the dining room. Hugo stirred and appeared to be coming round, and Olga spoke to him in a low voice. A newscaster appeared wearing a Santa hat. Kit thought bitterly of other families waking up to normal Christmas celebrations. "A freak blizzard hit Scotland last night, bringing a surprise white Christmas to most of the country this morning," the newscaster said.

"Shit," Nigel said with feeling. "How long are we going to be stuck here?"

"The storm, which left dozens of drivers stranded overnight, is expected to ease around daybreak, and the thaw should set in by midmorning."

Kit was cheered. They could still make it to the rendezvous.

Nigel had the same thought. "How far away is that four-wheel drive, Kit?"

"A mile."

"We'll leave here at first light. Have you got yesterday's paper?"

"There must be one somewhere—why?"

"Check what time sunrise is."

Kit went into his father's study and found *The Scotsman* in a magazine rack. He brought it into the kitchen. "Four minutes past eight," he said.

Nigel checked his watch. "Less than an hour." He looked worried. "But then we have to walk a mile in the snow, and drive another ten. We're going to be cutting it fine." He took a phone out of his pocket. He began to dial, then stopped. "Dead battery," he said. "Elton, give me your phone." He took Elton's phone and dialed. "Yeah, it's me. What about this weather, then?" Kit guessed he was speaking to the customer's pilot. "Yeah, should ease up in an hour or so . . . I can get there, but can you?" Nigel was pretending to be more confident than he really felt. Once the snow stopped, a helicopter could take off and go anywhere, but it was not so easy for the gang, traveling by road. "Good. So I'll see you at the appointed time." He pocketed the phone.

The newscaster said, "At the height of the blizzard, thieves raided the laboratories of Oxenford Medical, near Inverburn."

The kitchen went silent. That's it, Kit thought; the truth is out.

"They got away with samples of a dangerous virus."

Stanley spoke through smashed lips. "So that's what's in the perfume bottle . . . Are you people mad?"

"Carl Osborne reports from the scene."

The screen showed a photo of Osborne with a phone to his ear, and his voice was heard over a phone line. "The deadly virus that killed laboratory technician Michael Ross only yesterday is now in the hands of gangsters."

Stanley was incredulous. "But why? Do you imagine you can sell the stuff?"

Nigel said, "I know I can."

On television, Osborne was saying, "In a meticulously planned Christmas caper, three men and a woman defeated the laboratory's state-of-the-art security and penetrated to BioSafety Level Four, where the company keeps stocks of incurable viruses in a locked refrigerator."

Stanley said, "But, Kit, you didn't help them do this, did you?"

Olga spoke up. "Of course he did," she said disgustedly.

"The armed gang overcame security guards, injuring two, one seriously. But many more will die if the Madoba-2 virus is released into the population."

Stanley rolled over with an effort and sat upright. His face was bruised, one eye was closing, and there was blood down the front of his pajamas; yet he still seemed the most authoritative person in the room. "Listen to that fellow on TV," he said.

Daisy moved toward Stanley, but Nigel stopped her with a raised hand.

"You're going to kill yourselves," Stanley said. "If you really have Madoba-2 in that bottle on the table, there's no antidote. If you drop it and the bottle smashes and the fluid leaks out, you're dead. Even if you sell it to someone else and they release it after you've left, it spreads so fast that you could easily catch it and die."

On the screen, Osborne said, "Madoba-2 is believed to be more dangerous than the Black Death that devastated Britain in . . . ancient times."

Stanley raised his voice over the commentary. "He's right, even if he doesn't know what century he's talking about. In Britain in 1348 the Black Death killed one person in three. This could be worse. Surely no amount of money is worth that risk?"

Nigel said, "I won't be in Britain when it's released."

Kit was shocked. Nigel had not previously mentioned this. Had Elton also made plans to go abroad? What about Daisy and Harry Mac? Kit himself intended to be in Italy—but now he wondered if that was far enough away.

Stanley turned to Kit. "You can't possibly think this makes sense."

He was right, Kit thought. The whole thing bordered on insane. But then, the world was crazy. "I'm going to be dead anyway if I don't pay my debts."

"Come on, they're not going to kill you for a debt."

Daisy said, "Oh, yes, we are."

"How much do you owe?"

"A quarter of a million pounds."

"Good God!"

"I told you I was desperate, three months ago, but you wouldn't listen, you bastard."

"How the hell did you manage to run up a debt— No, never mind, forget I asked."

"Gambling on credit. My system is good—I just had a very long run of bad luck."

Olga spoke up. "Luck? Kit, wake up—you've been had! These people lent you the money, then made sure you lost, because they needed you to help them rob the laboratory!"

Kit did not believe that. He said scornfully, "How would you know a thing like that?"

"I'm a lawyer, I meet these people. I hear their pathetic excuses when they're caught. I know more about them than I care to."

Stanley spoke again. "Look, Kit, surely we can find a way out of this without killing innocent people?"

"Too late now. I made my decision, and I've got to see this through."

"But think about it, lad. How many people are you going to kill? Dozens? Thousands? Millions?"

"I see you're willing for me to be killed. You'd protect a crowd of strangers, but you wouldn't rescue me."

Stanley groaned. "God knows I love you, and I don't want you to die, but are you sure you want to save your own life at that price?"

As Kit opened his mouth to reply, his phone rang.

Taking it out of his pocket, he wondered whether Nigel would trust him to answer it. But no one moved, and he held the phone to his ear. He heard the voice of Hamish McKinnon. "Toni's following the snowplow, and she's persuaded them to divert to your place. She'll be there any minute. And there are two police officers in the cab."

Kit ended the call and looked at Nigel. "The police are coming here—now."

7:15 A.M.

CRAIG opened the side door of the garage and peeped out. Three windows were lit in the gable end of the house, but the curtains were drawn, so no casual observer could see him.

He glanced back to where Sophie sat. He had turned out the lights in the garage, but he knew she was in the front passenger seat of Luke's Ford, her pink anorak pulled close around her against the cold. He waved in her direction, then stepped outside.

Moving as quickly as he could, lifting his feet high as he stepped in the deep snow, he went along the blind wall of the garage until he came level with the front of the house.

He was going to get the Ferrari keys. He would have to sneak into the lobby at the back of the kitchen and take them from the key box. Sophie had wanted to go with him, but he had persuaded her that it was more dangerous for two people than for one.

He was more frightened without her. For her sake, he had to pretend to be brave, and that had made him braver. But now he had a bad attack of nerves. As he hesitated at the corner of the house, his hands were shaking and his legs felt strangely weak. He could easily be caught by the strangers, and then he did not know what he would do. He had never been in a real fight, not since he was about eight years old. He knew boys of his own age who fought—outside a pub, usually, on a Saturday night—and all of them, without exception, were stupid. The three strangers in the kitchen were none of them much bigger than Craig, but all the same he was frightened of them. It seemed to him that they would know what to do in a fight, and he had no idea. Anyway, they had guns. They might shoot him. How much would that hurt?

He looked along the front of the house. He was going to have to pass the windows of the living room and the dining room, where the curtains were not drawn. The snowfall was not as thick as before, and he could easily be seen by someone glancing out.

He forced himself to move forward.

He stopped at the first window and looked into the living room. Fairy lights flashed on the Christmas tree, dimly outlining the familiar couches and tables, the television set, and four oversize children's stockings on the floor in front of the fireplace, stuffed with boxes and packages.

There was no one in the room.

He walked on. The snow seemed deeper here, blown into a drift by the wind off the sea. Wading through it was surprisingly tiring. He almost felt like lying down. He realized he had been without sleep for twenty-four hours. He shook himself and pressed on. Passing the front door, he half-expected that it would suddenly fly open, and the Londoner in the pink sweater would leap out and grab him. But nothing happened.

As he drew level with the dark dining room windows, he was startled by a soft bark. For a moment his heart seemed to bang against his chest; then he realized it was only Nellie. They must have shut her in there. The dog recognized Craig's silhouette and gave a low let-me-out-of-here whine. "Quiet, Nellie, for God's sake," he murmured. He doubted whether the dog could hear him, but she fell silent anyway.

He passed the parked cars, Miranda's Toyota Previa and Hugo's Mercedes-Benz station wagon. Their sides as well as their tops were all white, so that they looked as if they might be snow all the way through, snow cars for snowmen. He rounded the corner of the house. There was a light in the window of the boot lobby. Cautiously, he peeped around the edge of the window frame. He could see the big walk-in cupboard where anoraks and boots were kept. There was a watercolor of Steepfall that must have been painted by Aunt Miranda, a yard brush leaning in a corner—and the steel key box, screwed to the wall.

The door from the lobby to the kitchen was closed. That was lucky.

He listened, but he could not hear anything from inside the house.

What happened when you punched someone? In the cinema they just fell down, but he was pretty sure that would not happen in real life. More important, what happened when someone punched you? How much did it hurt? What if they did it again and again? And what was it like to be shot? He had heard somewhere that the most painful thing in the world was a bullet in the stomach. He was absolutely terrified, but he forced himself to move.

He grasped the handle of the back door, turned it as gently as he could, and pushed. The door swung open and he stepped inside. The lobby was a small room, six feet long, narrowed by the brickwork of the massive old chimney and the deep cupboard beside it. The key box hung on the chimney wall. Craig reached to open it. There were twenty numbered hooks, some with single keys and some with bunches, but he instantly recognized the Ferrari keys. He grasped them and lifted, but the fob snagged on the hook. He jiggled it, fighting down panic. Then someone rattled the handle of the kitchen door.

Craig's heart leaped in his chest. The person was trying to open the door between the kitchen and the lobby. He or she had turned the handle, but was obviously unfamiliar with the house and was pushing instead of pulling. In the moment of delay, Craig stepped into the coat cupboard and closed the door behind him.

He had done it without thought, abandoning the keys. As soon as he was inside, he realized it would have been almost as quick to go out of the back door into the garden. He tried to remember whether he had closed the back door. He thought not. And had fresh snow fallen from his boots onto the floor? That would reveal that someone had been there in the last minute or so, for otherwise it would have melted. And he had left the key box open.

An observant person would see the clues and guess the truth in an instant.

He held his breath and listened.

NIGEL rattled the handle until he realized that the door opened inward, not out. He pulled it wide and looked into the boot lobby. "No good," he said. "Door and a window." He crossed the kitchen and flung open the door to the pantry. "This will do. No other doors and only one window, overlooking the courtyard. Elton, put them in here."

"It's cold in there," Olga protested. There was an air-conditioning unit in the pantry.

"Oh, stop it. You'll make me cry," Nigel said sarcastically.

"My husband needs a doctor."

"After punching me, he's lucky he doesn't need a fucking undertaker." Nigel turned back to Elton. "Stuff something in their mouths so they can't make a noise. Quick, we may not have much time!"

Elton found a drawer full of clean tea towels. He gagged Stanley, Olga, and Hugo, who was now conscious, though dazed. Then he got the bound prisoners to their feet and pushed them into the pantry.

"Listen to me," Nigel said to Kit. Nigel was superficially calm, planning ahead and giving orders, but he was pale, and the expression on his narrow, cynical face was grim. Beneath the surface, Kit saw, he was wound as tight as a guitar string. "When the police get here, you're going to the door," Nigel went on. "Speak to them nicely, look relaxed, the law-abiding citizen. Say that nothing's wrong here, and everyone in the house is still asleep except you."

Kit did not know how he was going to appear relaxed when he felt as if he were facing a firing squad. He gripped the back of a kitchen chair to stop himself shaking. "What if they want to come in?"

"Discourage them. If they insist, bring them into the kitchen. We'll be in that little back room." He pointed to the boot lobby. "Just get rid of them as fast as you can."

"Toni Gallo is coming along with the police," Kit said. "She's head of security at the lab."

"Well, tell her to go away."

"She'll want to see my father."

"Say she can't."

"She may not take no for an answer—"

Nigel raised his voice. "For crying out loud, what is she going to do—knock you down and walk in over your unconscious body? Just tell her to fuck off."

"All right," Kit said. "But we need to keep my sister Miranda quiet. She's hiding in the attic."

"Attic? Where?"

"Directly above this room. Look inside the first cupboard in the dressing room. Behind the suits is a low door leading into the roof space."

Nigel did not ask how Kit knew Miranda was there. He looked at Daisy. "Take care of it."

MIRANDA saw her brother speaking to Nigel and heard his words as he betrayed her.

She crossed the attic in a moment and crawled through the door into Daddy's suit cupboard. She was panting hard, her heart was racing, and she felt flushed, but she was not in a panic, not yet. She jumped out of the cupboard into the dressing room.

She had heard Kit say the police were coming and, for a joyful moment, she had thought they were saved. All she had to do was sit tight until men in blue uniforms walked in through the front door and arrested the thieves. Then she had listened with horror as Nigel rapidly devised a way of getting rid of the police. What was she to do if the police seemed about to leave without arresting anyone? She had decided she would open a bedroom window and start screaming.

Now Kit had spoiled that plan.

She was terrified of meeting Daisy again, but she held on to her reason, just.

She could hide in Kit's bedroom, on the other side of the landing, while Daisy searched the attic. That would not fool Daisy for more than a few seconds, but it might give Miranda just long enough to open a window and yell for help.

She ran through the bedroom. As she put her hand on the doorknob, she heard heavy boots on the stairs. She was too late.

The door flew open. Miranda hid behind it. Daisy stormed through the bedroom and into the dressing room without looking back.

Miranda slipped out of the door. She crossed the landing and stepped into Kit's room. She ran to the window and pulled back the curtains, hoping to see police cars with flashing lights.

There was no one outside.

She peered in the direction of the lane. It was getting light, and she could see the trees laden with snow at the edge of the wood, but no cars. She almost despaired. Daisy would take only a few seconds to look around the attic and make sure no one was there. Then she would check the rest of the upstairs rooms. Miranda needed more time. How far away could the police be?

Was there any way she could shut Daisy in the attic?

She did not give herself a second to worry about risks. She ran back to her father's room. She could see the door of the suit cupboard standing open. Daisy must be in the attic right now, staring around with those bruised-looking eyes, wondering if there were any hiding places big enough to conceal a grown woman, somewhat overweight.

Without forethought, Miranda closed the cupboard door.

There was no lock, but it was made of solid wood. If she could jam it shut, Daisy would have trouble busting it open, especially as she would have little room to maneuver inside the cupboard.

There was a narrow gap at the bottom of the door. If she could wedge something into it, the door would stick, at least for a few seconds. What could she use? She needed a piece of wood, or cardboard, or even a sheaf of paper. She pulled open her father's bedside drawer and found a volume of Proust.

She started ripping pages out.

KIT heard the dog bark in the next room.

It was a loud, aggressive bark, the kind she gave when a stranger was at the door. Someone was coming. Kit pushed through the swing door that led to the dining room. The dog was standing with her forepaws on the windowsill.

Kit went to the window. The snow had eased to a light scatter of flakes. He looked toward the woods and saw, emerging from the trees, a big truck with a flashing orange light on top and a snowplow blade in front.

"They're here!" he called out.

Nigel came in. The dog growled, and Kit said, "Shut up." Nellie retreated to a corner. Nigel flattened himself against the wall beside the window and peered out.

The snowplow cleared a path eight or ten feet wide. It passed the front door and came as close as it could to the parked cars. At the last moment it turned, sweeping away the snow in front of Hugo's Mercedes and Miranda's Previa. Then it reversed to the garage block, turned off the drive, and cleared a swath of the concrete apron in front of the garage doors. As it did so, a light-colored Jaguar S-type came past it, using the track it had made in the snow, and pulled up at the front door.

A figure got out of the car: a tall, slim woman with bobbed hair, wearing a leather flying jacket with a sheepskin lining. In the reflected light from the head-lamps, Kit recognized Toni Gallo.

"Get rid of her," said Nigel.

"What's happened to Daisy? She's taking a long time—"

"She'll deal with your sister."

"She'd better."

"I trust Daisy more than I trust you. Now go to the door." Nigel retreated into the boot lobby with Elton.

Kit went to the front door and opened it.

Toni was helping someone out of the back of the car. Kit frowned. It was an old lady in a long wool coat and a fur hat. He said aloud, "What the hell . . . ?"

Toni took the old lady's arm and they turned around. Toni's face darkened with disappointment when she saw who had come to the door. "Hello, Kit," she said. She walked the old woman toward the house.

Kit said, "What do you want?"

"I've come to see your father. There's an emergency at the laboratory."

"Daddy's asleep."

"He'll want to wake up for this, trust me."

"Who's the old woman?"

"This *lady* is my mother, Mrs. Kathleen Gallo."

"And I'm not an old woman," said the old woman. "I'm seventy-one, and as fit as a butcher's dog, so mind your manners."

"All right, Mother, he didn't mean to be rude."

Kit ignored that. "What's she doing here?"

"I'll explain to your father."

The snowplow had turned around in front of the garage, and now it returned along the track it had cleared, heading back through the woods toward the main road. The Jaguar followed.

Kit felt panicked. What should he do? The cars were leaving, but Toni was still here.

The Jaguar stopped suddenly. Kit hoped the driver had not seen something suspicious. The car reversed back to the house. The driver's door opened, and a small bundle fell out into the snow. It looked, Kit thought, almost like a puppy.

The door slammed, and the car pulled away.

Toni went back and picked up the bundle. It was a puppy, a black-and-white English sheepdog about eight weeks old.

Kit was bewildered, but he decided not to ask questions. "You can't come in," he said to Toni.

"Don't be stupid," she replied. "This is not your house. It's your father's, and he'll want to see me." She continued walking slowly toward him with her mother on one arm and the puppy cradled in the other.

Kit was stymied. He had expected Toni to be in her own car, and his plan had been to tell her she should come back later. For a moment, he considered running after the Jaguar and telling the driver to come back. But the driver would surely ask why. And the police in the snowplow might ask what the fuss was about. It was too dangerous. Kit did nothing.

Toni stood in front of Kit, who was blocking the doorway. "Is something wrong?" she said.

He was stuck, he realized. If he persisted in trying to

obey Nigel's orders, he might bring the police back. Toni on her own was more manageable. "You'd better come in," he said.

"Thanks. By the way, the puppy's name is Osborne." Toni and her mother stepped into the hall. "Do you need the bathroom, Mother?" Toni asked. "It's just here."

Kit watched the lights of the snowplow and the Jaguar disappear into the woods. He relaxed slightly. He was saddled with Toni, but he had got rid of the police. He closed the front door.

There was a loud bang from upstairs, like a hammer hitting a wall.

"What the heck was that?" said Toni.

MIRANDA had taken a thick sheaf of pages from the book and folded them into a wedge which she had shoved into the gap under the cupboard door. That would not hold Daisy for long. She needed a more solid barrier. Beside the bed was an antique commode chest used as a bedside table. With a huge effort, she dragged the heavy mahogany chest across the carpet, tilted it at a forty-five-degree angle, and jammed it against the door. Almost immediately, she heard Daisy pushing at the other side of the door. When pushing failed, she banged.

Miranda guessed Daisy was lying with her head in the attic and her feet in the cupboard, kicking the door with the soles of her boots. The door shuddered but did not fly open. However, Daisy was tough, and she would find a way. Nevertheless, Miranda had won a few precious seconds.

She flew to the window. To her dismay, she saw two vehicles—a truck and a sedan—driving *away* from the house. "Oh, no!" she said aloud. The vehicles were already too far for the people inside them to hear her scream. Was she too late? She ran out of the bedroom.

She stopped at the top of the stairs. Down in the hall, there was an old woman she had never seen before, going into the bathroom.

What was happening?

Next she recognized Toni Gallo, taking off a flying jacket and hanging it on the hat stand.

A small black-and-white puppy was sniffing the umbrellas.

Kit came into view. There was another bang from the dressing room, and Kit said to Toni, "The children must be awake."

Miranda was bewildered. How could this be? Kit was acting as if there was nothing wrong . . .

He must be fooling Toni, Miranda realized. He was hoping to make her think that all was well. Then he would either persuade her to leave, or overpower her and tie her up with the others.

Meanwhile, the police were driving away.

Toni closed the bathroom door on her mother. No one had yet noticed Miranda.

Kit said to Toni, "You'd better come into the kitchen."

That was where they would jump her, Miranda guessed. Nigel and Elton would be waiting, and they would take her by surprise.

There was a crash from within the bedroom: Daisy had broken out of the cupboard.

Miranda acted without thinking. "Toni!" she screamed.

Toni looked up the stairs and saw her.

Kit said, "Shit, no—"

Miranda yelled, "The thieves, they're here, they've tied Daddy up, they've got guns—"

Daisy burst out of the bedroom and crashed into Miranda, sending her tumbling down the stairs.

7:30 A.M.

FOR an instant, Toni froze.

Kit stood beside her, an expression of rage on his face, looking up the stairs. With a twisted mouth he said, "Get her, Daisy!"

Miranda was falling down the stairs, her pink nightdress billowing up to reveal plump white thighs.

Running after her was an ugly young woman with a shaved head and Gothic eye makeup, dressed in leather.

And Mother was in the bathroom.

In a flash of comprehension, Toni understood what was happening. Thieves with guns were here, Miranda had said. There could not be two such gangs operating in this remote area on the same night. These must be the people who had robbed the Kremlin. The bald woman at the top of the stairs would be the blonde Toni had seen on the security video—her wig had been found in the getaway van. Toni's mind raced ahead: Kit seemed to be in league with them—which would explain how they had defeated the security system—

As that thought struck her, Kit hooked his arm around her neck and pulled, trying to yank her off her feet. At the same time, he yelled: "Nigel!"

She elbowed him forcefully in the ribs, and had the satisfaction of hearing him grunt with pain. His grip on her neck eased, and she was able to turn and hit him again, this time a punch in the midriff with her left fist. He lashed out at her, but she easily dodged the blow.

She drew back her right arm for a real knockout punch but, before she could strike, Miranda reached the foot of the stairs and crashed into the back of Toni's legs. Because Toni was leaning back, ready to hit Kit, she fell backward. A moment later, the woman in leather tripped over Miranda and Toni and collided with Kit, and all four of them ended up in a heap on the flagstone floor.

Toni realized she could not win this fight. She was up against Kit and the woman he had called Daisy, and soon she might have others to contend with. She had to get away from these people, catch her breath, and figure out what to do.

She wriggled out of the scrum and rolled over.

Kit was flat on his back. Miranda was curled up in a ball, appearing bruised and winded but not seriously injured. As Toni looked, Daisy got to her knees and, apparently in a fury, punched Miranda, striking her on the arm with a fist encased, peculiarly, in a ladylike tan suede glove.

Toni leaped to her feet. She jumped over Kit, reached the front door, and threw it open. Kit grabbed her ankle with one hand, holding her back. She twisted, and kicked at his arm with the other foot. She connected with his elbow. He cried out in pain and released his grip. Toni jumped out through the doorway and slammed the door behind her.

She turned right and dashed along the track made by the snowplow. She heard a gunshot, and a crash as a pane of glass shattered in a window near her. Someone was shooting at her from inside the house. But the bullet missed.

She ran to the garage and turned onto the concrete apron in front of the doors, where the snowplow had cleared a space. Now the garage block was between her and the person with the gun.

The snowplow, with its two police officers in the cab, had departed at normal speed along the cleared road with its blade raised. That meant that by now the truck was too far away for her to catch it on foot. What was she going to do? While she was on the cleared path, she could easily be followed by someone from the house. But where could she hide? She glanced over to the woods. Plenty of cover there, but she had no coat—she had taken off her flying jacket just before Miranda yelled her warning—so she would not last long in the open. The garage itself would be almost as cold.

She ran to the other end of the building and looked around the corner. A few yards away, she could see the door to the barn. Did she dare to risk crossing the courtyard, in view of the house? She had no other choice.

As she was about to set off, the barn door opened.

She hesitated. What now?

A small boy emerged wearing a coat over Spider-Man pajamas and a pair of rubber boots too big for his feet. Toni recognized Tom, the son of Miranda. He did not look around, but turned left and trudged through the deep snow. Toni assumed he was heading for the house, and asked herself whether she should stop him; but after a moment she realized that her assumption was wrong. Instead of crossing the courtyard to the main house, he went to the guest cottage. Toni willed him to hurry, to get out of the way before trouble started. She imagined he was looking for his mother to ask if he could open his presents. In fact, his mother was in the main house, being punched by a woman gangster in tan suede gloves. But perhaps Miranda's fiancé was in the cottage. Toni thought it wiser to leave the boy to find out. The cottage door was not locked, and Tom disappeared inside.

Still Toni hesitated. Was there someone behind one of the house windows, covering the courtyard with a nine-millimeter Browning automatic pistol? She was about to find out.

She set off at a run but, as soon as she hit the deep snow, she fell. She lay there for a second, waiting for a gunshot, but none came. She struggled to her feet, cold snow chilling her through her jeans and sweater, and pressed on, walking more carefully but more slowly. She looked fearfully at the house. She could see no one at any of the windows. It could not take more than a minute to cross the courtyard, but each big step took painfully long. At last she reached the barn, stepped inside, and swung the door closed behind her, shaking with relief that she was still alive.

A small lamp revealed a billiard table, an assortment of elderly couches, a large-screen television set, and two camp beds, both empty. There appeared to be no one else in the room, though a ladder led to a loft. Toni made herself stop shaking and climbed the ladder. When she was halfway up, she peeped over the top. She was startled by several pairs of small red eyes staring at her: Caroline's rats. She climbed the rest of the way. There were two more beds here. The somnolent lump in one was Caroline. The other had not been slept in.

It would not be long before the gang in the house came looking for Toni. She had to get help fast. She reached for her mobile phone.

Then she realized she did not have it.

She shook her clenched fists at the ceiling in frustration. Her phone was in the pocket of the flying jacket, which she had hung up in the hall.

What was she going to do now?

"WE'VE got to get after her," Nigel said. "She could be on the phone to the police already."

"Wait," Kit said. He stepped across the hall to the hat stand. He was rubbing his left elbow where Toni had kicked him, but he stopped in order to search her jacket. Triumphantly, he produced a phone from one of her pockets. "She can't call the police."

"Thank God for that." Nigel looked around the hall. Daisy had Miranda facedown on the floor with her arm bent behind her back. Elton stood in the kitchen doorway. Nigel said, "Elton, get some more rope so Daisy can tie up this fat cow." He turned back to Kit. "Your sisters are a right bloody pair."

"Never mind that," Kit said. "We can get away now, can't we? We don't have to wait for daylight or fetch the four-wheel drive. We can use any car, and take the path cleared by the snowplow."

"Your man said there were coppers in that snowplow."

"The one place they won't look for us is right behind them."

Nigel nodded. "Clever. But the snowplow's not going all the way to . . . where we need to be. What do we do when it turns off our route?"

Kit suppressed his impatience. They had to get away from Steepfall at any cost, but Nigel had not yet figured that out. "Look out of the window," he said. "The snow has stopped. It will start to thaw soon, the forecast said."

"We could still get stuck."

"We're in worse danger here, now that the road has been cleared. Toni Gallo might not be the only visitor to show up."

Elton returned with a length of electric cable. "Kit's right," he said. "We can easily get there by ten o'clock, barring accidents." He handed the cable to Daisy, who tied Miranda's hands behind her back.

"Okay," Nigel said. "But first we have to round everyone up, including kids, and make sure they can't call for help for the next few hours."

Daisy dragged Miranda through the kitchen and shoved her into the pantry.

Kit said, "Miranda's phone must be in the cottage. Otherwise she would have used it by now. Her boyfriend, Ned, is there."

Nigel said, "Elton, go to the cottage."

Kit went on: "There's a phone in the Ferrari. I suggest Daisy goes to the garage to make sure no one is trying to use it."

"What about the barn?"

"Leave it till last. Caroline, Craig, and Tom don't have phones. I'm not sure about Sophie, but she's only fourteen."

"All right," Nigel said. "Let's get it done as fast as possible."

The bathroom door opened and Toni Gallo's mother came out, still wearing her hat.

Kit and Nigel stared at her for a moment. Kit had forgotten she was in there.

Then Nigel said, "Stick her in the pantry with the others."

"Oh, no," the old woman said. "I think I'd rather sit by the Christmas tree." She crossed the hall and went into the living room.

Kit looked at Nigel, who shrugged.

CRAIG opened the door of the boot cupboard a crack. Peeping out, he saw that the lobby was empty. He was about to step out when one of the gangsters, Elton, came in from the kitchen. Craig pulled the door an inch toward himself and held his breath.

It had been like this for a quarter of an hour.

One of the gang was always in view. The cupboard smelled mustily of damp anoraks and old boots. He worried about Sophie, sitting in Luke's Ford in the garage, getting cold. He tried to wait patiently. His chance would surely come soon.

A few minutes ago Nellie had barked, which must have meant someone at the door. Craig's heart had lifted in hope; but Nigel and Elton had stood inches away from Craig, talking in whispers that he could not quite make out. They must have been hiding from the visitor, Craig decided. He wanted to burst out of the cupboard and run to the door yelling for help, but he knew he would be seized and silenced the instant he revealed himself. It was maddeningly frustrating.

There was a banging from upstairs, as if someone was trying to bash a door down. Then there was a different bang, more like a firework—or a gun going off. It was followed instantly by the sound of breaking glass. Craig was dismayed and frightened. Until this moment, the gang had used guns only to threaten. Now that they had started shooting, where would it end? The family was in terrible danger.

At the gunshot, Nigel and Elton went, but left the door open, and Elton remained in sight at the far end of the kitchen, talking urgently to someone in the hall. Then he returned, but went out the back way, leaving the door wide open.

At last Craig could move without being seen. The others were in the hall. This was his chance. He stepped out of the cupboard.

He flipped open the key box and snatched the Ferrari keys. This time they came off the hook without snagging.

In two strides he was out of the door.

The snow had stopped. Somewhere beyond the clouds dawn was breaking, and he could see in black-and-white. To his left was Elton, trudging through the snow, heading for the guest cottage. Elton's back was turned and he did not see Craig. Craig went the other way and turned the corner, so that the house hid him from Elton.

He was shocked to see Daisy only yards away.

Fortunately she, too, had her back to him. She had obviously come out of the front door and was walking away from him. There was a cleared path, and he realized that a snowplow had been here while he was hiding in the boot cupboard. Daisy was heading for the garage—and Sophie.

He ducked behind his father's Mercedes. Peeping around the wing, he saw Daisy reach the end of the building, leave the cleared path, and turn the corner of the house, disappearing from view.

He went after her. Moving as fast as he could, he went along the front of the house. He passed the dining room, where Nellie stood with her forepaws on the windowsill; then the front door, which was shut; then the living room with its flashing Christmas tree. He was astonished to see an old lady sitting by the tree with a puppy in her lap. He did not pause to wonder who she was.

He reached the corner and looked around. Daisy was heading straight for the side door of the garage. If she went in there, she would find Sophie sitting in Luke's Ford.

She reached into the pocket of her black leather jacket and took out her gun.

Craig watched, helpless, as she opened the door.

7:45 A.M.

THE pantry was cold.

The Christmas turkey, too large to fit into the kitchen refrigerator, stood on a baking tray on a marble shelf, stuffed and seasoned by Olga, ready for roasting. Miranda wondered dismally if she would live to eat it.

She stood with her father, her sister, and Hugo, the four of them trussed like the turkey and crammed into a space three feet square, surrounded by food: vegetables in racks, a shelf of pasta in jars, boxes of breakfast cereals, cans of tuna and plum tomatoes and baked beans.

Hugo was in the worst state. He seemed to be drifting in and out of consciousness. He was leaning against the wall and Olga was pressing herself to his naked body, trying to keep him warm. Stanley's face looked as if he had been hit by a truck, but he was standing erect and his expression was alert.

Miranda felt helpless and miserable. It was heart-breaking to see her father, such a strong character, wounded and tied up. Hugo was a rotter but he hardly deserved this: he looked as if he might have suffered permanent damage. And Olga was a hero, trying so hard to comfort the husband who had betrayed her.

The others had tea towels stuffed into their mouths, but Daisy had not bothered to gag Miranda, presumably because there was no point in anyone shouting now that the police had gone. Miranda realized, with a spurt of hope, that she might be able to remove the gags. "Daddy, lean down," she said. He bent his tall figure over her obediently, the end of the gag trailing from his mouth. She tilted her head as if to kiss him. She was able to catch a corner of the tea towel between her teeth. She tugged, pulling part of it out; then, frustratingly, it slipped.

Miranda let out an exclamation of exasperation. Her father bent down, encouraging her to try again. They repeated the process, and this time the whole thing came out and fell to the floor.

"Thank you," he said. "By God, that was ghastly."

Miranda did the same for Olga, who said, "I kept wanting to puke, but I was afraid I would choke myself."

Olga removed Hugo's gag by the same method. "Try to stay awake, Hugo," she said urgently. "Come on, keep your eyes open."

Stanley asked Miranda, "What's going on out there?"

"Toni Gallo came here with a snowplow and some policemen," she explained. "Kit went to the door as if everything was all right, and the police left, but Toni insisted on staying."

"That woman is incredible."

"I was hiding in the attic. I managed to warn Toni."

"Well done!"

"That frightful Daisy pushed me down the stairs, but Toni got away. I don't know where she is now."

"She can phone the police."

Miranda shook her head. "She left her phone in her coat pocket, and Kit's got it."

"She'll think of something—she's remarkably resourceful. Anyway, she's our only hope. No one else is free, except the children, and Ned, of course."

"I'm afraid Ned won't be much use," Miranda said gloomily. "In a situation like this, the last thing you need is a Shakespeare scholar." She was thinking how feeble he had been yesterday with his ex, Jennifer, when she threw Miranda out of the house. What hope was there that such a man would stand up to three professional thugs?

She looked out of the pantry window. Dawn had broken and the snow had stopped, so she could see the cottage where Ned lay sleeping and the barn where the children were. She was horrified to see Elton crossing the courtyard. "Oh, God," she said. "He's heading for the cottage."

Her father looked out. "They're rounding people up," he said. "They'll tie everyone before they leave. We can't let them get away with that virus—but how can we stop them?"

Elton went into the cottage.

"I hope Ned's all right." Miranda was suddenly glad Ned was not the belligerent type. Elton was tough, ruthless, and armed. Ned's only hope was to come quietly.

"It could be worse," Stanley said. "That lad's a villain, but he's not a complete psychopath. The woman is."

"She makes mistakes because she's insane," Miranda said. "In the hall, a few minutes ago, she was punching me when she should have been catching Toni. That's why Toni got away."

"Why did Daisy want to punch you?"

"I locked her in the attic."

"You locked her in the attic?"

"She went there looking for me, and I closed the cupboard door behind her and jammed it shut. That's what made her so angry."

Her father seemed choked up. "Brave girl," he whispered.

"I'm not brave," Miranda said. The idea was absurd. "I was just so terrified that I was willing to do anything."

"I think you're brave." Tears came to his eyes, and he turned away.

Ned emerged from the cottage. Elton was close behind, holding a gun to the back of Ned's head. With his left hand, Elton held Tom by the arm.

Miranda gasped with shock. She had thought Tom was in the barn. He must have woken up and gone looking for his mother. He was wearing his Spider-Man pajamas. Miranda fought back tears.

The three of them were heading for the house, but then there was a shout, and they stopped. A moment later Daisy came into view, dragging Sophie by the hair. Sophie was bent double, stumbling in the snow, crying with pain.

Daisy said something to Elton that Miranda could not hear. Then Tom screamed at Daisy: "Leave her alone! You're hurting her!" His voice was a childish treble, made more high pitched by fear and rage.

Miranda recalled that Tom had a preadolescent passion for Sophie. "Be quiet, Tommy," she murmured fearfully, although he could not hear her. "It doesn't matter if she gets her hair pulled."

Elton laughed. Daisy grinned and yanked more viciously at Sophie's hair.

It was probably being laughed at that drove Tom over the edge. He suddenly went berserk. He jerked his arm out of Elton's grasp and threw himself at Daisy.

Miranda shouted: "No!"

Daisy was so surprised that when Tom crashed into her, she fell backward, letting go of Sophie's hair, and sat down in the snow. Tom dived on top of her, pummeling her with his small fists.

Miranda found herself shouting uselessly: "Stop! Stop!"

Daisy pushed Tom away and got to her feet. Tom jumped up, but Daisy hit him with her gloved fist on the side of the head, and he fell down again. She heaved him up off the ground and, in a fury, held him upright with her left hand while she punched him with her right, hitting his face and body.

Miranda screamed.

Suddenly Ned moved.

Ignoring the gun that Elton was pointing at him, he stepped between Daisy and Tom. He said something that Miranda could not hear and put a restraining hand on Daisy's arm. Miranda was astonished: weak Ned standing up to thugs!

Without letting go of Tom, Daisy punched Ned in the stomach.

He doubled over, his face screwed up in a grimace of agony. But when Daisy drew back her arm to punch Tom again, Ned straightened up and stood in her way. Changing her mind at the last instant, she punched Ned instead of Tom, hitting him in the mouth. Ned cried out, and his hands flew to his face, but he did not move.

Miranda was profoundly grateful that Ned had distracted Daisy from Tom—but how long could he stand this beating?

He continued to remonstrate with Daisy. When he took his hands away from his face, blood poured out of his mouth. As Miranda watched, Daisy punched him a third time.

Miranda was awestruck. Ned was like a wall. He simply stood there and took the blows. And he was doing it, not for his own child, but for Tom. Miranda felt ashamed of thinking he was weak.

At that moment Ned's own child, Sophie, acted. She had been standing still, watching in a stunned way, since Daisy let go of her hair. Now she turned around and moved away.

Elton made a grab for her, but she slipped through his grasp. For a moment, he lost balance, and Sophie broke into a run, crossing the deep snow with balletic leaps.

Hastily, Elton righted himself, but Sophie had disappeared.

Elton grabbed Tom and shouted at Daisy: "Don't let that girl get away!" Daisy looked disposed to argue. Elton yelled: "I've got these two. Go, go!"

With a malevolent look at Ned and Tom, Daisy turned and went after Sophie.

8 A.M.

CRAIG turned the key in the ignition of the Ferrari. Behind him, the huge rear-mounted V12 engine started, then died.

Craig closed his eyes. "Not now," he said aloud. "Don't let me down now."

He turned the key again. The engine fired, faltered, then roared like an angry bull. Craig pumped the throttle, just to be sure, and the roar turned into a howl.

He looked at the phone. It said: "Searching . . ." He jabbed at the number pad, dialing 999, even though he knew it was useless before the phone had connected to the network. "Come on," he urged. "I don't have much time—"

The side door of the garage flew open, and Sophie stumbled in.

Craig was taken by surprise. He thought Sophie was in the hands of the dreadful Daisy. He had watched as Daisy dragged her out of the garage. He had wanted desperately to rescue her, but he did not think he could beat Daisy in a fight even if she had not had a gun. He had struggled to remain calm as he watched Daisy maliciously dragging Sophie along by the hair. He kept telling himself that the best thing he could do for Sophie was to stay free and phone the police.

Now she seemed to have escaped unaided. She was sobbing and panicky, and he guessed that Daisy must be on her tail.

The passenger side of the car was so close to the wall that the door could not be opened. Craig threw open the driver's door and said, "Get in quick—climb over me!"

She staggered over to the car and fell in.

Craig slammed the door.

He did not know how to lock it, and he was too rushed to find out. Daisy could not be more than a few seconds away, he figured, as Sophie scrambled over him. There was no time to phone—they had to get out of there. As Sophie collapsed into the passenger seat, he fumbled under the dashboard and found the remote control device that opened the garage door. He pressed it, and heard behind him a squeak of unlubricated metal as the mechanism operated. He looked in the rearview mirror and saw the up-and-over door begin to move slowly.

Then Daisy came in.

Her face was red with exertion and her eyes were wide with rage. There was snow in the creases of her black leather clothes. She hesitated in the doorway, peering into the gloom of the garage; then her staring eyes locked on to Craig in the driving seat of the car.

He depressed the clutch and shoved the gearshift into reverse. It was never easy, with the Ferrari's six-speed box. The stick resisted his push, and there was a grinding of cogs; then something slipped into place.

Daisy ran across the front of the car and came to the driver's side. Her tan glove closed on the door handle.

The garage door was not yet fully open, but Craig could wait no longer. Just as Daisy opened the car door, he released the clutch and trod on the accelerator pedal.

The car leaped backward as if fired from a catapult. Its roof struck the lower edge of the aluminum garage door with a clang. Sophie gave a yell of fear.

The car flew out of the garage like a champagne cork. Craig stamped on the brake. The snowplow had cleared the thick overnight layer of snow from in front of the garage, but more had fallen since, and the concrete apron was slippery. The Ferrari went into a backward skid and stopped with a bump against a bank of snow.

Daisy came out of the garage. Craig could see her clearly in the gray dawn light. She hesitated.

The car phone suddenly spoke in a female voice. "You have one new message."

Craig pushed the gearshift into what he hoped was first. He eased the clutch out and, to his relief, the tires found purchase and the car moved forward. He turned the wheel, heading for the way out. If only he could make it onto the drive, he could get away from here with Sophie and summon help.

Daisy must have had the same thought, for she fumbled in the pocket of her jacket and brought out a gun.

"Get down!" Craig yelled at Sophie. "She's going to shoot!"

As Daisy leveled the gun, he stamped on the accelerator and swung the steering wheel, desperate to get away.

The car went into a skid, slipping across the icy concrete. Alongside his fear and panic, Craig had the feeling of déjà vu: he had skidded this car, in this place, only yesterday, a lifetime ago. Now he struggled to control the vehicle, but the ground was even more slippery after a night of steady snow and freezing temperatures.

He turned into the skid, and for a moment the tires gripped again, but he overdid it, and the car skidded in the opposite direction and spun around in a half circle. Sophie was flung from side to side in the passenger seat. He kept waiting for the bang of a gunshot, but none came yet. The only good thing, a part of Craig's terrified mind told him, was that it was impossible for Daisy to take steady aim at a vehicle that was being driven so erratically.

The car stopped, with great good luck, in the middle of the drive, facing directly away from the house and toward the lane. The path in front of Craig had obviously been swept by the snowplow. He had a clear road to freedom.

He pressed on the accelerator pedal, but nothing happened. The engine had stalled.

Out of the corner of his eye, he saw Daisy raise the gun and take careful aim at him.

He turned the key, and the car jerked forward: he had forgotten to take it out of gear. The mistake saved his life for, in the same instant, he heard the unmistakable firecracker bang of a gun, only slightly deadened by the soft snow covering everything; then the side window of the car shattered. Sophie screamed.

Craig knocked the stick into neutral and turned the key again. The throaty roar filled his ears. He could see Daisy taking aim again as he pressed the clutch and found first gear. He ducked involuntarily as he pulled away, and it was lucky that he did, for this time his side window smashed.

The bullet also went through the windshield, making a small round hole and causing the entire pane of glass to craze over. Now he could see nothing ahead but blurred shapes of darkness and light. Nevertheless he kept the accelerator depressed, doing his best to stay on the driveway, knowing he would die if he did not get away from Daisy and her gun. Beside him, Sophie was curled up in a ball on the passenger seat, hands covering her head.

On the periphery of his vision, he saw Daisy running after the car. Another shot banged. The car phone said: "Stanley, this is Toni. Bad news—a break-in at the lab. Please call my mobile as soon as you can."

Craig guessed that the people with guns must be connected to the break-in, but he could not think about that now. He tried to steer by what he could see out of the smashed side window, but it was no good. After a few seconds, the car went off the cleared path, and he felt the sudden drag as it slowed. The shape of a tree appeared in the crazed glass of the windshield, and Craig slammed on the brakes, but he was too late, and the car hit the tree with a terrific crash.

Craig was thrown forward. His head hit the broken windshield, knocking out shards of glass, cutting the skin of his forehead. The steering wheel bruised his chest. Sophie was flung against the dashboard and fell with her bottom on the floor and her feet up on the seat, but she swore and tried to right herself, so he knew she was all right.

The engine had stalled again.

Craig looked in the rearview mirror. Daisy was ten yards behind him, walking steadily across the snow toward the car, holding the gun in her suede-gloved hand. He knew instinctively that she was coming closer just to get a clear shot. She was going to kill him and Sophie.

He had only one chance left. He had to kill her.

He started the engine again. Daisy, five yards away now and directly behind the car, raised her gun arm. Craig put the gearshift into reverse and closed his eyes.

He heard a bang just as he stamped on the throttle. The rear window shattered. The car leaped backward, straight at Daisy. There was a heavy thump, as though someone had dropped a sack of potatoes on the boot.

Craig took his foot off the throttle, and the car rolled to a stop. Where was Daisy? He pushed broken glass out of the windshield and saw her. She had been thrown sideways by the impact and was lying on the ground with one leg at an odd angle. He stared, horrified at what he had done.

Then she moved.

"Oh, no!" he cried. "Why won't you die?"

She reached out with one arm and picked up her gun, lying on the snow nearby.

Craig put the car into first gear.

The car phone said: "To erase this message, press three."

Daisy looked into his eyes and pointed the gun at him.

He let out the clutch and stamped on the throttle.

He heard the bang of the gun over the bellow of the Ferrari engine, but the shot went wild. He kept his foot down. Daisy tried to drag herself out of the way, and Craig deliberately turned the wheel in her direction. An instant before the impact he saw her face, staring in terror, her mouth open in an inaudible scream. Then the car hit her with a thud. She disappeared beneath its curved front. The low-slung chassis scraped over something lumpy. Craig saw that he was headed straight for the tree he had hit before. He braked, but too late. Once again, the car crashed into the tree.

The car phone, which had been telling him how to save messages, stopped in midsentence. He tried to start the engine, but nothing happened. There was not even the click of a broken starter motor. He saw that none of the dials was working, and there were no lights on the dashboard. The electrical system had failed. It was hardly surprising, after the number of times he had crashed the car.

But that meant he could not use the phone.

And where was Daisy?

He got out of the car.

In the driveway behind him was a pile of ripped black leather, white flesh, and gleaming red blood.

She was not moving.

Sophie got out and stood beside him. "Oh, God, is that her?"

Craig felt sick. He could not speak, so he nodded.

Sophie whispered, "Do you think she's dead?"

Craig nodded again; then nausea overwhelmed him. He turned aside and vomited into the snow.

8:15 A.M.

KIT had a terrifying feeling that everything was coming unglued.

It should have been a simple thing for three tough crims such as Nigel, Elton, and Daisy to round up stray members of a law-abiding family. Yet things kept going wrong. Little Tom had made a suicide attack on Daisy; Ned had stunned everyone by protecting Tom from Daisy's revenge; and Sophie had escaped in the confusion. And Toni Gallo was nowhere to be seen.

Elton brought Ned and Tom into the kitchen at gunpoint. Ned was bleeding from several places on his face, and Tom was bruised and crying, but they were walking steadily, Ned holding Tom's hand.

Kit reckoned up who was still at large. Sophie had run away, and Craig would not be far from her. Caroline was probably still asleep in the barn. Then there was Toni Gallo. Four people, three of them children—surely it could not take long to capture them? But time was running out. Kit and the gang had less than two hours to get to the airfield with the virus. Their customer would not wait very long, Kit guessed. If something seemed wrong he would fear a trap and leave.

Elton threw Miranda's phone onto the kitchen table. "Found it in a handbag in the cottage," he said. "The guy doesn't seem to have one." The phone landed beside the perfume spray. Kit longed for the moment when the bottle would be handed over, never to be seen again, and he would get his money.

He was hoping that the major roads would be cleared of snow by the end of today. He planned to drive to London and check into a small hotel, paying cash. He would lie low for a couple of weeks, then catch a train to Paris with fifty thousand pounds in his pocket. From there he would make his leisurely way across Europe, changing small amounts of money as he needed it, and end up in Lucca.

But first, they had to account for everyone here at Steepfall, in order to delay pursuit. And it was proving absurdly difficult.

Elton made Ned lie on the floor, then tied him up. Ned was quiet but watchful. Nigel tied Tom, who was still sniveling. When Elton opened the pantry door to put them inside, Kit saw to his surprise that the prisoners had managed to remove their gags.

Olga spoke first. "Please, let Hugo out of here," she said. "He's badly injured and he's so cold. I'm afraid he'll die. Just let him lie on the floor in the kitchen, where it's warm."

Kit shook his head in amazement. Olga's loyalty to her unfaithful husband was incomprehensible.

Nigel said, "He shouldn't have punched me in the face."

Elton pushed Ned and Tom into the pantry with the others.

Olga said, "Please, I'm begging you!"

Elton closed the door.

Kit put Hugo out of his mind. "We've got to find Toni Gallo. She's the dangerous one."

Nigel said, "Where do you think she is?"

"Well, she's not in the house, not in the cottage because Elton's just searched it, and not in the garage because Daisy's just been there. So either she's out of doors, where she won't last long without a coat, or she's in the barn."

"All right," Elton said. "I'll go to the barn."

TONI was looking out of the barn window.

She had now identified three of the four people who had raided the Kremlin. One was Kit, of course. He would have been the planner, the one who told them how to defeat the security system. There was the woman whom Kit had called Daisy—an ironic nickname, presumably, for someone whose appearance would give a vampire a fright. A few minutes ago, in the prelude to the fracas in the courtyard, Daisy had addressed the young black man as Elton, which might be a first name or a surname. Toni had not yet seen the fourth, but she knew that his name was Nigel, for Kit had shouted to him in the hall.

She was half-scared and half-thrilled. Scared, because they were clearly tough professional criminals who would kill her if necessary, and because they had the virus. Thrilled, because she was tough, too, and she had a chance to redeem herself by catching them.

But how? The best plan would be to get help, but she had no phone and no car. The house phones had been cut off, presumably by the gang. No doubt they had also grabbed any mobile phones lying around. What about cars? Toni had seen two parked in front of the house, and there must be at least one more in the garage, but she had no idea where the keys were.

That meant she had to capture the thieves on her own.

She thought about the scene she had witnessed in the courtyard. Daisy and Elton were rounding up the family. But Sophie, the tarty kid, had escaped, and Daisy had gone after her. Toni had heard distant noises from beyond the garage—a car engine, breaking glass, and gunfire—but she could not see what was going on, and she hesitated to expose herself by going to investigate. If she let herself get captured, all hope was lost.

She wondered if anyone else was at liberty. The gang must be in a hurry to get going, for their rendezvous was at ten o'clock, but they would want to account for everyone before leaving, so that no one could call the police. Perhaps they would begin to panic and make mistakes.

Toni fervently hoped so. The odds against her were fearsome. She could not cope with all four villains at once. Three of them were armed—with thirteen-shot Browning automatic pistols, according to Steve. Her only chance would be to pick them off one by one.

Where should she start? At some point she had to enter the main house. At least she knew the layout—fortuitously, she had been shown around yesterday. But she did not know where in the house everyone was, and she was reluctant to jump into the dark. She was desperate for more information.

As she was racking her brains, she lost the initiative.

Elton emerged from the house and came across the courtyard toward the barn.

He was younger than Toni, probably twenty-five. He was tall and looked fit. In his right hand he carried a pistol, pointed down at the ground. Although Toni was trained in combat, she knew he would be a formidable adversary even without the gun. If possible, she had to avoid getting into a hand-to-hand fight with him.

She wondered fearfully if she could hide. She looked around the barn. No hiding place suggested itself. Besides, there was no point. She had to confront the gang, she thought grimly, and the sooner the better. This one was coming for her on his own, apparently confident he would not need help dealing with a mere woman. Perhaps that would turn out to be his crucial mistake.

Unfortunately, Toni had no weapons.

She had a few seconds to find some. She looked hurriedly at the things around her. She considered a billiard cue, but it was too light. A blow from one would hurt like hell, but would not render a man unconscious, or even knock him down.

Billiard balls were much more dangerous: heavy, solid, and hard. She stuffed two into her jeans pockets.

She wished she had a gun.

She glanced up at the hayloft. Height was always an advantage. She scrambled up the ladder. Caroline was fast asleep. On the floor between the two beds was an open suitcase. On top of the clothes was a plastic shopping bag. Next to the case was a cage of white rats.

The barn door opened, and Toni dropped to the floor and lay flat. There was a fumbling sound; then the main lights came on. Toni could not see the ground floor from her prone position, so she did not know exactly where

Elton was; but he could not see her, either, and she had
the advantage of knowing he was there.

She listened hard, trying to hear his footsteps over
the thunder of her heart. There was an odd noise that
she interpreted, after a few moments' puzzlement, as
Elton overturning the camp beds in case a child was
hiding underneath. Then he opened the bathroom door.
There was no one inside—Toni had already checked.

There was nowhere left to look but the hayloft. He
would be coming up the ladder any second now. What
could she do?

Toni heard the unpleasant squeak of rats, and was
struck by inspiration. Still lying flat, she took the shopping bag from the open suitcase and removed its contents, a gift-wrapped package labeled "To Daddy,
Happy Xmas from Sophie with love." She dropped the
package back in the suitcase. Then she opened the rats'
cage.

Gently, she picked the rats up one by one and put
them in the plastic bag. There were five.

She felt an ominous vibration in the floor that told
her Elton had started to climb the ladder.

It was now or never. She reached forward with both
arms and emptied the bag of rats over the top of the
ladder.

She heard Elton give a roar of shock and disgust as
five live rats dropped on his head.

His shout woke Caroline, who let out a squeal and
sat upright.

There was a crash as Elton lost his footing on the ladder and fell to the floor.

Toni sprang to her feet and looked down. Elton had
fallen on his back. He did not seem seriously hurt, but
he was yelling in panic and frantically trying to brush

rats off his clothing. They were as frightened as he, and trying desperately to cling to something.

Toni could not see his gun.

She hesitated only a fraction of a second, then jumped off the loft.

She came down with both feet on Elton's chest. He gave an agonized grunt as the air was knocked out of him. Toni landed like a gymnast, rolling forward, but still the impact hurt her legs.

From above, she heard a scream: "My babies!" Looking up, she saw Caroline at the top of the ladder, wearing lavender pajamas with a pattern of yellow teddy bears. Toni felt sure she must have squashed one or two of Caroline's pets as she landed, but the rats scattered, apparently unhurt.

Desperate to keep the upper hand, Toni struggled to her feet. One ankle gave her a stab of pain, but she ignored it.

Where was the gun? He must have dropped it.

Elton was hurt, but perhaps not immobilized. She fumbled in her jeans for a billiard ball, but it slipped through her fingers as she tried to pull it out of her pocket. She suffered a moment of pure terror, a feeling that her body would not obey her brain and she was completely helpless. Then she used both hands, one to push from outside her pocket and the other to grasp the ball as it emerged.

But the momentary delay had allowed Elton to recover from the shock of the rats. As Toni raised her right hand above her head, he rolled away from her. Instead of bringing the heavy ball down on his head in the hope of knocking him senseless, she was forced to change her mind at the last instant and throw it at him.

It was not a forceful throw, and in some part of her

brain she heard her ex, Frank, say scornfully, *You couldn't throw a ball if your life depended on it.* Now her life did depend on it, and Frank was right—the throw was too weak. She hit the target, and there was an audible thud as the billiard ball connected with Elton's skull, causing him to roar in pain; but he did not slump unconscious. Instead he got to his knees, holding his bruised head with one hand, then struggled to his feet.

Toni took out the second ball.

Elton looked at the floor all around him, searching in a dazed way for his gun.

Caroline had climbed halfway down the ladder, and now she leaped to the floor. She stooped and grabbed one of the rats that was hiding behind a leg of the billiard table. Turning to pick up another, she collided with Elton. He mistook her for his adversary, and punched her. It was a powerful blow that connected with the side of her head, and she fell to the floor. But it hurt him, too, for Toni saw him grimace in agony and wrap his arms around his chest, and she guessed she had broken some ribs when she jumped on him.

Something had caught Toni's eye as Caroline had reached under the billiard table for a rat. Toni looked again and saw the gun, dull gray against the dark wood of the floor.

Elton saw it at the same time. He dropped to his knees.

As Elton reached under the table, she raised her arm high above her head and brought the ball down with all her might, squarely on the back of his head. He slumped unconscious.

Toni fell to her knees, physically exhausted and emotionally drained. She closed her eyes for a moment, but there was too much to do for her to rest long. She picked up the gun. Steve had been right: it was a Browning automatic pistol of the kind issued by the British army to special forces for clandestine work. The safety catch was on the left side, behind the grip. She turned it to the locked position, then stuffed the gun in the waist of her jeans.

She unplugged the television and ripped the cable out of the back of the set, then used it to tie Elton's hands behind his back.

Then she searched him, looking for a phone; but, to her intense disappointment, he did not have one.

8:30 A.M.

IT took Craig a long time to work up the courage to look again at the motionless form of Daisy.

The sight of her mangled body, even viewed from a distance, had made him throw up. When there was nothing left in him to come out, he had tried to clean his mouth with handfuls of fresh snow. Then Sophie came to him and put her arms around his waist, and he hugged her, keeping his back to Daisy. They had stood like that until at last the nausea passed and he felt able to turn and see what he had done.

Sophie said, "What are we going to do now?"

Craig swallowed. It was not over yet. Daisy was only one of three thugs—and then there was Uncle Kit. "We'd better take her gun," he said.

Her expression told him she hated that idea. She said, "Do you know how to use it?"

"How hard can it be?"

She looked unhappy, but just said, "Whatever."

Craig hesitated a moment longer; then he took her hand and they walked toward the body.

Daisy was lying facedown, her arms beneath her. Although she had tried to kill Craig, he still found it horrible to look at a human being so mangled. The legs were the worst. Her leather trousers had been ripped to shreds. One leg was twisted unnaturally and the other was gashed and bloody. The leather jacket seemed to have protected her arms and body, but her shaved head was covered with blood. Her face was hidden, buried in the snow.

They stopped six feet away. "I can't see the gun," Craig said. "It must be underneath her."

They stepped closer. Sophie said, "I've never seen a dead person."

"I saw Mamma Marta in the funeral parlor."

"I want to see her face." Letting go of Craig's hand, Sophie went down on one knee and reached out to the bloodstained body.

Quick as a snake, Daisy lifted her head, grabbed Sophie's wrist, and brought her right hand out from under her with the gun in it.

Sophie screamed in terror.

Craig felt as if he had been struck by lightning. He shouted: "Christ!" and jumped back.

Daisy jammed the snout of the little gray pistol into the soft skin of Sophie's throat. "Stand still, laddie!" she yelled.

Craig froze.

Daisy wore a cap of blood. One ear was almost completely ripped from her head and hung grotesquely by a narrow strip of skin. But her face was unmarked, and now showed an expression of pure hatred. "For what you've done to me, I should shoot her in the belly and let you watch her bleed to death, screaming in agony."

Craig shook with horror.

"But I need your help," Daisy went on. "If you want to save your little girlfriend's life, just do everything I tell you, instantly. Hesitate, and she dies."

Craig felt she really meant it.

"Get over here," she said.

He had no choice. He stepped closer.

"Kneel down."

Craig knelt beside her.

She turned her hateful eyes on Sophie. "Now, you little whore, I'm going to let go of your arm, but don't you try to move away, or I'll shoot you, and enjoy it." She took her left hand off Sophie's arm, but kept the gun pushed into the flesh of Sophie's neck. Then she put her left arm around Craig's shoulders. "Hold my wrist, lad," she said.

Craig grasped Daisy's wrist as it dangled over his shoulder.

"You, lassie, get under my right arm."

Sophie changed her position slowly, and Daisy put her right arm over Sophie's shoulders, managing all the time to keep the gun pointed at Sophie's head.

"Now, you're going to lift me up and carry me to the house. But do it gently. I think I've got a broken leg. If you jog me it might hurt, and if I flinch I might accidentally pull the trigger. So, easy does it . . . and lift."

Craig tightened his grip on Daisy's wrist and raised himself from the kneeling position. To ease the burden on Sophie, he put his right arm around Daisy's waist and took some of her weight. The three of them slowly stood upright.

Daisy was gasping with pain, and as pale as the snow on the ground all around them; but, when Craig looked sideways and caught her eye, he saw that she was watching him intently.

When they were upright, Daisy said, "Forward, slowly."

They walked forward, Daisy dragging her legs.

"I bet you two were hidden away somewhere all night," she said. "What were you up to, eh?"

Craig said nothing. He could hardly believe that she had enough breath and malice left to rail at them.

"Tell me, laddie," she jeered. "Did you put your finger in her little pussy, eh? You dirty little bastard, I bet you did."

Craig *felt* dirty when she talked like that. She was able to sully an experience that had been carefree. He hated her for spoiling his memory. He longed to drop her on the ground, but he felt sure she would pull the trigger.

"Wait," she said. "Stop." They halted, and she put some of her weight on her left leg, the one that was not twisted.

Craig looked at her terrible face. Her black-lined eyes were closed in pain. She said, "We'll just rest here for a minute. Then we'll go on."

TONI stepped out of the barn. Now she could be seen. By her calculations, there were two of the gang in the house—Nigel and Kit—and either of them might look out of a window at any moment. But she had to take the risk. Listening for the shot that would kill her, she walked as fast as she could, pushing through the snow, to the guest cottage. She reached it without incident and dodged around the corner of the building, out of sight.

She had left Caroline searching tearfully for her pet rats. Elton was trussed up under the billiard table, blindfolded and gagged to make sure that when he came round he could not talk dopey Caroline into untying him.

Toni circled the cottage and approached the main house from the side. The back door stood open, but she did not go in. She needed to reconnoiter. She crept along the back of the building and peeped in at the first window.

She was looking into the pantry. Six people were crammed in there, bound hand and foot but standing: Olga; Hugo, who seemed to be naked; Miranda; her son, Tom; Ned; and Stanley. A wave of happiness washed over Toni when she saw Stanley. She realized she had feared, in the back of her mind, that he might be dead. She caught her breath when she saw his bruised and bloody face. Then he spotted her, and his eyes widened with surprise and pleasure. He did not appear to be seriously wounded, she saw with relief. He opened his mouth to speak. Quickly, Toni raised a finger to her lips for silence. Stanley closed his mouth and nodded understanding.

Toni moved to the next window and looked into the kitchen. Two men sat with their backs to the window. One was Kit. Toni felt a surge of pity for Stanley, having a son who would do something like this to his family. The other man wore a pink sweater. He must be the one Kit had called Nigel. They were looking at a small television set, watching the news. The screen showed a snowplow clearing a motorway in the light of early morning.

Toni chewed her lip, thinking. She had a gun now but, even so, it could be difficult to control the two of them. But she had no choice.

As she hesitated, Kit stood up, and she quickly ducked back out of sight.

8:45 A.M.

NIGEL said, "That's it. They're clearing the roads. We have to go *now*."

"I'm worried about Toni Gallo," Kit said.

"Too bad. If we wait any longer, we'll miss the rendezvous."

Kit looked at his watch. Nigel was right. "Shit," he said.

"We'll take that Mercedes outside. Go and find the keys."

Kit left the kitchen and ran upstairs. In Olga's bedroom, he pulled out the drawers of both bedside tables without finding any keys. He picked up Hugo's suitcase and emptied the contents onto the floor, but nothing jingled. Breathing hard, he did the same with Olga's case. Then he spotted Hugo's blazer draped over the back of a chair. He found the Mercedes keys in the pocket.

He ran down to the kitchen. Nigel was looking out of

the window. "Why is Elton taking so long?" Kit said. He could hear a note of hysteria in his own voice.

"I don't know," said Nigel. "Try to stay calm."

"And what the hell's happened to Daisy?"

"Go and start the engine," Nigel said. "Brush the snow off the windshield."

"Right."

As Kit turned away, his eye was caught by the perfume spray, in its double bag, lying on the kitchen table. On impulse, he picked it up and stuffed it into his jacket pocket.

Then he went out.

TONI peeped around the corner of the house and saw Kit emerge from the back door. He went in the opposite direction, to the front of the building. She followed him and saw him unlock the green Mercedes station wagon.

This was her chance.

She took Elton's pistol from the waist of her jeans and moved the safety catch to the unlocked position. There was a full magazine in the grip—she had checked. She held the gun pointing skyward, in accordance with her training.

She breathed slowly and calmly. She knew how to do this kind of thing. Her heart was pounding like a bass drum, but her hands were steady. She ran into the house.

The back door gave onto a small lobby. A second door led to the kitchen proper. She threw it open and ran in. Nigel was at the window, looking out. "Freeze!" she screamed.

He spun around.

She leveled the gun at him. "Hands in the air!"

He hesitated.

His pistol was in the pocket of his trousers—she could see the lumpy bulge it made, the right size and shape for an automatic just like the one she was holding. "Don't even think about reaching for your gun," she said.

Slowly, he raised his hands.

"On the floor! Facedown! Now!"

He went down on his knees, hands still held high. Then he lay down, his arms spread.

Toni had to get his gun. She stood over him, transferred her pistol to her left hand, and thrust its nose into the back of his neck. "The safety catch is off, and I'm feeling jumpy," she said. She went down on one knee and reached into his trousers pocket.

He moved very fast.

He rolled over, swinging his right arm at her. For a split second she hesitated to pull the trigger; then it was too late. He knocked her off balance and she fell sideways. To break her fall, she put her left hand flat on the floor—dropping her gun.

He kicked out at her wildly, his shoe connecting with her hip. She regained her balance and scrambled to her feet, coming upright before he did. As he got to his knees, she kicked him in the face. He fell back, his hand flying to his cheek, but he recovered fast. He looked at her with an expression of fury and hatred, as if outraged that she should fight back.

She snatched up the gun and pointed it at him, and he froze.

"Let's try again," she said. "This time, *you* take the gun out. Slowly."

He reached into his pocket.

Toni stretched her arm out in front of her. "And please—give me an excuse to blow your head off."

He took the gun out.

"Drop it on the floor."

He smiled. "Have you ever actually shot a man?"

"Drop it—now."

"I don't think you have."

He had guessed right. She had been trained to use firearms, and she had carried a gun on operations, but she had never shot at anything other than a target. The idea of actually making a hole in another human being revolted her.

"You're not going to shoot me," he said.

"You're a second away from finding out."

Her mother walked in, carrying the puppy. She said, "This poor dog hasn't had any breakfast."

Nigel raised his gun.

Toni shot him in the right shoulder.

She was only six feet away, and she was a good shot, so it was not difficult to wound him in exactly the right place. She pulled the trigger twice, as she had been taught. The double bang was deafening in the kitchen. Two round holes appeared in the pink sweater, side by side where the arm met the shoulder. The gun fell from Nigel's hand. He cried out in pain and staggered back against the refrigerator.

Toni felt shocked. She had not really believed she could do it. The act was repellent. She was a monster. She felt sick.

Nigel screamed: "You fucking bitch!"

Like magic, his words restored her nerve. "Be glad I didn't shoot you in the belly," she said. "Now lie down."

He slumped to the floor and rolled over on his face, still clutching his wound.

Mother said, "I'll put the kettle on."

Toni picked up Nigel's dropped gun and locked the

safety catch. She stuffed both guns into her jeans and opened the pantry door.

Stanley said, "What happened? Was someone shot?"

"Nigel," she said calmly. She took a pair of kitchen scissors from the knife block and cut the washing line that bound Stanley's hands and feet. When he was free, he put his arms around her and squeezed her hard. "Thank you," he murmured in her ear.

She closed her eyes. The nightmare of the last few hours had not changed his feelings. She hugged him hard for a precious second, wishing the moment could last longer; then she broke the clinch. Handing him the scissors, she said, "You free the rest." She drew one of the pistols from her waistband. "Kit's not far away. He must have heard the shots. Does he have a gun?"

"I don't think so," Stanley replied.

Toni was relieved. That would make it easier.

Olga said, "Get us out of this cold room, please!"

Stanley turned to cut her bonds.

Kit's voice rang out: "Nobody move!"

Toni spun around, leveling the gun. Kit stood in the doorway. He had no gun, but he was holding a simple glass perfume spray in his hand as if it were a weapon. Toni recognized the bottle that she had seen, on the security video, being filled with Madoba-2.

Kit said, "This contains the virus. One squirt will kill you."

Everyone stood still.

KIT stared at Toni. She was pointing the gun at him, and he was pointing the spray at her. He said, "If you shoot me, I'll drop the bottle, and the glass will break on these tiles."

She said, "If you spray us with that stuff, you'll kill yourself as well."

"I'll die, then," he said. "I don't care. I've put everything into this. I made the plan, I betrayed my family, and I became a party to a conspiracy to murder hundreds of people, maybe thousands. After all that, how can I fail? I'd rather die." As he said it, he realized it was true. Even the money had diminished in importance now. All he really wanted was to win.

Stanley said, "How did we come to this, Kit?"

Kit met his father's gaze. He saw anger there, as he expected, but also grief. Stanley looked the way he had when Mamma Marta died. Too bad, Kit thought angrily; he brought this on himself. "Too late now for apologies," he said harshly.

"I wasn't going to apologize," Stanley said sadly.

Kit looked at Nigel, sitting on the floor, holding his bleeding right shoulder with his left hand. That explained the two gunshots that had caused Kit to arm himself with the spray before coming back into the kitchen.

Nigel struggled to his feet. "Ah, bollocks, it hurts," he said.

Kit said, "Hand over the guns, Toni. Quick, or I'll press this nozzle."

Toni hesitated.

Stanley said, "I think Kit means what he says."

"On the table," Kit said.

She put the guns on the kitchen table, beside the briefcase that had contained the perfume bottle.

Kit said, "Nigel, pick them up."

With his left hand, Nigel picked up a gun and stuffed it into his pocket. He took the second, hefted it, then, with sudden speed, smashed it across Toni's face. She cried out and fell back.

Kit was furious with him. "What do you think you're doing?" he cried. "There's no time for that! We have to get going."

"Don't you give me orders," Nigel said harshly. "This cow shot me."

Kit could tell from Toni's face that she thought she was about to die. But there was no time to enjoy revenge. "That cow ruined my life, but I'm not hanging around to punish her," Kit said. "Knock it off!"

Nigel hesitated, staring malevolently at Toni.

Kit said, "Let's go!"

At last Nigel turned away from Toni. "What about Elton and Daisy?"

"To hell with them."

"We should tie up your old man and his tart."

"You stupid fool, don't you realize we're out of time?"

The stare Nigel gave Kit was sulfuric. "What did you call me?" Nigel wanted to kill someone, Kit realized, and right now he was thinking of shooting Kit. It was a terrifying moment. Kit raised the perfume spray high in the air and stared back, waiting for his life to end.

Then Nigel looked away and said, "All right, let's get out of here."

9 A.M.

KIT ran outside. The engine of the Mercedes was throbbing low, and the snow on its hood was already melting from the heat. The windshield and side windows were partly clear where he had hastily swept them with his hands. He jumped in, stuffing the perfume spray into his jacket pocket. Nigel clambered into the passenger seat, grunting with the pain of his gunshot wound.

Kit put the automatic gearshift into drive and touched the accelerator pedal. The car seemed to strain forward, but did not move. The plow had stopped a couple of feet away, and snow was piled two feet high in front of the bumper. Kit increased pressure on the pedal as the car labored to move the snow out of the way. "Come on!" Kit said. "This is a Mercedes. It ought to be able to shift a few pounds of snow! How big is the damn engine, anyway?" He pressed a little harder, but he did not want the wheels to lose traction and begin to spin. The car eased forward a few inches, and the piled-up snow seemed to crack and shift. Kit looked back. His father and Toni stood outside the house, watching. They would come no closer, Kit guessed, because they knew Nigel had the guns.

The car suddenly sprang forward as the snow gave way.

Kit felt a soaring elation as he accelerated along the cleared driveway. Steepfall had seemed like a jail from which he would never escape—but he had. He passed the garage—and saw Daisy.

He braked reflexively.

Nigel said, "What the hell?"

Daisy was moving toward them, supported by Craig on one side and by Ned's sulky daughter, Sophie, on the other. Daisy's legs dragged uselessly behind her, and her head was a mass of blood. Beyond them was Stanley's Ferrari, its sensuous curves battered and deformed, its gleaming blue paintwork scraped and scratched. What the hell had happened there?

"Stop and pick her up!" Nigel said.

Kit remembered how Daisy had humiliated him and almost drowned him in her father's pool only yesterday. "Fuck her," he said. He was at the wheel, and he was not going to delay his escape for her. He put his foot down.

THE long green hood of the Mercedes seemed to lift like the head of an eager horse, and it leaped forward. Craig had only a second to act. He grabbed the hood of Sophie's anorak with his right hand and pulled her to the side of the drive, moving the same way himself. Because they were tangled up with Daisy, she moved with them, and all three fell into the soft snow beside the track, Daisy screaming in pain and rage.

The car shot past, missing them by inches, and Craig

glimpsed his uncle Kit at the wheel. He was flabber-gasted. Kit had nearly killed him. Was it intentional, or had Kit known that Craig had time to get out of the way?

"You bastard!" Daisy screamed after the car, and she leveled her pistol.

Kit accelerated past the crashed Ferrari and along the curving driveway that ran beside the cliff top. Craig watched, frozen, as Daisy took aim. Her hand was steady, despite the pain she was in. She squeezed off a shot, and Craig saw a rear side window shatter.

Daisy tracked the speeding car with her arm and fired repeatedly, cartridge cases spewing from the ejection slot of the gun. A line of bullet holes appeared in the car's side; then there was a different kind of bang. A front tire blew out and a strip of rubber flew through the air.

The car continued in a straight line for a second. Then it slewed sideways, its hood plowing into the piled snow at the side of the drive, sending up a fantail of white. The back swung out and crashed into the low wall that ran along the cliff edge. Craig heard the metallic scream of tortured steel.

The car skidded sideways. Daisy kept firing, and the windshield shattered. The car went into a slow roll, tilting sideways, seeming to hesitate, then toppling over onto its roof. It slid a few feet upside down then came to a stop.

Daisy stopped shooting and fell backward, her eyes closed.

Craig stared at her. The gun fell from her hand. Sophie started to cry.

Craig reached across Daisy. He watched her eyes, terrified that they would open at any moment. His hand closed over the warm gun. He picked it up.

He held it in his right hand and put his finger into the trigger guard. He pointed it at a spot exactly between Daisy's eyes. All he cared about was that this monster should never threaten him and Sophie and their family ever again. Slowly, he squeezed the trigger.

The gun clicked on an empty magazine.

KIT was lying flat on the inside roof of the overturned car. He felt bruised all over, and his neck hurt as if he had twisted it, but he could move all his limbs. He managed to right himself. Nigel lay beside him, unconscious, possibly dead.

Kit tried to get out. He pulled the handle and pushed at the door, but it would not move. Something had jammed in the crash. He hammered madly at it with his fists, with no result. He jabbed at the button of the electric window, but nothing happened. He thought frantically that he might be imprisoned until the fire brigade arrived to cut him out, and he suffered a moment of panic and despair. Then he saw that the windshield was crazed. He shoved at it with his hand and easily pushed out a big section of broken glass.

He crawled through the windshield. He was careless of the broken glass, and a shard cut the palm of his hand painfully. He cried out and sucked the wound, but he could not pause. He slithered out from under the hood of the car and scrambled to his feet. The wind off the sea blew madly in his face. He looked around.

His father and Toni Gallo were running along the drive toward him.

TONI stopped to look at Daisy. She seemed to be out cold. Craig and Sophie appeared scared but unhurt. "What happened?" Toni said.

"She was shooting at us," Craig replied. "I ran over her."

Toni followed Craig's gaze and saw Stanley's Ferrari, dented at both ends and with all its windows smashed.

Stanley said, "Good God!"

Toni felt for a pulse in Daisy's neck. It was there, but weak. "She's still alive—just."

Craig said, "I've got her gun. It's empty, anyway."

They were all right, Toni decided. She looked ahead to the crashed Mercedes. Kit had climbed out. She ran toward him. Stanley followed close behind.

Kit started to run away, along the drive, heading for the woods; but he was battered and shaken by the crash, and he ran erratically. He was never going to make it, Toni could see. After a few paces he staggered and fell.

He seemed to realize that he could not escape that way. Scrambling to his feet, he changed direction and turned toward the cliff.

Toni glanced into the Mercedes as she passed it. Nigel lay in a crumpled heap, eyes open with the blank stare of the dead. That accounted for the three thugs, Toni thought: one tied up, one unconscious, and one dead. Only Kit was left.

Kit slipped on the icy drive, staggered, regained his balance, and turned around. He took the perfume spray from his pocket and held it out like a gun. "Stop, or I'll kill us all," he said.

Toni and Stanley stopped.

Kit's face was all pain and rage. Toni saw a man who had lost his soul. He might do anything: kill his family, kill himself, destroy the world.

Stanley said, "It won't work out here, Kit."

Toni wondered if that were true. Kit had the same thought, and said, "Why not?"

"Feel this wind," Stanley said. "The droplets will disperse before they can do any harm."

"To hell with it all," Kit said, and he threw the bottle high in the air. Then he turned around, jumped over the low wall, and ran full tilt at the cliff edge a few feet away.

Stanley jumped after him.

Toni caught the perfume bottle before it hit the ground.

Stanley leaped through the air, hands stretched out in front of him. He almost got Kit by the shoulders, but his hands slipped. He hit the ground, but managed to grab one leg and grip it tight. Kit fell to the ground with his head and shoulders jutting out over the edge of the cliff. Stanley jumped on top of him, holding him down with his weight.

Toni looked over the edge, down a hundred-foot drop to where the sea boiled among jagged rocks.

Kit struggled, but his father held him down, and eventually he became still.

Stanley got slowly to his feet and pulled Kit up. Kit's eyes were shut. He was shaking with emotion, like someone in a fit. "It's over," Stanley said. He put his arms around his son and held him. "It's all over now." They stood like that on the edge, with the wind blowing their hair, until Kit stopped shaking. Then, gently, Stanley turned him around and led him back toward the house.

THE family was in the living room, stunned and silent, still not sure that the nightmare was over. Stanley was talking to the Inverburn ambulance service on Kit's mobile phone while Nellie tried to lick his hands. Hugo lay on the couch, covered in blankets, while Olga bathed his wounds. Miranda was doing the same for Tom and Ned. Kit lay on his back on the floor, eyes closed. Craig and Sophie talked in low voices in a corner. Caroline had found all her rats and sat with their cage on her knees. Toni's mother sat next to Caroline with the puppy in her lap. The Christmas tree twinkled in the corner.

Toni called Odette. "How far away did you say those helicopters were?"

"An hour," Odette replied. "But that was then. As soon as the snow stopped, I moved them. Now they're at Inverburn, waiting for instructions. Why?"

"I've caught the gang and I've got the virus back, but—"

"What, on your own?" Odette was amazed.

"Never mind that. The important man is the customer, the one who's trying to buy this stuff and use it to kill people. We need to find him."

"I wish we could."

"I think we can, if we act fast. Could you send a helicopter to me?"

"Where are you?"

"At Stanley Oxenford's house, Steepfall. It's right on the cliff exactly fifteen miles north of Inverburn. There are four buildings in a square, and the pilot will see two crashed cars in the garden."

"My God, you have been busy."

"I need the chopper to bring me a bug, a miniature radio beacon, the kind you plant on someone you need to follow. It has to be small enough to fit into a bottle cap."

"How long does the transmitter need to operate?"

"Forty-eight hours."

"No problem. They should have that at police headquarters in Inverburn."

"One more thing. I need a bottle of perfume—Diablerie."

"They won't have *that* at police headquarters. They'll have to break into Boots in the High Street."

"We don't have much time— Wait." Olga was saying something. Toni looked at her and said, "What is it?"

"I can give you a bottle of Diablerie, just like the one that was on the table. It's the perfume I use."

"Thanks." Toni spoke into the phone. "Forget the perfume. I've got a bottle. How soon can you get the chopper here?"

"Ten minutes."

Toni looked at her watch. "That might not be fast enough."

"Where's the helicopter going after it picks you up?"

"I'll get back to you on that," Toni said, and she ended the call.

She knelt on the floor beside Kit. He was pale. His eyes were closed, but he was not asleep: his breathing was shallow and he trembled intermittently. "Kit," she said. He did not respond. "Kit, I need to ask you a question. It's very important."

He opened his eyes.

"You were going to meet the customer at ten o'clock, weren't you?"

A tense hush fell on the room as the others turned and listened.

Kit looked at Toni but said nothing.

She said, "I need to know where you were going to meet them."

He looked away.

"Kit, please."

His lips parted. Toni leaned closer. He whispered, "No."

"Think about it," she urged. "You might earn forgiveness, in time."

"Never."

"On the contrary. Little harm has been done, though much was intended. The virus has been recovered."

His eyes moved from side to side as he looked from one family member to the next.

Reading his mind, Toni said, "You've done a great wrong to them, but they don't yet seem ready to abandon you. They're all around you."

He closed his eyes.

Toni leaned closer. "You could begin to redeem yourself right now."

Stanley opened his mouth to speak, but Miranda stopped him with a raised hand. She spoke instead. "Kit, please," she said. "Do one good thing, after all this rottenness. Do it for yourself, so that you'll know you're not all bad. Tell her what she needs to know."

Kit closed his eyelids tight, and tears appeared. At last he said, "Inverburn Flying School."

"Thank you," Toni whispered.

10 A.M.

TONI sat in the control tower at the flying school. With her in the little room were Frank Hackett, Kit Oxenford, and a local police detective. In the hangar, parked out of sight, was the military helicopter that had brought them here. It had been close, but they had made it with a minute to spare.

Kit clutched the burgundy briefcase. He was pale, his face expressionless. He obeyed instructions like an automaton.

They all watched through the big windows. The clouds were breaking up, and the sun shone over the snow-covered airstrip. There was no sign of a helicopter.

Toni held Nigel Buchanan's mobile phone, waiting for it to ring. The batteries had run out at some point during the night, but it was the same kind as Hugo's, so she had borrowed his charger, which was now plugged into the wall.

"The pilot should have called by now," she said anxiously.

Frank said, "He may be a few minutes late."

She pressed buttons and discovered the last number Nigel had dialed. It looked like a mobile number, and it was timed at 11:45 p.m. yesterday. "Kit," she said. "Did Nigel call the customer just before midnight?"

"His pilot."

She turned to Frank. "This will be the number. I think we should call it."

"Okay."

She- pressed SEND, and handed the mobile to the local police detective. He put it to his ear. After a few moments, he said, "Yeah, this is me. Where are you?" He spoke with a London accent similar to Nigel's, which was why Frank had brought him along. "That close?" he said, looking through the window up at the sky. "We can't see you—"

As he spoke, a helicopter came down through the clouds.

Toni tensed.

The police officer hung up. Toni took out her own mobile and called Odette, who was now in the operations room at Scotland Yard. "Customer in sight."

Odette could not repress the excitement in her voice. "Give me the tail number."

"Just a minute . . ." Toni peered at the helicopter until she could make out the registration mark, then read the letters and numbers to Odette. Odette read them back, then hung up.

The helicopter descended. Its rotors blew the snow on the ground into a storm. It landed a hundred yards from the control tower.

Frank looked at Kit and nodded. "Off you go."

Kit hesitated.

Toni said, "Just do everything as planned. Say, 'We had some problems with the weather, but everything worked out okay in the end.' You'll be fine."

Kit went down the stairs, carrying the briefcase.

Toni had no idea whether he would perform as instructed. He had been up for more than twenty-four hours, he had been in a car crash, and he was emotionally wrecked. He might do anything.

There were two men in the front seats of the helicopter. One of them, presumably the copilot, opened a door and got out, carrying a large suitcase. He was a stocky man of medium height, wearing sunglasses. Ducking his head, he moved away from the aircraft.

A moment later, Kit appeared outside the tower and walked across the snow toward the helicopter.

"Stay calm, Kit," Toni said aloud. Frank grunted.

The two men met halfway. There was some conversation. Was the copilot asking where Nigel was? Kit pointed to the control tower. What was he saying? *Nigel sent me to make the delivery,* perhaps. But it could just as easily be *The police are up there in the control tower.* There were more questions, and Kit shrugged.

Toni's mobile rang. It was Odette. "The helicopter is registered to Adam Hallan, a London banker," she said. "But he's not on board."

"Shame."

"Don't worry. I wasn't expecting him. The pilot and copilot are employees of his. They filed a flight plan to Battersea Heliport—just across the river from Mr. Hallan's house in Cheyne Walk."

"He's Mr. Big, then?"

"Trust me. We've been after him for a long time."

The copilot pointed at the burgundy briefcase. Kit

opened it and showed him a Diablerie bottle in a nest of polystyrene packing chips. The copilot put his suitcase on the ground and opened it to reveal stacks of banded fifty-pound notes, closely packed together. At least a million pounds, Toni thought, perhaps two million. As he had been instructed, Kit took out one of the stacks and riffled it.

Toni told Odette, "They've made the exchange. Kit's checking the money."

The two men on the airfield looked at each other, nodded, and shook hands. Kit handed over the burgundy briefcase, then picked up the suitcase. It seemed heavy. The copilot walked back to the helicopter, and Kit returned to the control tower.

As soon as the copilot got back into the aircraft, it took off.

Toni was still on the line to Odette. "Are you picking up the signal from the transmitter in the bottle?"

"Loud and clear," Odette said. "We've got the bastards."

BOXING DAY

7 P.M.

LONDON was cold. No snow had fallen here, but a freezing wind whipped the ancient buildings and the curled streets, and people hunched their shoulders and tightened the scarves around their necks as they hurried to the warmth of pubs and restaurants, hotels and cinemas.

Toni Gallo sat in the back of a plain gray Audi beside Odette Cressy. Odette was a blond woman Toni's age, wearing a dark business suit over a scarlet shirt. Two detectives sat in the front, one driving, one studying a direction-finding radio receiver and telling the driver where to go.

The police had been tracking the perfume bottle for thirty-three hours. The helicopter had landed, as expected, in southwest London. The pilot had got into a waiting car and driven across Battersea Bridge to the riverside home of Adam Hallan. All last night the radio transmitter had remained stationary, beeping steadily from somewhere in the elegant eighteenth-century house. Odette did not want to arrest Hallan yet. She wanted to catch the maximum number of terrorists in her net.

Toni had spent most of that time asleep. When she lay down in her flat just before noon on Christmas Day, she felt too tense to sleep. Her thoughts were with the helicopter as it flew the length of Britain, and she worried that the tiny radio beacon would fail. Despite her anxieties, she had dropped off in seconds.

In the evening, she had driven to Steepfall to see Stanley. They had held hands and talked for an hour in his study; then she flew to London. She slept heavily all night at Odette's flat in Camden Town.

As well as following the radio signal, the Metropolitan Police had Adam Hallan and his pilot and copilot under surveillance. In the morning Toni and Odette joined the team watching Adam Hallan's house.

Toni had achieved her main objective. The deadly virus samples were back in the BSL4 laboratory at the Kremlin. But she also hoped to catch the people responsible for the nightmare she had lived through. She wanted justice.

Today Hallan had given a lunch party, and fifty people of assorted nationalities and ages, all wearing expensive casual clothes, had visited the house. One of the guests had left with the perfume bottle. Toni and Odette and the team tracked the radio beacon to Bayswater and kept watch over a student rooming house all afternoon.

At seven o'clock in the evening, the signal moved again.

A young woman came out of the house. In the light

of the streetlamps, Toni could see that she had beautiful dark hair, heavy and lustrous. She carried a shoulder bag. She turned up the collar of her coat and walked along the pavement. A detective in jeans and an anorak got out of a tan Rover and followed her.

"I think this is it," Toni said. "She's going to release the spray."

"I want to see it," Odette said. "For the prosecution, I need witnesses to the attempted murder."

Toni and Odette lost sight of the young woman as she turned into a Tube station. The radio signal weakened worryingly as the woman went underground. It remained steady for a while. Then the beacon moved, presumably because the woman was on a train. They followed the feeble signal, fearing it would fade out and she would shake off the detective in the anorak. But she emerged at Piccadilly Circus, the detective still tailing her. They lost visual contact for a minute when she turned into a one-way street. Then the detective called Odette on his mobile phone and reported that the woman had entered a theater.

Toni said, "That's where she'll release the spray."

The unmarked police cars drew up outside the theater. Odette and Toni went in, followed by two men from the second car. The show, a ghost story with songs, was popular with visiting Americans. The girl with beautiful hair was standing in the queue for collection of prepaid tickets.

While she waited, she took from her shoulder bag a perfume bottle. With a quick gesture that looked entirely natural, she sprayed her head and shoulders. The theatergoers around her paid no attention. Doubtless she wanted to be fragrant for the man she was meeting, they would imagine, if they thought about it at all. Such beautiful hair ought to smell good. The spray was curiously odorless, but no one seemed to notice.

"That's good," said Odette. "But we'll let her do it again."

The bottle contained plain water, but all the same Toni shivered with dread as she breathed in. Had she not made the switch, the spray would have contained live Madoba-2, and that breath would have killed her.

The woman collected her ticket and went inside. Odette spoke to the usher and showed him her police card; then the detectives followed the woman. She went to the bar, where she sprayed herself again. She did the same in the ladies' room. At last she took her seat in the front orchestra and sprayed herself yet again. Her plan, Toni guessed, was to use the spray several times more in the interval, and finally in the crowded passages while the audience was leaving the building. By the end of the evening, almost everyone in the theater would have breathed the droplets from her bottle.

Watching from the back of the auditorium, Toni listened to the accents around her: a woman from the American South who had bought the most beautiful cashmere scarf; someone from Boston talking about where he pahked his cah; a New Yorker who had paid five *dollars* for a cup of cawfee. If the perfume bottle had contained the virus as planned, these people would by now be infected with Madoba-2. They would have flown home to embrace their families and greet their neighbors and go back to work, telling everyone about their holiday in Europe.

Ten or twelve days later, they would have fallen ill. "I picked up a lousy cold in London," they would have said. Sneezing, they would have infected their relations and friends and colleagues. The symptoms would have gotten worse, and their doctors would have diagnosed flu. When they started to die, the doctors would have realized that this was something much worse than flu. As the deadly infection spread rapidly from street to street and city to city, the medical profession would have begun to understand what they were dealing with, but by then it would be too late.

Now none of that would happen—but Toni shuddered as she thought how close it had been.

A nervous man in a tuxedo approached them. "I'm the theater manager," he said. "What's happening?"

"We're about to make an arrest," Odette told him. "You may want to delay the curtain for a minute."

"I hope there won't be a fracas."

"Believe me, so do I." The audience was seated. "All right," Odette said to the other detectives. "We've seen enough. Pick her up, and gently does it."

The two men from the second car walked down the aisles and stood at either end of the woman's row. She looked at one, then the other. "Come with me, please, miss," said the nearer of the two detectives. The theater went quiet as the waiting audience watched. Was this part of the show? they wondered.

The woman remained seated, but took out her perfume bottle and sprayed herself again. The detective, a young man in a short Crombie coat, pushed his way along the row to where she sat. "Please come immediately," he said. She stood up, raised the bottle, and sprayed it into the air. "Don't bother," he said. "It's only water." Then he took her by the arm and led her along the row and up the aisle to the back of the theater.

Toni stared at the prisoner. She was young and attractive. She had been ready to commit suicide. Toni wondered why.

Odette took the perfume bottle from her and dropped it into an evidence bag. "Diablerie," she said. "French word. Do you know what it means?"

The woman shook her head.

"The work of the devil." Odette turned to the detective. "Put her in handcuffs and take her away."

CHRISTMAS DAY
A YEAR LATER

5:50 P.M.

TONI came out of the bathroom naked and walked across the hotel room to answer the phone.

From the bed, Stanley said, "My God, you look good."

She grinned at her husband. He was wearing a blue toweling bathrobe that was too small for him, and it showed his long, muscular legs. "You're not so bad yourself," she said, and she picked up the phone. It was her mother. "Happy Christmas," Toni said.

"Your old boyfriend is on the television," Mother said.

"What's he doing, singing carols in the police choir?"

"He's being interviewed by that Carl Osborne. He's telling how he caught those terrorists last Christmas."

"*He* caught them?" Toni was momentarily indignant. Then she thought, What the hell? "Well, he needs the publicity—he's after a promotion. How's my sister?"

"She's just getting the supper ready."

Toni looked at her watch. On this Caribbean island it was a few minutes before six o'clock in the evening. For Mother, in England, it was coming up to ten o'clock at night. But meals were always late at Bella's. "What did she give you for Christmas?"

"We're going to get something in the January sales. It's cheaper."

"Did you like my present?" Toni had given Mother a cashmere cardigan in salmon pink.

"Lovely, thank you, dear."

"Is Osborne okay?" Mother had taken the puppy to live with her, and he was now full-grown, a big shaggy black-and-white dog with hair that covered his eyes.

"He's behaving very well and hasn't had any accidents since yesterday."

"And the grandchildren?"

"Running around breaking their presents. I must go now. The Queen's on the telly."

"Bye, Mother. Thank you for calling."

Stanley said, "I don't suppose there's time for a bit of . . . you know . . . before dinner."

She pretended to be shocked. "We just had a bit of *you know*!"

"That was hours ago! But if you're tired . . . I realize that when a woman gets to a certain age—"

"A certain age?" She leaped onto the bed and knelt astride him. "A certain age?" She picked up the pillow and beat him with it.

He laughed helplessly and begged for mercy, and she relented and kissed him.

She had expected Stanley to be fairly good in bed, but it had come as a surprise to her that he was such a pistol. She would never forget their first holiday together. In a suite at the Ritz in Paris, he had blindfolded her and tied her hands to the headboard. As she lay there, naked and helpless, he had stroked her lips with a feather, then with a silver teaspoon, then with a strawberry. She had never before concentrated so intensely on her bodily sensations. He caressed her breasts with a silk handkerchief, with a cashmere scarf, and with leather gloves. She had felt as if she were floating in the sea, rocked gently by waves of pleasure. He kissed the backs of her knees, the insides of her thighs, the soft undersides of her upper arms, and her throat. He did everything slowly and lingeringly, until she was bursting with desire. He touched her nipples with ice cubes, and put warm oil inside her. He carried on until she begged him to enter her; then he made her wait a little longer. Afterward, she had said, "I didn't know this, but all my life I've wanted a man to do that."

"I know," he had said.

Now he was in a playful mood. "Come on, just a quickie," he said. "I'll let you be on top."

"Oh, all right." She sighed, pretending to feel put-upon, as she adjusted her position over him. "The things a girl has to do, nowadays—"

There was a knock at the door.

Stanley called out: "Who is it?"

"Olga. Toni was going to lend me a necklace."

Toni could see that Stanley was about to tell his daughter to go away, but she put a hand on his mouth. "Just a minute, Olga," she called.

She detached herself from Stanley. Olga and Miranda were coping well with having a stepmother their own age, but Toni did not want to push her luck. Best if they were not reminded that their father was having hot sex.

Stanley got off the bed and went into the bathroom.

Toni pulled on a green silk robe and opened the door. Olga strode in, dressed for dinner in a black cotton dress with a low neckline. "You said you'd lend me that jet necklace."

"Of course. Let me dig it out."

In the bathroom, the shower ran.

Olga lowered her voice, an unusual event. "I wanted to ask you—has he seen Kit?"

"Yes. He visited the prison the day before we flew out here."

"How is my brother?"

"Uncomfortable, frustrated, and bored, as you would expect, but he hasn't been beaten up or raped, and he isn't using heroin." Toni found the necklace and put it around Olga's neck. "It looks better on you than me— black really isn't my color. Why don't you ask your father directly about Kit?"

"He's so happy. I don't want to spoil his mood. You don't mind, do you?"

"Not in the least." On the contrary, Toni was flattered. Olga was using her the way a daughter would use a mother, to check on her father without bothering him with the kind of questions men did not like. Toni said, "Did you realize that Elton and Hamish are in the same jail?"

"No—how awful!"

"Not really. Kit's helping Elton learn to read."

"Elton can't read?"

"Barely. He knows a few words from road signs— motorway, London, town center, airport. Kit is teaching him 'The cat sat on the mat.' "

"My God, how things work out. Did you hear about Daisy?"

"No."

"She killed another inmate of the women's prison, and she was tried for murder. A young colleague of mine defended her, but she was convicted. She got a life sentence added to her existing term. She'll be in jail until she's seventy. I wish we still had the death penalty."

Toni understood Olga's hatred. Hugo had never completely recovered from the beating Daisy had given him with the blackjack. He had lost the sight in one eye. Worse, he had never regained his old ebullience. He was quieter, and less of a rake, but he was not so funny, and the wicked grin was rarely seen.

"A pity her father is still at large," Toni said. Harry Mac had been prosecuted as an accomplice, but Kit's testimony had not been enough to convict him, and the jury had found him not guilty. He had gone straight back to his life of crime.

Olga said, "There's news of him, too. He's got cancer. Started in his lungs, but now it's everywhere. He's been given three months to live."

"Well, well," said Toni. "There is justice, after all."

MIRANDA put out Ned's clothes for the evening, black linen trousers and a check shirt. He did not expect her to do it but, if she did not, he might absentmindedly go down to dinner in shorts and a T-shirt. He was not helpless, just careless. She had accepted that.

She had accepted a lot about him. She understood that he would never be quick to enter a conflict, even to protect her; but, to compensate for that, she knew that in a real crisis he was a rock. The way he had taken punch after punch from Daisy to protect Tom proved that.

She was dressed already, in a pink cotton frock with

a pleated skirt. It made her look a bit wide across the hips, but then, she was a bit wide across the hips. Ned said he liked her that way.

She went into the bathroom. He was sitting in the tub, reading a biography of Molière in French. She took the book from him. "The butler did it."

"Now you've spoiled the suspense." He stood up.

She handed him a towel. "I'm going to check on the kids." Before she left the room, she took a small package from her bedside table and tucked it into her evening bag.

The hotel rooms were individual huts along a beach. A warm breeze stroked Miranda's bare arms as she walked to the cabin her son, Tom, was sharing with Craig.

Craig was putting gel in his hair while Tom tied his shoelaces. "Are you boys okay?" Miranda asked. The question was superfluous. They were both tanned and happy after a day spent windsurfing and waterskiing.

Tom was not really a little boy anymore. He had grown two inches in the last six months, and he had stopped telling his mother everything. It made her sad. For twelve years she had been all in all to him. He would continue to be dependent on her for a few more years, but the separation was beginning.

She left the boys and went to the next hut. Sophie was sharing it with Caroline, but Caroline had already left and Sophie was alone. She stood at her wardrobe in her underwear, choosing a dress. Miranda saw with disapproval that she was wearing a sexy black half-bra and matching thong panties. "Has your mother seen that outfit?" Miranda said.

"She lets me wear what I like," Sophie said sulkily.

Miranda sat on a chair. "Come here, I want to talk to you."

Reluctantly, Sophie sat on the bed. She crossed her legs and looked away.

"I'd really prefer your mother to say this but, as she's not here, I'll have to."

"Say what?"

"I think you're too young to have sexual intercourse. You're fifteen. Craig is only sixteen."

"He's nearly seventeen."

"Nevertheless, what you're doing is actually illegal."

"Not in this country."

Miranda had forgotten they were not in the UK. "Well, anyway, you're too young."

Sophie made a disgusted face and rolled up her eyes. "Oh, God."

"I knew you'd be ungracious, but it had to be said," Miranda persisted.

"Well, now you've said it," Sophie rejoined rudely.

"However, I also know that I can't force you to do what I say."

Sophie looked surprised. She had not been expecting concessions.

Miranda took the package out of her evening bag. "So, if you decide to disobey me, I want you to use these condoms." She handed them over.

Sophie took them wordlessly. Her face was a picture of astonishment.

Miranda stood up. "I don't want you getting pregnant when you're in my care." She went to the door.

As she went out, she heard Sophie say, "Thanks."

GRANDPA had reserved a private room in the hotel restaurant for the ten members of the Oxenford family. A waiter went around pouring champagne. Sophie was late. They waited a while for her; then Grandpa stood up, and they all went quiet. "There's steak for dinner," he said. "I ordered a turkey, but apparently it escaped."

They all laughed.

He went on in a more somber tone. "We didn't really have a Christmas last year, so I thought this one should be special."

Miranda said, "And thank you for bringing us, Daddy."

"The last twelve months have been the worst year of my life, and the best," he went on. "None of us will ever completely get over what happened at Steepfall one year ago today."

Craig looked at his father. He certainly would never recover. One eye was permanently half-closed, and the expression on his face was amiably blank. He often seemed just to tune out, nowadays.

Grandpa went on, "Had it not been for Toni, God alone knows how it would have ended."

Craig glanced at Toni. She looked terrific, wearing a chestnut brown silk dress that showed off her red hair. Grandpa was nuts about her. He must feel almost the same way I do about Sophie, Craig thought.

"Then we had to relive the nightmare twice more," Grandpa said. "First with the police. By the way, Olga, why do they take statements that way? They ask you questions, and take down your answers; then they write out something that isn't what you said, and is full of mistakes, and doesn't sound like a human being at all, and they call it your statement."

Olga said, "The prosecution likes things phrased a certain way."

" 'I was proceeding in a westerly direction,' and so on?"

"Yes."

Grandpa shrugged. "Well, then we had to live it all over *again* during the trial, and we had to sit and listen to suggestions that somehow *we* were at fault for injuring people who had come into our house and attacked us and tied us up. Then we had to read the same stupid innuendos in the newspapers."

Craig would never forget it. Daisy's advocate had tried to say that Craig had attempted to murder her, because he had run over her while she was shooting at him. It was ludicrous, but for a few moments in court it had sounded almost plausible.

Grandpa went on. "The whole nightmare reminded me that life is short, and I realized that I should tell you all how I felt about Toni and waste no more time. I need hardly say how happy we are. Then my new drug was passed for testing on humans, the future of the company was secured, and I was able to buy another Ferrari— and driving lessons for Craig."

They laughed, and Craig flushed. He had never told anyone about the *first* time he had dented the car. Only Sophie knew. He was still embarrassed and guilty about it. He thought he might confess when he was really old, like thirty or something.

"Enough of the past," said Grandpa. "Let's drink a toast. Merry Christmas, everybody."

They all said, "Merry Christmas."

Sophie came in as the first course was being served. She looked wonderful. She had put her hair up and wore small dangling earrings. She looked so mature, at least twenty. Craig's mouth went dry at the thought that she was his girl.

As she passed his chair, she stooped and whispered in his ear, "Miranda gave me some condoms."

He was so surprised that he spilled his champagne. "What?"

"You heard," she said, and she took her seat.

He smiled at her. He had his own supply, of course. Funny old Aunt Miranda.

Grandpa said, "What are you grinning at, Craig?"

"Just happy, Grandpa," he said. "That's all."

ACKNOWLEDGMENTS

I was privileged to visit two laboratories with BSL4 facilities. At the Canadian Science Center for Animal and Human Health in Winnipeg, Manitoba, I was helped by Stefan Wagener, Laura Douglas, and Kelly Keith; and at the Health Protection Agency in Colindale, London, by David Brown and Emily Collins. Further advice on BSL4 laboratories and procedures came from Sandy Ellis and George Korch.

On security and biosecurity I was advised by Keith Crowdy, Mike Bluestone, and Neil McDonald. For insight into possible police responses to biohazards, I talked to Assistant Chief Constable Norma Graham, Superintendent Andy Barker, and Inspector Fiona Barker, all of the Central Scotland Police in Stirling.

On gambling I spoke to Anthony Holden and Daniel Meinertzhagen, and I was permitted to read the typescript of David Anton's book *Stacking the Deck: Beating America's Casinos at Their Own Game*.

Many of the above experts were located for me by Daniel Starer of Research for Writers in New York City.

For comments on drafts of the book, I'm grateful to my editors Leslie Gelbman, Phyllis Grann, Neil Nyren, and Imogen Tate; to my agents Al Zuckerman and Amy Berkower; to Karen Studsrud; and to my family, especially Barbara Follett, Emanuele Follett, Greig Stewart, Jann Turner, and Kim Turner.

IT was the most romantic plane ever made.

Standing on the dock at Southampton, at half past twelve on the day war was declared, Tom Luther peered into the sky, waiting for the plane with a heart full of eagerness and dread. Under his breath he hummed a few bars of Beethoven over and over again: the first movement of the *Emperor* Concerto, a stirring tune, appropriately warlike.

There was a crowd of sightseers around him: aircraft enthusiasts with binoculars, small boys and curiosity seekers. Luther reckoned this must be the ninth time the Pan American Clipper had landed on Southampton Water, but the novelty had not worn off. The plane was so fascinating, so enchanting, that people flocked to look at it even on the day their country went to war. Beside the same dock were two magnificent ocean liners, towering over people's heads, but the floating hotels had lost their magic: everyone was looking at the sky.

However, while they waited they were all talking about the war, in their English accents. The children were excited by the prospect; the men spoke knowingly in low tones about tanks and artillery; the women just looked grim. Luther was an American, and he hoped his country would stay out of the war: it was none of America's business. Besides, one thing you could say for the Nazis, they were tough on communism.

Luther was a businessman, manufacturing wool cloth, and he had had a lot of trouble with Reds in his mills at one time. He had been at their mercy: they had almost ruined him. He still felt bitter about it. His father's menswear store had been run into the ground by Jews setting up in competition, and then Luther Woolens was threatened by the Commies—most of whom were Jews! Then Luther had met Ray Patriarca, and his life had changed. Patriarca's people knew what to do about Communists. There were some accidents. One hothead got his hand caught in a loom. A union recruiter was killed in a hit-and-run. Two men who complained about breaches of the safety regulations got into a fight in a bar and finished up in the hospital. A woman troublemaker dropped her lawsuit against the company after her house burned down. It only took a few weeks: since then there had been no unrest. Patriarca knew what Hitler knew: the way to deal with Communists was to crush them like cockroaches. Luther stamped his foot, still humming Beethoven.

A launch put out from the Imperial Airways flying-boat dock, across the estuary at Hythe, and made several passes along the splashdown zone, checking for floating debris. An eager murmur went up from the crowd: the plane must be approaching.

The first to spot it was a small boy with large new boots. He had no binoculars, but his eleven-year-old eyesight was better than lenses. "Here it comes!" he shrilled. "Here comes the Clipper!" He pointed southwest. Everyone looked that way. At first Luther could see only a vague shape that might have been a bird, but soon its outline resolved, and a buzz of excitement spread through the crowd as people told one another that the boy was right.

Everyone called it the Clipper, but technically it was a Boeing B-314. Pan American had commissioned Boeing to build a plane capable of carrying passengers across the Atlantic Ocean in total luxury, and this was the result: enormous, majestic, unbelievably powerful, an airborne palace. The airline had taken delivery of six and ordered another six. In comfort and elegance they were equal to the fabulous ocean liners that docked at Southampton, but the ships took four or five days to cross the Atlantic, whereas the Clipper could make the trip in twenty-five to thirty hours.

It looked like a winged whale, Luther thought as the plane came closer. It had a big blunt whalelike snout, a massive body and a tapering rear that culminated in twin high-mounted tailfins. The huge engines were built into the wings. Below the wings was a pair of stubby sea-wings, which served to stabilize the aircraft when it was in the water. The bottom of the plane had a sharp knife-edge like the hull of a fast ship.

Soon Luther could make out the big rectangular windows, in two irregular rows, marking the upper and lower decks. He had come to England on the Clipper exactly a week earlier, so he was familiar with its layout. The upper deck comprised the flight cabin and baggage holds and the lower was the passenger deck. Instead of seat rows, the passenger deck had a series of lounges with davenport couches. At mealtimes the main lounge became the dining room, and at night the couches were converted into beds.

Everything was done to insulate the passengers from the world and the weather outside the windows. There were thick carpets, soft lighting, velvet fabrics, soothing colors and deep upholstery. The heavy sound-proofing reduced the roar of the mighty engines to a distant, reassuring hum. The captain was calmly authoritative, the crew clean-cut and smart in their Pan American uniforms, the stewards ever attentive. Every need was catered to; there was constant food and drink; whatever you wanted appeared as if by magic, just when you wanted it, curtained bunks at bedtime, fresh strawberries at breakfast. The world outside started to appear unreal, like a film projected onto the windows; and the interior of the aircraft seemed like the whole universe.

Such comfort did not come cheap. The round-trip fare was $675, half the price of a small house. The passengers were royalty, movie stars, chairmen of large corporations and presidents of small countries.

Tom Luther was none of those things. He was rich, but he had worked hard for his money, and he would not normally have squandered it on luxury. However, he had needed to familiarize himself with the plane. He had been asked to do a dangerous job for a powerful man—very powerful indeed. He would not be paid for his work, but to be owed a favor by such a man was better than money.

The whole thing might yet be called off: Luther was waiting for a message giving him the final go-ahead. Half the time he was eager to get on with it; the other half, he hoped he would not have to do it.

The plane came down at an angle, its tail lower than its nose. It was quite close now, and Luther was struck again by its tremendous size. He knew that it was 109 feet long and 152 feet from one wingtip to the other, but the measurements were just numbers until you actually saw the goddamn thing floating through the air.

For a moment it looked as if it were not flying but falling, and would crash into the sea like a dropped stone and sink to the bottom. Then it seemed to hang in the air, just above the surface, as if dangling on a string, for a long moment of suspense. At last it touched the water, skipping the surface, splashing across the tops of the waves like a stone thrown skim-wise, sending up small explosions of foam. But there was very little swell in the sheltered estuary, and a moment later, with an explosion of spray like the smoke from a bomb, the hull plunged into the water.

It cleaved the surface, plowing a white furrow in the green, sending twin curves of spray high in the air on either side; and Luther thought of a mallard coming down on a lake with spread wings and folded feet. The hull sank lower, enlarging the sail-shaped curtains of spray that flew up to the left and right; then it began to tilt forward. The spray increased as the plane leveled out, submerging more and more of its whale's belly. Then at last its nose was down. Its speed slowed suddenly, the spray diminished to a wash, and the aircraft sailed the sea like the ship it was, as calmly as if it had never dared to reach for the sky.

Luther realized he had been holding his breath, and let it out in a long relieved sigh. He started humming again.

The plane taxied toward its berth. Luther had disembarked there a week ago. The dock was a specially designed raft with twin piers. In a few minutes, ropes would be attached to stanchions at the front and rear of the plane and it would be winched in, backward, to its parking slot between the piers. Then the privileged passengers would emerge, stepping from the door onto the broad surface of the sea-wing, then onto the raft, and from there up a gangway to dry land.

Luther turned away, then stopped suddenly. Standing at his shoulder was someone he had not seen before: a man of about his own height, dressed in a dark gray suit and a bowler hat, like a clerk on his way to the office. Luther was about to pass on; then he looked again. The face beneath the bowler hat was not that of a clerk. The man had a high forehead, bright blue eyes, a long jaw, and a thin, cruel mouth. He was older than Luther, about forty; but he was broad-shouldered and seemed fit. He looked handsome and dangerous. He stared into Luther's eyes.

Luther stopped humming.

The man said: "I am Henry Faber."

"Tom Luther."

"I have a message for you."

Luther's heart skipped a beat. He tried to hide his excitement, and spoke in the same clipped tones as the other man. "Good. Go ahead."

"The man you're so interested in will be on this plane on Wednesday when it leaves for New York."

"You're sure?"

The man looked hard at Luther and did not answer.

Luther nodded grimly. So the job was on. At least the suspense was over. "Thank you," he said.

"There's more."

"I'm listening."

"The second part of the message is: Don't let us down."

Luther took a deep breath. "Tell them not to worry," he said, with more confidence than he really felt. "The guy may leave Southampton, but he'll never reach New York."